"FUN!"
Susan Elizabeth Phillips

SUSAN
ANDERSEN

**"SASSY, SNAPPY, AND
SIZZLING HOT!"**
Janet Evanovich

**"YOU CAN'T GO WRONG WITH
A SUSAN ANDERSEN BOOK."**
Jayne Ann Krentz

Dear Reader,

I have this great vision of myself penning books as birds tweet and the heavens smile down upon me. The reality of my writing process is probably closer to chainsaw juggling. What's scary is that this seems perfectly reasonable to me—right up until the point in every book when my characters wrest the story from my hands and run with it. Then I'm pretty sure it's going to be a bloodbath.

My troublemakers in *Getting Lucky* are Zach Taylor, a tough-minded marine on a mission, and Lily Morrisette, a chef who might *look* like a party girl but is more than equal to the task of matching wits with a stubborn soldier. I was convinced when I started their story that this time I had a firm grasp on my cast of characters. What a dreamer—as always, they took me in directions I never envisioned. I'm pleased to announce, however, that in the end the book came together with a minimum of nicks and cuts to my tender psyche. Now that it's finished and I've survived to write another day, I'm just so, so wild about Zach and Lily. It's my fondest wish that you'll fall in love with them, too.

Susan Andersen

SUSAN ANDERSEN

GETTING LUCKY

AVON BOOKS

An Imprint of HarperCollinsPublishers

This is a work of fiction. Names, characters, places, and incidents are products of the author's imagination or are used fictitiously and are not to be construed as real. Any resemblance to actual events, locales, organizations, or persons, living or dead, is entirely coincidental.

AVON BOOKS
An Imprint of HarperCollins*Publishers*
10 East 53rd Street
New York, New York 10022-5299

First Avon Books paperback printing: March 2003

Avon Trademark Reg. U.S. Pat. Off. and in Other Countries, Marca Registrada, Hecho en U.S.A.
HarperCollins® is a registered trademark of HarperCollins Publishers Inc.

Printed in the U.S.A.

10 9 8 7 6 5 4 3 2 1

*In memory of a rare, special night
when I finally got two of
my very favorite people together,
this is dedicated, with love,
to my cousin Colleen
and my best friend, Mimi.
Here's to
French manicures and ice cream,
plots to convert Christopher into a Babs fan,
and conversations both serious enough
to make us cry and so hysterical
we nearly wet our pants.*

I adore you both.

Susie

1

LILY MORRISETTE PAUSED WITH HER WATER GLASS suspended halfway to her lips as she stared in fascination at the big man letting himself in through the kitchen door. The granite tiles beneath her feet were smooth, and around her, the huge Laguna Beach oceanfront house was silent, the only sound the distant ticking of the antique mission clock in the living room. Cool, salt breezes with an underlying hint of April flowers blew in on the man's wake. But *cool* wasn't the first word to pop to Lily's mind. He had to be about the hottest thing she'd ever clapped eyes on.

She knew who he was, of course, from the photographs Glynnis Taylor had shown her. But none of those came *close* to doing him justice, and Lily was caught flatfooted by the sheer impact of his physical presence.

He was six feet of dark and dangerous—you could tell the latter just by the way he held himself. As for the rest—the midnight-black hair and dark jaw stubble, the long legs, and those wide shoulders straining the navy material of his T-shirt—well, heck, it was overkill, pure and simple.

Lily considered pouring her glass of water where it would do the most good to cool her down. She didn't, naturally, but *ho*ly petunia. She'd finally met her fantasy man in the flesh.

Then he opened his mouth and wrecked the illusion.

"Who the hell are you?" he demanded, swinging an olive-drab duffle bag off his shoulder and down to the tiled floor. "And what are you doing in my kitchen? Where's Glynnis?"

His eyes were a clear, pale gray, the irises ringed in charcoal. Intense and unflinching, they narrowed between thick, dark lashes to rake over her, taking in her thin cotton, peppermint ice cream–colored drawstring pajama bottoms and tank top. The scrutiny served to remind Lily of every one of the extra ten pounds she could never seem to shed, no matter what. She set her glass down on the countertop with a sharp click, but refrained from responding in kind to his rudeness.

"You must be Zach." She stepped forward, extending her hand to Glynnis's brother. "She's away right now, but I'm Lily—Lily Morrisette. I've heard a lot about you since I started renting a room here."

"The hell you say," he growled, ignoring her proffered hand. His voice was so deep she could practically feel its vibration through the soles of her feet, the way she always registered the bass thumping from the car of the teenage boy who lived down the block whenever he drove past. It was also nearly as frigid as those iceberg eyes of his when he continued, "Glynnis has always been a sucker for every con artist with a sad story to tell, but I didn't think she'd go so far as to actually install one in our house while I was gone."

"*Excuse* me?"

"I hope you got whatever you were angling for while the opportunity was ripe, lady." His gaze was so scornful it took all Lily's starch not to recoil. "But don't let that shapely little ass get too comfortable, because the free ride is officially over. Go pack your bags."

He thought her bottom was shapely? And *little*? Then she gave herself a sharp mental shake. Good God, what was the *matter* with her? His opinion of her butt was hardly the point. Straightening her shoulders, she tipped up her chin. "No," she said firmly, and crossed her arms over her breasts.

"What?" He went very still, as if no one ever contradicted him.

Perhaps no one ever did, Lily surmised, recalling that he was some hotshot Marine who specialized in reconnaissance missions. Then his mouth went hard, and part of her attention got distracted by the thin white scar that bisected his upper lip.

Funny the difference a few minutes and an insulting attitude could make. What she undoubtedly would have considered sexy as all get-out a moment ago struck her now as vaguely sinister. *Pretty is as pretty does*, Grandma Nell would've said, and for the first time Lily understood on a bone-deep, fundamental level exactly what her grandmother had meant. This guy's behavior wasn't pretty at all, and she refused to be the first to flinch in the strange game of chicken they played. "What part of the word don't you understand?" she inquired sweetly. Then her voice adopted the authority she'd acquired from years of dealing with the temperamental chefs who'd taught her her craft. "I'm not going anywhere, so get used to it."

The next thing she knew, she had a hundred and ninety pounds of irate male looming over her, making her painfully aware of her own less-than-impressive stature. "We can do this the easy way, or we can do it tough," Zach said, and the deep timbre of his voice registered up and down her spine. "But one way or another, sister, you *will* be leaving."

Lily's head snapped back to meet his storm-gray eyes. "Back off, soldier boy. And let me make myself perfectly clear: You lay one hand on me, and I'll have the cops crawling down your throat so fast it'll make your head twirl." She *hated* it when people used their size to try to intimidate her.

"Yeah, I quake in fear of a little operator like you calling in the local heat." But he eyed her as if unable to figure out where she got her brass and stepped back. The retreat must not have sat too well with him, though, because those mile-wide shoulders of his immediately adopted a stubborn set, his square jaw did the impossible and became even harder, and he leaned into her just enough to invade her personal space without actually crowding her to the point where she could warn him off again.

"Tell you what," he said with soft menace, "I'll save you the trouble and give them a call myself. Then *they* can escort you off the premises, and I can get a good night's sleep. After playing hurry-up-and-wait on military transports for the past two days, I'm in no mood to deal with a wheeler-dealer out to fleece my sister of her inheritance."

Oh, for—

Tired of the slurs against her character, Lily turned on her heel. She caught a glimpse of his satisfied expression out of the corner of her eye and had to grit her teeth against the frustration that burned like chipotle pepper in the back of her throat. Refusing to give vent to her ire, however, she stalked out of the kitchen and down the adobe hallway to her room, where she headed straight for the little fireproof safe she kept in the nightstand next to her bed.

Her blood raced so hot through her veins she was surprised steam didn't rise through her pores, and her nerves jangled just below the surface of her skin. Then her knees abruptly buckled, and she collapsed onto the coverlet. Perching her bottom on the edge of the bed and clutching the small box in her lap, she took several slow, deep breaths. How on earth had everything gotten so far out of hand so flipping fast?

The truth was, aside from his being a complete idiot regarding her role in his sister's life, Zachariah Taylor probably had valid reasons for his concern. Glynnis was only a week or so from her twenty-fifth birthday, when she was supposed to come into a sizable trust fund, the source of which Lily didn't know. It had something to do with a family-owned corporation and Glynnis's grandfather, she thought, but wasn't actually sure of the details, since her younger friend had a tendency to go off on incoherent tangents whenever she came to that point in a conversation. What Lily did know was that

Glynnis didn't have a great track record picking her friends—at least when it came to men. Actually, that had recently changed, but the point was that Glynnis had been burned more than once by guys chasing after her for her money, and it was no secret she was an easy touch for anyone with a hard-luck story.

No doubt brother Zach had a tough time believing her ability to read character applied solely to the male gender.

Lily also conceded she may have been the tiniest bit predisposed to think the worst of Zach before they'd ever met. Glynnis adored her brother, but from everything she'd ever said about him Lily had formed an impression of one of those macho, overly dominant types who live to keep their womenfolk dependent. She'd been momentarily sidetracked by his Greek god physique, but Zach's insulting assessment of her character had immediately plunged her right back into that mindset.

But perhaps it was time to draw back and regroup. He was clearly stressed and likely worn to a nub from travel frustration. That sort of thing could prey on a person and turn even the easiest-going disposition nasty. So perhaps they ought to start over again. She opened the box on her lap, withdrew what she'd come looking for, then returned the box to its drawer and headed back to the kitchen. She'd show him this, then calmly explain how she had come to be living here.

Her willingness to give him another shot, however, didn't render her so full of comradeship that she was ready to start tossing flowers at Zach's oversized feet. She had her work cut out, in fact, not to lapse into defensiveness the moment she walked back into the room and found herself once again the cynosure of those take-no-prisoners eyes of his. So although she politely extended the document to him rather than slapping it against his hard abs the way she might've done five minutes ago, her posture as she faced him was screw-you erect.

"What's this?" Not waiting for an answer, he opened the thrice-folded paper and began to read. His dark eyebrows suddenly gathered like thunderclouds above his nose, and his gaze snapped up from the document to pin her in place.

"A contract?" he said in a dangerously low tone. "You've got a *contract* to stay here? I don't have to ask whose idea this was."

Lily felt her good intentions slipping away. She didn't like his tone of voice, much less what he insinuated. It was particularly insulting in light of the fact that she'd come up with this idea as a way of teaching Glynnis a little financial accountability—something Mr. Commando here might have taken the time to do himself. But she held on to her temper with both hands. "I'm not sure I understand your objections," she said with hard-won equanimity. "As you can see, I'm paying a fair, market-value rent, not staying here for free."

He simply looked at her, and she said in exasperation, "You just read the contract—you must have seen for yourself that it doesn't favor my interests over those of your sister. And it's not as if *I* drew the thing up; Glynnis and I went to a perfectly reputable lawyer."

"And he was—what? Let me guess." His gaze took a

leisurely up-and-down tour of her body, lingering over specific curves. "A very good 'friend' of yours?"

"I don't *believe* you! How can someone as sweet as Glynnis have such a pig of a brother?" *And how could I have harbored even a momentary fantasy about this guy?* Lily concentrated the full force of her contempt on him, but he merely returned an expressionless stare. Expecting steam to come whistling out of her ears at any moment like some enraged cartoon character, she snatched the contract from his hand. "I've had it. I'm going to my room. You just stay the heck away from me."

She heard him sweep his bag up off the tiles as she stalked stiff-legged from the kitchen. And although he moved as quietly as a cat, she sensed him padding along in her wake and had to bite back the urge to scream. Fists clenched at her sides, she picked up her pace, eager to reach the haven of her own space.

She wasn't quite quick enough, however, to avoid hearing him snarl, "Oh, that just fucking figures. You've even got my room."

Mortification sent scalding heat up Lily's throat. She'd offered to take the smaller bedroom down the hall when she'd first moved in, but Glynnis wouldn't hear of it. She'd insisted that if Lily paid rent she ought to at least get her money's worth by having an ocean view. The younger woman hadn't once mentioned that the room she'd assigned Lily was her brother's.

Not wanting to see his expression, Lily refused to look around as she pushed open the door. "I'll have my stuff moved down the hall in five minutes."

"Forget it," he said sarcastically. "I wouldn't want to put you out. I'll crash in the guest room."

A disbelieving sound escaped her. "And let you add that to my list of supposed crimes? I don't think so." She stalked across the room to grab her big suitcase off the shelf in the closet, then pulled the clothes that hung from the rod below it off their hangers. Tossing them into the case, she then gathered a dozen pairs of shoes off the closet floor, and swept the highboy clear of her framed photographs and perfume bottles. Next she emptied the dresser drawers and added their contents to the mix. She stuffed her jewelry box into one corner, looked around to be sure she hadn't forgotten anything, then went into the attached bathroom to collect her makeup and toiletries.

When she came out it was to see Zach standing over her case staring down at its contents. Scorching heat settled in her cheeks. What was it, Murphy's Law or something, that the lacy, silky contents of her undies drawer had to be right on top? Shouldering him aside, she added her armload from the bathroom. Then she snatched the case up in both hands. She'd crammed enough stuff in it for three suitcases—much too much to ever close it.

"I think that's everything," she said with hard-won civility, and carefully holding the case level to prevent any liquids from leaking from the bottles within, carried it toward the door. "The room is officially all yours." *So grown up,* a little voice in her head commended her. *And polite. Yes, indeed—you're nothing if not polite.*

But she refrained from mentally issuing herself any self-congratulatory pats on the back for such mature handling of the situation. Because the sad truth was, had both of her hands not been fully occupied, she would have been hard pressed to keep from slamming the bedroom door so violently behind her it'd rattle the big goon's pearly white teeth.

Zach strung obscenities in creative combinations as he prowled the hacienda-style house, locking up as he went. Irritation rode him hard, and he decided that this was just one more crime he could lay at Lily Morrisette's dainty little feet—the fact that she had simply waltzed off without bothering to secure the house.

Then the absurdity of the notion brought him up short. *Yeah, right.* That was kind of like worrying that the fox hadn't locked up the hen house, wasn't it? Trouble from without was the *least* of his problems when it was already entrenched with a capital T right here inside the compound with him.

But he stood foursquare by the fox analogy, since that was exactly what she reminded him of. Wily, slick, and shrewd. Dangerously intelligent. *All pink and gold and built like a—*

He gave his head a furious shake and headed for his room. He wasn't going to accomplish anything tonight when he was so damn tired he could barely see straight. Might as well catch some zs and figure out in the morning how to get little Ms. Morrisette out of here.

That left him Glynnis to fret about. Where was she? And just when the hell did he get to quit worrying about her, anyway? It wasn't as if she were a kid. Or that he wasn't a liberated kind of guy—hey, he firmly believed that women were *every* bit as capable of looking out for themselves as men were. More so, many of them.

Only . . . Glynnie was different. There had always

been something sort of sweet and innocent and a little bit clueless about his baby sister that made it just plain impossible *not* to worry. She'd been nineteen years old to his thirty when she'd come to live with him at Camp Lejeune in North Carolina, where he'd been stationed at the time. She'd never known their parents, Grandfather had just died, and she'd been in need of someone to bolster her emotional fragility. Since he was all the family she had left, that job had fallen to him, and he'd been happy to oblige—when he was available. But he'd been in and out of the country on a pretty regular basis, so he'd had to leave her on her own quite a bit. She'd hardly been a child, though. Hell, she'd been a year older than he had been when he'd left that cold mausoleum of a mansion in Philadelphia to join the Marines, so he refused to feel guilty about his inability to be there on a constant basis. He did sometimes wonder, though, if she might not have become a little more savvy during the past six years had he been around more to ride herd on her.

Especially when it came to money. Glynnis was dead hopeless in the finance department. He couldn't remember a single month since she'd moved in with him that she'd managed to live on the allowance from her trust fund. Maybe that was his fault for always bailing her out. He probably shouldn't have let her get away with "borrowing" from him, particularly when nine times out of ten she'd just turned right around and shelled out his money to one of her lost causes. She was too damn trusting for her own good.

Which brought Zach's thoughts swinging right back to the very curvy little Lily. Ruthlessly cutting them short, he ripped his clothes off and padded naked into the bathroom, ditty bag in hand. *Don't even go there.* He washed up and brushed his teeth, then headed back to the bedroom with the full intention of getting some much-needed rest.

But exhausted as he was, sleep was slow in coming. He had a month's leave, and his plan had been to use the time to catch up with his sister and figure out how to hang on to the only billet he'd ever cared to have for the final two years he had left in the service. Now Glynnis wasn't home, he was struggling with the fact that he needed to worry about his career at all, and to top it all off he was half hard from the scent on his pillow left by some Marilyn Monroe lookalike out to bilk his sister of her fortune. This wasn't the way he'd envisioned his homecoming.

He flipped over onto his back, cradled his head in his clasped hands, and stared up at the ceiling. Big deal, so he was suffering a random surge of lust—that would get the zero attention it deserved. And since he wasn't willing to go pound on Lily's door to demand his sister's whereabouts, there wasn't much he could do about Glynnis tonight. But the remainder of his military career was a subject he could devote some attention to.

Nothing was the same as it used to be. He was the only one left from his original unit, for starters. His closest friends, Coop Blackstock, whom he'd met his first day of boot camp, and John "the Rocket" Miglionni, whom he'd met not long after that, had both been out of the service for several years now. Since their discharge, Coop had gone on to become a best-selling author of military-techno thrillers and Rocket was a private detective with his own agency. And all the other grunts in their unit had either retired, transferred, or died.

Zach had somehow ended up as the old man in a new recon unit full of eighteen-, nineteen-, and twenty-year-olds. *Jesus.* He scrubbed his hands over his face. *How the hell had that happened?* In any other business a thirty-six-year-old in his physical condition would be considered in his prime. But reconnaissance was a young man's game and the brass was beginning to hint he should think about giving up field work to teach the younger men its finer points. To teach, for crissake!

Sure, the younger men could go for days on end without sleep and never have it catch up with them, and at some point during the last year or so he had lost that ability. And yes, this last assignment in South America had been a bitch. But, hell, it had been a hundred and ten fucking degrees with humidity to match. Even the day-care kids, as he sometimes thought of them, had gotten their asses kicked.

So, screw it. He could keep up with them any day of the week. Maybe lately he hadn't liked being in the field as much as he used to, but that was surely temporary. He was just a little discouraged over the way the last assignment had shaken out.

All he needed was a little R&R and he'd be back in fighting trim. He'd always seen himself in a recon unit right up until the day he mustered out of the service for good, and that's exactly what he planned to do until he had his twenty years in and was eligible for retirement.

How to get the brass off his back in the meantime was the question.

He realized, though, that there was no use worrying about it tonight. Flipping onto his side, he pounded the pillow into submission, and stuffed it under his head, only to have another subtle waft of fragrance rise to tease his nose. An image of Lily immediately popped to mind and this time refused to be dislodged.

She was such a little thing—he'd be surprised if she topped out at five-two. But inch for inch, pound for pound, she was pure sex on the hoof. It was more than the sum total of that froth of blonde hair, those blue eyes, and that golden skin. It was the way she moved and the sheer femaleness of her. It was the pheromones she exuded. And it was those curves.

Man, oh, man. Those *curves*.

She had what used to be referred to as an hourglass figure: round breasts, tiny waist, and full, lush hips. Like a top-of-the-line Cadillac, hers was a chassis designed for a smooth ride—a guy only had to take one look at it to get all sorts of ideas.

The wrong kind of ideas. Zach whipped the pillow out from under his head and hurled it across the room. He rolled onto his other side and pillowed his head on his biceps, swearing another blue streak beneath his breath when the scent he'd thought to rid himself of merely drifted up from the sheets instead. It had been a long couple of days, and he was beat—no doubt that was why he was feeling so susceptible.

But he didn't try to fool himself. Lily Morrisette was the type of woman who could tie a man's thoughts in knots without lifting so much as one single, dainty, rose-tipped finger. And that made her more dangerous than a field full of land mines.

So first thing in the morning, after he'd had a decent night's sleep and his brain was once again working at its usual brisk pace, he'd find a way to send her packing.

2

LILY STOOD IN FRONT OF THE MIRRORED CLOSET door the next morning and studied her naked body. The longer she looked, the closer together her eyebrows inched. Who invented the full-length mirror, anyway? She'd lay odds on a man with a sadistic streak.

Okay, maybe that wasn't fair. Perhaps he was a perfectly nice fellow—one so moon-faced in love with his sylphlike wife that he'd invented the thing so she could admire her svelte and no doubt hipless body from head to toe whenever her little heart desired. Besides, it wasn't as if the reflection looking back at her was *that* bad. If she were seeing it strictly through her own eyes, in fact, she'd probably think, *Not fabulous. Could definitely stand improvement. But, all in all, not bad for a thirty-five-year-old who's fond of food.*

Unfortunately, her observation was tainted by the re-membrance of Zach Taylor's cool gray eyes tracking over her, as well as the knowledge that *he* had clearly never had to sweat cellulite. Sucking in her stomach, standing as tall as she possibly could, she turned side to side, scowling at the not-much-improved-upon reflection. She was simply so darn . . . *round*.

Blowing out a breath, she studied the various components that comprised the whole. It wasn't all bad news. She liked her shoulders, and her arms had nice definition. She had good skin, and her breasts were fairly decent. They were a bit larger than she would've chosen had it been left up to her, but they weren't show-stopper huge, thank goodness. And they were still right up where they were supposed to be—there was something to be said for that.

That was the plus side of the ledger; then things got a little dicey. She was short-waisted and her hips and bottom were the bane of her existence, both being several inches fuller than she cared to contemplate, never mind acknowledge. And being only five feet, three inches tall (well, darn near—five-two and three-quarters, anyhow) her legs obviously weren't the kind that reached to heaven. Thank God for nicely squared shoulders or she'd look like one of those roly-poly punching-bag dolls that always popped right back up no matter how often one pushed the thing down.

And God bless, too, the benefit of cosmetics and all the other accoutrements of being a woman. *Heck*, she thought, as she reached for one of her favorite lingerie sets, *everyone looks better in clothing, anyway*. She stepped into the tiny electric-blue panties and pulled them into place, then shimmied her breasts into the lace demi-cups of its matching bra. She adjusted the straps and swept up a pair of freshly ironed designer jeans. Donning them, she then stepped into a pair of strappy, red spiked heels that added three and a half inches to her stature, and pulled a color-coordinated sleeveless V-necked tunic on over her head. She added a narrow gold chain belt over the slinky jersey material, made a few adjustments until she was satisfied with its loose drape between hip and waist, then stood back and nodded. The glitter of gold was always a welcome addition to any outfit, and the belt helped hint at her contours while maintaining the always stylish, straighter silhouette.

She sashayed into the bathroom and plugged in her hot rollers. While waiting for them to heat, she applied liquid foundation with a light hand, powdered her T zone, added a hint of blush to the apples of her cheeks, then carefully made up her eyes with neutral colors, all to achieve a luminous no-makeup look.

The light that indicated the rollers were ready blinked off a few minutes later, just as she was tossing her eyelash curler and mascara back into the vanity drawer. She threw a few rollers into her hair, brushed her teeth, applied a nice cheery, rosy lipstick, and took the rollers out. After waiting a sec to let her hair cool, she pulled a brush through it, then tossed the brush in the drawer, bent from the waist, and mussed her hair vigorously with both hands. Straightening, she tweaked the 'do here and there, then walked back into the bedroom. She stopped in front of the mirror once again to give herself another appraisal.

"Much better," she murmured. "I swear, only the airbrushed look truly good stark naked."

Still, she mused as she made her way to the kitchen, it certainly wouldn't hurt to get back on the diet wagon. Perhaps she'd cut up a little fruit and limit herself to that for breakfast.

It was a worthy goal—and one that lasted until she opened the refrigerator a moment later and spied the full carton of eggs. She did get out an orange, but along with it retrieved two eggs, a large crimini mushroom, a green onion, and half a small tomato. She set them all on the counter next to the stove. Remembering there was a nice smoked Gouda in the dairy drawer, she grabbed that, too, and cut off a small hunk. She drizzled olive oil into a frying pan, set the pan on the burner, and turned the gas on beneath it. As blue flames licked the rim of the pan's bottom, she broke the eggs into a bowl she'd grabbed out of the cupboard. Adding a splash of half-and-half and a dash of salt and pepper, she whipped them to a froth with a wire whisk, then set them aside to quickly chop the rest of the ingredients.

She adored good food. She loved everything about it: its scents, its tastes, its textures. Reverence for the world of edibles and everything that could be done with them had sent her first to a culinary academy straight out of high school, then through advanced training and a series of apprenticeships with some of California's most prestigious chefs.

She hummed as she poured the egg mixture into the hot pan and evenly distributed the vegetables, tomato, and finely cubed cheese on top of it. While waiting for it to set up enough to fold, she set the table with a pretty plate, a linen napkin, and silverware. Then she made herself a cup of tea, cut two thin slices from the middle of the orange, and arranged them in decorative twists on either side of her plate. She ate the remainder leaning over the sink.

A few minutes later she slid the omelet onto her plate

and sat down to her meal. For a moment she simply breathed in the aroma and appreciated the omelet's aesthetic appeal against the blue plate and orange garnish. Then she picked up her fork, sliced off a bite, and slipped it into her mouth. Her eyes slid closed. Oh, my. She did so love good food. There was never a time she *didn't* enjoy eating. Well, her appetite did disappear on those rare occasions when she was upset, but fortunately for her—or perhaps unfortunately, given the way everything that passed her lips seemed to settle directly on her hips—she was a natural-born optimist.

A condition that threatened to die a natural death when halfway through her omelet her neck began to tingle, and she looked up to see Zach lounging in the archway.

He stood with one big shoulder propped negligently against the stucco jamb, watching her with the oddest look on his face. Then in the blink of an eye, the indecipherable look disappeared, and he pushed away from the arch and sauntered into the kitchen. Stopping next to the table, he regarded her without favor. "You still here?"

Lily set down her fork. "Yes," she said. "And just so we don't have to keep having this conversation over and over again, let me see if I can put this in words simple enough for you to understand. I. Am not. Leaving. Certainly not because you have some ridiculous notion that I'm out to cheat Glynnis of her inheritance. Your sister was kind enough to offer me a place to stay when my apartment went condo, and unless *she* asks me to leave, this is exactly where I plan to remain." At least until the last week in May, when her next stint as chef for a corporate yacht was scheduled to begin—but Lily didn't feel any burning need to share that information with Glynnis's brother.

She looked him over. Why did the guy have to be such eye candy? He had that flushed, moist glow of the freshly showered, and his hair was still damp, his cheeks smooth and shiny from a recent shave. He was just plain fan-yourself attractive, and lordy, didn't it just *figure* that the first man to rev her engine in way too long would turn out to be a judgmental oaf? Life was so unfair.

Never did it seem more so than when he asked in a silky baritone, "Did my sister happen to mention that the house is in *my* name, not hers?"

Zach watched as Lily absorbed the news. She looked stunned for a moment, but he had to hand it to her, she recovered quickly. Her fine-boned little chin lifted, and her eyes were cool as they met his head-on.

"And I assume you mean to challenge the legality of my contract with her?"

"Maybe." He crossed his arms over his chest and gazed down at her. But she looked way too good, so he transferred his attention to the plate in front of her, which held the most delicious-looking omelet he'd ever seen. Its tantalizing scent had been responsible for pulling him to the kitchen in the first place, and actually seeing its golden-brown perfection made saliva pool in his mouth. His stomach growled.

"Then I guess we'll see each other in court," Lily said, snapping his attention back to her. Cheeks flushed and eyes so bright a blue he suspected colored contact lenses, she pushed back from the table and rose to her feet. She carried her plate over to the sink where she scraped its contents, giving him a long, level look over her shoulder. "Because I'm still not leaving."

For one brief moment Zach didn't care. He watched the perfect omelet disappear down the garbage disposal and wanted to howl. Just because she couldn't finish it didn't mean it had to go to waste. He would have taken care of it for her. He couldn't *remember* the last time he'd eaten a proper meal, but it sure as hell hadn't been during the past twenty-four hours. Hunger, lack of sufficient sleep, and worry over his sister sent him across the space separating them. "Where's Glynnis?" he snarled, even though he knew damn well that hotheaded demands were destined to fail.

Lily didn't reply, but something in her eyes confirmed Zach's suspicion that she knew the answer, and with a lack of control that wasn't at all like him he wrapped his hands around her upper arms and pulled her up onto her toes. Bending his head, he got right in her face. "Where the hell is she?"

The warmth and the softness of her skin registered first. Then he saw her crystalline blue eyes go wide, and the genuine fear that flashed through them struck him like a punch to the gut. With an oath, he set her free. He stepped back and plowed a hand through his hair. "I just want to know where my sister is." Hearing the apologetic tone in his voice, he snarled, "For all I know, finagling yourself a cushy berth here wasn't enough to keep you satisfied."

"Meaning what—that now you think I've *harmed* her? For heaven's sake! She's gone on a trip!" Crossing her arms over her breasts, she rubbed her arms. "You might want to consult a professional about that paranoia."

Shoving down the flash of guilt he felt seeing her hands pat the flesh he'd just manhandled as if searching for bruises, he honed in on the pertinent information. "A trip where? With who?"

"North," she replied coolly. "With a friend." Eyes narrowed, she thrust her jaw up at him. But she couldn't quite hold his gaze.

It told him louder than words could have that the "friend" was someone he wouldn't approve of. "Aw, crap. She's off with *another* fortune hunter, isn't she?"

"Insinuating that I'm one too, I take it?"

"If the high heel fits, honey chile." Although, taking in that tousled blonde hair and those kiss-me-daddy lips, he'd grant that gulling a naive young woman might be a departure for her. Little Miss Lily's wiles were probably more often practiced on the dick-bearing segment of the moneyed set.

"My gawd." She blew out a disgusted breath and shot him a look that should have dropped him in his tracks. "You are some piece of work."

"And don't you forget it. Now let's you and I sit down and get nice and comfy. Then you can tell me exactly *where* up north Glynnis has gone—and just who the hell her travel buddy is."

"Can I now," she said flatly. "And is there anything *else* I can do for you while I'm at it?"

"I wouldn't say no to one of those omelets."

"Oh, you bet—I'll get right on that. Meanwhile, I tell

you what." She cocked a hip at him, gave one pretty, rounded cheek a resounding smack, and tendered him a sweet smile. "Kiss this."

He gave the anatomy in question a comprehensive perusal, then slowly raised his gaze. "Wouldn't say no to that, either."

A soft shriek of frustration escaped her, and pivoting on her toe, she stalked from the room—or at least that was the impression conveyed by the unyielding set of her golden-skinned shoulders as she left the kitchen. Genuine stalking had to be a tough act to pull off in heels that tall.

He watched the rhythmic twitch of her hips as she walked away. *How can someone as sweet as Glynnis have such a pig of a brother?* Her words from last night whispered in his mind, and he scowled. What was it about her, anyway, that loosened every restriction that ordinarily guarded his tongue? Two lousy minutes in her company seemed to be all it took to destroy years of having manners drummed into his head.

This wasn't how he'd been raised to talk to women. Grandmother must be spinning in her grave—she'd had very concrete ideas of how gentlemen dealt with ladies, and she would've skinned him alive to hear the disrespect he'd tendered Lily.

But, *damn*, the woman had annoying ways of getting to him! Like dabbing on just enough of that scent she wore to make him want to get closer to sniff out more. Or doing whatever it was she did to make herself look as if she'd just tumbled out of bed after a bout of really hot sex. Not to mention the way she walked, with those hip swinging, tippy-toed little steps. Hell, she even *ate* seductively. The look on her face when she'd been forking that omelet into her mouth had practically knocked him on his butt. He'd seen women in the midst of an orgasm who hadn't looked half as ecstatic.

He shook his head, trying to get the image out of his mind. He didn't get it. What the hell was it about her that drew him so? It wasn't as if Lily were the most beautiful woman he'd ever met. Or even the sexiest, when it came right down to it. But just let her be in the same room and, without any effort on her part it seemed, she kept his attention trained squarely on her.

And you think that's by accident, genius?

Zach swore. Well, duh. Keep a guy's attention focused on disheveled blonde hair and a well-rounded little fuck-me body, and it sure as hell won't be his *mind* doing the thinking. Lily Morrisette might be about the girliest female he'd ever clapped eyes on, but she had a habit of meeting both gazes and situations head-on, a way of refusing to ever back down, that was almost masculine in its determination. She knew precisely what she was doing.

He didn't think he was jumping to any hasty conclusions by questioning her motives. Glynnis certainly had a record of trusting the wrong people. She'd run afoul of some real losers in her life, and more than one young buck had thought to score himself a free ride by attaching himself to her. But they hadn't *all* been out to take her, so it wasn't as if he automatically suspected every person she came into contact with. She'd managed to make some regular friends; he'd give her that. Every one of his sister's girlfriends he'd met up until now, though, had been her own age—young women in their early twenties who'd tended either to start giggling or to flirt blatantly whenever he tried to have anything resembling an intelligent conversation with them.

They were nothing like Lily. They lacked that aura she had of knowing the score, for one thing. It took years and experience to gain that kind of worldliness. He might not be the greatest judge of age, but he'd put money on Lily being quite a bit older than his sister—somewhere closer to his own thirty-six than to Glynnis's not-quite twenty-five.

And all things considered, he had to wonder: What would someone as self-assured as Lily want with an ingenuous girl who was nine or ten years younger if it wasn't her money?

The origins of their association definitely bore closer examination.

Lily paced her room, seriously irritated. And to think she used to dream of having a big brother! If Mr. I-Am-the-Commandant-of-All-I-Survey was any example, she could count herself fortunate she'd been an only child.

She made a conscious effort to unclench her teeth. But, really! She'd excused his rudeness last night because he'd obviously been tired and not thinking clearly, but how dare he continue to heedlessly assume she had no integrity? Yes, she was a busty, blue-eyed blonde who loved makeup and jewelry; so rarely in her life had any man bothered to look deeper than that. But there was a big difference between being considered a dumb blonde and Zach's careless assassination of her character.

She plopped down on the edge of the bed and concentrated on regaining her equilibrium, trying to look at the situation without all the emotion that had her blood churning. It took her a while, but her pulse finally began to settle down.

Then the pounding on her door commenced. Lily jerked and to her disgust made a sound like a startled screech owl. Popping off the bed, she faced the closed door with her hands fisted on her hips, all her high-minded promises forgotten as her heart once again pounded double time. "Go away!"

"Open up, Lily. I want to talk to you."

"Oh, well, then," she muttered. "Let me just trot right over and let you in. Your wishes make *all* the difference in the world."

"I heard that." He had the effrontery to sound amused. But his good humor apparently didn't last. He thumped the portal. "Open the damn door."

She crossed the room in several angry strides, ripped the door open, and stared up in annoyance at his tanned face. "Are you incapable of completing one lousy sentence without cursing?"

He blinked, then to her surprise gave her a sheepish look. "Sorry," he rumbled in that deep voice. "I've been a soldier so long I sometimes forget that conversations are more refined in the civilian world. I'll try to do better." Then he seemed to recall he was conversing with the enemy. He stepped into the room, forcing her to take a step back before she caught herself and stood her ground. "But that's not why I'm here," he said. "Tell me how you met my sister."

He was back to being his imperious, give-me-the-facts-and-give-'em-to-me-*now* self, and Lily's knee-jerk reaction was to invite him to kiss her rosy red cheeks. Recalling she'd already done that, however, sent blood hot enough to blister rushing through her veins—particularly when she thought of his response. A better idea would be to get a handle on this anger once and for all. So she took a deep breath, eased it out, and told him the truth. "We met at a yoga class."

"Where?"

"At Headlands, over on Harbor Drive in Dana Point."

"And who joined the class first?" He snapped out his questions for all the world as if he were a drill instructor and she his raw recruit. "You, or Glynnis?"

"Glynnis," she said through her teeth.

He looked down at her as if she'd just confirmed his lowest suspicion. "Uh-*huh*."

"What do you mean, *uh-huh*?" As if it took a wizard to see where *this* was going. Her back went ramrod straight. "I lived about a mile away at the time, between San Juan Capistrano and Dana Point. Glynnis is the one who travelled out of her way to attend that particular class. Does your paranoia know no *bounds*?"

"Well, let me see," he said, looking down at her. "A thirtysomething woman with no visible means of support just happens to join the same yoga class as my very wealthy twenty-four-year-old sister—and the next thing we know, she's moved right in with her." He raised his eyebrows. "Oh, yeah, sounds paranoid to me, all right. The two of you having so much in common, and all."

"I've told you I'm paying rent! Your 'very wealthy sister' is flat broke half the time, and this has been a way for both of us to benefit until I find a new place! Besides, you've known me one day! What makes you just assume I don't support myself?"

"You're right, that remains to be seen. But today's a workday, lollipop, and as far as I can see, you've gotten yourself all dolled up to lounge around the house." His cool, gray gaze did a fast slide over her before coming back to meet her own. "But, hey, if you're subsidizing Glynnis's trust fund, there's an easy enough way to prove it, isn't there? Show me a canceled check."

Oh, swell. Lily's heart sank. "The bank doesn't return my canceled checks. I can request photocopies, but it might take a day or two."

"I just bet it will."

Itching for the first time in her life to strike a person, she closed the distance separating them. "I've had enough of your attitude. I want you to leave my room."

He looked down at her and didn't move until she poked him in the chest. Then he took a slow, indolent step backward and didn't take another until she poked him again. He stepped over the threshold out into the hall.

Lily stared up at him. "You want to know what Glynnis and I have in common, soldier boy?"

He raised an eyebrow.

"We both marvel at what absolute cretins some men can be," she said and recited the complaints of every woman she'd ever known who'd been on the dating circuit for a while. "It seems they either want to change you, take you for a ride, or run your life. You oughtta be able to identify with that." With a sharp little click, she closed the door in his face.

There was silence from the other side for a moment. Then Zach said, "I want to know where my sister is."

"And I want an end to world hunger. Looks like we're both going to be disappointed."

"No, ma'am. Maybe you've got your work cut out to meet your goal, but I don't intend to fail in mine. You *will* tell me. Count on it."

Not blooming likely, she thought, staring at the closed portal. There was no way on earth she intended to be the one to break the news to Control Freak Taylor that the sister he apparently thought was too clueless to be left to her own devices was on her way to Washington state to meet her new fiancé's family.

3

"WHY DON'T YOU JUST TELL THE BIG JERK WHAT YOU do for a living and be done with it?"

Lily looked at her friend Mimi across the restaurant table and smiled ruefully. "That would be the reasonable thing to do, I'm sure. But he makes me so darn mad that reason just flies right out the window whenever I'm anywhere near him."

"Which is exactly why you should let me guide you back to the smart side of the street." Mimi moved aside her leopard-skin handbag to make room for her elbows on the ecru linen tablecloth and leaned forward earnestly. "Show him one of your pay stubs, Lil, and enjoy yourself when he's forced to eat his words. Seeing all those zeros is bound to make him feel like an idiot."

"If I had my way, they'd make him *choke*," Lily muttered. Then taken aback by her own savagery, she said, "Okay, maybe not literally." She shook her head in confusion. "Good Grief. Until I met Zach Taylor, I always considered myself to be a live-and-let-live sort of person. But he just makes me so . . . so darn . . ."

"Passionate?"

"Furious!" Amid the clink of silverware, the muted conversations, and the classical music purling out of hidden speakers, she sat ramrod straight on her tapestry upholstered chair. "And you know what? I don't owe him any explanations. He's the one who jumped to the idiotic conclusion I'm some sort of larcenous bimbo. Why should I knock myself out providing him proof that I'm not?"

"Because it'd make life easier?" Then Mimi shook her head. "Okay. I recognize that mulish look. For someone usually so mellow, you sure can dig your heels in once you've got your back up."

"I know, it's stupid and no doubt adolescent as well; but that's the way I feel. Maybe after a nice relaxing luncheon with you, my outlook will be more mature."

"Then just let me ask you this and I'll drop it: don't you think there's an elegant sort of irony at work here? I mean, if there's *one* thing you're particularly good at, it's money management."

"It's what comes from having grown up poor," Lily agreed. "I was probably only eight when I swore I'd find a way to make myself financially secure when I grew up."

"And you've achieved that," Mimi said gently. "You've met every one of your short-term goals and you're well on your way to realizing most of your long-term ones as well."

Lily's spine unbent a little. It was true. The career she'd forged for herself netted her very good money, and the investments she'd made over the years had paid off even more handsomely. So to *hades* with Zachariah

Taylor and his unfounded accusations! Let him stew in his own suspicions. As long as she knew that contrary to his nasty little digs she'd actually been teaching his sister a little financial responsibility, what did it matter what he believed? Her mouth curved up on one side. "So what you're saying is I oughtta lighten up?"

"Listen, sweetie, I know that's easy for me to say when it's not my integrity under attack, but maybe just a little. Or at least try not to take his crap so much to heart. What are you going to do about the sister?"

"Glynnis?"

"Yes. Taylor sounds like a first-class bastard, but to play devil's advocate for a minute, you said yourself he probably has experience on his side when it comes to dealing with his sister's character judgment skills. Her track record in that department sounds less than impressive."

"It is, and I did." Despite her newfound resolve, however, Lily realized she still wasn't in the mood to give him the benefit of the doubt. "Is this going somewhere, Mimi?"

"Not in a straightforward manner, apparently." Her friend laughed. "I guess what I'm trying to say is, maybe his wanting to know her whereabouts is more than a control issue. What if he's just genuinely concerned for her welfare? How do you balance that against his hounding you for information?"

"By keeping out of it. Glynnis can be too wide-eyed for her own good sometimes—heck, we got to talking in the first place because she was torn up from discovering the very charming young man currently sweeping her off her feet had his eye firmly on her bank account.

But the fact is, she's of age. If she'd wanted her brother to know her plans, she would have left him a note or called by now, so it's sure as sugar not up to me to fill in the blanks. Plus, I really like David, and I genuinely think he'll be good for her." She took a sip of wine. "If the commando king learns David dared whisk her away, though. . . . Well, I shudder to think what he'll do. Frothing at the mouth would just be the beginning." She looked across the table at her friend. "Boy, I'm starting to think maybe I should've just bought the darn apartment when it went condo. At least then I wouldn't be smack in the middle of this opera."

"No, you'd be thirty grand short of your goal, instead. And for what? Not your dream digs, that's for sure. Your place was a nice enough, but they wanted way too much for a piece of real estate that's not even seven hundred square feet. Hell, I usually equate an asking price like that with something that provides at least a partial view, even if it's one you have to hang out a window to see."

It cheered Lily to hear her decision validated. "You're right. Bless you for reminding me I wasn't particularly attached to it—not enough, at least, to dig into my savings for the down payment and closing costs."

Brilliant sunshine poured through the window. And glancing out at the palm trees rustling their green fronds in the gentle breeze, she let her long-held dream of finally settling in one place to open her own restaurant give her a moment's peace before turning back to the problem at hand. "One thing's for sure," she told her friend. "I'm gonna have to step up my search for somewhere else to live. I was hoping to hold off until I got back from my next gig aboard the *Argosy*, but the writing's on the wall. Much as I detest letting him get away with driving me off, there's just no living with the guy."

"Now that's not necessarily so." A long skein of artfully streaked butterscotch-colored hair slipped over Mimi's shoulder and she scooped it back behind her. "I'm telling you, sweetie, tell the man the truth. He'll probably be so mortified by how badly he misjudged you that he'll offer you room and board for free." She flashed a cheeky grin. "Then your restaurant kitty will be that much closer to a grand opening."

Lily's laugh was short and skeptical. "I doubt Zach Taylor's spent an embarrassed moment in his life. Besides, I think we're way beyond the kiss-and-make-up stage." A fleeting image of that mouth of his with its thin white scar reminded her libido it still possessed a few red corpuscles capable of generating heat, and she shifted in her seat. "No," she said with extra firmness to make up for it. "My dream will simply have to wait a month or two."

"Well, okay," Mimi said, "but I think you're making a mistake."

Lily gave her a lopsided smile. "Like *that* would be a first." Then she picked up the menu. "So. Do you know what you're going to have for dessert? I keep hearing great things about the tiramisu here. I have really got to check it out."

Zach opened the front door in response to an authoritative knock and froze in surprise when he saw who stood on the other side. Of all the people he might have expected to land on his porch, John Miglionni wouldn't have even made the top twenty.

But there stood his former Marine buddy all the same, one muscular shoulder propped against the stucco arch, his hands shoved in his slacks pockets as he proffered a lazy smile, teeth startlingly white against his olive-skinned complexion. "Midnight, you ugly son of a bitch," he said easily. "Long time, no see."

"Rocket!" A surge of genuine pleasure shattered Zach's paralysis. Breaking into a huge smile, he stepped forward, and the two men pounded each other on the back in greeting. As they stepped back, Zach's hand whipped out to grasp the other man's sleek black ponytail and give it a tug. "What's this? I may be ugly, but at least I'm a clean-cut American guy. When did you turn into a pinko radical chick?"

"Screw you, Taylor."

"I don't think so, pal. Some of us still go for the ladies."

They grinned at each other, satisfied to be exchanging insults once again, and for the first time since arriving home, Zach felt like his old self. He waved his friend through the doorway. "Haul your ass in here," he commanded. "God, what's it been, nearly two years? What brings you to my neck of the woods?"

"I had a case that ended up in L.A." John followed Zach into the kitchen, where Zach retrieved a couple of beers from the refrigerator. "Once it was wrapped up, I figured I could hardly be this close and not drop by to say hello."

"You got that right, buddy." He passed the other man

a beer and they twisted off the caps, snapped their fingers to send the tops zinging toward the sink, then moved to the kitchen table. "Damn. It's good to see you, John." Gesturing to his friend to take a seat, he pulled out a chair for himself. "How've you been—still getting a big charge out of doing the Sam Spade thing?"

"Yeah, I really like it." Rocket lounged back, his long legs stretched out in front of him and his beer bottle cradled against his flat stomach. "Most of the time, anyhow. Can't say I was crazy about it when it prevented me from making Coop's wedding, but I was right in the middle of a couple of cases that paid the overhead, and I couldn't afford to leave them dangling. Sure hated to miss out on the big event, though. I was dying to meet the bride, since I'm having a hard time picturing the woman capable of getting Ice to the altar."

"You'd like Veronica. She looks a lot like Snow White would've if she'd been getting any."

"You mean she *wasn't*?" Rocket stared at him as if he'd just been told Santa Claus was dead. "You can't tell me she wasn't messing around with the dwarves, man. Why the hell you think Dopey had that goofy grin?"

"Lack of oxygen at birth, maybe?" Zach laughed. "You gotta admit she was pretty damn good at keeping up the virginal façade. Or maybe it was just the high, trilly voice that had me fooled. As for Veronica, think our girl Snow with hot blood, and that would be her. She's cute, she's fun, and she's talented. And she's just wild about Coop."

"Sweet. Still, the only way she'll ever get the Miglionni stamp of approval is if I meet her for myself." He took a drink of his beer, then smiled. "Which I actually finally get to do. The case I just finished put me between jobs for the first time in over a year and a half, and I'm taking a little vacation to go up to Fogey, Washington, and spend a few days with them."

"Fossil, you moron," Zach corrected automatically. Then he realized what John's vacation meant for his own plans and swore. When Rocket's jet-black eyes leveled on him and his dark eyebrows raised in easygoing inquiry, however, he merely shrugged. "Sorry," he said. "That'll be good for you. It's just not so great for me. I was about to call you about running a check on someone."

"Hey, I can run checks any time, anywhere. Have laptop, will travel—I'm never far from my trusty titanium. Who do you want investigated?"

"A woman by the name of Lily Morrisette." He explained the situation.

"And you're absolutely sure she's pulling a con?" Rocket asked when he finished.

"About as sure as I can be without your background check. I gave her a chance to prove otherwise and she put me off." He rubbed the back of his neck. "I don't know, John, maybe this is my fault."

"How do you figure that?"

"Look at this place. I wanted to give Glynnie what she gave up when she came to live with me at Lejeune. But I might as well have taken out an advertisement that read, 'Naive rich girl, left on her own a lot. Come and get it.' "

Rocket shook his head. "I'd tell you to cut yourself some slack here, bud, but I know you when it comes to your sister. So give me everything you know about Morrisette."

Zach provided what he knew, which admittedly wasn't a lot. The only thing he didn't tell John was what a struggle he found it to resist the pull of Lily's sexuality. It wasn't pertinent anyhow. The attraction was strictly involuntary, and he planned to get a grip on it.

But he must be slipping, because when he finished laying everything out Rocket crossed his ankles beneath the table, sank a little deeper onto his tailbone, and studied him intently as he sipped his beer.

And Zach knew he'd somehow given himself away.

For a moment, John didn't say a word. Then he scratched the tip of his thumbnail across his chin. "From what I've seen since hitting L.A., these California girls are something else again. The solution seems like a no-brainer to me."

"Give me a clue then, Miglionni, because I'm not seeing it."

"She's built, she's blond, and she's no better than she oughtta be, right?"

"Yeah. So?"

He shrugged. "So, why not make her an offer she can't refuse? Hell, Zach, she sounds like every girl you've ever pursued. Buy the chick a few baubles. Become her sugar daddy for a while."

Zach snapped upright in his chair. "What are you, *crazy*?"

"Crazy like a fox, maybe." Rocket's grin was all teeth. "It's a win-win situation. You've got the funds to keep her happy; sounds to me like she's got the goods to keep *you* happy; and if she's occupied taking care of your needs, she won't have the time or energy to hustle Baby Sis."

For several heartbeats the urge to take his friend's suggestion and run with it was sweeter than the sing of narcotics through a junkie's veins. The sheer temptation of it caught Zach by surprise.

Then he came to his senses.

"I prefer not to buy my women," he said with a coolly sardonic smile. But he had to take a long pull on his beer to wet his suddenly dry throat.

"Ah, well, if you're gonna be *fussy* about it." Rocket shrugged. "Now, me, I'll take the little darlins any way I can get 'em. Just as long as the end result is me getting my hands on them."

Zach laughed. "You're so full of shit, John." Raising his beer bottle to his lips, he studied his friend over the top of the amber glass for a moment. "Though, come to think of it, you never were all that discriminating, were you? Still chasing skirts as fast as you can?"

"Nah. I've slowed down some. Hell, I don't even brag about my conquests anymore."

"Get outta here. The guy who used to regale Coop and me in pornographic detail of whatever girl had ridden the rocket the night before—now keeping it all to himself? Son of a bitch, boy."

"I know; the world as we once knew it has ceased to exist. This growing up is a spooky business." He killed off his brew and set the bottle on the table. "Speaking of growing up, when you plan on giving up field work?"

"Goddamn never." Because it hit a nerve too close to

the surface, his voice was flatter than he might have wished.

But John didn't seem to mind; he merely hitched one shoulder in an easy shrug. "The twenty-year-olds haven't managed to run you into the ground yet, then?"

"They try, but I'm hanging tough." Although maybe not bouncing back as fast as he used to. "Jesus, Rocket, were we ever that young? Or that stupid? I just got back from a detail in South America where I had to ride herd on a bunch of horny teenagers bent on chasing the local señoritas. We damn near had ourselves an international incident by the time we pulled out."

"One of your men compromise a local girl?"

" 'Ruined' her is how her betrothed put it." He shook his head in disgust. "We went down to extract a hostage from a drug cartel, then stayed to defend the local village against retaliation. It was supposed to be quick and professional. We were to get the hostage out, set up defensible parameters around the village and show the villagers the basics of maintaining them, then select a few of their young men to bring back to Pendleton."

"To train in the rudiments of warfare?"

"Yeah; you know how it works."

"Sure." John shrugged again. "Teach 'em everything you can cram into six weeks, then send them back to educate the rest of the village and hope for the best. So, was it actually your man getting his rocks off that nearly caused the incident, or was this just one of those ops that are fucked from start to finish?"

"No, the recon and extraction went great. My unit is young, but they're good. The problems didn't start until we got to the village. That's when they turned from a corps of highly trained professionals into a bunch of pussy-chasing morons."

"And this is something new? Hell, Midnight, there's always shit like that to rein in whenever young soldiers are exposed to nubile sweet young things. Or to any female with a pulse when it comes to that—particularly following a successful mission."

"I know, but this time one of my men diddling with a local girl damn near meant the difference between a village getting the training to defend itself and not. And I sure as hell wouldn't have enjoyed having to explain why to the brass."

"What happened?"

Zach noticed John's empty beer bottle and got up to get two more longnecks out of the fridge. "The best candidate for the program by far," he said, "was a young man named Miguel Escavez. He had the most raw talent, the greatest determination to protect what's his, and unquestionable leadership potential." Handing Rocket a beer, he sat back down, then stopped in the midst of twisting the cap off his own to look at his friend across the table. "Unfortunately, he was also the girl's fiancé."

"Oh, shit."

"Tell me about it. After talking to the girl and determining the sex with Pederson was consensual, I got the happy job of telling Miguel that since that was so, and she was of age, I didn't have jurisdiction to punish my soldier-cum-stud of the hour." Zach got a sudden flashback to swarming flies and thick, steamy heat, saw again the outraged ego burning in the young Latino's eyes.

He finished twisting the bottle cap off and took a

swig of beer to wash the vision away. "A couple days later we found Pederson outside the village, beaten to a pulp. I know damn well Escavez was responsible, but lacking concrete proof, there wasn't a helluva lot I could do about that, either." His jaw set. "Which pretty much summed up the entire detail. I didn't do a helluva lot."

John shrugged. "Some missions are like that—there's just not much you can do. And it's probably just as well you didn't find evidence against Escavez anyway."

"How do you figure?"

"We've both spent more hours than we can count in these villages. If there's one thing you can depend on in some of the more macho cultures, it's the store they place in saving face. Is Pederson okay?"

"Yeah. He's still not one hundred percent, but you know how fast a nineteen-year-old heals."

"There you go, then. Your soldier survived and might even think twice before he messes with another villager's woman. Escavez got his retribution, which probably helped him save face in front of his village."

"True." Zach felt some of the weight he'd been carrying slide away. "And in the end Miguel even volunteered to be part of the three-man delegation we brought back with us." He saluted Rocket with his beer bottle. "So all's well that ends well, I guess."

He heard the sound of the front door opening. Knowing it had to be Lily, he looked toward the archway, waiting for her to pass by. It bugged him to realize his blood was pumping a little hotter and faster through his veins than it had been a few moments ago. Then, recalling his friend's words, he took a slow, controlled breath and gave himself a break.

Rocket was right. Lily *was* the exact type of woman that usually drew his attention—at least in the physical sense. *I'll be damned,* he thought with a little surge of relief. *I'm not turning into the world's worst brother, after all. I merely need to get laid.*

He almost laughed out loud. As John had said, successful reconnaissance missions had a way of getting a guy's juices flowing. Combine that with the fact that it had been a long time since he'd been within belly-rubbing distance of a woman—even before the South American detail had come up—and any woman would look good to him, never mind a hot little number like Lily Morrisette. Just give him the chance to rectify the sexual limbo he'd been in, though, and she'd likely lose whatever small hold she had over his senses.

He kept that thought firmly in mind when Lily sashayed into view, all cotton-candy hair and swinging hips as she strutted toward the archway. Still his temperature cranked another notch higher. Then, just as he was thinking he'd better start trolling the bars pretty damn soon, Lily glanced up from the tiny handbag into which she dropped her keys.

With a little yelp of surprise she stopped in her tracks, a splayed hand slapping the full swell of her breasts. A half dozen narrow gold bangles clinked and jingled as they slid down her arm from wrist to forearm. Her eyes locked with Zach's.

"You startled me!" she exclaimed breathlessly, and more jingling ensued as her hand patted her chest as if to contain a racing heart. "I didn't realize anyone was here." Then she jerked her gaze away and glanced at Rocket, offering him a tentative smile.

It pushed all Zach's buttons, and he laughed harshly. "Right," he snarled. "Like you can't smell fresh meat a block away." *Jesus, what an actress.* He jerked his head toward Rocket. "So meet John. He can't afford you."

You would have thought he'd pissed in the middle of a tea party, the way she looked at him. Without a word, she turned on her heel and walked away.

His blood flat-out boiled. How did she do it? How did she make him feel as if *he* was in the wrong when he knew damn good and well that she was the one playing all the angles?

"So that's Lily, huh?"

Zach blew out a breath and turned to look at his friend. "Yeah."

"*Hoo*-ahh," Rocket breathed. "Now that's lethal stuff." He reached over to punch Zach on the arm. "But my money's on you, buddy. You'll have her disarmed in no time." He cocked a dense black eyebrow. "That is, if you start thinking with something besides your dick. What's the matter with you, anyway? I've never seen you like this, never heard you be anything but polite to a woman, no matter what her agenda. You gotta quit letting this one mess with your head."

Then he bared his teeth. "Lucky for you, you've got me at your back. You've established you're the bad guy. Now it's time for ol' brother John to see what he can learn."

4

LILY WAS PANTING IN ABSOLUTE FURY BY THE TIME she closed the door at her back. He was a *pig*! A pig, a pig, a *pig*! Where did he get off treating her like that?

Well, he won. She'd pack her bags and start looking for another place this afternoon. It just chapped her hide to let him run her off this way, but she couldn't take it any more. She simply wasn't built for this kind of confrontation.

Unlike last night, when she'd thrown everything she owned into her case, she began gathering together only the nonessentials she could live without for a while, so she'd be ready to move at a moment's notice. But she made a face as she retrieved her luggage from the closet. This was way too reminiscent of her life growing up, when a year rarely went by without her restless parents telling her to pack her things because they were moving on. She'd learned at a young age never to get too comfortable in any one place, so heaven knew she had a decent grasp on what was necessary in order to get by for a day or two, and what were just extras.

She'd really thought all that was finally behind her, though. Until her apartment went condo, she'd lived in the same place for seven years, a record for someone who had gone to eleven different schools in six different states—and that wasn't counting two culinary schools. When Glynnis invited her to stay in this lovely ocean-front home, she'd appreciated it more than she could say and had truly hoped her next move would be her last. Ideally, when she found her restaurant, it would combine a living area with the commercial space. She'd planned to search for the perfect spot as soon as she got back from her next cruise.

Lily gave herself a mental shake. Well, sometimes things didn't work out; no one knew that better than she. That didn't mean she intended to go off half-cocked and storm out without a plan. Mimi would undoubtedly let her camp out on her couch for a few days, but she wanted to reserve that option as a last resort. First, she'd check out the ads to see what was available without a lease.

Merely thinking about it made her tired, though, so she flipped open her luggage on the bedspread and began filling it. She'd start with something a little less stressful.

She was piling most of her collection of pretty lingerie into one corner of the case, thinking she really ought to rummage through the three-car garage for some boxes, when her gaze was caught by an envelope sticking up out of one of the suitcase's little gathered pockets.

Her hands stilled for a moment over the heap of silkies and lace. Funny, she didn't remember tucking anything away in there. Then she shrugged. It was probably an old greeting card that had gotten swept up and tossed wily-nilly into the case when she was snatching up stuff last night. Since she rarely hung on to things—a habit left over from her days of keeping extras to a minimum—it was likely not even hers.

She was just reaching for it to check it out when a knock sounded at the door. She whirled to face it, the card promptly forgotten. "Go away," she snapped, her heart renewing its pounding rhythm as if it had never slowed down. "I'm through talking to you."

"It's John Miglionni, ma'am. Please. I won't take up much of your time, but I'd like to speak to you for a moment."

She crossed the room and yanked the door open. Folding her arms militantly beneath her breasts, she glared up at the man on the other side of the threshold. "What makes you think I'm interested in anything you have to say?" Then she blinked. She'd been so furious with Zach earlier she'd barely gotten more than a quick impression of his friend. Seeing John clearly for the first time, she murmured, "What *is* this place, anyhow, Testosterone Central?"

Then she gave him a second, closer inspection and wasn't sure where that first impression had come from. He didn't look so tough. He was an inch or two over six feet, and aside from muscular shoulders, looked as lean and lanky as a young Jimmy Stewart beneath his pricey silver-gray silk T-shirt and impeccably pressed black slacks. Even the brawny shoulders appeared somehow less powerful than she'd first thought when she looked at him slouched against the doorframe.

He was dark-skinned and had hair so black and shiny it contained blue highlights even in the dim hallway. He wore its thick length pulled back in a ponytail, a style that accented his high cheekbones, hawklike nose, and the spare angularity of his face. But it was his dark eyes and smile that grabbed her—both were as bashful and self-effacing as a monk's.

"I don't know about the testosterone," he said softly, "but I do want to apologize for Zachariah. He's been under a lot of pressure lately, and he's worried sick about his little sister, but that's no excuse to treat you so rudely. He was completely out of line, and I told him so."

His soft-spoken apology was balm to her offended sensibilities, and her combative pose eased. "That's very gallant of you."

He ducked his head. "Not at all, ma'am. Zach's insinuations were insulting, and I wanted you to know that although he's my friend I don't endorse his behavior." Thrusting his hands in his pockets, he hunched his shoulders and shot her a glance full of shy, male interest. "Are you from around here?"

The movement starkly defined the sinews of his arms for a moment, and Lily realized there was more muscle to him than she'd thought. Silky black hair feathered his forearms, and a small patch of color on his left one caught her attention. "I guess you could say I'm from everywhere," she admitted slowly, shooting what was undoubtedly a tattoo a covert glance to see if she could figure out what it depicted. "But for the past seven years I've lived in—" Sudden comprehension chopped her sentence in two.

Oh. He was good. She should have remembered the quick impression she'd gotten in the kitchen of intelligent, watchful eyes, but his polite, soothing manners and low-key interest had suckered her completely.

"Well," she continued smoothly, flapping a dismissive hand. "You don't care about that."

"Of course I do. I'd love to hear everything about you."

"You're awfully kind. It's just so *nice* to talk to a gentleman after dealing with that horrid—" She grimaced. "I'm sorry. I forgot for a moment he's your friend."

"Don't worry about it." He dug a shoulder into the doorjamb and smiled that monk's smile at her. "You were going to tell me about all those places you've been and how the last seven years you've lived in . . . ?"

"Oh, let's not talk about me." She gave him an aren't-you-just-the-sweetest-thing look. "Where are *you* from?"

"I've been all over, too." He leaned a little closer. "Maybe we've been to some of the same places."

"Gee, do you think? That would be something, wouldn't it?" With a glance up from under her lashes, she murmured, "John is such a nice, strong name. What's your sign?"

"Aries. How about you?"

"Oh, dear, not one that's compatible with yours. And you seemed so perfect, too." With a regretful sigh, she started to close the door.

"Wait!" Straightening, he gave her a self-deprecating smile. "You can't hold that against me. Heck, you don't even know what house my moon is in, or anything. It could make all the difference."

"Why, that's true. What time were you born?"

He told her and she gave a thoughtful, "Hmm," then reached out to touch his wrist. "What do you do for a living, John?"

"I'm an accountant."

Her brow furrowed. "Oh."

"And a financial planner."

"*Really.* Oooh, I just love money." Leaning against the edge of the open door, she slid her hand up the smooth wood until her arm curved overhead, her palm flat against its interior panel. "So tell me," she said, watching him eye the outside curve of her breast that the pose exposed. "When it comes to long-term investment, what mix of high, medium, and low caps do you recommend for a stock portfolio? And what's your take on index mutual funds?"

His gaze snapped up to meet hers. "Uh . . ."

"Don't," she admonished gently, "confuse blond hair and breasts with stupidity."

He gave her a perplexed look. "Ma'am?"

"At least Zach's up front in his enmity. The next time you try out your aw-shucks-golly routine, I suggest you cover up that." She nodded at the mostly red tattoo on his arm, which his change in position had made clearly visible. Outlined in black, it contained the words *Swift, Silent,* and *Deadly* on three sides of a white skull with black and yellow markings, and 2d Recon Bn inscribed across the bottom. Looking up into eyes gone abruptly hard, she assured him crisply, "It truly does detract from the image." Then, giving the panel beneath her hand a push, she closed the door in his face.

She had a feeling her blood pressure was in the red zone. As if things weren't bad enough already, the lousy ratfinks were double-teaming her! Too restless to go back to her packing, she paced her room for several tense moments.

Then she abruptly stopped in the middle of the room. She had to get out of here before she did something stupid like scream her head off. A walk on the beach would cool her down, but if she wanted to kill two birds with one stone she should probably grab a newspaper and head up the coast highway to the Koffee Klatch, where she could read the apartment listings in peace. A nice, nonhostile environment sounded like just the ticket. She grabbed her purse from the dresser top where she'd tossed it a short while ago and let herself out of the room.

When she let herself back in several hours later, the sun had disappeared over the horizon in a blazing ball of orange and red, and she was calmer—if no closer to having another place to stay than when she'd left. There had only been one apartment in the ads worth pursuing, and by the time she'd gotten over to check it out someone else had already snatched it up.

Well, there was always the internet, but she'd get to that later. The walls of her room were already closing in, and unwilling to act as if she had anything to hide, she marched down the hall, braced to brave the duel condemnation of Zach and his underhanded friend. But the kitchen was empty and the entire house had a deserted feel. She dished up a bowl of ice cream and took it into the den, where she settled into a chair and turned on the news. A short while later, she turned it off again. Beyond a fleeting impression of an impending air-traffic controllers' strike and a murder-suicide in Newport Beach, she had no idea what she'd just viewed. She cleaned her dish in the kitchen, then went out on the terrace to listen to the surf.

Usually she found the susurrus of waves against sand a hypnotic lullaby, but tonight it failed to soothe her, and she decided to call it a day. Tomorrow would be soon enough to log on to the internet to see what it offered in the way of rentals. At the moment she desperately needed the oblivion of sleep.

It wasn't until late the following morning, as she was transferring most of the items she'd packed the day before into some boxes she'd found in the garage, that she remembered the envelope in the suitcase. She dug it out and extracted a single sheet of stationary. Unfolding it, she began to read.

Nooo! She abruptly sat down on the edge of the bed, and for one of the few times in her life, she wished she were a swearing woman. Her few, pitiful expletives simply didn't cover the depth of her feelings. But, *poop*!

The note was from Glynnis. Lily didn't know how she'd missed it but that wasn't the issue. What mattered was Glynnis's specific request that Lily tell Zach where she had gone, with whom, and why.

Poop, poop, poop, poop, *poop*! Why was that *her* job?

But there was simply no help for it; she had to honor Glynnis's wishes. Hating not only that necessity, but the knowledge that Zach was going to blow it *all* out of proportion, she girded her loins and went looking for him.

She didn't quite do the cha-cha upon discovering he wasn't home, but it was a near thing. *Well, that's a crying shame,* she thought insincerely, and dug a package of phyllo dough out of the fridge to make herself a nice veggie turnover to go with that apple chutney she'd made the other day. *And after lunch*, she decided, *I really should hit the real estate agents.*

When the back door rattled open a short while later as she was still eating, however, she sighed in defeat, knowing she could kiss a clean getaway good-bye. Rats.

Zach closed the door behind him and looked at Lily, who gazed back at him calmly for a moment before returning to her lunch. Like yesterday, she was dolled up right down to the spike-heeled shoes on her feet—this pair open-toed and blue to match her top, which she had no doubt chosen to match her eyes. He watched her rosy lips close around a bite of something with a wonderful fragrance, and jerking his gaze away, he looked at the steam rising off a flaky pastry-looking thing full of wild rice, vegetables, and what looked to be cranberries. His stomach immediately protested that a single piece of peanut-butter toast was no kind of breakfast for a grown man. "I'll say this for you, lollipop. You sure can cook."

"Yes, I can." She hesitated, then jutted her chin toward the stove. "There's another one in the oven, if you'd like it."

She didn't have to ask him twice. He grabbed a plate, singed his fingers grabbing the goodie out of the oven, then got a fork from the drawer and poured himself a glass of milk. Carrying everything to the table, he pulled out a chair and sat down across from her. She passed him a little bowl of some spicy-smelling sauce with chopped apples in it, and he dumped a spoonful on top of his turnover. Before he dug in, though, he shot her a suspicious glance. "Why are you being so accommodating all of a sudden?"

"For exactly the reason you think," she said with a shrug that had him struggling not to watch the resultant jiggle of her breasts. "To soften you up, of course." She waved at his plate. "Don't let it get cold."

Knowing he wasn't likely to get more than that, he took a bite. One taste was all it took, and he was a goner. "Damn," he breathed when he came up for air half a turnover later. Forgetting who he was dealing with for an instant, he gave her a genuine smile. "This is *good*." He immediately forked up another bite, savoring the rich textures and the flavors that exploded on his tongue.

"So was my nefarious plot successful?" Lily asked when he finished. "Did my cooking turn you into Mr. Mellow?"

"Yep." And surprisingly, it was true. He'd spent the morning at Camp Pendleton getting the South American contingent situated for their training program, and he was now officially on leave. Add to that a stomach full of exceptional food, and he really did feel pretty damn mellow.

"Good." Lily passed him a sheet of paper that had been folded in half.

"What's this?" He took it and shook it open. Recognizing his sister's handwriting, his eyebrows furrowed. Then he read it, and his head snapped up. He didn't like the sound of this at all, and he pinned the curvy little blonde sitting across the table in his sights. "Okay, spill it."

Lily drew a breath and then released it in a long sigh. "The reason that Glynnis isn't here is that she's gone up to Washington state . . . to meet her fiancé's family."

Zach reacted every bit as badly as Lily feared he would.

He cursed succinctly as he pushed to his feet with such force his chair tumbled over. Slapping his hands on the tabletop, he leaned his weight on his splayed fingers and thrust his face forward until they were nose to nose. "I don't *believe* you, lady. You've known exactly where she is all this time and you're just now getting around to telling me?"

They were so close she could smell the chutney on his breath, hear the clicking pop of his TMJ joint as his teeth clenched and unclenched. His tension was contagious, but she forced herself to meet his furious eyes serenely. "I only just discovered the note."

"So if you hadn't found it, you wouldn't have ever told me?"

She lifted her chin. "Your sister is an adult, Taylor. It isn't up to me to tell you her business. If she'd wanted you to know, she would have said so—and considering what a control freak you are, I wasn't exactly bowled over when she didn't." She gave him a level look. "As it turns out, you're still a control freak, but apparently one she wants kept informed, so here's the scoop. The young man's name is David Beaumont. They met when he was down here on business, and they're driving up to his home in Washington state so Glynnis can meet his family. Then they plan to get married." A corner of her mouth crooked up in a faint smile. "I'm sure you'll be invited."

"The hell you say." Pushing off the table, Zach straightened and glared down at her.

"Then again, maybe not, if that's going to be your attitude."

"Hell, yes, it's my attitude. Damned if I'll allow some two-bit hustler break my baby sister's heart!"

"For Pete's sake!" She stared at him in exasperation. "You haven't even met David. He loves her!"

"Loves her money, you mean."

"No, Rambo, loves *her*. I've seen them together, and—" She found herself abruptly talking to thin air when Zach turned on his heel and strode from the room. She followed him to the den, where he was flipping through an address book.

He made a sound of satisfaction and picked up the telephone. Seeing her standing in the doorway he gave her a smug smile. "I knew I could trust Glynnis to jot down his cell phone number." He punched out the numbers.

Then the smile dropped away and he banged down the phone. "Shit. Out of the service area." He shot her one of his my-wish-is-your-command looks. "What's the Beaumonts' phone number?"

"I have no idea. The only thing Glynnis gave me was his address."

He dialed information, and she watched his face turn grimmer yet as he tried unsuccessfully to talk the operator into giving him an unlisted number. He then reached for the yellow pages, pausing only long enough to glare at her. "I want that address," he snapped. "I'll book a flight to Seattle for now, but I expect the exact address in my hand before I leave."

The impending air-traffic controller's strike popped

into Lily's mind. She opened her mouth to tell him about it, then pursed her lips closed. As if he'd believe her anyway. But judging by his language when he slammed down the phone a short while later, she'd say the strike was no longer imminent.

"The hell with it," he suddenly declared. "I'll drive." He looked at her. "Get me that address."

"Yes, master," she said as he stalked away—presumably to go pack for his trip.

As she headed down the hallway to her room, Lily fully intended to get Zach his address, and then get the heck out of his way. The threat he posed to Glynnis and David's wedding plans was none of her business. Glynnis was a big girl; if she was old enough to get married, she was certainly old enough to stand up to her brother regarding her choice of husband.

This is actually a good thing for me, she assured herself as she tried to remember in which box she had just packed her address book. *Heck, it's a reprieve, extra time to find a new place to live without Mister Personality breathing down my neck.*

She pushed aside the guilt that tickled the edges of her conscience. She and Glynnis had hit it off, and she truly thought David was good for the younger woman. But Glynnis's problems with her brother were her own, and none of Lily's.

"Lily!" The impatient shout came from outside, and she crossed the room to snap open the shutters. Zach stood on the parking apron outside the garages, glaring up at her window. As soon as he saw her, his hand slapped down on the roof of a black SUV with tinted windows. "Hurry up with that address!" he yelled.

Irritation shot through her as she stared down at his hard, belligerent face. He really was a bulldozer. She thought again of Glynnis and the fragile happiness she'd had the past couple months with David. He was wonderfully gentle with her—and the two of them would be no match at all for Zachariah Taylor. It was a crying shame, really. True love was hard enough to find without GI Joe roaring around smashing everything apart.

She glanced at her open suitcase and made a decision. Probably the worst decision of her life, but one she knew she would follow through on just the same.

"Oh, *poop!*"

5

ZACH DRUMMED AN IMPATIENT TATTOO AGAINST
the top of his Jeep. What the hell was keeping Lily with
that address?

He was too edgy just to stand around cooling his jets
this way; he had to act before his sister made a mistake
it might take her years to recover from. Realizing Lily
had wiggled her way into Glynnis's life had been bad
enough. But he didn't even know how long his sister
had been gone, and the lost time that little golddigger
had cost him by keeping Glynnis's news to herself
could well make the difference between him getting to
Beaumont's house in time to stop this farce or not.

*Considering what a control freak you are, I wasn't
exactly bowled over when Glynnis didn't tell you her
plans,* whispered Lily's voice in his brain, stilling
Zach's fingers on the rooftop. Then, slapping both
hands against the hot metal, he pushed away and began
to pace.

Bullshit. It had nothing to do with control; he just

wanted to protect his little sister. Someone had to prevent her from making the biggest mistake of her life.

Experience was on his side, and this time the situation was even worse than usual. Glynnis was too big-hearted for her own good, but no one had ever brought her to the point where *marriage* sounded like a good idea. Zach thrust his hands through his hair as he paced. Somehow this Beaumont guy had gotten her to that stage, though. Somehow he'd convinced her he was the man for her, the one she could trust to supply her with the happily-ever-after she'd always wanted. Zach had to save her from getting her soft, generous heart stomped into paste. For if she'd been crushed in the past when she'd discovered she'd been used by the people she'd trusted, what would it do to her to learn her true *love* was playing her for a fool?

Love. Zach made a rude noise. As if *that* was an emotion anyone could trust.

Turning to pace in the other direction, he saw Lily headed his way. "It's about damn time," he snarled, so busy trying not to notice the ultra-girly hip-swinging, breast-bouncing walk of hers that it took him a moment to register she was burdened with a purse and train case and was pulling a suitcase in her wake. "What the—"

She sashayed right up to the passenger side of his Jeep, opened the door, and tossed her stuff in the backseat while he stood there with his mouth open. Looking at him across the top of the SUV, she gave the vehicle a slap. "What are you waiting for? Let's go." And she climbed into the car.

He ripped open his own door and leaned in to glare at

her across the seats. "What the *hell* do you think you're doing?"

"I would think that would be obvious even to you." She gave him a cool look out of those clear blue eyes. "I've decided to go with you."

"Over my cold and rotting corpse, lady."

"Works for me—that'd save me a trip. But failing that, your sister has a real shot at happiness with David, and I've resolved not to let you wreck it for her."

"You've *resolved*," he said scornfully. "What, you afraid you'll lose your meal ticket if I talk some sense into her?" His brain tried to tell him there was a flaw in that logic, but he couldn't puzzle it out over the roar of his anger. And that made him even more livid, the knowledge that she could make him lose his temper without any effort at all. No one else had ever been able to do that. "Haul your little butt out of my car."

"No."

"Then I'll haul it for you." He straightened, fully prepared to follow through on his threat.

"Not if you want David's address."

Zach had to remind himself he was disciplined, that a soldier did not react without thinking. He'd already tried calling Rocket, but his friend must be serious about this being a vacation and had turned off his cell phone for the trip up to Coop's. Zach bent back down and looked at Lily. "I'll have that address if I have to tear your purse and bags apart to find it," he said flatly. He gave her a slow up-and-down appraisal. "If I have to strip you naked."

She didn't even blink. "Could be fun, I suppose—but it still won't get you the address." She tapped her temple. "It's in here, bud. So unless you're a mind reader . . ."

Swearing in defeat, he climbed into the Jeep and slammed the door.

Miguel Escavez raced back to the car he'd won off a soldier yesterday and started the engine. When Master Sergeant Taylor drove away from the opulent ocean-front property a moment later, Miguel patiently waited until the other man reached the bend in the road before pulling away from the shoulder to trail in the black SUV's wake. His impulse to follow the commander from Camp Pendleton this morning had paid off with even faster results than he'd expected—a sure sign his mission was just.

But then, he'd never doubted that for a moment. He was, after all, Miguel Hector Javier Escavez, only son of the mayor of Bisinlejo. And this was just one more in a series of signs he'd received already. Why, just last night he'd won a fortune from several of the gringo soldiers.

That filled him with satisfaction—and for more reasons than simply the money that enabled him to finance his plans. They thought because he came from a small Colombian village he was dumb, that he was a—how did one of them put it?—a spic. Miguel spit out the car window. Arrogant fools. How many of *them* spoke two languages? He had learned English from Father Roberto, the mission priest who had also taught him the finer points of five-card stud. If the Norte Americanos were so damn smart, how was it that most of their recently cashed paychecks had ended up in *his* pocket?

They knew nothing. He was an important man; his life was charmed.

At least it had been until the American soldiers had sent everything spinning out of control. He had *admired* Taylor when the marine had first come to Bisinlejo, but now the master sergeant was his enemy. Pedersen, under Taylor's command, had sullied Emilita, but it was the master sergeant who had compounded the insult by demeaning *him*—Miguel Escavez—in front of the entire village. And of the two transgressions, that was the one he couldn't forgive.

Taylor must pay.

Miguel smiled to himself, for having seen the marine's eyes go hot when the blond woman had jiggled her breasts and swung her hips crossing the courtyard, he knew what to do. He hadn't been close enough to hear the conversation inside the car, but clearly the *puta* was the commander's woman.

The church preached an eye for an eye, so retribution seemed simple enough to Miguel. He had lost his woman. Emilita may as well be dead for the dishonor she'd shown him, and he held Master Sergeant Taylor directly responsible. He would therefore see to it that the marine lost his woman in exchange.

It was only just.

Lily eyed Zach's grim profile. They'd been traveling for over two hours, and he hadn't said a word to her. Not one. Not wanting to be the first to cave, she turned to stare out at the almond groves whizzing past the window. But a few minutes later she found herself turning back to him again. "Are you going to sulk all the way to Washington?"

The glance he spared her before returning his attention to the long, straight stretch of freeway should have singed the eyebrows right off her face. "You blackmailed me into letting you come along. I don't feel a burning need to entertain you as well."

"Oh, yeah," she scoffed. "You being such an entertaining guy and all." If personalities equaled looks, Zach Taylor would be a dung beetle. It seemed the height of unfairness that instead he could probably get work as an underwear model, darn him.

Being a sociable woman, though, she didn't think she could bear thirteen hundred miles of the silent treatment. So she wracked her brain for a subject he might respond to. Beauty makeovers were probably out. Politics and religion were risky at the best of times, and the weather had been consistently fair for the past several days—not a lot to discuss there. Food was always a good topic, of course, but Zach struck her as more the *let's-eat* type than the *you-have-got-to-tell-me-how-you-prepared-this* kind of guy. That left just one subject—the relationship between Glynnis and David. And the only thing discussing *that* was likely to get her was a huge headache.

Heck, silence wasn't so bad.

Another thirty miles farther on, though, she couldn't stand it any longer. As they blew past a long row of evenly spaced eucalyptus trees, she shifted in her seat to face him once again. "David Beaumont isn't the cad you're making him out to be, you know."

Zach grunted.

Lily had never realized such a brief sound could convey so much skepticism. "He's not," she insisted. "Not unless he's the best darn actor in the world—and, frankly, I don't think anyone could sustain an act that good twenty-four hours a day for several days running. Which is what he'd have to do since he and Glynnis planned to take their time and see some of the sights along the way. Don'tcha think in that case Glynnis would figure out for herself he's not the man for her?" This time she didn't even get a grunt in response, and she swallowed her sigh. "I doubt it will come to that, though. I know it was a pretty fast decision since they've only been dating for a couple of months, but David struck me as simply a decent guy who fell head over heels in love with your sister and thought he was the luckiest man on earth when she returned his feelings."

"I guess I can just turn right around and go home, then."

His tone, of course, suggested otherwise, and blowing out a disgusted breath, she gave up. In the silence that followed, she shifted in her seat, trying to restore circulation to her travel-deadened bottom and legs. Gradually she became aware of another discomfort. She looked over at him. "I need to use a restroom."

He emitted another of those charming sounds and she turned her attention back to the scenery outside the window, determined to hold her tongue for real this time. She would patiently await the next service station if it killed her. She was nevertheless relieved a short while later to see a sign announcing a rest stop at the next exit, for she was beginning to grow uncomfortable.

Zach whizzed right past it.

Lily's temper climbed into the red zone, and she had to clench her teeth against ranting and railing and telling him exactly what she thought of his crummy tactics. For that's what this was—a way of letting her know he hadn't wanted her along in the first place and he wasn't about to allow her so-called "blackmail" to dictate the terms of the drive. She forced herself to breathe deeply until she found a measure of control. Then she stroked her hand admiringly over the fine leather of her bucket seat. "Nice upholstery," she murmured. "What a shame my bladder's about five minutes away from destroying it."

He looked over at her, and his charcoal-ringed gray eyes seemed to weigh her determination. "Okay, hold your water. I'll find you a bathroom."

Service stations were few and far between along this stretch of farm country, however, and Lily was practically dancing in her seat by the time Zach roared off the exit and rolled to a stop in front of a gas pump. She left her door hanging open in her rush to the restroom.

When she came out several minutes later, Zach was just reseating the nozzle in its holder. Pulling his wallet from his back pocket, he headed for the small minimart. "You'd better come in and pick out what you want to eat, because I'm not stopping again."

Most of the store's offerings ran toward grease, salt, and sugar, but Lily selected a bottle of water, two apples, an orange, and a small package of presliced cheese. She added a candy bar at the counter. Then she fished through her purse for her wallet, but by the time she'd dug to the bottom and located it, Zach had already paid for everything.

"C'mon," he said and strode back to the Jeep.

She sighed as she picked her way over the cracked concrete parking lot in her needle-heeled shoes. This was going to be a *long* trip.

Miguel hurried to pay for his petrol, watching through the market window as the sergeant major drove out of the lot. Where the hell was he headed?

This wasn't what he'd anticipated. He'd expected Taylor to take his woman out for a meal in the small beach town where he lived. Or maybe up to Los Angeles. He certainly hadn't expected him to just keep driving and driving and driving. Miguel had nearly run out of petrol before Taylor had finally pulled in here—and then he'd counted himself lucky that this was America, where gas pumps lined two sides of the small market. In Bisinlejo they had one pump—and the truck to fill *that* only came once every couple of months or so. Here he was able to fill his car at the same time as the commander and still avoid being seen.

Shoving his change in his pocket, he headed for his car. He didn't want to let Taylor get too far ahead. If the marine took an exit before Miguel could catch up, this would be a wasted trip, and he'd have to wait for another day to start all over again. He'd just as soon not have to do that. Too bad he hadn't had the opportunity to talk to the blonde this stop, but Father Roberto used to say that good things came to those who wait.

And he had all the time in the world.

Lily had no idea what time it was when she awoke several hours later to find the Jeep had finally stopped moving. It was pitch dark, and she struggled upright when she heard sounds coming from the back of the vehicle. "What?" she mumbled, trying to shake off the stupor that still had her in its grip. Her bottom was numb, and her neck had a crick in it from falling asleep sitting up.

"We're stopping for the night," Zach's deep voice rumbled from the direction of the cargo space.

"Oh. Okay." Yawning, she reached for her purse with one hand and the door handle with the other. "I'll give you some money for my room."

He gave a short, unamused laugh, and that was when she woke up enough to look around and realize this was no parking lot of a nice hotel, or even a cracked courtyard of the fleabag, motor-court variety. They were in the middle of nowhere.

And it was cold. She shivered as she opened the door and chill air rushed in. Teeth chattering, she closed it again and turned to kneel on the seat, reaching in back for her suitcase. She pulled out a sweater, donned it, then gingerly climbed out of the car. "Where are we?" She heard the back hatch close and squinted to see through the darkness.

"At a campground near Shasta."

"Shasta, as in the mountain?"

"That would be the one."

"And we're *staying* here?" She took an imprudent step forward, and her heels, not designed for their current surroundings, caught on something underfoot. She went flying.

The free-fall sensation sent her stomach swooping toward her throat, but her tumble to the ground was stopped when her upper arms were suddenly caught in hard-skinned hands. She was jerked upright, and her breasts flattened against rigid muscle with a force that knocked her breath from her lungs. Her chin bounced off Zach's hard chest, clicking her teeth together.

For a moment she simply dug her fingers into his muscular arms and clung, leaning against the comfortingly solid body propping her up. He smelled of laundry soap and man, and as she ran a quick check to make sure all her parts were still in working order, it occurred to her that being held in his arms this way felt very . . . safe. And warm—mercy, so blessedly warm.

Then his hands tightened on her arms and he moved her back, holding her steady until she found her balance. "Put on some sneakers before you kill yourself."

Chilled again, she peered into the darkness, trying to see him as he moved away. "I don't own any sneakers." God, he couldn't be serious about camping here, could he?

"What was I thinking?" He laughed shortly. "Of course you don't. Do you have *any* shoes in that bag that don't have four-inch heels?"

"I have a pair of sandals," she said with great dignity.

"You might want to put them on, then, so you don't break your neck."

She turned to go back to the car, only to realize she'd gotten turned around by her near spill. "Which direction is the Jeep? And how come *you* can see stuff when I can't see a blessed thing? Are you wearing a pair of those night goggles or something?"

"No, I've just got excellent night vision. Take a half turn to your right; the car's a few steps in front of you."

She very carefully made her way to the vehicle and almost wept with relief when she finally located the handle, opened the door, and the dome light came on. She admitted it; she wasn't a huge nature lover. Sunsets from a deck were about her speed. She could hear a lot of rustling going on out there in the dark, and she didn't even want to contemplate what type of nocturnal creatures might be causing it. She cast a longing glance to the keys dangling from the ignition before reluctantly giving up the fantasy they inspired of leaving Captain Commando to play soldier by himself while she flew down the highway in search of motels, hot showers, and clean sheets.

After changing her shoes, she rummaged in the glove box, whispering a fervent "thank goodness" when she found a flashlight. She climbed out of the car and went in search of GI Joe.

She found him stretched out on the ground in a sleeping bag and she stopped in her tracks, staring down at him in disbelief. "You're gonna just go to sleep?"

"Yeah. I'm beat. Get that damn light out of my eyes."

She ran it down the length of his sleeping bag, thinking how warm it looked. "What about me?"

"I didn't know you were coming along for the ride when I packed, did I, sugar britches? But you're welcome to join me in my bag."

For one heart-stopping instant she was seriously tempted, remembering the heat he'd generated during the brief moment she'd spent in his arms. She was *cold*, darn it, and he'd been as toasty as a convection oven on baking day.

But she wasn't so cold that she didn't know climbing

into a sleeping bag built for one with Zach Taylor would be a huge mistake. Against all reason, given his insulting behavior, the man generated some serious chemistry with her. "Is there a blanket I can use?"

"There might be one in the back of the Jeep."

"You could have said so right away." Mumbling about inconsiderate men who kept women standing around freezing while they were nice and cozy, she made her way to the back of the vehicle and felt as if she'd struck gold when she located a thick fleece blanket. Wrapping it around her, she went back to stand over Zach. "I need to wash my face."

"You'll find a water jug back in the cargo space."

She shivered at the thought of using cold water. "It needs to be *warm*."

His big shoulders moved beneath the bag. "Pans and the camp stove are back there, too. Knock yourself out."

Blowing out a disgruntled breath, she turned back to the Jeep, stopping on the way to fish a stick out of her sandal. The stove he'd mentioned wasn't like anything she'd ever seen; a regular camp stove she at least might have figured how to use. This one was little more than a propane canister with a pump and a ring. She gave up on the idea of hot water and slathered her face with moisturizer instead, wiping it off with a tissue in hopes of removing her makeup.

She was returning her toothbrush to her train case when she spotted Zach's duffel. She reached out and pulled it to her, then guiltily dropped her hand to her side. But guilt didn't stand up against a skinny little cashmere sweater that wasn't designed to resist more than a summer evening breeze. She'd bet Mr. Preparedness owned something more appropriate for spring nights in the mountains. She grabbed the duffel bag, slammed the cargo door, then climbed into the backseat of the Jeep. She'd been a good girl who'd played by the rules—and just look where that had gotten her.

The first thing she did after settling in was lock all the doors. She recognized a horror flick situation in the making when she saw one, and she did not intend to be one of those stupid heroines who left herself wide open to a knife-wielding maniac or, worse, some backwoods boy looking to make this city girl squeal like a pig. Then she pulled Zach's duffel onto her lap and opened it.

At first she tried not to disturb anything as she riffled through it. But that was absurd—*he* certainly wouldn't be so forbearing if the situation were reversed. So she upended the bag, and moaned in ecstasy at all the goodies that tumbled out. Oh, man, socks. Warm, woolen socks. She kicked off her sandals and pulled on a pair over her frozen feet. The rest of his underwear didn't offer much in the way of protection, so she tossed it over her shoulder into the cargo area. His jeans went the same way. But he had some luscious thermal T-shirts, and she peeled off her ineffectual little sweater and pulled one on. Then another. She topped off both with a wonderfully cozy Northface fleece pullover. Feeling a spurt of euphoria as she finally began to thaw, she pushed up the too-long sleeves and bent to check out the rest of his goodies in the weak illumination cast by the dome light.

She found a small zipper bag, but except for a con-dom whose worn and dented foil packet looked as though it had been rattling around the bottom of the bag for a while, his toiletries were pretty boring. Just a toothbrush and toothpaste, floss, a razor, nail clippers, aspirin, and a small tube of triple antibiotic cream. Oh, and wait. A small pocket knife. She pried open the lat-ter's various blades and implements.

As she was checking out the tiny corkscrew and won-dering where a good bottle of wine was when you really needed it, she grew aware that her finally warm body had released Zach's scent from the clothes she'd donned. Heat that didn't originate from wearing sufficient cloth-ing crawled through her veins, and she scowled, her mo-mentary pleasure dissipating. Great. Just what she needed to make her day complete—sexual awareness of Gunga Din. She'd never understood women who were drawn to good-looking men who treated them like dirt, so darned if she was cheered by the thought of joining their ranks.

It was late; that was her problem. She needed to call it a day. Grabbing the fleece blanket, she folded the empty duffel to use as a pillow, turned off the overhead light, then wrapped up and stretched out on the backseat.

She couldn't relax, though. The longer she lay there, the spookier the sounds she heard outside the car. She thought woods were supposed to be *quiet*. Then, as if the situation wasn't already about as lousy as it could get, nature called. Well, she wasn't answering. She'd let her bladder explode before she'd venture into the trees surrounding this small camping spot. Nervous, stiff, and miserable, she tried to talk herself out of jumping at every unexplained noise.

But it was only by thinking of the various ways she could make Zach pay that she eventually lulled herself to sleep.

6

Zach woke up to snow. Swearing, he sat up and threw back his sleeping bag, which was weighed down with half an inch of the sloppy, wet stuff. He reached beneath the Jeep for his shoes. This frigging trip was cursed.

At least he'd had the foresight to throw his Marine-issue poncho over his bag before going to sleep last night. Being spared the scent of wet sleeping bag was a small blessing to be sure, but he'd take his boons where he could get them.

Not that he'd *gone* right to sleep. He'd twisted and turned in that damn narrow bag for a good forty-five minutes after Lily had finally quit messing around and turned off the light in the Jeep. Twisted, and turned, and relived, over and over again, that brief moment he'd held her. Burned everywhere her soft weight had touched him. And didn't that just take the fucking cake?

Cold, clammy, and pissed off, he donned his shoes, then snapped out the poncho wet-side down over the spot where he'd lain, using it as protection against the soggy ground while he rolled up his bag. Tucking the roll beneath his arm, he strode to the Jeep, shivering when a wet flake found its way down his neck just as he reached for the cargo hatch handle.

The hatch was locked, and he slapped his pants' pockets for the keys before remembering he'd left them in the ignition. Rounding the vehicle, he tried the driver's door handle, but it didn't budge either. He swore under his breath and peered in the windows just as dawn broke through the trees, marginally brightening the ash-gray sky. Well, great. All the doors were locked up tight, and Lily was asleep in the backseat, covered from stem to stern by the purple fleece blanket. Wisps of blonde hair were the only part of her he could see.

He rapped on the window, and felt an unworthy sense of satisfaction when she startled beneath the blanket. She raised her head, then slowly pushed up on one elbow, glancing around as if wondering where she was. Their gazes met through the window, and she blinked and gave him a sleepy smile.

It was a friendly smile, a *sweet* smile, and something jerked in his gut. Something else clamored for attention in his brain. Gritting his teeth, he ignored them both. "Unlock the door."

He saw the exact moment her mind engaged enough to remind her he wasn't her friend. She was in the midst of stretching for the mechanism to comply with his command when she suddenly stilled. Her hand dropped to her side and she struggled upright, wrapping the fleece blanket tightly around her. What the hell—was that his Northface she was wearing? "Will you *move* it?" he growled. "Let me in."

"No," she said.

"Dammit, Lily, open the door! It's snowing out here."

"I can see that. Are you *cold*?"

"Yes!" And that *was* his jacket. The giveaway was the fact that it was about ten sizes too big for her.

"Well, gee, that's a crying shame. Although as I recall it, you didn't care that I was cold last night."

"Hey, I offered to share my bag." Big mistake. Not only did her upper lip curl in disdain, but his dick had a déjà vu moment of the instant just after he'd proposed the option, when the ramifications of a possible acceptance had left him in a half erect state. He rattled the door. "Lemme in!"

"There are some things we need to discuss first."

He regarded her warily. "Like what?"

"I want a few concessions."

"Shit." But he knew he probably wouldn't get in without them—not without a lot of bother on his part. Mentally calculating how far he was willing to go, he demanded, "What do you want?"

"Bathroom stops I don't have to fight for, for starters."

"Oh." It caught him by surprise . . . then left him feeling guilty. Denying her those yesterday *had* been petty of him. "Okay, sure."

"And your word that you'll behave civilly from now on."

Now, that was a tougher one, especially considering his less-than-cheerful frame of mind lately. Still, he nodded. "You've got it." He watched through the window as she pulled her heels up on the seat next to her round little butt, pinched the toes of her socks—no, *his* socks, by God—and pulled them off her feet, trading them for her sandals. It was a sad day when·a woman's naked *feet* got him itching. He raked his fingers through his hair. "What else?"

Dropping her feet to the floor, she straightened and fixed him with a stern glare. "I want water so I can wash up. *Hot* water."

"I'll· get right on that—the minute I have access to the camp stove."

"Okay, then." She stretched over the front seat to flip the mechanism that opened all the locks.

That was easier—not to mention a whole lot cheaper—than he'd expected. He went around to the cargo hatch and popped it open just as Lily tumbled out of the jeep and trotted awkwardly toward the stand of trees, a wad of tissues clenched in one fist. The sight brought a sardonic smile to Zach's lips, and he reached for the camp stove to heat her water. Dàmned if he hadn't been out-bluffed.

His amusement fled when he saw his belongings scattered all over the cargo area, and it suffered a further downturn when he went looking for a dry shirt to put on and discovered his two long-sleeved thermal T's were gone. It was all he could do not to glare at Lily when she returned a short while later. "Give me back my shirts."

"Excuse me?" She cocked an expectant eyebrow at him.

Words he forced himself to swallow went down like ground glass. "Please."

To his surprise she immediately removed his North-face, laying the jacket inside the hatch. Then she reached for the hem of his burgundy T and peeled it off over her head. When she removed the silver one beneath it, her own top came partway with it, hitching up to expose a golden slice of skin just above her jeans waistband.

"Here, you wear this one," she said amiably, handing him the silver, waffle-weave shirt. "It does the most for your eyes. But I get to keep the burgundy one—at least until I warm up." She put it back on, then had to reroll the sleeves several times to prevent them from flopping over her fingertips.

Without her usual sky-high heels, the top of her head barely reached his chest, and his shirt wasn't simply long in the sleeves on her; it hung clear down to her knees. "You look like a damn kid playing dress-up," he muttered insincerely. No way in hell would anyone ever mistake her for a child. Not with those round hips or the sweet curve of her breasts pushing against his T.

He hated it that he was so physically aware of her. But when she pressed a hot wash cloth to her face a moment later and moaned in pure pleasure, he immediately thought of sex, down-and-dirty sex, in one position after another, each one of which flashed raunchier than the last across the screen of his mind. Disgusted, he stomped away and went to stand with his face lifted to the sluggishly falling snow.

Shit. Being rude to women might not be the way he was raised, but it had sure been a dandy cushion between him and the pull of Lily's sexuality. Now, because a deal was a deal, and he always kept his word, that cushion was gone.

Busy dealing with the nasty suspicion that this civility business just might be the death of him, he failed to notice the old Ford LTD parked behind the big wooden site map when he drove past it soon after.

.   Hours later Zach conceded that sometimes a man would just as soon not be right. His jaw ached from gritting his teeth as he drove through the sweeping ranch land of southern Oregon. *Dammit, did I call this or what? A guy honors his word to be polite and just look where it gets him—ass-deep in sexual frustration.*

It was the very thing he'd feared, and observing Lily's feminine rituals sure as hell hadn't helped. At the campsite earlier she'd accommodated his need to hit the road by merely washing her face and brushing her teeth, then immediately restoring order to his trashed duffel bag without him saying a word. As soon as they'd gotten underway, though, she'd balanced her train case in her lap and started doing the girly thing.

She'd applied lotions and scents and war paint with a skill and feminine appreciation for the process that was downright erotic. From the corner of his eye he'd seen her mouth drop open slightly as she leaned into the mirror to apply mascara, watched her lips purse as she stroked on lipstick. She'd combed and teased her hair, then applied something to it and mussed it all up again until it looked as if a man's hands had just lost their grip on it in the wake of some world-class oral servicing.

Jesus, Taylor. He shifted in his seat. *What're you, a masochist? Don't even go there.*

It was the direction in which his mind kept wandering, though. A short while ago she'd decided she was finally warm enough and had peeled off his thermal

T-shirt. It was a fairly utilitarian stripping, but he couldn't have been more affected if she'd been working the stage pole at the Pussy-Kat Club. That was approximately the same time he'd begun to notice that the silver T-shirt he wore—the one that "did the most for his eyes," for crissake—bore her scent. Man, he was beginning to lose it. But why the hell couldn't she be a tall brunette? None of this would be an issue if she were a tall, dark-haired woman, since for some odd reason they'd never held much attraction for him.

And why didn't she *say* something? Yesterday he'd been perfectly content to spend the entire drive without exchanging a word, but today he needed a distraction from all this awareness. Hell, at this point he'd even welcome a dialogue about David Beaumont, sister-hustling, money-grubbing little pissant that he was. But although Zach's body kept hearing the whisper of *come on and get me, big boy* from Lily's lush curves, except for a single request for a pit stop about forty minutes ago, she hadn't uttered one word in the three hours they'd been on the road.

To be fair, she was probably waiting for him to demonstrate good faith and start the conversation himself. But he couldn't think of a thing to say.

Then, almost as if she could read his thoughts, Lily suddenly shifted in her seat to look at him. "Glynnis once told me she was born in Africa."

All right! This is more like it. "Yeah, she was."

"She said she was too young to remember it, but that you actually lived there for quite a while?"

"Yep." *Not exactly chatty, bud.* He'd better improve

on the monosyllabic responses or he'd be right back where he'd started—and that was a situation he wanted to avoid at all costs. "I lived in numerous small villages on the veldt of south and east Africa until I was eleven."

"The veldt of Africa," she repeated dreamily. "It sounds like something out of a Karen Blixen novel. That must have been so fascinating. And your parents! Your sister mentioned they were doctors whose specialty was working with the natives. I know she's terribly proud of them. You must have been, too."

"Proud? Yeah, I suppose so." Mostly, though, an unsatisfied yearning was the feeling that came to mind when he thought of his parents. Their grand passion for each other and for their work hadn't left much over for anyone else, and the benign neglect that had been his childhood had taught him early on that you couldn't rely on others for your emotional well-being. But if he'd often felt left out, even forgotten, at least he'd had the freedom of the veldt. Running with the nomadic Maasia tribesmen in the high open grasslands had given him his first taste for adventure and gone a long way toward alleviating his loneliness.

Then, that too, had been denied him shortly after Glynnis was born, when his mother and father, who'd claimed to love them so much, had shipped him and his infant sister back to the states. "Glynnis never actually had the opportunity to know our parents," he heard himself admit. "I might have romanticized them a bit for her benefit."

"How so?"

He had to hand it to her; she was all big-eyed curiosity. Yet even the cynical suspicion that she couldn't possibly be that interested didn't prevent him from responding to all that intense attention being focused on him. "They were rabid about the plight of the natives, which made them excellent doctors. But they weren't exactly the most attentive mom and dad in the world. They packed us off to our grandparents in Philadelphia when Glynnie was less than six months old, and they only ever bothered to come see her a handful of times after that. Yet I could hardly tell her that other people obviously mattered more to them than she did, could I? They were the only parents she had." He shrugged to make clear his supreme indifference. "So I emphasized the great demands put on them by their humanitarian deeds." He shot her a quick sideways glance, then turned his attention back on the road. "For Glynnis's sake I always hoped the situation would someday change, but as you already know, a fever swept through the village where they worked when Glynnis was eight, and it killed them both."

"Yes, I'm sorry."

He shrugged again. "Given the conditions they routinely worked in, it was bound to happen."

But Lily watched a flash of pain come and go across his face, and her stomach performed a funny little somersault. *Okay, so maybe he's not the demon spawn I pegged him to be.* Observing his profile from beneath her lashes, she deduced that his hopes for a change in his parents' situation probably hadn't been merely for Glynnis's sake. And Lily had to wonder: Where the heck had *he* come into the equation? He'd talked about other people mattering more to his parents than his sister, but what about him? He'd lived with them for eleven years before Glynnis was even born—what had happened during that decade that their only son seemed not to expect any attention for himself? For the first time since clapping eyes on him in his Laguna Beach kitchen, she found herself regarding him not as a gorgeous hunk or an insulting Neanderthal, but as an intriguing puzzle she'd very much like to figure out.

Before she could decide what it would take to do so, however, Zach surprised her by saying, "What about you? Are your parents still around?"

"Oh, yeah." She laughed. "Very much so." For a second she considered not saying anything else to see if he was interested enough to ask for details, but decided against it. If he hadn't said a word for almost two hundred miles, what were the chances of him suddenly demanding all the details of her life? Clearly he'd be perfectly happy to travel in silence for the rest of the day.

She couldn't claim the same; the last couple of hours had nearly driven her up the wall. "My folks sound the polar opposite of yours, at least as far as education goes. They had to get married when they were both seventeen, so they barely made it through high school."

He didn't take his eyes off the road. "Was that because of you?" he asked, "or do you have an older sibling somewhere who forced that marriage?"

"No, that would be me. Conceived, I've been told, in the backseat of a '62 Buick at the Sunset Drive-In Theater in a little one-horse town in Idaho I'm sure you've never heard of."

"So which parent did you end up with?" He deigned

to take his eyes off the road long enough to slide a fast glance over her. "I'm guessing your mother."

She looked at him in surprise. "I lived with both of them."

"They're still married? Isn't that against every statistic for couples that wed so young?"

"Yeah, well, the statisticians never met my folks. Until I took over their finances, they might not have had two nickels to rub together, but one thing they always have had is true love." She caught Zach's eye roll. "I'm not saying they didn't occasionally indulge in a scream-the-house-down fight. But there was never any doubt that their marriage was solid."

This time when he took his eyes off the road, it was to give her a look she couldn't even begin to decipher. "So you had yourself a white-picket-fence upbringing?"

Lily couldn't help it—she threw back her head and laughed herself silly. "I'm sorry," she said in the face of his irritation once she'd collected herself. "I'm not laughing at you. It's just—a white-picket-fence upbringing is about the farthest thing from the truth. My folks led a restless lifestyle. We moved a lot. Usually once, often twice, and sometimes even three times a year. I *dreamed* of a house with a white picket fence." She made a wry face. "I never actually got to live in one."

"Huh." He fell silent, his eyes narrowing in concentration as he swung around a semi. More and more traffic began to clog the interstate the closer they got to Salem, and Zach seemed focused not only on getting through it, but making good time as well.

Lily found herself shooting him frequent glances,

wondering what he was thinking beyond the fact that Oregon's fifty-five-mile-an-hour speed limit clearly didn't sit well with him. They stopped occasionally for her to use the restroom, or to grab something to eat, but Zach's growing impatience was all but palpable. Surprisingly, rather than annoying her, his restlessness made Lily long to reach across the console and give him a little there-there pat on the knee. She managed to engage him in a couple more brief exchanges, but it was like trying to detangle hair from a fine chain necklace at the back of one's neck, difficult and painstaking.

He pulled into the first gas station he saw after they'd crossed the Oregon border into Washington later in the day. "Here." He shoved a handful of bills into Lily's hand. "Go get us something to eat. I'm gonna fill up the tank now that we're finally in a state where you can pump your own."

She felt a smile crook her lips as she went into the minimart. Zach had taken Oregon's law that prohibited the pumping of one's own gas as a personal affront. No doubt the service station attendants weren't fast enough to suit his exacting standards.

Picking over the store's selection for something that wasn't loaded with preservatives, she experienced a sudden surge of homesickness for a real kitchen. She was tired of fast food and minimart fare. She'd give a bundle to be able to whip up something with ingredients she knew to be fresh. A pragmatic woman at heart, though, she did the best she could with the limited resources at hand.

She was headed back to the car with a small bag of

provisions when a dark-haired young man suddenly materialized at her side.

"Mees?" He was handsome and well built . . . and perhaps just the tiniest bit too aware of both facts. But the smile he gave her was polite and endearingly hesitant. "H'excuse me; I'm sorry for bothering you. But I wonder if I might trouble you for some help."

"Sure. What can I do for you?"

"My H'english is not so good—"

"On the contrary, your English is quite excellent."

"*Gracias*, but I cannot seem to make myself h'understood to—" He gave a vague wave in the direction of the minimart, or perhaps to the pumps on the far side of it—"and I wondered if you might trouble yourself to assist me?"

"I'd be happy to do what I can. What exactly seems to be the misunder—"

"*Lily!* Get your butt over here now, or I'm leaving without you!"

The sheer impatience of Zach's roar had her shifting the bag and shrugging at the young man. "I'm sorry, those dulcet tones belong to my ride, so I'm afraid I won't be able to help you after all. But truly," she assured him as she headed for the Jeep, "your English is much better than you seem to believe. Just speak slowly to whomever you're having the problem with and I'm sure everything will work out just fine.

"Threats, Zach?" she asked a moment later as she climbed into the car. "That's hardly what I call being civil."

"Hey, I've been gracious as an old lady at a frigging tea party the whole damn day," he growled as she buckled her seatbelt. "But I'm not waiting around while you flirt with the local boys. Do that on your own time. I've got a schedule to keep." And punching the accelerator, he sent them roaring out of the station.

7

ZACH'S SCHEDULE SMACKED UP AGAINST THE WASHINGton state ferry system in Anacortes several hours later and promptly came out the loser. He stared at the ticket seller incredulously. "A *three-hour* wait?"

"Yes, sir. Three hours and thirty-five minutes, to be precise."

"You're kidding me, right?"

"No." The man in the booth gave him a slight smile. "You're not from around here, I'm guessing."

"No."

"Well, sir, we're still operating on the non–peak season schedule, so this isn't unusual. You just missed a boat to Orcas Island, and the next one to stop there is the *Illahee*, so I'm afraid you won't make that either, because it only has a seventy-five car capacity and there are more than that already ahead of you."

"Those cars can't all be going to Orcas."

"No, sir. Many of them are going to Lopez and Shaw. Orcas is the third stop on the San Juan route, although not every boat stops at each island." The man shrugged.

"In any case, the next superclass boat will be here in three hours and"—he consulted the clock over his head—"thirty-four—nope, make that thirty-*three*—minutes." He passed the ticket out the window along with a schedule. "You'll want lane five."

Zach had to swallow the urge to curse a blue streak. But the man clearly wasn't high on the chain of command, and Zach's eighteen years in the service had taught him not to take out his frustrations on someone who has no control over the circumstances. Thanking the man for his time, he accepted the ferry ticket and pulled away from the booth.

He knew better than to take the delay personally anyway, but it had been a long, tense trip, and it was aggravating to be stopped when he was finally so close to his objective. "An island," he groused as he pulled up behind the last car in line and killed the engine. Clipping the ticket on the visor, he checked out all the other lanes, most of which were full of cars. "Glynnis had to pick a guy who lives on a frigging island?"

Lily looked up from the fingernail she was filing. "You're such a cheery guy." She arched an eyebrow at him. "I suppose now probably wouldn't be a good time to point out we would've had plenty of time after all to stop at that Liz Claiborne outlet we passed."

He turned his head slowly and gave her his deadliest master sergeant stare, the one that made raw recruits tremble in their boots.

It had about as much effect on Lily as every other attempt he'd made to put her in her place. "Guess not," she said cheerfully, and dropped the file into her purse before opening the passenger door. "Well, look on the bright side. At least we can stretch our legs. I don't know about you, but my tush passed numb and headed straight for rigor mortis about fifty miles back."

He couldn't help it; he smiled ruefully. Then he, too, climbed out and did what she suggested. He took the opportunity to stretch his legs.

Miguel pulled into lane five three cars behind the Jeep and slouched down in his seat when he saw Taylor and his woman headed his way. This was getting complicated. Who would have thought, when he'd followed the master sergeant from the Marine base yesterday, that this evening would find him more than a thousand miles away, in line for a vessel going only *Dios* knew where?

Reading a board outside the booth a few moments ago while awaiting his turn to buy a ticket, he'd seen that in addition to four island destinations, there were two boats a day that went to Canada. For an instant, he had frozen, wondering which destination he was supposed to buy a ticket for, and realizing that if it was Canada he was in trouble. Then his natural confidence had returned. The Canadian boats appeared to leave early in the day, so this was not likely to be a problem, and to—how did the saying go?—borrow trouble was unacceptable.

When his turn came at the booth, he'd considered simply pointing out Taylor's Jeep and telling the ticket seller he was part of the master sergeant's party and wanted to go where the other man was going. But what if the seller didn't remember where that was? There were several cars between Miguel's and Taylor's, and the last thing he needed was to be brought to the commander's attention. In the end, he had simply bought a ticket for the last island in the chain.

So here he sat, hemmed in on all sides by other cars. It was pointless to grab the woman at this juncture, since it was impossible to get off the dock even if he could separate her from the marine. Hence, his current slouch—he had no intention of relinquishing the element of surprise by allowing himself to be spotted.

But it didn't please him. Miguel Escavez did not slide down in seats to avoid confrontations; he met them head on! He didn't appreciate feeling out of his element, but this quite frankly was far beyond what he had anticipated when he'd set out on his mission. If he had had just one more minute at that petrol station this afternoon, the woman would be in his possession now, and this furtiveness would be unnecessary. He had been so close . . . until the commander barked out an order and the gringa had jumped to do his bidding.

Miguel had half expected the marine to get out of his vehicle and confront him then and there. But Taylor had driven off the minute the blonde woman had climbed into the Jeep, so clearly he hadn't bothered to note who she was talking to.

Proving my superiority over the U.S. Marines once again, he thought smugly. *He* would have noted who talked to his woman. But that led to thoughts of Emilita in another man's arms, which led to the injustice of his treatment by Taylor, and before he knew it, he was grinding his teeth in fury. Determinedly, he shook it off, taking several deep, calming breaths. He needed to concentrate his energy on the positive.

After all, he was about to accomplish his objective; he could feel it in his bones. It would be beneficial to know where they were headed, but surely an island destination meant this endless road trip was about to reach its culmination. And not a moment too soon, if you asked him.

He didn't like driving these American highways. Gringo drivers were too quick with the rude gestures whenever he made a mistake. He spit on them—*they* made mistakes all the time, so he ought to be allowed a minor one or two. At least he had the excuse of unfamiliar thoroughfares that were much busier, if a lot smoother, than those to which he was accustomed. What excuse had they?

Finding himself once again growing tense, he drew yet another deep breath and forced himself to relax. He need only practice patience for a short while longer. For, soon, the opportunity would present itself to him.

Then the master sergeant would see how it felt to lose *his* woman.

Lily's forehead furrowed as she glanced over at Zach. Had his shoulders grown wider since the last time she'd looked? She could swear that the longer they were confined in the car, the more space he took up.

Watching his hands as they tapped a restless rhythm against the steering wheel made her strangely itchy. They were tanned, tough-skinned, and sort of beat-up-looking, marred by nicks and calluses. His nails were clean and clipped, but his left thumb sported a nail that was ripped below the quick on one side.

She looked down at her own hands with a rueful

smile. They weren't exactly smooth as silk themselves. But she was a chef, so cuts and burns were a hazard of the job. Besides, compared to Zach's, hers could have belonged to some pampered magnolia blossom on one of those old-time southern plantations. With his wide palms and large-knuckled fingers, Zach's hands were just so indisputably *male*.

A moment later she snuck a peek at his mouth, and found her gaze lingering on the thin, pale scar that bisected his upper lip. Her nipples tightened to attention, and the spot deep between her thighs went all tight and achy, and she jerked her gaze away. Oh, man. This was not good. This was not good at all.

She was suddenly hornier than a convict out on parole, and where the heck had *that* come from? She'd never tried to deny Zach's hunk appeal, but she had sort of blithely assumed his insulting attitude toward her would act like a vaccine against it. Surely regular booster shots of his lousy personality would render her permanently immune.

But he'd played nice today. Well, nicer, anyway, but when one was used to dealing with Baboo the Barbarian, almost human behavior made an amazing difference, and she'd found her opinion of him softening considerably. The deciding factor, of course, had been that hint of vulnerability he'd displayed this morning talking about his parents. It had tugged at every sensibility she possessed, worming its way more deeply into one of her soft spots every time her thoughts drifted back to it.

And wasn't that just too pathetic for words? Good grief, women had been falling for that tough-guy-disguising-the-hurt-inner-boy ploy for centuries. She shifted in her seat, straightening her spine defensively. Well, if she couldn't be smarter than that, she'd simply have to be vigilant. Because no way on earth did she plan to fall victim to *that* sorry cliché.

Still, sneaking looks at his mouth, she couldn't help but speculate. Zach was well traveled and came from a monied background that usually landed its brethren deep in the Old School Tie network. So how in heaven's name had he gotten from *there* to the macho Marine thing he had going? And why did the conviction keep sliding into her mind that far from preppie polite, he'd kiss like a guy from the wrong side of the tracks?

She pressed her spine hard into her seat back. *Good glory, Lily, are you out of your cotton-picking mind? The man thinks you're a money-grubbing slut, and you're wondering how he* kisses*? Why not just bash your head against the nearest concrete surface while you're at it? It would involve about the same level of intelligence.*

Swiveling to glare at Zach as if he'd been the one to suggest she rate his sex appeal, she snapped, "If you're so darned concerned about your sister being taken to the cleaners by every Tom, Dick, and Harry she encounters, why the heck didn't you ever bother to teach her some basic money management skills?"

Zach's hands, which he had consciously been keeping occupied to prevent himself doing something real stupid with them, froze on the steering wheel midtap. Then he turned to stare at Lily. Where the hell had *that* come from? Was this the same woman who'd been so relentlessly, annoyingly cheerful all day? It didn't take

Sigmund Freud to know what *his* problem was, but what had gotten *her* panties in a twist all of a sudden?

When it came right down to it, however, he really didn't give a good goddamn what her reasons were. All he knew was that he was ripe for a fight . . . and she'd just obligingly hand-delivered one right to his door.

Turning, he braced his arm along the back of the seat and gave her a slow, insolent appraisal. Not until hot color flooded the surface of her skin did he drawl, "And you consider this to be your business *why*, sweetheart?"

"I consider it to be my business, bud, because Glynnis is only a few days shy of her twenty-fifth birthday, and she didn't even know the bare bones of handling her finances until I started giving her some pointers a couple of months ago."

"Oh, yeah, I can just imagine how *that* worked. It takes a real humanitarian to point her money into your bank account."

"*What* money? Have you ever paid the slightest attention to your sister's struggle to make ends meet? Yes, she lives in that lovely beach house, and her allowance is generous for a young woman her age. But it must be obvious even to you that she barely has a rudimentary grasp of economics. She was sent to European finishing schools and raised to expect the very best. No one ever bothered to tell her the reasons she couldn't keep spending in the manner to which she was accustomed before I sat down with her and explained why it was no longer viable. For heaven's sake, Zach, where her contemporaries are shopping Nordstrom Rack if they're lucky, she's still buying couture. She didn't even know how to balance her darn checkbook until I taught her!"

He stared at her. There was a ring of truth in her voice that he didn't want to hear, so he shoved it away with a flatly stated, "Bullshit." But agitation, born from an old familiar guilt, began to churn in his gut.

"It is *not* bull crap," she said hotly. "You know what I think? I think you must be one of those control freaks who *likes* keeping his womenfolk in ignorance. What is it, some kind of power trip that provides your kicks or something?"

His sister was the only family he had left, and Zach had been on edge for three days, worrying about her. Anger and guilt and a sense of his own failure exploded in his gut and rose in a red tide to erode his control, and reacting for perhaps the first time in his adult life without considering the consequences of his actions, he grasped Lily by the shoulders and hauled her half out of her seat. Pulling her toward him over the console, he bent his head until their noses were a fraction of an inch apart and rasped, "You are full of shit, lady, you know that? If I was even *half* the control freak you accuse me of being I'd *still* have more candidates for victims than I'd know what to do with. I've got big, tough Marines to push around—I sure as hell don't need to dominate my little sister to get my rocks off."

To his surprise she didn't have an immediate smart-ass comeback, and he was on the verge of congratulating himself for finally scoring a point off her when he became aware that she was staring fixedly at his mouth. He stilled . . . and felt the quiver that ran through her.

Slowly, her gaze rose to meet his. She swallowed and her tongue stole out to slick across her lower lip, and his dick shot from dormant to raging hard-on so fast he was surprised his little head didn't get a concussion rapping against his fly. He dropped her so quick her breasts bounced as she plopped back in her seat, and he reared back against his door, scrubbing his fingers across his forehead.

Jesus. What the hell just happened here? Had she really been looking at his mouth like she'd like to take a big bite out of it, or had the strain he was under finally popped a vein in his brain? Then his eyes narrowed. Or maybe she was switching her attention from his sister to him. After all, he had a lot more money than Glynnis.

That theory would have held together a lot better if Lily looked anything like a woman who controlled men through sex right this moment. Instead, she sat there blinking, and when their eyes met, scalding color climbed her throat.

Then she seemed to gather herself.

"Okay," she squeaked. Clearing her throat, she started over. "Okay, so maybe I was wrong about the control-freak thing. If so, I apologize. But I'm not wrong about Glynnis's financial ignorance." She sat up straighter. "She *didn't* know how to balance a check-book until I showed her, and she didn't have the vaguest idea about managing her allowance."

Zach's hand dropped. "That doesn't make sense. She's an extravagant shopper, sure, but Grandfather must have taught her *something* about handling her finances. He was sure as hell all over me to learn financial responsibility so I'd be in position to take over the family corporation. When I refused to fall in with his plans and joined the Marines instead, I just figured he'd eventually start grooming Glynnis for the position." Surreptitiously adjusting himself, he gazed across the seat at her. "Now *he* was a controlling son of a bitch."

Then he stilled. "He *was* a control freak," he reiterated slowly. "And I wouldn't put it past the old bastard to have set it up to keep Glynnis ignorant on purpose."

A pucker formed between Lily's slender brows. "Why would he do such a thing?"

"Hell, I don't know. It pissed him off when I refused to toe the line—maybe he thought when I saw what he was doing it would bring me home to take care of her, and by extension, the business, just the way he wanted. God, that man was cold. He detested not getting his way, and if it hadn't been for Grandmama, life in that frigging mausoleum would have been unbearable." But warmth stole through him at the memory of his grandmother, and he felt a soft smile tug at his lips. "She was the best, though—that's where Glynnie gets her sweetness."

"Glynnis said your grandmother died when you both were still quite young."

"Yeah, the same year as my folks, just days after I graduated prep school. Then it was just me and Grandfather, since Glynnis had been sent to a year-round boarding school in Geneva when Grandmama got sick. She hated that, but that was the old man for you. He didn't give a shit what we wanted. *He* wanted Glynnie out of the way, so Glynnie was sent off. And he decided that I would be trained to take over the family corporation." Feeling the weight of those suffocating expectations all over again, he tugged at the neckline of his thermal T.

"So you ran away and joined the Marines?"

He frowned at her. "I didn't *run* away. I was eighteen years old; I simply exercised my right to choose my own career path. And it sure as hell wasn't gonna be one that left me sitting in an office day after day."

Her lips curled up in a small, empathetic smile. "No," she agreed solemnly. "I can't envision that at all. I have no doubt an office job would have driven you straight up the wall."

Her comment caught him by surprise. He would have thought she'd be all for a guy taking whatever job brought in the most money. A vagrant thought that she might not fit so handily into the role he'd assigned her crawled uneasily through his mind, but he shoved it away. *Don't go there,* he told himself.

And didn't allow himself to question why not.

The sun had set behind the mountains to the west a few hours later when a tap on the window jerked Miguel out of the light doze he'd fallen into. He sat upright, adrenaline pumping through his veins as he half expected to see the sergeant major on the other side of the glass furiously demanding to know what Miguel was doing here. But the young woman who bent down to peer in his window was a stranger. Miguel cracked the window.

"I need your ticket, sir."

It took a second to change mental gears; then he blinked, yawned, and plucked the ticket from the dashboard. He handed it to the woman.

She looked at it and frowned. "You're in the wrong line."

"Que?"

"This ticket is for San Juan Island. You're in line for Orcas."

Swearing to himself, he nodded emphatically at the young woman. *"Sí.* Orcas."

"Your ticket is for San Juan. You spent more on it than you had to for passage to Orcas."

He pretended not to understand, hoping she'd go away.

She sighed. "You *paid* too much," she said loudly, as if he were deaf instead of a foreign national, and tried to hand the ticket back to him. "If you take it up to the booth you can exchange it and get some money back."

People were starting to look this way, and Miguel wanted her *gone* before one of them was Taylor. *"Sí,"* he said again. "Orcas."

"Oh, for crying out loud," she said. "Whatever. You can't say I didn't try." Then, adding the ticket to the stack in her hand, she shrugged and moved on to the next car.

She obviously thought he was an idiot, and Miguel glared first at her retreating back in the side-view mirror, then at the Jeep three cars forward. For this indignity, too, Taylor would pay. He was going to pay, and pay, and pay.

8

FULL NIGHT HAD FALLEN AND CLOUDS OBSCURED THE moon by the time they debarked the ferry at Orcas Island. Once past the lights of the landing's tiny village, the darkness was absolute, and Lily's first impression of the island was of a great mass of trees. Deciduous hard- and softwoods crowded the spaces between towering evergreens, which in turn soared overhead, their tangled branches meeting to form a tunnel over the road. Within the sweep of the Jeep's headlights, their dark shapes gained color and texture, only to fade back into sooty shadows against the night sky like a multidimensional tone-on-tone onyx frieze.

She turned from the window and looked at Zach. His eyes were impenetrable pools in the glow from the dash, and his face was all harsh angles. "We really should see if there are rooms available in Eastsound. It's too late to just show up unannounced on David's doorstep."

He didn't even take his gaze off the road, but merely said tersely, "Let it go, Morrisette. We've had this conversation before."

And they had. They'd had it while he'd pored over the map of the island as they'd eaten Ivar's clam chowder in the dining area on the boat's upper deck. They'd had it while facing each other across bench seats as the ferry glided through narrow passages between dark islands. And they'd had it again while standing at the rail in the brisk early April breeze watching cars debark and load onto the boat at Lopez Island. When Lily had insisted one didn't simply barge in on people at eleven o'clock at night, Zach had said *watch me.*

"Yes we have," she agreed now. "And you're *still* wrong."

He didn't flick so much as a glance her way, and her shoulders twitched irritably. She blew out an exasperated breath. "You are the *stubbornest* man I have ever met. And probably the rudest, too. I should have waited until tomorrow to give you the address."

His mouth tightened. His voice was cool and uninvolved, though when he said, "But you didn't. And I didn't invite you on this junket, lady; I'd be more than happy to head over to Eastsound and dump you off."

She made a rude noise. "Oh, right. Like I came all this way because I'm so fond of *your* jolly company." She stared at him, willing him at least to glance at her, but not surprised when he didn't. He'd been aloof since shortly after he'd caught her staring at his mouth in that brief moment of madness on the Anacortes ferry dock. *Man*, but she'd wanted to know what it would taste like—a momentary mania that was *so* far from smart she couldn't believe it. Her face burned as it belatedly occurred to her that he might be acting this way to keep her from getting any funny ideas. She cleared her throat.

"Nice try. But I plan to be right by your side to lend whatever damage control I can when you start throwing your weight around."

"Good. I'll let you pass the tissues when Glynnie throws herself on my chest in gratitude for rescuing her from Trailer Town Tommy."

She felt her mouth drop open. "My gawd. What a snob you are." She probably shouldn't be shocked by the discovery, but she was.

For the first time he took his gaze off the road long enough to look at her, and even in the murky light she could tell he was steamed. "It's not snobbery, you little—" Cutting himself off, he gave her a strong look. "I've been through this shit before."

"Get out! Glynnis has *never* taken off with another guy." At least . . . *had* she?

"Did *I* say she had? But guess where the last guy she fancied herself in love with was waiting for his ship to come in when I tracked him down?"

"Oh, let me take a wild stab, here. A trailer park?"

"Damn right. And before you get on your high horse, I know living in a trailer park doesn't automatically make a person trash, okay? I'm sure they're filled with hard-working people, but *this* guy didn't happen to be one of them. He maintained a few pieces of expensive clothing, but otherwise he lived like a pig. And he flat-out lied to Glynnis. Until I took her out there to see for herself, she fully believed the reason they'd always had to meet at her place was because his beach condo was being renovated."

Poor Glynnis, Lily thought. But aloud she merely said, "David's not like that. He *loves* her."

Zach made a derisive sound and stepped on the gas.

Twenty minutes later he pulled up to a rural mailbox close to the entrance of a driveway. Rolling down the window, he aimed a flashlight on the address printed on its side. "This is it."

Headlights from a car that had turned onto the road behind them swept the interior of the Jeep, then just as quickly disappeared, and Lily turned from staring at the thick stand of Douglas firs that provided the Beaumont property with privacy. She opened her mouth to try one last time to talk Zach out of descending on David's family at this late hour, but before she could say a word, he put the Jeep in gear.

"I'm through debating this with you," he said, as if she'd actually presented her argument, and wheeled the vehicle into the drive.

They drove down a long ribbon of asphalt that unfurled through dense woods. Then the surrounding trees gave way to an acre of meticulously maintained lawn. But it was the lodgings perched midway between the woods and a bluff overlooking the water that caught Lily's attention, and a startled laugh escaped her.

"Oh, my." She turned delighted eyes on Zach. "So much for your he-only-wants-my-sister-for-her-money theory."

Far from the trailer of Zach's imagination, David's home was an estate. Built of fieldstone and weathered shingles, it looked more like a sprawling country inn than a single-family dwelling. Angled to face the cliff and the water below, it had stubby wings on either side of the main structure, several chimneys, and shutters that framed exquisitely crafted windows . . . every one of which was currently lit up.

Zach didn't look the least bit embarrassed to have jumped to what was clearly a wrongheaded conclusion. He merely shrugged at her jibe, pulled the Jeep to a halt at the top of the circular drive, and killed the engine. He spared Lily a single glance before reaching for the door handle. "Yeah, but everyone appears to still be up. So I guess it's not too late to come calling, after all." He climbed out of the car.

Lily rolled her eyes as she, too, got out, but she couldn't prevent a tiny smile from curling up the corners of her lips. Soldier Boy was wrong, wrong, wrong, and soon he'd be forced to eat his words. She did a little dance and promised herself a ringside seat for the occasion.

She was still smiling as she followed him to the front of the house, and they climbed the stone steps of a generously proportioned veranda. A minute later he rang the bell. When that didn't garner a quick enough response to suit him, he raised a big fist and pounded on the solid portal.

"For heaven's sake, Zach," she remonstrated, but when the front door abruptly opened, pure shock clogged her throat as they found themselves looking down the business end of a double-barreled shotgun.

Whoa, shit! Holding his hands away from his body to demonstrate his harmlessness, Zach stepped in front of Lily. Not that putting himself between her and the shotgun would shield her from a helluva lot if the guy facing them decided to pull the trigger. At this range, two barrels worth of shot would rip a hole through him the size of a volleyball and plow right into her.

Voices rose within the house, most of them feminine, one of them perilously close to hysteria, but Zach didn't take his eyes off the young man with the shotgun. Stowing away the brief regret of having packed his Marine-issue nine-millimeter in his duffel bag before leaving the campground this morning, he said calmly, "Hi. How ya doin'? I know it's a little late to be dropping by, but even so, this is a bit excessive, don't you think? Or is this how you always greet visitors?"

The man's hands tightened on the stock of the gun. "Who the hell are you? And what the hell do you want?"

The guy was nervous, and he was an amateur, neither of which was a condition Zach appreciated in someone pointing a gun at him. Seeing the young man's finger slide off the trigger to tap restlessly against the stock, Zach whipped out a hand and wrenched the shotgun sideways, relieving him of it with a single, supple twist of his wrist.

The man swore and made a grab for it in an attempt to regain possession.

Fending him off, Zach broke open the barrel, slid out the two rounds of shot, then snapped the barrels back into place and passed the shotgun back to the other man. "My name is Zachariah Taylor," he said. "Master Sergeant, U.S. Marines," he added, hoping the fact he had the authority of the United States government behind him would help to cool the other man's jets. The guy looked as if he were about to jump out of his skin. "I'm here to see my sister Glynnis."

He felt Lily unhook her fingers from his waistband where she'd anchored herself, and the warmth of her breasts dissipated as she peeled herself off his back. He barely had time to register the fact, however, before a woman in her late fifties materialized in the doorway.

"Oh my God, oh my God," she said as tears trembled on her lower lashes and her pale, fine-boned hands systematically shredded a lace-and-lawn handkerchief between them. Then she bunched the hankie in one hand as she reached out and grasped his arm with the other. She tugged him into the foyer, then stared up at him hopefully as the young man closed the door behind them. "Have you *heard* from him, then? Have you news of my David?"

Damn. He didn't like the sound of this. "No, ma'am."

"Oh, no!" An unchecked noise escaped her, and he realized this was the voice he'd heard on the edge of hysteria.

"Take a deep breath, ma'am," he ordered in the same I-*will*-be-obeyed tone he'd used throughout the years to get more than one green recruit over a hurdle of nerves. "Take nice, deep breaths and let them out slowly. Then tell me what's going on here."

She sucked in air but didn't look appreciably steadier for her efforts once she'd exhaled it. Nevertheless, she drew in and exhaled another, then faced him as calmly as she was able. "They've been kidnapped," she said, her chin immediately beginning to wobble. "Oh, God, oh, God. David and his little girlfriend have been *kidnapped*."

* * *

Dios, it was cold. Miguel rubbed his hands up and down his arms and wished he had warmer clothing. He missed his beloved Colombia, where the heat sank into a man's bones, and wondered in dissatisfaction if Master Sergeant Oh-Such-a-Big-Man Taylor and his anemic woman had *finally* reached the destination they'd been heading for ever since leaving California. He certainly hoped so, because the sooner he accomplished his mission, the sooner he could reclaim his rightful status and return to his village with his pride intact.

He was tempted to get out of the car and make his way down the driveway where the master sergeant had parked a short while ago, to see if that was where the marine was now. Except it was the dilemma last night at the campground all over again. He didn't dare abandon his car for fear he'd be caught unprepared should the commander suddenly return. And he couldn't park too close for the same reason that had kept him a respectable distance for two long days—an unwillingness to give the game away before he was ready to make his move. As it was, he'd practically driven right up the Jeep's back bumper in his race to catch up earlier, when he'd feared he'd lost them and had instead came across the vehicle unexpectedly parked in the middle of the road. He'd wheeled into the first private drive he'd seen and waited until he'd heard their car drive away before pulling out again. Then he'd found a better place from which he could not only keep an eye on this road but screen his car from the casual glance.

As soon as he determined this was indeed the master sergeant's final destination, he planned to make a quick trip to the nearest town to outfit himself properly for the climate. It wouldn't be long now before the opportunity arose to grab the woman and get out of here, but he needed appropriate supplies while he waited. He pulled the thin blanket he'd found in the trunk around him and turned the car on for a short while to use the heater. The thought of the master sergeant's face when he was relieved of his woman made Miguel smile. Soon, he promised himself. It would be very soon now.

But when he turned off the car's engine to conserve his remaining petrol a moment later, the cold settled right back in his bones. And he knew it couldn't *be* soon enough. For if he didn't make his move before long, he was likely to freeze his buttocks off in this unaccustomed, inhospitable climate.

Zach felt as if he'd taken a direct hit to the gut, and he stared at the stylish matron in front of him. "Kidnapped?"

The young man who'd greeted them at the door with the shotgun stepped forward, sliding a supporting arm around the older woman's shoulders. He flipped his shiny brown hair off his brow with a toss of his head that had the unconscious look of habit. "That was the reason for this," he said, giving the now empty gun in his hand a small heft. "When you showed up practically on the heels of the note we received, we thought you must be them. I'm Richard Beaumont," he added, thrusting out his hand. "David's cousin. And this is David's mother, Maureen."

Two other women and a man came out of a connecting room to join them in the foyer, and Richard introduced them as his sisters Cassidy and Jessica, and Jessica's husband Christopher.

Zach filed away his impression of a flashy brunette, a plain brunette, and a guy who could've stepped off the pages of *Gentleman's Quarterly* to be examined later as Mrs. Beaumont said, "David called us several days ago. He said he'd met his future wife in California and was bringing her home to meet us. It seemed so sudden—we were concerned she'd turn out to be one of those awful, flashy, starlet types, or a golddigger who'd latched on to him for his money." Then, obviously recalling the female in question was Zach's sister, color flooded the older woman's face.

Lily's abrupt whoop of laughter echoed in the pocket of silence that followed, and shock rippled through the assembled group as everyone turned to look at her. Even after two solid days of travel, with most of her makeup worn off and her hair tousled and slightly flattened on one side, she still had that last-of-the-red-hot-mamas look about her, and it occurred to Zach that *she* probably appeared to be the exact type the Beaumonts had feared his sister would be. As it was, Mrs. Beaumont regarded Lily as if she'd stepped directly out of Bimbo Central Casting, and if his stomach hadn't been tied up in about ten kinds of knots, he might have gotten a real kick out of her predicament.

It was just as well he was in no mood, however, for it would have been premature anyway. Aside from that one brief moment this afternoon, he'd never seen Lily at a loss for words, and she wasn't now. She directed a gentle smile at David's mother.

"I'm sorry," she said softly. "That was terribly inappropriate, and I'm not making light of the situation. It's just that Zach spent the entire drive from California fearing the exact same thing—that David was after his sister's money," she clarified when the older woman just stared at her blankly. "Glynnis is about to come into a considerable fortune of her own."

Mrs. Beaumont blinked. "Oh," she said. Then she turned pale. "Oh, dear. I wonder if the people who have them know that. You can't stay here," she said in a sudden panic, turning to Zach. She made agitated shooing motions with her hands. "You have to leave."

Zach focused the full force of his attention on her. "I'm not going anywhere until I find my sister, ma'am," he informed her levelly. He'd camp out on her lawn if he had to.

"You must!" She looked beside herself with fear as she stared up at him. "They'll think we *called* you, and they said not to call the police if we want to see David again. What if they're watching the house? If they *see* you, they'll think we ignored their warning."

Not about to be run off before he knew the entire story—and probably not even then, since after one look at this crew he'd decided he was the best candidate for getting Glynnis and David back in one piece—Zach took Mrs. Beaumont's restless hands between his own and stroked his thumbs over them as he said slowly and calmly, "That kind of threat is a common ploy intended to keep the victim off kilter, ma'am. Extortionists count on your emotions clouding your ability to reason, but it's important that you use this time to think as rationally as you can. For instance, take a good, hard look at

Lily. Can you honestly imagine anyone ever confusing her for a cop?"

Too late, he remembered Lily's level-eyed way of meeting even the most disapproving scrutiny head on. But she played along as if she knew just how much he needed to stay here in order to exert some control over the situation. With every eye in the house turned on her, she stood with one hip cocked, studying her manicure as if she were alone in the foyer. Her jaw moved subtly, and if he hadn't known better he would have sworn she was chewing gum.

When Zach saw Mrs. Beaumont relax marginally, he eased out a breath, and said, "I need you to tell me exactly what led you to believe your son and Glynnis were abducted."

"We received a note about twenty minutes before you showed up." She hesitated, then gestured toward the room the others had come out of a moment ago. "Let's go in the parlor."

The entire gathering trooped into a large room with a set of French doors and two windows that undoubtedly looked out over the water, although at the moment it was too dark to see beyond a grouping of wicker chairs out on the lighted veranda. The top third of the windows was comprised of leaded, beveled glass, lending them a richness that was echoed in the cool, sage-green, silk-covered walls. By contrast, the room's couch, loveseat, and chairs were mostly homey overstuffed pieces upholstered in unbleached canvas and hunter green chintz. A fire crackled cozily in the stone fireplace on the north wall.

Mrs. Beaumont gestured for them to take a seat, but

Zach remained standing. What he really wanted was to pace, but he stood at-ease as she turned to her nephew.

"Show him the note, Richard."

Richard went to a built-in cupboard, where he retrieved a piece of paper. He brought it over to Zach.

Looking down at it, Zach realized that until this moment, he hadn't fully believed in the Beaumonts' claim. In a far-flung corner of his mind he must have hoped they'd misunderstood or had somehow panicked over nothing. But this single sheet of paper with its three sentences formed of letters cut from magazines disabused him of the notion.

It was brief and to the point.

WE HAVE YOUR SON. IF YOU WANT TO SEE HIM AND HIS GIRLFRIEND AGAIN, YOU'LL AWAIT INSTRUCTIONS. CALL THE COPS AND THEY'RE DEAD.

Over the years, Zach had been point man with his friend Cooper Blackstock on numerous recon missions involving kidnap victims. He understood the value of fear. But he learned now that the greasy slide in his gut that kept him alert and cautious wasn't nearly as easy to control when the hostages under consideration included his baby sister. He sucked in quiet, even breaths to keep the feeling in check, and looked over at Maureen Beaumont, who was perched on the edge of a loveseat.

"Where was this found?"

"In the mailbox out on the road with the rest of the mail," she said. "Jessie offered to collect it earlier in the day, but I wanted the exercise. Then I got busy and didn't walk up the drive until later."

"You walked in the dark?"

"Yes, I quite often do. I've always felt safe on this island." Then her face crumpled, and Zach knew she must be realizing she'd probably never recapture that feeling of absolute safety again. "Oh, God," she said.

"Breathe," he reminded her.

She inhaled and exhaled, and when she'd composed herself somewhat, she sat a little straighter in her seat and eyed him curiously. "How can you stay so calm?"

"I've spent eighteen years in a specialized unit—extracting kidnap victims is part of what I do. This is different, of course, because it involves my sister, and I don't know where Glynnis and your son are being held, so I can't simply slip in and get them out. But I *will* see to it that both of them get home safe and sound, ma'am. You can count on that."

She nodded, then turned to the plain brunette seated next to her. "Master Sergeant Taylor and Miss"—she turned to Lily—"I'm sorry, I don't know your last name."

"Morrisette," Lily said. "But please, Mrs. Beaumont, won't you call me Lily?"

"And I'd be honored if you'd call me Zach, ma'am," Zach agreed.

"Very well." She turned back to the brunette. "Jessica, Zach and Lily will need rooms. Would you see about preparing them?"

9

ZACH MANAGED TO MAINTAIN HIS CALM, PARADE-ground face right up until the moment he shut the door to the room he'd been assigned. Alone at last, he dumped his duffel bag on the floor, walked to the side of the bed, and sat. He barely noticed either the room's pleasing color scheme or its opulent appointments. He only knew that his hands had developed a fine tremor, and he stared at them as he clenched and unclenched his fists in an attempt to stop the shaking.

His baby sister had been kidnapped.

"No," he whispered in fierce denial. He couldn't lose her. He'd been looking after her one way or another since the day his mother had put her into his arms and then put the two of them on an airplane, and he could not, would not, lose her now.

Except he hadn't exactly done a stellar job of looking after her, had he? Maybe Lily was right. Maybe he *had* been concentrating on all the wrong things. Take Beaumont, for example. It appeared he wasn't after Glyn-nie's money after all. And even if he had been, suddenly that didn't seem like the worst situation in the world. Zach had plenty of money—he'd happily provide for his sister and whoever else her little heart desired. Hell, he'd give up every red cent he owned if that would guarantee her safe return.

It didn't help knowing that this was far from his first screw-up with her. He'd been happy enough to skip out on her the minute he'd turned eighteen. He'd delegated responsibility without a backward glance, and hadn't once bothered to make sure Grandfather was teaching her the most elementary of life skills.

Nor had he bothered to really get to know her when he'd resumed charge of her after Grandfather's death. He'd been so damned bent on protecting her from potential con artists out to drain her inheritance that he'd neglected to realize it was her own lack of knowledge that was probably her greatest vulnerability.

He'd made certain assumptions about Glynnis without taking the time to discover who she'd become. And now he was faced with a fair possibility he'd never get that opportunity.

No. Zach rose to his feet, teeth gritted. *No, by God, that is* not *an option, so don't even think it*. He *would* get Glynnie back. And Beaumont as well, if that would make her happy. Damned if he was going to lose anyone else he cared about—his life had been filled with too many good-byes as it was. He'd lost his parents, his grandmother, and more men whom he'd fought beside and counted as friends than he cared to think about. There hadn't been anything he could do to govern those circumstances. But he'd move heaven and earth to get his sister back.

Not that he'd exactly made a grcat start. He should have insisted the police be called as soon as he'd learned about the kidnapping. Then again, his entire focus had been locked on not getting bounced from this house, because to do so would have cost him any chance of gaining control over the situation. Tomorrow morning he'd rectify that. Meanwhile, he wasn't without resources of his own.

He picked up the telephone from the nightstand and punched in his calling card number with one hand while he fished his address book out of his duffel with the other.

A moment later the phone on the other end of the line rang three times before it was picked up by a machine. His friend Cooper Blackstock's recorded voice began a spiel telling him to leave a message, then was abruptly replaced by a live voice that impatiently snarled, "Whataya want?"

Zach glanced at the clock and grimaced. "Oh, shit, Coop. Sorry. I didn't realize it was so late."

"Zach?" Coop's voice warmed considerably. "That you?"

"Yeah."

"Well, sonuvabitch, Midnight. How's it going? I hear your sister has some woman who's an absolute babe living off her. I think Rocket dug up some information on said babe, but he won't discuss it with me, so I'll have to let him tell you what it is for himself. And don't that beat all? Who would've thought the guy who used to tell us way more than anyone ever wanted to know about his sex life could suddenly be so discreet?"

"Coop—"

"Yeah, I know." His warm laugh rumbled down the line. "Even Peter Pan's gotta grow up sometime. But back to your sis, Rocket tells me she ran off with some guy. You disentangle her yet?"

Zach's hand tightened around the receiver. Suddenly he didn't want to say this out loud, because to do so seemed to make it more real. But there was no help for it. "I've got a situation here, Ice. I'm at her boyfriend's home now on Orcas Island, and it seems Glynnie and Beaumont were kidnapped on their way here."

"What?" The humor left Coop's voice. "Jesus. What can I do to help?"

"I don't suppose there's a chance you've interviewed someone in the Seattle FBI for one of your books?"

"No, man; I'm sorry. I don't have a single contact there."

"Then I think you'd better let me talk to John. I need him to tap some of his sources for me."

"You got it. Hang on a second."

Zach heard him calling Rocket's name, then a low-voiced conversation in which Cooper must have explained the situation, for John picked up the phone a moment later and said without preliminary, "I'll make inquiries with the Seattle feds, Zach—find out from the field agents there if their SAC is reliable and discreet, or one of those assholes who cares more about grabbing headlines than the safety of the abductees."

It was an important distinction. Most of the kidnap victims their type of unit was charged with extracting were military, so it wasn't often they dealt with the FBI. But they'd liberated enough snatched ambassadors and businessmen to know the personal agenda of the special agent in charge could make the difference between a victim being returned alive or shipped home in a body bag. The possibility of placing his sister's life in the hands of some hotdogger out to make his name made Zach's blood run cold.

As if John could tell, he said with unsentimental briskness, "Give me the particulars so I can figure out what else needs to be done."

Zach recited them as if giving a report to a senior officer, and Rocket was silent for a moment. Then he said in a carefully neutral tone, "So you're telling me *Beaumont* is the primary target?"

"That would be an affirmative." Then he took the stick out of his ass. "Ironic, isn't it? In light of my allegations against him?"

"Yeah. There seems to be a whole lot of that ironic shit going on around here lately."

Whatever the hell that meant. Ordinarily, Zach would have demanded to know. He also would have picked up on the odd note in John's voice and hounded him unmercifully until he discovered what had put it there. But right now he had more important matters on his mind. "You have any contacts you can tap around here? I know this is out of your usual area, but I need to know if there are whispers of anything going down." He rammed his fingers through his hair. "God, John, I'm groping around blind—I don't even know *where* Glynnie and her boyfriend were snatched. It could have been anywhere between here and home. The guy's mother was too hysterical to give me any details."

"So hopefully she'll slam down a tranq or two that'll guarantee her a good night's sleep, and you'll learn more in the morning when she's had time to calm down," John said. "Meanwhile, you try to get some rest, too, and I'll get cracking and see what I can find. Let me have a number where I can reach you. No, wait, that's probably not a great idea—you'll want to keep the lines clear so the kidnappers can get through. Jesus, Zach, you gotta drag yourself into the twenty-first century here; you're about the only guy I know who still doesn't own a cell phone. But, okay, never mind that," he muttered, and Zach could practically smell the circuits burning in Rocket's brain. "We can work around it. Give me a call tomorrow, late morning, and I'll let you know what I've found."

"Thanks, John." His gratitude was profoundly sincere, but to counteract the almost embarrassing degree of emotion that swept through him, he cleared his throat and said with deliberate lightness, "I could just plant a big wet one right on your lips."

"Not in this lifetime, pal." Then John's voice went dead serious. "You keep the faith, Zachariah. And let me and Coop know if you require our physical presence up there. He says it's about a five-hour drive from here. What?" A quiet exchange occurred off John's end of the line, then he spoke back into the receiver. "Ice said to tell you we can be there a helluva lot sooner than that if we charter a plane. So let us know."

When they said good-bye and hung up a moment later, Zach felt better. It didn't make sense, since he wasn't any closer to getting his sister back than he'd been ten minutes ago. But at least he'd started the ball rolling. And it was . . . comforting, somehow, to touch base with friends.

He paced his room for a while, then prepared for bed. He didn't expect to get much sleep, but at least it gave him a goal, and after stripping down to his skivvies, he grabbed his ditty bag and headed for the bathroom.

He stopped inside the door. Wonderful. *Just* his freaking luck. It wasn't bad enough he and Lily had been given rooms right next door to each other, but they shared this bath, too, and she'd obviously already put it to use before him. It was warm, steamy, and fragrant with woman-scent, and she had stuff spread out from one end of the counter to the other. Zach simply stood and stared at the clutter for a moment, recalling Coop saying that John had information on her, which Zach had then failed to collect. It wasn't like him to let the details slide.

Then his shoulders hitched in a minute shrug. So big whoop. He'd find out what it was tomorrow. Reaching out, he picked up a fancy little pot and turned it end for end to peer at its labels. He unscrewed its lid and sniffed the contents before closing it up again and setting it back where he'd found it. Next, he picked up a shiny golden tube. Damn. He shook his head as he pulled the top off a creamy red lipstick and swivelled it up to its full extension. Women sure as hell packed a heap of shit with them. His own ditty bag was downright spartan in comparison.

Carefully he restored and replaced the lipstick, then took a step back with his hands up to keep from messing with anything else. He reached for his own bag and hauled out a toothbrush and toothpaste, then brushed his teeth and knocked back three aspirin. Glancing at the damp towel spread out over the curtain rod across the tub, and at the water-massage shower-head beyond it, he decided to put off his own shower until tomorrow.

But around four in the morning, when he got tired of flip-flopping from one side to the other for what felt like the hundredth time, he got up and took a long, hot shower after all. By the time he finally dropped off it was nearly five A.M.

The sun beat down on Zach's head, and the airfield's tarmac beneath his feet felt soft and gooey in the fierce African heat. He was hot and sweaty, and his arms ached from holding his squirmy, five-month-old baby sister. She'd drooled all over his chest, she kept chewing on the pocket's flap, and everywhere her sturdy little body touched his, a furnace-like heat molded his white cotton shirt and khaki shorts to his skin in soggy, misery-producing patches. To top it off, the bug bite on his left leg just below her drumming foot itched like crazy. His stomach churned with such queasy anxiety he feared he might throw up.

He swallowed to hold down the nausea and ignored his discomfort as he stared up at his parents. "Don't make me go," he pleaded one last time. They were send-ing him away from the only home he knew, and he'd give anything, do anything, to change their minds. "The flight attendants can take care of Glynnie." He stared imploringly at his father, then his mother. When he caught her glancing at her watch, he knew his entreaty had fallen on deaf ears in that quarter. So he concen-trated on his dad. "Please, Papa. You said yourself that Grandfather will be waiting to meet the plane. Let the flight attendants hand Glynnie over to him. You don't need me there for that."

"She'll be growing up in a strange land, son, and you're her big brother. I'm counting on you to keep her safe."

Zach's chin jutted. "It's not fair! I'm eleven; what the heck can I do? It's not like I know this Philadelphia place the way I do the veldt. It's Grandfather's territory. Let him keep her safe."

"He will. But he's getting up there in years, so she'll need your strength and stamina as well."

"But if he's old, don't you think two kids might be too much for him? Girls are easy—just send him Glynnie. Boys are nothing but trouble. They wear a body down." He should know, he'd heard his mother say so often enough.

She frowned down at him now. "Don't argue with your father. You're going, and that's the end of this discussion." But, bending, she kissed his forehead, and he closed his eyes to savor the unusual caress.

When she straightened she smoothed back a lock of his hair that had fallen forward. "It won't be so bad, darling." Then she looked at his father. "Peter, we should be going; I want to check that appendix in the village. Zachariah, be a good boy for your grandparents. Take care of your sister. We'll come see both of you very soon."

Suddenly he was on the airplane, buckled into his seat with the damn baby back to gnawing on his pocket as he pressed his face to the porthole window. He watched his parents walk away before the plane even *taxied to the runway. Turning from the sight of their departing backs, he glared down at his sister, hot resentment rising in his throat. This was all her fault. Things had been fine before she was born. If it wasn't for her . . .*

But when her lip quivered and she started to whimper as the plane hurtled down the runway and rose into the sky, he pulled her up against his chest to comfort her. Her damp little arms clung around his neck, and he cuddled her close and whispered reassurances as, staring out the small window, he watched everything he'd ever known dwindle to the size of a dime, then disappear.

With a sharp inhalation of air, Zach jerked awake. He blinked, his eyes stinging with unshed tears and his stomach hollow with a remembered sense of abandonment. Then he just lay there, staring blankly up at the ceiling as he sucked in and blew out deep, even breaths to bring his heart rate back down within its normal range.

Christ. Back when he was a kid, he'd relived that awful time in so many dreams he'd lost count. Loneliness had been a way of life in those days, with only his grandmother's sweetness and his baby sister's laughter to alleviate his sense of isolation. Mother's promise to come see them had turned out to be just so much hot air.

He had really hoped, during his first and even second year in the much-hated Philadelphia mansion, that his parents would suddenly arrive out of the blue and admit they had made a mistake sending him and Glynnie away. Eventually, though, he'd become a teenager and put away his childish dreams. His folks had abdicated the role of parenthood to Grandfather and Grandmama. They'd only ever bothered to visit a grand total of four times, and hadn't hidden their impatience to get back to their work all that well even then. The plight of a bunch of strangers in remote African villages clearly held more importance for them than Glynnie or he ever would.

But that was then. He was no longer a scared eleven-year-old and hadn't been for what seemed like a thousand years now. It had been a fucking age since he'd woken up crying like a baby over an event so far in the past he could barely even remember it—except in his dreams.

Irritated, he rolled over and looked at the clock. Great. Seven forty-five—he hadn't even gotten three hours sleep. But there was work to be done, so he crawled out of bed and made his way into the bathroom, where he shook out more aspirin for his headache and tossed them back with a glass of water. It didn't take a shrink to guess what had resurrected the dream after all these years. The face reflected in the mirror was grim as he reached for his razor and the travel-sized can of shaving gel. Once again he'd failed his sister—and this time it had potential life and death consequences.

But it wasn't a failure written in stone, and he would, by God, rectify the situation come hell or high water. Ten minutes later, he let himself out of his room.

As he reached the bottom of the stairs, the plainer of the two sisters he'd met last night was just entering the foyer carrying a fully loaded tray. She looked up and gave a start, which made the items shift with an ominous rattle.

"Oh, my goodness," she said. "You gave me a start."

"Sorry. Here, let me take that for you." He relieved her of the tray. "You're Jessica, right?"

"Yes. I was just taking breakfast into the dining room." Eyeing the tray he now held, she grimaced. "Such as it is. Won't you join us?"

"Sure." He followed her into the room across the foyer. Mrs. Beaumont and Richard were seated at a long cherrywood table, and they looked up at his entrance, giving him subdued greetings.

Jessica directed him to a sideboard where she unloaded the tray he carried of its pitchers of milk and orange juice, a silver salver stacked with toast, and a crystal bowl of jam.

"It's not much, I'm afraid." She waved him to a stack of plates and bowls. "But there's cereal over there, if you'd like, and fresh coffee."

Zach shrugged. "It's fine." He didn't particularly feel like eating, but supposed having something in his stomach might help his headache. He discarded the tray, then slapped a dollop of jam on a piece of toast, poured himself a cup of coffee, and carried his meal over to the table.

He ate the toast, then looked across at Mrs. Beaumont as he sipped his coffee. "You look more rested," he observed. "Are you up to discussing strategy for getting Glynnis and David back?"

She gave a regal nod. "Certainly."

"Good. Then the first thing we need to do is alert the authorities."

Panic immediately transformed her bearing. "No!"

"Mrs. Beau—"

"You saw the note yourself. They said they'd *kill* David if we called in the police!"

They said they'd kill both David and Glynnis, and Zach wasn't exactly wild about having his sister's endangerment ignored. But he reined in his impatience. It was clear Mrs. Beaumont's hysteria wasn't as well under control as he'd first assumed. "That's standard op for this type of crime, ma'am," he informed her patiently. "Of *course* they don't want the police involved—the chances of getting caught go up exponentially whenever they're brought in."

"They said they'd *kill* him!"

"*Them*," Zach corrected in a hard voice. "Kill *them*. It's not only your son whose life is threatened." Then he shook his head and softened his tone. "But that's not the point. The threat itself is pure terror tactic, ma'am, specifically designed to keep you from calling in the police, or in this case—since state lines may have been crossed—the FBI. Historically, though, victims have always stood a better chance when the law is involved. The authorities need to be informed."

"*No.*"

"Yes," he said flatly. "This is not negotiable."

"How dare you tell me what is and isn't negotiable, young man! I will *not* put my darling David in jeopardy. And if you call the police over my objections, I'll . . . I'll . . ." She seemed to look inward for a moment in search of a threat big enough, then suddenly raised her chin and looked him straight in the eye. "I'll deny they've even been kidnapped!"

Zach stilled. "You'll do what?" he demanded in a dangerously even tone.

"I'll tell the police I don't know what you're talking about. And I'll ask them to remove you from the premises."

It took everything he had not to come out of his chair. He wanted to reach across the table and grab her by the neck—and wasn't *that* a sorry state of affairs. He'd taken verbal abuse from the best, had drill instructors who'd yelled in his face that he was lower than the shit on their boots, and he'd never so much as blinked an eye. But this middle-aged woman strained his patience to the limit.

Even so, this was no time to go off half-cocked. He took a couple of deep, steadying breaths. "That would be a mistake, ma'am," he said with quiet authority. "Who do you imagine they'll be more likely to believe—a hysterical mother, or the man who's spent his entire adult life dealing with just this sort of situation? More importantly, Mrs. Beaumont, removing me will put your son and my sister at unnecessary risk, and the idea here is to lessen the jeopardy they already face, not exacerbate it."

"Please, Aunt Maureen," Jessica said in her very soft, I-don't-want-to-bother-anyone voice. "I think you should listen to what he has to say."

"Why?" Mrs. Beaumont demanded querulously. "What makes *him* more qualified than, say, Richard here?"

Was she freaking *nuts*? Zach stared at her incredulously for an instant before composing his expression to display nothing beyond a cool professionalism. But his voice was flat when he said, "Eighteen years in the

United States Marines, ma'am, during which a large portion of my job was extracting kidnap victims."

"Yes, but—"

"And excuse me for pointing this out, but it took me less than a minute last night to disarm your nephew. What makes you assume he'd fare any better with a criminal?"

Richard flushed, but to his credit he patted his aunt's hand and said, "He has a point, dear."

Her lips trembled, but her eyes were stubborn. "I will *not* have the police called."

"All right," Zach agreed. "We won't call them." *For now*. He could tell this was a deal breaker for her and if he had to bring the feebs in over her objections, it could conceivably add to the danger Glynnie and David already faced. So he'd back off for today, find out what Rocket had to say, then hit her with his demands again tomorrow. "But understand that I'm in charge of this, and that is *not* up for debate. I have the best chance of bringing David and Glynnis home safely." He gave her a hard look. "Are we agreed?"

She nodded begrudgingly, but it was an agreement nonetheless, and he became all business. "Good. Then we need to lay out some ground rules. I don't care who answers the phone, but no one talks to the kidnappers, no one negotiates with them, but me."

"But what if that makes them angry? They could hurt David."

She was starting to seriously piss him off. What the hell did it take for her to understand her fucking precious David wasn't the only one who stood to get hurt?

But his voice was calm when he said, "They won't be angry if you handle it right. Pretend you're the maid, pretend you're the butler, pretend you don't speak English." He gave each of the Beaumonts his sternest listen-up-and-listen-good master sergeant stare. "I don't care how you do it. But if I'm not right here, you put them off and come get me."

∽10

LILY WAS PROUD OF HERSELF FOR ONLY GETTING LOST once as she made her way down to the main floor of the Beaumont mansion. But that wrong turn and her stomach's inelegant protests over the holdup since its last meal made her wish wryly for a trail of breadcrumbs. Not only would the guidance come in handy, but she could use a little something to tide her over until breakfast, and even crumbs off the floor were beginning to sound pretty darn good. This place was immense, and her starting point had been somewhere deep in the heart of the west wing, where she and Zach had been given rooms.

That took her mind off her grumbling stomach, and an ironic smile crooked her lips. No doubt whoever chose their cheek-to-jowl accommodations assumed she was granting the two of them a discreet favor. Little did the Beaumonts know that putting her and Zach in such close proximity was more likely a homicide waiting to happen.

Then again, maybe not. She mulled it over as she descended the central staircase. Yesterday she'd caught glimpses of a different Zach, and last night she'd seen the professional, competent, and determined side of what she began to suspect was a more multifaceted personality than she'd originally thought. Granted, she was already highly familiar with the "determined" part, since Zach made no secret of his resolution to get her out of his sister's life. But last night Lily had actually found the authority with which he'd assumed command admirable.

She might think Zach wrongheaded where Glynnis was concerned, but she didn't doubt his devotion to her. And to Lily's surprise, she was learning to read the subtle signs that provided a bit of insight into the way he thought. For instance, even though he hadn't displayed any overt distress, she had known instinctively that he was worried sick about his sister's safety.

She reached the bottom of the staircase, and the civilized clink of sterling against china and the low murmur of voices drew her toward a room opposite the parlor they'd occupied last night. She crossed the foyer.

As she paused in the doorway, all conversation ceased. Then Jessica gave her a hesitant smile. "Good morning," she said in a soft voice. "Come in; we don't stand on ceremony around here. Are you hungry?" Without awaiting a reply, she indicated the sideboard. "Breakfast is a help-yourself affair. You'll find plates and bowls on the other side of the coffee service."

Lily took a covert head count as she crossed to the sideboard. Besides Jessica, Zach, Richard, and Mrs. Beaumont were present. The only ones not in attendance were Jessica's husband, Christopher, and her more flamboyant sister, Cassidy. But as it was Monday morning, chances were they'd already left for work. Eager for breakfast, she turned her attention from the missing two people to the food arrayed before her. Only to have her heart sink. The selection was surprisingly meager.

It embarrassed her to realize her dismay at the scant arrangement of cold cereal and equally cold toast must have shown, for Mrs. Beaumont said in her well-bred voice, "I do apologize for the inadequate selection, but I'm afraid Ernestine, our cook, is quite overcome and has taken to her bed." Her bottom lip quivered. "David is her favorite, you know."

"Have you heard anything this morning?"

"Not a word. And if anything should happen to my darling David, I simply don't know what I'll do."

Zach shifted in his seat. The uncharacteristic abruptness of his movement drew Lily's attention, and a thrill of alarm shot through her. For although he didn't speak and he appeared coolly contained, with the same flash of telepathy that had told her last night how worried he was about Glynnis, she knew this morning that he was dangerously on edge. No one else seemed to notice anything amiss in his manner, but it couldn't have been clearer to her if he'd suddenly begun waving semaphores over his head. The tomato-red Henley he wore seemed appropriate, for as far as she was concerned he was one great big warning flag.

His agitation appeared to be linked to Mrs. Beaumont, so partly to divert the woman from doing whatever it was that was putting his back up, and partly because Lily couldn't abide one more day eating second-rate food, she left the sideboard to approach the older woman.

"I'm sorry," she said. "You must think I'm terribly rude. It's just that I adore food, and we've been eating such catch-as-catch-can meals since leaving California that I was looking forward to a real breakfast. But I have a suggestion that might suit everyone's needs. I love to cook, and I'd be happy to fill in until Ernestine is feeling more herself."

The offer was clearly tempting, but Mrs. Beaumont said politely, "Oh, no. You're our guest. We could never ask you to slave in the kitchen."

Lily laughed. "You didn't ask, and to me it isn't slaving. Zach and I showed up on your doorstep unannounced, and you've been gracious enough to offer us lodging. So, please. Allow me to repay you, if only a little, by doing this in return."

Richard, who had been quietly sipping coffee across the table, tossed his shiny brown hair out of his eyes and reached over to give the older woman's hand a squeeze. "It's a generous offer, Aunt Maureen. Take her up on it."

Mrs. Beaumont looked from him to Lily. "Well, if you're sure you wouldn't mind . . ."

"I truly wouldn't. In fact I'd enjoy it, and if someone will simply point me in the direction of the kitchen, I'll go put together a nice hot breakfast. Everyone's under a great deal of stress. Keeping fueled is an essential part of dealing with it."

Jessica set her half-eaten slice of toast on her plate. "I'll show you."

As she rose from the table, Zach leaned back in his chair and regarded Lily with raised eyebrows. "I know

"I think you should feel very sorry
idea what a sad tale I have to tell."
ted pulling ingredients out of the
a wry look as she passed the items
to set on the counter. She twirled
granting an audience. "So spill."
, and I are—are you prepared for
itions in the Beaumont clan."
gasp.
smile that transformed her face
pretty. "I know. Shocking, isn't it?
se women for whom appearance is
rse we had a cook, as did everyone
rence was, while we merely ap-
, they actually were. If there had
in our part of the family, I might
n the kitchen. But only genuinely
to behave as if they don't have a
. What *we* had," she said with a
ons." Then, with the slightest hint
ed to herself, "Yes indeed. We cer-
ll important connections."
her well enough to ask what that
merely said lightly, "Well, I don't
my name outside the restaurant in-
n me, kid, and I can at least teach

tely."
nd by her side. "What are you go-

ry basic this morning, since we're

you can cook," he said as his gaze ran over her, pausing a moment on the multistrand necklace of glittery crystals that spilled across her breasts. "But there's a difference between cooking for one or two people, and a group this size. Are you sure you're up to this?"

Cooking for *seven*? Not even that, if Cassidy and Christopher didn't eat breakfast. She managed not to roll her eyes. "Oh, I think I can muddle through somehow."

As she followed Jessica down a short hallway off the foyer, she heard the other woman murmur wonderingly to herself, "A 'group this size'?"

She laughed. "I know," she agreed. "Why is it men so often think that because we wear lipstick and have parts that jiggle, our competency must be in inverse proportion? Oh!" she breathed as she stepped into the kitchen. "This is *fabulous*." It was a state-of-the-art work space, her personal idea of heaven.

"At least you *have* jiggly parts," Jessica said under her breath. "I should be so lucky. As for lipstick . . ."

Her soft voice pulled Lily away from an ecstatic inspection of the Viking range, and she really looked at the other woman for the first time. "You should wear it," she said decisively, after giving her a thorough inspection. "Most women would kill for bee-stung lips like yours. In fact, I've got a lipstick I bet would be perfect for you. It's a shade called Pink Smooch that I fell in love with in the store, but when I got it home I discovered it was all wrong for my coloring. I'll dig it out for you after I get breakfast on the table."

Jessica gave her such a helpless look that Lily couldn't help but smile. "I'm guessing you don't share my passion for makeup." She splayed her fingers across her chest. "Be still my heart. I find that completely shocking."

"According to my sister, it's nothing short of heresy." Lily laughed. "At the very least."

"Yes, well, not all of us are slaves to fashion."

"Oh, honey, of course we are. You obviously just haven't met the right consultant yet." *Until now.* There was nothing more frustrating to Lily than untapped potential, and seeing Jessica's made her itch to do a complete makeover.

Not only was the other woman's face devoid of makeup, her medium-brown hair was much too long and bushy for her narrow face, overwhelming its delicate bone structure. Lily didn't need labels to recognize quality clothing when she saw it, and she could tell at a glance that Jessica's sweater was an expensive one. But the color was all wrong for the brunette, muddying her fair complexion, and it was too bulky for her slender frame. Her jeans were fine, but those shoes were a nightmare. They looked like a potato farmer's brogues.

It wasn't up to her to barge in and start rearranging anyone's life, however, so she simply smiled and turned back to the marvelous kitchen she'd been given permission to play in. But wiggling her painted toes appreciatively in her own Cuban-heeled, open-toed, retro pumps, she thought dryly, *So I won't barge. I can hold off for a day.*

She was immersed in deep admiration for all the wonderful gadgets and the well-stocked pantry when Jessica said uncertainly, "Well, you'd probably like me to get out of your way."

Lily swung around. "Oh, no; don't go. I could use

your help
is. That is
ing you d
ordinarily
have to, a

Jessica
sound, as
joke. "No
pressing t
would be
for spendi
one respo
room this
should be

Lily gr
what she
leap here
as I am."

"As a
ally enjoy
find out."

"Wait,
always ha

"Some

"Well,
of sympat
left her m
jolt, it occ
with the
Laguna, v
to give he

To her

"Actually," she said
for me. You have no

"Yeah?" Lily sta
fridge, giving Jessic
to the other woman
one hand like royalt

"Richard, Cassi
this?—the 'poor' re

Lily gave a mock

Jessica flashed
from plain to almos
Mama was one of th
everything, so of co
in our set. The dif
peared to be wealth
been any real mone
have been allowed
rich girls can affor
bean to their name
shrug, "was connec
of bitterness, she ad
tainly do have those

Lily didn't know
was all about, so sh
have a connection to
dustry. But stick wi
you to cook."

"Really?"

"Oh, yeah. Absol
Jessica came to s
ing to make?"

"Just something

a little pressed for time. We'll do scrambled egg-stuffed breakfast pitas and a cantaloupe-blueberry salad. Will your husband and sister be joining us?"

"I . . . imagine."

"I wasn't sure if they'd already left for work."

"Oh, no, the office for B Networks is upstairs in the east wing."

"Okay, then, we'll plan on seven." She indicated the eggs, mushrooms, red pepper, onion, and cheese assembled on the counter. "You see anything here that anyone can't eat?"

"No."

"Excellent. I'll make a poppyseed dressing for the salad first so it can chill while I get everything else ready."

"What can I do?"

"Cut the cantaloupe and assemble the salads," Lily replied, reaching for a bowl. "Do crosswise slices."

Jessica raised her eyebrows, and Lily demonstrated what she meant, cutting the melon the long way, then handing the other woman the knife. She turned back to her own station and scraped a carton of vanilla yogurt into the bowl and added some lemon juice and poppyseeds. A few minutes later she glanced up from grating orange zest in the bowl. "I think I saw some Boston lettuce leaves in the fridge, so when you're done there, get those out and put a few on each plate to make a bed. Then add four or five slices of cantaloupe and sprinkle them with a handful of blueberries." She whipped the dressing, covered it with plastic wrap, and placed it in the freezer for a quick chill. Then she went to work chopping the vegetables.

"How do you *do* that?" Jessica demanded a moment later.

"What?"

"Chop that fast without slicing off a finger."

Lily laughed. "Practice. Training."

"Can you teach me how to do it?"

"Sure. C'mere." When Jessica joined her, she held up her left hand. "The trick is keeping your fingers tucked under. See?" She demonstrated how to pin down the green onions in such a way that there were no horizontal protrusions to accidentally cut off. Finishing the onions, she julienned the red pepper, then offered the knife to Jessica. "You want to try it on the these?"

Jessica did better than she'd anticipated, but in no way did she attain anything close to Lily's speed. She laughed and went back to removing the last of the rinds from the cantaloupe slices. "I can see it'll take a little practice."

Lily wagged her eyebrows. "Meet me here an hour before each meal and I can give you plenty of that."

"I just might." Jessica smiled and scraped the rinds into the compost bucket Ernestine kept next to the sink. She hadn't expected this, she realized as she washed and dried her hands, then collected salad plates from the cupboard and set them out on the counter to adorn with lettuce leaves. She hadn't expected to like Lily this much, to feel this almost instant sense of kinship with her, as if they were best friends from grade school who'd just met up again and taken right up where they'd left off.

And wasn't that amazing? With Lily's blonde bombshell looks, sparkly jewelry, and wiggly walk, she was exactly the sort of woman who usually made Jessica feel about as exciting as yesterday's leftovers. She was one of the girly-girls, those ultrafeminine types who seemed to know instinctively all the things that escaped Jess. What colors to wear, which makeup to buy, how to put together an ensemble that made the most of one's assets. A woman like Cassidy.

Except Lily didn't make her feel inadequate. She made her laugh, Jessica thought warmly. She made her feel . . . useful.

"Those look great." Lily nodded at the arrangement of fruit on the lettuce leaves. She grabbed the poppy-seed dressing out of the freezer and handed it to Jessica. "Stir that up and then spoon it down the middle of the fruit. And if you'll point me to a platter, I'll stuff this egg mixture into the pitas, and we'll be ready to go."

A few minutes later, carrying a tray on which she'd carefully balanced all the salads, Jessica followed Lily back into the dining room. She felt as flushed with ac-complishment as if she'd devised the menu herself.

The first person she saw when she entered the room was Christopher, and her smile widened with the in-stinctive flash of joy the sight of her husband invariably gave her. She noted that her sister had yet to put in an appearance—not that *that* had anything to do with any-thing. Cassidy was always late . . . and surely the fact that Christopher had also been late getting to the dining room this morning was strictly coincidental.

Circling the table, she offered a salad first to the dark, silent Marine who quite frankly rather unnerved her, then to the members of her family.

"My word," Aunt Maureen said, looking up from the

prettily arranged plate to Lily, who was placing a break-fast pita on everyone's bread plate. "This is amazing. You were only gone ten minutes. How on earth did you manage something so nice in such a short amount of time?"

Lily shrugged. "It's what I do—I'm a chef by trade. Besides, I had a terrific assistant." She shot Jessica a grin, then turned back to Maureen. "Your niece actually made the salads."

"Well, I followed directions, anyway," Jess amended. Setting the rest of the plates down in the vacant places at the table, she propped the tray against the sideboard and took her seat next to Christopher.

"Yes, Jessie's a good little direction follower." Cassidy breezed into the room, wearing just the right outfit, complete with chunky jewelry, her hair twisted up in a messy, casual do that Jessica knew took her forever to arrange. "Good morning, all." She slid into the vacant chair next to Zach that Lily had been heading toward and looked down at the salad plate in front of her. "So what was your contribution, Jess? Washing the lettuce?"

Jessica felt herself start to disappear, simply fading away until she became part of the surroundings, the way she so often did around her younger sister.

Then simultaneously, Christopher squeezed her thigh beneath the table while Lily sat down and leveled a look at Cassidy as she reached for her linen napkin and shook it open. "Actually, she pretty much did it all. Cut the fruit, arranged it, dressed it. And as you can see, she did a lovely job of the presentation. What is it that *you* do, Ms. Beaumont?"

The question was asked in a perfectly polite tone of

voice, but Cassidy's cheeks mottled red beneath her impeccable makeup. And suddenly Jess didn't feel quite so much like a part of the wallpaper.

"Cassidy shops," Richard supplied, and picked up his pita. He took a bite and hummed a little in appreciation.

Cassidy shot her brother a sour look. Then she turned to Lily with a superior smile. "Actually, my real forte is fund-raising. Someone has to look after the less fortunate." She glanced down at the plate in front of her but made no move to pick up her fork. "Being a cook is certainly a useful little job, though. If you're looking for work, I'm sure I could find you a place on someone's staff. Our crowd is always looking for good help."

Jessica winced at her sister's rudeness and Aunt Maureen said, "*Cassidy,*" in a remonstrative tone.

But Lily merely smiled. "That's very kind of you, but I have a job."

"*Do* you. Do you work for a good family, dear? Or perhaps cook for a nice little diner?"

"No. I'm a corporate chef."

Cassidy shrugged impatiently. "Cook, chef, what's the difference?"

"Training, chiefly—a chef has a great deal more of it. I got mine at the Culinary Academy in San Francisco and in Le Cordon Bleu at the California School of Culinary Arts in Pasadena. Then I apprenticed for several years with two of the top chefs in Los Angeles."

Zach abruptly set down his fork. It clattered against his china, and Jessica looked over in time to see him push his chair back from the table.

With his shuttered eyes and unsmiling mouth, he appeared completely intimidating to her, but obviously her sister didn't agree. She reached out to run her beautifully manicured fingers down his arm, and sent him a flirtatious glance from beneath her long lashes. "You're not leaving already, are you?"

"Yes." His face expressed no emotion as he stared down at her fingers tracing the soft veins that stood beneath the tanned skin of his forearm. "I have some calls to make." Withdrawing his arm from beneath her hand, he stepped back, circled the table, and walked out of the room.

No one said a word for an instant, then Lily, too, set her napkin aside and rose to her feet. "Excuse me, won't you?" she murmured. "I need to talk to Zach for a moment, then I'll be back to clean up the kitchen."

"Oh, dear, you needn't do that," Aunt Maureen said with a little flutter of her hands.

"I don't mind, Mrs. Beaumont, really. It's just another part of the job."

"What?" Cassidy demanded sweetly. "The big, important chef doesn't have a little helper-bee to do the dirty work for her?"

"Shut up, Cassidy," Jessica snapped.

Her sister turned cool eyes on her. "Well, well, the mouse speaks." Then she turned away, and Jessica watched her watch Lily walk out of the room.

As soon as the petite blonde disappeared, however, Cassidy turned back to her, and something about her air of satisfaction made Jessica's stomach churn.

"So," Cassidy said. "Did Christopher tell you about the . . . service . . . he performed for me this morning?"

🔗 11

A CHEF! ZACH STALKED ACROSS THE FOYER AND up the graceful central staircase, taking the stairs two at a time. *And not just a line cook giving herself a fancy title, either, from the sound of it, but a highly trained professional.* He swore with inspired creativity beneath his breath. Because, as much as he'd love to scoff at the notion, it made an awful sort of sense.

Nothing like having your fuck-ups come home to roost. All of a sudden he couldn't even convince himself that, in spite of having a career, the possibility still existed that Lily was the golddigger he'd repeatedly accused her of being. For, too late, he figured out the fault in his logic that had bothered him the other day when he'd demanded to know if she was worried his stopping Glynnis from marrying David would lose Lily her meal ticket. He smacked himself in the forehead. *It never occurred to you, genius, that if a meal ticket had been her big concern she would've been all for you breaking up the big romance? Once Glynnie has a husband to moni-*

tor her finances, chances of wriggling money out of her are pretty much shot.

Zach blew out a breath and squared his shoulders. So all right, big deal. He'd been wrong, and as a consequence he'd leveled a bunch of unfounded accusations at her. What the hell—he'd apologize.

Even if he still did wonder what was in it for her. There had to be something. Gainfully employed or not, no one put herself out to the extent that Lily had for someone she'd known as short a time as she had his sister. No one outside of the Corps, anyway.

"Zach."

He spun around at the sound of her soft voice and watched her jiggle down the corridor with that hip swiveling, feminine walk of hers, looking like every Marine's wet dream as she perambulated toward him on yet another pair of her ubiquitous high heels. He marched over to meet her. "Well, you really got me good, didn't you? I'm sure you're pretty damned pleased with yourself."

She had the brass to laugh. "I gotta admit, not being regarded for once as the Slut of Golddigger Gulch is a nice change of pace."

Grasping her upper arms, he backed her against the nearest wall. "Just who the hell are you, lady?"

She didn't pretend confusion. Palms pressed flat against the wainscoting at her back, she tilted her chin up and looked him straight in the eye. "Exactly who I claimed to be right from the start, Soldier Boy. Glynnis's friend."

"Right. And you just ditched your career out of the goodness of your heart so you could come along and keep me from wrecking the so-called love match of the century?"

"I'm not ditching anything. I'm a chef for a corporate yacht, and my next trip doesn't leave port until the last week in May. But, yes." She shrugged. "That's precisely why I came along. I tried to tell you David was different, but you refused to listen."

The firm feel of her shoulders shifting beneath his hands reminded him that touching her—especially right now when his feelings were so screwed up—wasn't the wisest idea in the world, and he released her like a hot spud. "I might have been more inclined to pay attention if you'd bothered to let me know you actually *worked* for a living." Then he mentally winced. *This is your big apology?* As bad-tempered and burdened as he felt this morning, it didn't escape him that he was being unreasonable. And the real pisser was, his mood didn't even have all that much to do with the revelation that Lily wasn't the little money grubber he'd accused her of being. Discovering he'd been acting like a jerk toward her was merely the sprinkles on his cupcake.

Somehow Lily seemed to know it, too. "I don't feel a burning need to justify myself to people who make idiotic assumptions," she said with a commendable lack of rancor for someone who had every right to be dancing around taking pokes at him and singing *na-na-na-na-na*. "I have a feeling that's not your biggest beef, anyhow," she said, staring up at him. "What is this really all about, Zach?"

Gut churning, he stepped back. "I don't know what you're talking about."

"Yes, you do. You were already tense when I came

down to breakfast. Does it have anything to do with Mrs. Beaumont?" She reached out and touched his arm, a sudden anxiety scudding across her eyes. "Did she say something? Discover something about Glynnis and David's situation?"

The ire that had been eating him alive all morning came boiling to the surface, and he slapped his hand down on the wall next to her shoulder. "Finally. Someone who acknowledges that Glynnie, too, is at risk."

Her eyes widened. "Well, of course she is."

"No one else around here seems to think so! They're all so friggin' worried about their precious *David*—but I have yet to hear a single word of concern for my sister. Jesus, Lily. It's as if she doesn't exist."

"I'm sure it's just because they don't know her, Zach."

Incensed, he leaned into her. "I don't know Darling David either, but at least I have the decency to *pretend* I care."

Lily's lips twitched, but she merely said, "No, what I mean is, I imagine Glynnis probably doesn't seem quite real to them, since none of them has ever actually met her."

"I don't want to hear any lame excuses—there's no justification for their behavior!" Bracing both forearms on the wall on either side of her head, he bent his knees and leaned into her so closely they only escaped a full body press by a hair's-breadth. Such close proximity had him sucking in the warm, lemony-sugary scent of her, and suddenly all his pent-up agitation veered off in a brand new direction. Or maybe not so new. Either way, feeling jumpy and restless and in need of a safe outlet to blow off some steam, he found himself dipping his nose until it almost touched the contour of her neck, where he inhaled deeply. Her fragrance seemed to emanate from her skin rather than any one particular pulse point, but he wasn't fussy about the source. He merely breathed her in, then had to slick his tongue across lips suddenly gone dry. "Ah, man. I want to kiss you."

She froze. "What?"

He pulled his head back far enough to look down at her, aware of the heavy drumming of his heart against his ribs. "I want to kiss you. Have *wanted* to kiss you since practically the first minute I laid eyes on you."

"Yeah, right," she scoffed. "My *tush*, you have."

"Hey, it's no lie. But since I have this ironclad rule about never making time with women out to steal my sister's inherit—" He trailed off. *Oh, good going, Romeo. Be sure to remind her of all the insults you've hurled at her—that oughtta put her in a lather to jump your bones.* "What I mean to say is, I couldn't act on it."

"Uh-huh," she said neutrally. "So, I've officially been cleared, then, of only wanting to be friends with Glynnis for her money?"

"Yes. I guess I owe you a pretty big apology for some of the things I've said."

"Gee, ya think?" She regarded him with those brilliant blue eyes. "Have I been cleared of the slut charges, too? Or, wait. Maybe it's the fact you *do* still think I'm one that's fueling this sudden desire to kiss me."

"No—I mean, yes. Shit." He looked down at her and shrugged helplessly. It was exactly this sort of female doublespeak that drove him up the wall, and by rights, having to deal with it now on top of everything else going on ought to banish his hard-on right into soprano country.

But it didn't seem to be working that way. "Let me try this in English. No, that's not the reason I want to kiss you," he clarified. "And yes, you've been cleared of that charge." As if getting to kiss her was a likely prospect, anyway. Why the hell was he giving her the opportunity to get her rocks off by rejecting him? The smart money said he should just turn and walk away.

Lately, however, smart wasn't exactly the first word he'd use to describe himself—so why start now? He stayed where he was, staring down at her in frustration.

"So let me see if I've got this straight." She drew a slow, deep breath, and the action brushed her breasts against his diaphragm, sending him sucking for a breath of his own.

Then she ticked off the points on her fingers. "I'm off the hook for the charge of trying to lead Glynnis astray in order to get my mitts on her moolah. I apparently no longer top the Ten Tawdriest Sluts list. And you have a sudden urge to kiss me." A small, crooked smile tugged at her lips as she looked up at him.

He lowered his head until his mouth was a fraction of an inch from hers. "There's nothing sudden about it, Lil. But, affirmative. That about covers it."

"Well, I've only got one thing to say to that, bud." Her tongue stole out to moisten her bottom lip.

Watching the movement, he had to rein in the impulse to simply take what he wanted, and political correctness be damned. He dragged his gaze up to meet her eyes. "Let me guess. Get bent?"

"That's two words, Taylor, and I only need one. It's short; it's sweet. It's—"

" 'No.' I *get* it."

"—Okay."

"The only damn service I provided your sister," Christopher said, tugging Jessica into their suite, "was offering to jump-start the battery in her car."

"Yes, so you said downstairs." Jessica watched him as he set her loose and began pacing their bedroom. God, he was handsome. With his sculpted cheekbones, gold-streaked brown hair, and leaf-green eyes, he could have been a model, and she knew perfectly well what people thought whenever they saw the two of them together—how on *earth* had such a Greek God ever ended up with someone as plain and dowdy as she? Not that Jessica blamed them. She often wondered the same thing herself . . . and very much feared she knew the answer, that he'd married her for her connections.

They'd met two years ago at a thousand-dollar-a-plate fundraiser, the decorations of which had been designed by her committee. It was a night she'd never forget, because she'd never realized until then that a person could meet someone and feel such instant recognition, as if their souls spoke to one another. After just one conversation with the tall, unbelievably handsome guy in the perfectly fitted tux, she'd known he was the man for her.

Ordinarily someone with his good looks would have made her feel tongue-tied and self-conscious, but it was as if he didn't realize how devastatingly gorgeous he was, and he'd made her feel pretty and witty, too. Then, in the days that followed, he'd given her a rush that had simply swept her off her feet. They'd gotten married four short months later, and Christopher had promptly given up his apartment in Bellingham to move into the Beaumont estate and had exchanged his job for a post in the family business.

He walked over to stare down at her now, and when his golden eyebrows gathered over his nose she thought for an instant that he'd read her thoughts. But apparently that wasn't the case.

"So I'm repeating myself," he growled with a shrug of one muscular shoulder. "So sue me—I know how easily you allow Cassidy to undermine your confidence. But I swear to you, Jess, the instant I concluded my business call, my intention was to head down to breakfast like I told you I would. I didn't anticipate Cassidy waylaying me in the upstairs hall to moan about her dead BMW and an appointment she simply *had* to make."

"Yet, there she was at breakfast, with all the time in the world to insult our guest." And that didn't even address the sinking feeling in the pit of her stomach that Christopher's telephone call had given her. When he'd covered the mouthpiece and urged her to go down to breakfast without him, she'd had the uneasiest feeling that he didn't want her overhearing his end of the conversation.

But her husband had a way of allaying all her fears, and he did so now. "What can I say?" he asked smoothly. "It was typical Cassidy bullshit. As soon as I determined her problem was only a rundown battery because as *usual* she hadn't bothered to make sure the driver's door was fully closed, I offered to jump-start the car. But no; all of a sudden she's no longer in a big galloping hurry and decided she simply had to have breakfast." He ran his fingertips down Jessica's cheek as he gazed earnestly into her eyes. "We both know she's just trying to cause trouble."

And darned if it wasn't working, too, Jessica thought unhappily. She could literally feel all her insecurities kicking in, but she drew a deep, quiet breath, then slowly eased it out again, refusing to let them get the better of her. Helping with the breakfast preparations this morning had made her feel good about herself, and she wanted to hang on to the sensation, to experience again that boost to her confidence. She looked up at Christopher and changed the subject. "Lily said she could teach me how to cook."

"She did, huh? And that appeals to you?"

"Yes." She laughed. "Isn't that silly?"

"Hell, no. Not if it gives you pleasure." He studied her face. "You like her, don't you?"

"Yes, I do. She's nice, and she makes me laugh."

"There's not many who can claim that distinction these days." He sounded almost bitter, but before she could decide if she were imagining things or not, he asked, "What's your take on her relationship to Taylor?"

She looked at him in surprise. "They're lovers," she said immediately. Then hesitantly, "Don't you think?"

"Did she say as much?"

"Well, no, but look at her. Look at him. And there's that . . . electricity when the two of them are in the same room. I simply assumed—"

Christopher shook his head. "I don't know, babe. I

don't deny the chemistry, but he has a way of looking at her that makes me believe they haven't actually done the deed yet."

And just like that, Jessica's feeling of well-being collapsed. "Well, perfect," she said flatly. Stepping back, she pushed her hair out of her eyes with both hands and stared up at her husband in frustration. "Once again my sterling ability to read people and situations shines through."

Bewilderment drew his golden eyebrows together as Christopher looked down at her. "Why would you feel an investment in their love life?"

She blew out a disgusted breath. "Because, helpful me, I arranged for them to be in adjoining rooms."

Braced for rejection, Zach took a moment to change gears. "What d'you mean, *okay*?" he demanded, shoving back in order to stare down at Lily. "Okay, as in that's your response to my 'I get the rejection' comment? Or okay, as in yes?"

"Okay, as in yes. I'm curious, all right?" But even as bravado tilted Lily's chin up, she wondered what the heck she was doing. This was *sooo* not smart and immediately she tried to backpedal. "Look, just forget it. It was one of those impetuous speak-before-you-think things, but it's a dumb idea. An *extremely* dumb—"

"Oh, no you don't," he growled. "You said 'okay.' Too late to change your mind now." And hooking a warm hand behind her neck, he pulled her away from the wall, lowered his head, and rocked his mouth over hers.

Pleasure splintered through her in amazing abundance, considering it wasn't some deep, wet soul kiss.

Zach's lips were slightly parted, and his mouth worked hers masterfully, but he kept his tongue to himself. Even without it, however—*boy*, the man could kiss! His lips teased, and then delivered on every promise. They brushed hers lightly . . . then not so lightly . . . then firmly rubbed her lips apart. When his mouth suddenly sealed itself over hers and lightly sucked, she came right up onto her toes. Wrapping her arms around his neck, she offered up her mouth for more and impulsively skimmed the tip of her tongue along the slick, inner curve of his bottom lip where it adhered to her own.

Making an uncivilized sound, Zach slanted his mouth over hers with just the slightest hint of roughness and pressed her back against the wall. He spread his thighs and bent his knees until he was on a more equitable level with her much shorter stature, then plunged his hands into her hair to hold her head firmly. His kiss grew more insistent but still remained relatively chaste. Until, with a rumble of frustration, his hot tongue suddenly slid past her teeth to probe her receptive mouth.

Lily felt as if she'd plunged her fingers into a live socket—electricity shot from the damp thrust of Zach's tongue straight to her nipples, her fingertips, her toes. Muscles deep between her thighs tightened. She moaned and kissed him back for all she was worth, chasing the aggressive pump of his tongue with her own until the two slid and retreated from each other in a damp, fervent tango.

Lifting his mouth a moment later, he whispered a ragged curse, turned his head to come at her from another angle, then dove back into the kiss. His fingers tangled in her hair for a second, then slowly slid free to stroke down the sides of her neck, over the curves of her shoulders and along the hollows of her underarms. The heels of his hands lightly skimmed the sides of Lily's breasts, but before she could fully inhale the breath she'd sucked in, his clever hands had already continued on to smooth along her ribcage, to trace the dip of her waistline, then slide onto the fullness of her hips. There his fingers sank in, and he suddenly lifted her up as he straightened to his full height.

With a startled exclamation, she pulled her mouth free and tightened her grip around his neck. But Zach obviously had no intention of letting her slip, and the next thing Lily knew, she was pressed between the hard wainscoting and his even harder body, her feet dangling a good foot off the floor as he recaptured her lips. Not about to hang there like a rag doll, she wrapped her legs around his narrow hips.

He made a satisfied noise deep in his throat, and his hands slid around to grasp the full curves of her bottom. Continuing to kiss her senseless, he made minor adjustments to her position. Then all of a sudden the achy notch between her legs aligned with the hard length of his erection. Nerves sang throughout Lily's entire body, and involuntarily, her pelvis surged forward to maintain the delicious contact.

And control of the kiss abruptly went up in flames.

Zach's mouth turned fierce, and the sheer pressure against Lily's lips ground her head back against the wall. She barely noticed. All she was truly cognizant of was the taste of his kiss, the heat of his body, and the hardness of his sex rocking, rocking, rocking against hers.

Then, without warning, he ripped his mouth free and,

his breath sawing harshly, whispered a foul word. A second later, Lily was dumped back on her feet. Blinking like a mole suddenly flung into the light, she leaned weakly against the wall and peered up at him. "Zach?"

Then she, too, heard what his sharper ears had obviously already picked up. Footsteps tapped rapidly up the stairs. Smoothing her hair back, then nervously running her hands over herself to make sure all her clothing was still in place, she watched as Jessica's bitchy sister raced into view.

"Good, you're here," Cassidy said breathlessly. "The kidnapper just called."

☌12

ZACH SWORE AND HEADED FOR THE STAIRS WITH ground-eating strides. What the *hell* was the matter with him? He was a trained strategist, for God's sake, but when his sister was in the clutches of a kidnapper and he should be manning, or at the very least somewhere in the *vicinity* of a telephone, what was he doing? Making out with little Lily Morrisette, that's what! It made him furious, not only with himself and the kidnapper, but with her, too, for being the constant temptation that she was.

And yet . . .

Lily wasn't the one who'd initiated that red-hot necking session. *She* wasn't the one who'd said "I want to kiss you," and then picked him up and dry humped him against the nearest wall. *This one's all on you, cowboy.*

Big mistake. Big, *big* mistake. Yet even so, he found he couldn't completely regret having gotten his mitts on something as purely delicious as she was—no matter how irresponsible. Reaching the bottom of the stairs, he hesitated, and hearing her clattering down the steps be-hind him, twisted around.

She caught up in that instant, arriving in his wake slightly out of breath—no doubt from racing after him in those silly-ass shoes. She faltered to a stop one step above him, which put them on a more equitable level than usual, and staring at him, she was all hot pink cheeks, mussed-up hair, and guilty eyes.

He grasped her chin. "You okay?" he demanded, and couldn't quite prevent his thumb from making a brief pass over her bottom lip. It was soft and damp.

She nodded.

"Good." Turning her loose, he then did what years in the military had taught him to do: He compartmental-ized, putting her firmly out of his mind as he walked into the parlor.

Mrs. Beaumont was there, once again in hysterics. He gritted his teeth, not wanting the kidnappers to hear her panic. He opened his mouth to shut her up, then snapped his teeth closed when he looked at the phone and saw that wouldn't present a particular problem today.

The receiver was firmly on the hook.

He about-faced smartly to look at her. "What the hell is this?"

"I *tried* to get him to hold on until you got here," she cried. "I *did!*"

"That's right, she did," Cassidy said, strolling into the room behind Lily. "She told him she was the *maid*, of all things." She shook her head as if lowering one's standards to such a degree was simply beyond her comprehension, then shrugged and stepped in close to Zach. "She also sent me after you. And let me tell you"—reaching out, she trailed a fingernail from his collarbone to his chest—"I haven't run that fast since . . . well, I've never run that fast." She lightly traced a downward path over the ridges of his abdomen.

He snatched her hand before it reached his belt and pressed it back against her own midsection. "Lady, don't waste my time."

Ignoring the sudden anger that replaced her seductive expression, he turned his attention back to Mrs. Beaumont. He had some anger of his own to deal with, but he sucked it in. This wasn't the time. In truth, were he to do a quick soul search, he had the unsettling thought he might discover that his own anger had been misplaced just a little too often recently.

He swallowed a curse, then a sigh, and admitted to himself that he hadn't handled this situation very well. He'd been commanding soldiers for so long he'd sort of forgotten that a middle-aged woman wasn't a recruit to be slapped into shape. Standing in front of him was a distraught mother, and he should never have taken her disregard of his sister's danger personally. *He* was all shook up at suddenly finding himself on the relative-of-the-victim end of the spectrum, and at least he had some experience with the sort of tactics kidnappers used. He could only imagine how terrified they'd made her. So he bit back the harsh words on the tip of his tongue and asked gently, "You attempted to convince him you were the maid?"

"I did. I really tried, Zach, but he said 'don't give me that, you old bitch,' and called me other horrid names, and he kept hammering at me and *hammering* at me to admit who I was. He told me over and over again what he'd do to David if I didn't confess who I was and start talking to him—if I didn't do exactly as he said. And I got so rattled, I didn't know if I was coming or going."

Her face was deathly white, her breathing too rapid and shallow, and Zach stepped forward and rubbed his hands up and down her arms. "Take slow, deep breaths, Mrs. B.," he said. "I want you to listen to me. You gave it your best, and that's all anyone can ask of you. Remember what I told you about terror tactics. The kidnapper *wants* you rattled, so let's work on not letting him win. We can beat him if you don't fall apart on me."

She stared up at him pleadingly, and he said firmly, "We *are* going to get David and Glynnis back—you can take that to the bank. That's right," he commended as she finally drew in a breath that was deep enough to be steadying and then slowly exhaled it. "Breathe. Now another." Once her respiration slowed and a little color returned to her cheeks, he held her at arm's length. "Tell me as concisely as you can everything that was said. You can leave off the parts you've already told me," he added hastily when her breathing promptly sped up and grew choppy again. "For instance, are we definitely dealing with a man?"

"Yes, of cour—" She gave him a startled look. "That is—I just assumed he was. But he never actually spoke above a whisper."

"So it's not impossible it was a woman?"

"No, but—" She cut herself off, waving her hand as if to push her objection aside. "Never mind. You'll think I'm silly."

"Tell me anyhow."

"Well . . . it's just that I got the *feeling* it was a man." Color touched her cheeks. "I told you it was silly."

"Not necessarily. I'm a soldier, ma'am; I never discount the gut. Quite often a hunch, or woman's intuition, or whatever you want to call it, is actually an observation that you can't put an exact name to, but which the subconscious has noted all the same. So, for now, we'll go with your feeling and assume our kidnapper's a man. Did he make any demands?"

Lily's scent curled around his senses a nanosecond before her manicured hand came into view with a cup of coffee that she offered to the older woman. "Here, Mrs. B.," she said. "I poured this from the thermal pot in the dining room. It's hot and it's bracing. Take a sip—the caffeine will do you good."

"Thank you." Mrs. Beaumont wrapped her hands around the eggshell-thin china cup. Although she didn't immediately drink the coffee, she seemed to take comfort from the warmth that emanated from its container. She stared down into it as if mesmerized for a moment, then looked back up at Zach. "He said he wants a million dollars, and he wants it in bills of small denomination. Nothing larger than a fifty."

"Do you have that kind of money?" If she didn't, he could sell off enough of the Taylor holdings so that, between them, they could come up with it.

She nodded. "Yes. But it will probably take a few days to liquidate part of the business in order to put that much together. Christopher and Richard would know more about that aspect of it than I do."

"Did you tell the kidnapper that it would take a few days?"

"Yes."

"And what was his response?" No doubt a recitation of all the painful things he'd do to her son if she didn't produce it sooner. The kidnapper's desire would be to keep her properly alarmed—that was standard operating procedure for these jokers. Zach could swear sometimes that there must be a *Kidnapping 101* textbook out there advising thugs to always keep the families of their victims off balance—even if nine times out of ten they fully intended to allow them the time necessary to raise the money.

"He told me we have five days to get it together."

"He told you—" Cutting himself off to keep his incredulity from showing, he said smoothly, "That's good news. Excellent, really."

So why did it give him an uneasy feeling in the pit of his stomach?

Probably because you're a suspicious sonuvabitch by nature, pal. But still . . . five days? He squared his shoulders and tried to tell himself that just because this differed from the way these scenarios generally played out, it didn't make this one dubious.

But when his gut told him something was wrong, he went with it. And he sure as hell didn't screw around trying to convince himself it was because he couldn't do much until the kidnapper called again.

He paced a few steps away, then turned back to look at her. "Are Richard and Christopher still around?"

"Yes, I'm sure they are."

"I need them down here."

She looked almost pathetically grateful to have something to do and promptly walked over to the telephone. Picking up the receiver, she ran a fingertip down a row of buttons and pressed one.

Watching her, Zach realized for the first time that it was the type of system one usually saw in offices. Very efficient for a mansion this size. Speaking urgently into the phone for a second, she informed the person on the other end that the kidnapper had called, then disconnected, punched another button, and spoke urgently once again. A moment later, she replaced the receiver and nodded to him.

"They'll be down in a minute."

Lily brought him a cup of coffee while they waited, and he carried it over to the French doors, staring out into the yard as he sipped it. He wasn't sure when it had begun to rain, but a fine, steady drizzle turned the world outside the windows a misty gray. It soaked the terrace furniture and formed a murky curtain that obscured the bluff and the straits beyond.

Richard arrived breathless a minute later, and a moment after that Christopher barreled through the door with Jessica in tow. Since Maureen had only told them the bare bones on the phone, Zach filled them in on the details of what had transpired. Richard immediately left to gather the ledgers from the office, and Christopher ran back upstairs for his laptop computer. As soon as both men returned, they sat down to figure out which aspects of the family business could be liquidated and how long it would take to do so.

Zach watched them for a while, then paced the perimeters of the room, covertly studying the dynamics of the Beaumont family.

Both men were obviously well trained and business-minded, but Christopher seemed to have a more concrete idea of which assets were expendable, and without discussion he assumed the dominant role. Richard didn't appear to have any problem with the pecking order, but Zach noted it all the same.

Down by the fireplace at the other end of the room, Cassidy sat in an overstuffed chair and flipped through the pages of a magazine, her legs crossed and one foot tapping the air impatiently. Jessica fussed over her aunt on an adjacent couch, keeping the older woman anchored with whatever she was saying to her in her soft voice.

And then there was Lily. She wasn't a part of the family dynamics, of course, but of them all, she was the one his eyes were drawn to most often.

She bustled around the room, jewelry jingling as she saw to it that everyone had coffee. Now that he no longer viewed her through the narrow end of his own misconceptions, he was beginning to notice things he'd missed before. He saw, for instance, that for all that she looked like some rich man's trophy squeeze, she had a down-to-earth basic kindness about her.

When she topped off Mrs. Beaumont's cup, she reached out and patted the older woman's shoulder. She squeezed Jessica's hand as she spoke quietly to both women. Yet the men, he noted as he watched her go over to refill Christopher's and Richard's cups, she didn't touch at all. She talked to them easily, but kept her hands strictly to herself.

As early as this morning he would have expected it to be just the opposite. Then again, earlier this morning he also probably would have expected her to sit around like Cassidy, exhibiting an air of entitlement as she waited for someone else to attend to her needs. Instead, Lily was the one waiting on everyone, and it obviously didn't make her feel the least bit diminished to do so.

Discovering yet more evidence of just how far off base he'd been with her was about as welcome as a case of the clap. He ground the heels of his hands into his eyes, then dropped his hands to his sides and watched as she brushed a spill of sugar off a table into her cupped palm and walked over to toss it into the fireplace. He wasn't a man who ordinarily jumped to hasty, ill-thought-out conclusions. Nor was he accustomed to being in the wrong.

He hated that lately he'd been both.

"Okay, that seems to be it," Christopher said, and Zach turned to him in relief. He'd think of a way to apologize later. Hell, maybe he should just kiss her again; that had worked pretty slick the last time he'd felt the need to admit he was wrong.

Are you out of your mind? He managed not to pound his head against the nearest wall, but just barely. *Jesus, Taylor. You keep your damn distance from that dame before she completely screws up your head.* Besides, wouldn't this apology simply be more of the same old, same old anyway? He was getting confused. Was he in the wrong again or in the wrong *still*?

His headache was starting to come back—he couldn't think about this any more. Right here, right now—*thank you, Jesus*—he had a situation that needed his attention, and it was something with which he actually had some experience. Walking over to where the two men were tossing their pencils onto the table and pushing their chairs back, he demanded, "You've projected a timetable for getting the money together?"

"Yes." Christopher plowed his hands through his expensively barbered hair and stretched his elbows toward the ceiling as he dug all ten fingers into the muscles at the base of his skull. "If I get started right away, we ought to be able to liquidate everything we need in four days. Five at the outside."

Zach froze. Well, well. What an amazing coincidence. That was the exact amount of time the kidnapper had generously allowed them to raise the ransom money.

Funny thing, though. Zach had never been the type of man who believed in coincidences.

And suddenly this reeked to him of an inside job.

Miguel dashed back to his car through the rain. He let himself in and turned on the engine, immediately cranking the heater to high. Then, shivering, he shook out his hands like a wet cat, flicking drops of water all over the dash. *Dios*, it was cold! More than anything—more than the mellifluous language of his country, more than its foods so full of flavor and spice—he missed the bone-melting heat of Colombia. He was ready to go home.

He didn't intend to go back, though, with his tail tucked between his legs. When he returned to his village, he'd do so walking tall—the people of Bisinlejo would not see a man who allowed great wrongs to go unpunished. No indeed, what they would see was a man who avenged his honor.

But first the blonde *puta* had to come out of the big house.

Leaning over the steering wheel, he wiped a circle in the windshield with his sleeve to clear the fogged glass, and peered out. But the haze wasn't all on the inside of the car. The weather was socked in.

He'd never seen anything like it. In Bisinlejo when it rained, it came down in violent torrents that pelted the ground and pummeled the surrounding foliage, but just as quickly stopped. One could always count on the sun to come out again and evaporate the moisture until nothing remained but vagrant wisps of steam rising from the ground. This rain, though—it was a thick, almost mistlike drizzle that quickly soaked everything in its path. It seemed to find its way into every crack and crevice, no matter how well you thought you defended against it, and it sank to the bone, chilling and stiffening the joints.

A short while ago he'd pulled out a package of crackers left over from one of the petrol stops he'd made on the way here and had eaten them for breakfast. Although they'd been well wrapped, they were completely limp and soggy.

Still, he could live with that. But he was dressed all wrong, he was running out of food, and what provisions he did have were in pitiful condition. Worse, no one in the big house had ventured out of doors all morning long, and even if the master sergeant's woman should come outside, Miguel's teeth were chattering so loudly, she'd probably hear him a kilometer away and run for the hills!

With sudden decision, he reached for the shift lever, put the car in gear, and released the emergency brake. Leaning forward to peer cautiously in all directions, he inched the car out of its hiding place and started down the narrow country road. Since he didn't have any idea what Taylor's plans might be or how long this might take, he could very well be stuck here for a good long while yet.

But regardless whether that turned out to be the case or he accomplished his mission tomorrow, it was definitely time to find the nearest town and properly outfit himself.

13

ALONE IN THE KITCHEN, LILY CHOPPED, DICED, AND minced everything that wasn't nailed down. Restlessness burned through her veins and along her skin like a fast-spreading rash. Try as she might, she couldn't seem to get the session with Zach in the upstairs hallway out of her mind.

Whoever would have guessed that a guy so hard-edged aggressive could kiss with such devastating subtleness and restraint? At least at first he had. But then he'd really got cooking, and . . .

Heat suffused her. She stared blindly across the kitchen as she relived those too few moments, her knife suspended over the potatoes she was currently reducing to uniform cubes. Again she experienced the hunger with which he'd kissed her, recalled the hard length of him wedged solidly between her thighs, remembered the friction and heat she'd felt as he'd rocked and ground against her, generally driving her insane.

The knife slipped from her fingers with a clatter. Startled, she jerked back to reality, and reached for a napkin to blot the perspiration that dotted her forehead, her cleavage, her upper lip. What *was* it about that man?

A different president had been in office the last time she'd had sex, and she'd never been the sort of woman to tumble into bed with a guy simply because she liked the cut of his jeans. Even if he was a great kisser.

So she was safe. It was a case of momentary lust, that was all. Refuse to give into it, and it would pass.

Only . . .

What if that *wasn't* all? A small moan escaped her. It hardly seemed credible, but she had an awful feeling she was starting to harbor feelings for Zach. Genuine, caring feelings.

She tried to push the thought aside, for the very idea scared her silly. She *couldn't* care for him. Not only had she not known him long enough, but to care—*stop thinking the word, darn it!*—would threaten her lifelong dream to settle down in one place and open her own restaurant. The last thing she wanted was to fall for some soldier whose very profession was synonymous with moving. She'd had a bellyful of that lifestyle already.

Besides, you had to really know a person in order to care for him, and she didn't have a clue who the real Zachariah Taylor was. Was he the guy who could be totally rude and crude and talk to her as if she were some no-account bimbo? The devil who'd kissed her like his soul was on the brink of damnation and she was his salvation—or more realistically, like he was determined to pull her into the Dark Side with him? Or was he the man who'd stopped for a second at the bottom of the stairs to make sure she was all right?

Maybe he was all three. Right this moment, though,

it was the man who'd kissed her senseless who, quite frankly, kept drawing her thoughts off track. Oh, Lord, that mouth. That hot and talented mouth—

Holy smokes, enough already! Yanking off her apron, she found some containers, scraped the various mounds of vegetables into them, and put everything into the fridge. She had to get out of here. Get her mind on something else. *Now.*

Moments later, after a quick detour to her room for her purse, she knocked on Jessica's door. It was obvious the other woman was surprised to see her standing there, but Jessica had gracious behavior down to a fine art, and she quickly masked her reaction.

"Well, hi," she said and stepped back from the door. "Please. Come in."

Lily waved away the invitation. "I don't mean to intrude on your private time. I just wanted to bring you this"—she extended the lipstick she'd promised earlier—"and ask directions to a decent grocery store. I was doing some meal planning and realized I'm going to need a few supplies. Especially the fresh stuff like veggies and fruit, and milk and eggs."

Jessica grasped her arm and tugged her over the threshold. "Come in," she repeated. "Let me just put on some shoes, and I'll drive you into Eastsound."

"Oh, you don't have to—" But Lily cut off her protest as she followed Jessica into a cozily furnished suite. No sense in working overtime to sabotage herself; Jessica's help would be much appreciated. "That is—if you're sure it's not too big a bother?"

"Not at all. I wouldn't mind getting out for a while, myself." She peered uncertainly down at the lipstick in her hand. "I'll just go brush my teeth and apply a little of this, and then we can take off. Make yourself comfortable; I'll be right back."

She left the room, and Lily gazed around curiously, happy for the opportunity to get a closer look at the touches that gave the room its welcoming warmth. She was admiring two small quilts that hung over the navy velvet couch and one that was draped over the back of an antique rocking chair when Jessica returned wearing shoes and lipstick, and carrying a small purse in her hand. Lily gave her a quick smile, then went back to studying the craftsmanship in the wall quilts. "Are these your work?"

"Yes."

"My God, Jessica, they're fabulous. *These* are what you called your little hobby? I'm surprised you're not selling them professionally."

Jessica joined her in front of the exquisitely crafted blue, sand, and bronze-toned pair. Her expression was skeptical as she gazed at them. "You really think they're good enough to sell?"

"Yes! My goodness, I've seen quilts that aren't half this nice selling for hundreds of dollars. Do you have any others?"

Jessica emitted a sound that in a less mannerly woman might have been considered a snort and walked over to an old leather and brass humpbacked trunk. She opened it and removed its top tray to reveal the stack of quilts within, an eclectic conglomeration of patterns, colors, and sizes.

Lily sank to her knees on the hardwood floor in front of the trunk. Reaching in, she pulled out several quilts and examined them avidly. "Wow." She tore her gaze away long enough to look up at their creator. "I feel like I'm in the yuppy version of Santa's workshop."

Jessica's cheeks turned pink with pleasure. "You really like them that much?" At Lily's enthusiastic nod, she asked, "You want one?"

"Are you crazy? You can't just *give* these away!"

"Sure I can. You gave me a lipstick."

"Yeah, worth fifteen bucks. This"—her hands hovered over the rich terra cotta, black, and clay colored primitive-style quilt that was her favorite—"*this* has to be worth hundreds of dollars. Maybe even tens of hundreds."

Jessica grinned. "Boy, you're good for my ego."

"Yeah? Well, as long as I'm doing such a bang-up job, I gotta tell ya, you look really great in that lipstick." Then Lily laughed. "Okay, that's actually a stroke for *my* ego, since I called it right when I said the color would be perfect for you. But still. You've got pretty lips—you should showcase them all the time."

"Oh, my." Jessica laughed too, and pulled the quilt Lily had admired out of the stack and thrust it at her. "Here, you take this. I think you overestimate its worth, but even if you haven't, just hearing somebody say that something about me is pretty is worth—how did you put it?—tens of hundreds of dollars."

Lily hugged the quilt to her breast. "I passed up your first offer, but I only do my martyr act once. Don't even *try* to get this back now." She studied Jessica curiously as the other woman closed up the trunk and they let themselves out of the suite. "I imagine your husband must tell you you're pretty."

"Oh, well, sure, but . . . you know." She shrugged and looked uncomfortable. "Isn't it almost a *rule* that he has to say so? I think it's in the Official Husband's Handbook, or something."

"I wouldn't know about that; I've never been married. And I obviously don't know your husband well enough to form an ironclad opinion, but just offhand, he doesn't strike me as the type of guy to say stuff he doesn't mean." Lily realized that something about this conversational tack was making Jessica feel awkward, though, so she changed the subject. "Let's go drop this off in my room, and then we can hit the grocers. Are there any clothing stores where we're going? I could sure use something warmer than what I brought with me. If we hadn't left California in such a hurry, I might've taken a minute to realize the weather up here was bound to be colder than I'm used to."

She'd also left home without a lot of cash, so they hit the ATM machine first thing when they got to the small, picturesque town of Eastsound. Then, deciding to save the grocery shopping until last to avoid having to leave unrefrigerated food in the car, they dashed through the drizzle to the nearest clothing boutique.

Jessica watched Lily in baffled wonder as the other woman selected two warm sweaters and a lightweight rain jacket in about seven minutes flat, and some of her enjoyment in this unexpected shopping trip drained away. "Well, that's certainly demoralizing."

Lily paused on her way to the cash register to look back at her. "What is?"

"The way every woman in the world except me seems to be born knowing these things." At Lily's raised eyebrows, Jess waved a hand to indicate the garments the little blonde was about to purchase. "Everything you chose is perfect for you, and you didn't even have to think about it. How did you know exactly what to buy?"

Lily shrugged. "I figured out a long time ago what works best with my coloring and body type, and I just stick within the range I came up with."

"See what I mean? I wouldn't even have a clue what my range is."

Lily simply looked at her for a moment, then asked, "Who decorated your apartment at the house, Jessica?"

It seemed like an abrupt and odd switch in the conversation, but rather than let on Jessica politely admitted, "I did."

"And do you select all the fabrics for your quilts?"

"Yes, of course."

"Then you're certainly capable of learning what your range is. You have exquisite taste."

Jessica stared at her for a moment in arrested amazement; she had never considered that the one had anything to do with the other. Then she blinked, and reality once again reared its ugly head. "But that's entirely different."

"No, it's not. You've created a comfortable environment to live in. This is simply a matter of expanding that comfort and style to include the things you wear, the makeup you choose, and the way you style your hair. You figure out both your good and your not so good points and shoot for ways to accentuate the first and disguise the second."

Jessica's mind went utterly blank, leaving her incapable of coming up with even a hint of what her points were, good or bad.

But Lily didn't get impatient with her the way Cassidy always did when she wasn't quick enough on the fashion uptake. She simply said, "Let me give you an example. I'm busty and way too hippy, but my waist is nice and little, so the dilemma is how to accentuate the waist without bringing attention to the hips. My compromise is no-fuss clothing. I stay away from busy patterns and ruffles and puffs and the like. I tend toward straight, long lines with accessories that hint at my curves. And I love heels, partly because I'm short and they make my legs look longer and give me more height, and partly just because they're so darn pretty." She smiled unrepentantly and shrugged.

Jessica began to get a glimmer of what the other woman was talking about when she truly examined Lily for the first time and realized the petite blonde's figure *wasn't* perfect. She simply knew how to give the impression that it was.

"Also my complexion is mostly olive," Lily continued. "That gives me the option of wearing a variety of colors. But I've learned to steer clear of the brighter oranges and the yellower greens, because they make my skin look sallow." She fingered her necklace. "I adore jewelry, and you can probably tell I'm not your basic outdoorsy kind of woman. I rarely wear rings, though, because I do have a career that can be very messy, especially on the hands, and I lean toward jeans for both work and everyday use, because I can press them to make them look a little dressier, but they're still a practical garment that can take a lot of abuse." Lily steered Jess over to the three-way mirror in the corner of the shop and gently turned her to see her own reflection. "Now you try it."

Jess studied herself for a minute, then blew out a breath. "I'm an indoor-outdoor woman," she said softly. "I spend most of my time inside, but I also like to tramp the cliffs. I don't have a career, or even a job, but like Cassidy, I volunteer on a number of charitable committees that call for dressier day wear and some evening apparel." Then she faltered. Saying what she did was easier than assessing her pluses and minuses—especially when she felt she had more minuses.

"You have a delicate bone structure," Lily prompted.

Jess met her gaze in the mirror. "That's a very diplomatic way of putting it. I'm *skinny*."

"Yeah? I'd love to hear you ask the nine out of ten American women who constantly struggle with their weight how sorry they feel for you because you think you're too slender."

"Easy for you to say," Jess snapped, and it didn't even occur to her to be appalled by her abrupt lack of manners. "You're stacked."

"*Boobs*, you're talking about?" Lily made a rude noise. "Please. You can buy those anywhere. Every lingerie department from Victoria's Secret to Walmart offers some form or another of padded, water-filled, or gel-filled bras. You can *always* beef up that area, but trust me on this, you cannot subtract excess curves to get the kind of slinky little hips that you've got. Neither can those of us who are more height challenged add inches to get those long legs. So quit your whining."

Jessica laughed in surprised gratification and studied herself more closely. "Okay, I have"—she cleared her throat—"delicate bone structure. And long legs and slender hips."

"And pretty lips."

"Yes, and pretty lips that look good in this shade of lipstick." Beginning to see she did possess pluses, she gained confidence. "I have nice skin, but . . ." She plucked at her sweater. "This color is all wrong for me, isn't it?"

"Too pastel," Lily agreed. "It washes you out. And a style less bulky would be more flattering. Something like these." She led Jess over to a stack of chenille sweaters that zipped up the front and had a different type of stitching through the midsection that lent a hint of a waistline. "Yep, I bet these would look good on you. What color grabs your fancy?"

Jessica reached for a rich golden brown, but then dropped her hand to her side, figuring it'd probably make her look like a big brown wren. But Lily pulled it out of the stack.

"I think most of us tend to be drawn to the colors that look good on us," she said. "Not always, of course, but more often than not." She held the sweater up to Jessica. "Look, you have excellent instincts. This brings out the highlights in your hair and makes your skin look really creamy. Try it on."

By the time they finished shopping that afternoon, Jessica found herself the proud owner of two new sweaters, new makeup, and even a new pair of shoes. She'd tried to protest the latter, citing the practicality of her current pair of casual oxfords.

But Lily had merely looked at her with raised eyebrows and demanded, "Practical for what, plowing the lower forty? I'm not suggesting you toss them away, Jess, just save them for tramping the cliffs. Meanwhile, buy yourself these darling ballerina flats for the less athletic moments. Heck, if you're looking for practicality, slip-ons have that in spades. Think about it: For someone who likes to go barefoot in her own apartment, this style is much easier to kick off and slide back into. Not to mention how good *pretty* can be for your health. It relieves stress. I can testify that seeing you wear something other than those big old clodhoppers has dropped *my* stress level considerably."

So Jess laughed and bought them, secretly delighted. She knew her new purchases and a few quick lessons in applying makeup wouldn't magically transform her into a beauty. And it certainly wouldn't address her worries concerning her marriage. But for nearly the first time in her life, she felt stylish. Not just passable or neat, but genuinely stylish. And that made her feel attractive. It was as if a light had come on, as if the secrets that other women took for granted had finally decided to reveal themselves to her, too. And even knowing that sooner or later Lily would go back to California, Jess felt confident she was actually learning the skills to continue *making* choices that would highlight her assets.

There was a surprising amount of power in that.

It was getting late when Zach heard the knock, and he swore softly into the phone. "Someone's at my door."

"Then I'll let you go," Rocket promptly replied.

"And don't worry; I'll start looking into the background of Beaumont's family right away."

"You're the man, Miglionni. Something is sure as hell fishy here, and if anyone's got the juice to dig me up a motive, it's you." They settled on a time for him to call back for the results, and Zach hung up just as another knock sounded at his door.

"I'm coming, already," he growled, and strode over to yank it open. "Hold your damn hors—" At the sight of the woman on the other side of the door, the words dammed up in his throat.

Because the last person he expected—or wanted—to see was Lily.

And the last place he wanted to see her was in his bedroom.

But there she stood, all five and a third feet of her in her crazy sky-high heels, looking like sin incarnate and smelling like heaven. He didn't want to let her in, and he opened his mouth to make an excuse—any excuse—so he could shut the door in her face and safely keep her on the other side. But before a single word left his lips, she sashayed right past him into his room. The next thing he knew, she was crossing within a foot of his bed and bringing with her every damn memory he'd struggled all day long to suppress.

He shoved his hands in his pockets. "Well, hey, c'mon in," he said with carefully understated irony. "Make yourself right at home."

She turned to him. "I've been thinking."

"Ah. I thought I smelled something burning."

She gave him a look that was surprisingly repressive

for a woman who was anything but repressed. "Very funny. You need a minute to get all your blonde jokes out of your system, or do you wanna hear what I have to say?"

He could use a minute, all right, but not to assemble his arsenal of jokes. The woman scrambled his brain. He'd been raised to be polite to women, yet every time he turned around he found himself acting rude as hell toward this one.

Still . . . did he want to hear what she had to say? *No.* He didn't want to have to deal with her, period. Then again, she looked as if she were about two seconds away from walking over and taking a poke at him with one of those competent little fingers of hers, and he *really* didn't think he could handle her touching him right now. He didn't trust what he'd do if she laid hands on him—and wasn't that a hell of a thing for a trained warrior to have to admit? Yet it was nothing short of the truth. It was all he could do just to squelch the fantasy that raced through his mind of the various ways he could keep those capable hands busy. So he gave her a brisk, impersonal nod and said, "My apologies. What have you been thinking?"

"That somebody really ought to call the police about the kidnapping."

That actually took his mind off wondering what it would be like to lay her down on the bed just a few steps behind her.

At last. Someone who showed a little common sense. He gave her a wholly approving look that for once didn't have a thing to do with her sex appeal. "You and me both, sweetheart."

"You agree?"

"Hell, yes. You heard me arguing this morning wi—
No, I guess that was before you came downstairs." He
rolled his shoulders. "Anyway, I had this very argument
with Mrs. Beaumont. Christ, Lily, I'm a soldier—I *believe* in the system. But not only did Mrs. B. threaten to
kick my butt out of here if I called in the feds over her
objections, she said she'd deny Glynnie and David were
even kidnapped!"

Lily looked properly horrified, and he was filled with
a sudden comradely warmth toward her. He took a few
steps closer.

"That's just plain foolish!" she said indignantly.

"Amen to that." He couldn't believe he hadn't realized before how intelligent she was.

"So what do we do?"

"We proceed cautiously. We've got five days to work
on her, and Rocket—" At her furrowed brow, he cut
himself off to say, "You remember my friend John
Miglionni who stopped by the house?" He got a flash of
Rocket laughing himself silly on the phone a few minutes ago after he'd started to tell Zach he'd discovered
Lily was exactly who she'd claimed to be, and Zach'd
had to admit he'd already found that out for himself.
Then, recalling his behavior when he'd introduced them
back in Laguna Beach, not to mention the way he and
John had double-teamed her, he braced himself for an
acid response.

But she merely nodded. "Of course. Mr. Sensitivity.
You call him Rocket?"

"Yeah, it's his Marine handle. He's a private detective
now, and he's checking out the reliability of the local

FBI." He patted her shoulder with companionable bon-homie as he explained the reason for John's inquiries.

Big mistake. She was soft and warm beneath his fingers, and it took an effort to remove his hand. He rubbed the back of his neck in an attempt to eradicate the feel of her and groped for the hail-brothers-well-met emotions of a moment ago. He cleared his throat. "Don't, uh, worry about it, okay? One way or the other—hopefully with the feds' help, but even without it—I *will* see to it that everything works out all right."

Lily stared up into his eyes, and blinked when she saw their normal gray watchfulness all warmly avuncular as he gazed back down at her. She didn't get this guy—she didn't get him at all.

Oh, not the trust-me-I-can-take-care-of-everything attitude—that struck her as pretty typical of the Zach she'd come to know. But earlier today he'd kissed her like she was the hottest woman in the known universe—and now he was patting her like a decrepit old dog? Good Lord. And to think she'd hesitated to come to his room for fear he'd jump to the wrong conclusion. Talk about worrying over nothing.

And how immature was it to be a little bent out of shape that the need had been removed? Heck, it wasn't as if she *wanted* to pick up where they'd left off. She stared at the pale scar that bisected his upper lip. Did she?

No, of course she didn't. But really, was she the only one who remembered the way they'd been all over each other just a few short hours ago?

Impulsively, she reached out and touched his chest. "Zach," she said . . . then realized she didn't have the first idea where to go from there.

Before she could decide, Zach's hand whipped out to grip hers. He jerked it away from the soft red material covering those hard, muscular planes. "You don't want to be doing that," he growled. "Or maybe you do. Either way, be damn careful what signals you send out, Lily, because I'm not in the mood to be teased."

His eyes, when hers snapped up to meet them, were no longer the least bit avuncular. They were molten and intense, and seemed to see right down to her skin.

And suddenly she didn't have a doubt in the world that he remembered every single thing about that encounter.

14

ZACH REMEMBERED, ALL RIGHT. HE REMEMBERED every single second. And staring down at Lily, with that curvy body that made his fingers itch, and those electric-blue eyes that seemed to see into his darkest corners, he wanted nothing more than to pick her up, toss her on the bed, and have at her.

Jesus. He was a man who took pride in his self-control—so what the Sam Hill was it about her that brought him so close to throwing it all away, time after frigging time? To prevent himself from grabbing her, he crossed his hands behind his back and assumed the time-honored "at ease" position. But damned if she got to wiggle off the hook and just bebop on her merry way.

"Why are you really in my room?" he demanded. "You looking to pick up where we left off?" *Say yes,* he thought fiercely. *Just say the word, sweet thing, and I'll be happy to oblige you.*

"No, of course not," she snapped indignantly. "I told you—" Cutting herself off, she shook her head and blinked up at him thoughtfully. Then she shrugged. "I don't know," she admitted with the inherent honesty he was beginning to understand was an integral part of her. "Maybe. I'd like to say you're crazy even to suggest it . . . but maybe I am."

His hands came out from behind his back and he took a step forward, crowding her so closely she had to tip her head way back just to maintain eye contact. But she didn't step away, and triumph exploded in his chest. "Good," he said in a low, intense voice. "Because that's sure as hell what I'd like to do. I'd like to pick right up where we left off before we were interrupted—and then some. I want to strip you naked and touch you every place I've ever thought of touching you. Spread you out on that bed and lick you from head to toe." His gaze took a slow, leisurely journey down her body, and the sheer lust that roared through his gut tempted him to jettison his control, if only for a while. Hell, self-restraint was probably overrated, anyhow.

Christ, Taylor. Wise up. "Or maybe"—he snapped his gaze back up to pin her in place—"I should leave you in those cock-teasing shoes you always wear and just lick you from head to ankle."

There. That oughtta do it. He'd noticed that Lily never swore, so his deliberate crudeness ought to put some distance between them. And as much as it galled him to admit it, he needed her to be the one to do it, because he simply didn't have the strength to voluntarily pass up the chance to get naked with her.

Her eyes flared hot, and she made a soft, yearning sound low in her throat. "Maybe . . ." She licked her lips. Cleared her throat. "Maybe you should go with that idea."

Zach's much prized constraint hit the skids. His right hand whipped out and hooked her by the back of her neck. Pulling her flush against his body, he bent and rocked his mouth over hers.

It was like splashing white lightning over the coals of a fire believed to be extinguished, but which had only been banked. When Lily's mouth immediately opened beneath his own, red-hot lust exploded in his veins and incinerated the last bit of common sense he had left. He was all urgent need as he licked into her, all burning sensation as he felt her plush breasts flatten against him when she rose onto her toes and wrapped her arms around his neck. With a rough sound deep in his throat, he picked her up by her hips, took two giant steps forward, and toppled them both onto the bed.

Immediately, he rolled until he was half on top of her, throwing one leg over her thighs to pin her in place and pressing his forearms to the mattress on either side of her shoulders. He plunged his hands into that soft, cotton-candy hair and held her head still for his kisses. Triumph rolled through him when she kissed him back with unbridled enthusiasm—until a soft sound that struck him as more anxious than aroused purled in her throat. Frowning, he raised his head and looked down at her.

Lily's eyes were still closed, the fine skin of her eyelids looking fragile and vulnerable. Her Marilyn Monroe 'do clung in soft strands to his fingers, and her mouth was reddened and swollen. Shit. He was behaving with all the finesse of a high school geek who'd suddenly found himself getting lucky with the hottest cheerleader in town.

"Lily?" He stroked his thumb slowly over her cheek-bone and down to her full bottom lip. "Are you all right?"

Lily was slow to drag herself from the hot quagmire of sexual enthrallment, but surprise at the question pried her heavy-lidded eyes open, and she blinked up at him. His pale gray irises, ringed in darker charcoal, were full of fire. They stared back at her, hot, horny . . . and full of concern.

Ah, jeez. How was she supposed to *not* care about this guy, when he disrupted his own gratification in order to worry about her welfare? There was no question that Zachariah Taylor could be tough, hard-nosed, and occasionally downright impossible to get along with. But the man was also a caretaker right down to his big old size-thirteen combat boots. And more than anything else—more than his hard body and knowledgeable mouth, more than his propensity for smart-aleck remarks and his occasional loss of temper—*that* was the thing about him that really got under her skin.

So just how the heck am I supposed to stop myself from caring?

A cool dribble of unease trickled through her hot blood, but she shoved it aside. It wasn't a crime to care; heck, she'd probably never be able to feel this level of attraction if she *didn't*. That didn't mean she was in *love*, or that this was anything more than a temporary fling. Whatever this thing was that she and Zach had going between them, it would no doubt end once Glynnis was brought home safe and sound.

So until then, why not enjoy it? Did it really matter that flings weren't her usual style? Zach could be her exception.

Face it, the man was in a class all his own, anyhow.

Parting her lips, she gave the rough-skinned pad of Zach's thumb a tiny suck, then curled her arms around his strong neck and arched slightly to press her breasts against his chest. "Are you *worried* about me?" she asked with a slight smile. "I'm not sure how we got from 'lick you from head to ankle' to being anxious about—"

"I'm not *anxious*," he growled. "But when you made that little noise in your throat, it sounded as if you were—I don't know—in pain or something. I don't want to hurt you, or push you somewhere you don't want to go."

"Why, Zach, that's so *sweet* of you." And it was—sweet and accountable. But sweetness from him was the last thing she wanted at this juncture. Thankfully, as she suspected, simply using *sweet* and *you* in the same sentence made him react as if she'd just complimented the size of his penis by squealing, "Isn't that *precious*?"

"Sweet?" His head reared back and his eyes darkened. He was fully upon her now, and when he pressed his hips forward she felt the hard bulge behind his fly. "Men aren't *sweet*."

His erection felt solid and competent, and it hit just the right spot between her legs. She managed to keep her eyes from crossing, but her voice emerged more breathy than the ironic she was shooting for as she suggested, "Responsible, then?"

"Yeah. Responsible's good. A helluva lot better than *sweet*." He lowered his head and touched his lips to a vulnerable spot behind her ear, then moved his mouth along her neck. "That's a good word for you, though. Considering that's the way you smell, the way you taste." His lips moved back up to her mouth. "*God*, you taste sweet," he repeated hoarsely before his mouth once again claimed hers.

Lily clung to his broad shoulders and allowed herself to be enveloped by his heat and his strength, to be seduced by his mouth. She retained just enough presence of mind to warn herself not to become addicted to Zach's kisses. But they were soft and lingering, then strong and fierce, and it would be so easy to become dependent upon them, especially when his tongue went from teasing hers gently to demanding full capitulation as he boldly countered her every parry and thrust.

Absorbing his heat, she undulated restlessly beneath the weight of his body. The scent of him surrounded her, an amalgamation of the triple-milled soap from the bathroom they shared, laundry detergent from his T-shirt and jeans, and the healthy musk of aroused man radiating from his hot skin. Excitement burned in Lily's veins, and with a need to touch him, to feel the strength and heat of his muscular body, she reached down to tug his red Henley tee from his pants.

It had barely cleared his waistband when he slid off her onto the mattress, and without breaking their kiss, propped himself half over her. He disentangled a hand from her hair and stroked his fingertips down the side of her throat and along the V neckline of her thin sweater. Lily stiffened a little, waiting for him to transfer all his attention to her breasts. It had been her experience that where those particular curves were concerned, men often forgot there was an actual woman attached to them.

But she should have remembered from her session

with him in the hallway that Zach never did the expected. Instead of diving into her cleavage, or enthusiastically fine-tuning her nipples like a radio operator trying to dial in a static-filled station, he seemed perfectly content to trace lightly along her sweater's neckline. When his fingers did stray lower, it was with a touch so gentle she found herself holding her breath and thrusting her breasts out for closer attention. Behind the lace of her bra, her nipples distended.

When a moment later, he removed the only true source of satisfaction she had going for her by raising his head until their mouths were connected only by the light play of his tongue, Lily growled in frustration. Lifting up she kissed him hard, then grabbed the hand that teased her and dragged it over the aching swell of her breast.

The impact kicked Zach like a mule. Finally, he had his hands on her. When he'd felt her stiffen a moment ago, he'd forced himself to go slowly, but *damn*, the temptation had been strong to fill his hand with her breast. Now that he finally had, its tactile impression was everything he'd known it would be. It was firm and round with that marvelous inner jiggle that made tits such a magnet for men. A guttural groan rumbled in his throat, and he returned her kiss with a strength that drove her head back into the coverlet as his fingers massaged her breast's full softness. He moved his palm lightly to feel the fluid movement beneath it, and was so enthralled with the result that it was a moment before he even noticed the thrust of her nipple trying to drill a hole through his palm.

He ripped his mouth free to look down at her. "I've

been a good boy scout, Lily; I've been patient and true. But you have on way too many clothes, and I want to see you."

Hot color washed up her throat and onto her face, but she coolly raised her eyebrows and met his gaze with the directness he expected from her. "I'll show you mine if you'll show me yours."

"Oh, honey, now that's what I call a sweetheart deal." Pushing back to sit on his heels, he reached for the hem of his T-shirt.

By the time he'd tugged it over his head, Lily had divested herself of her pullover sweater, and Zach's shirt fell from suddenly nerveless fingers. "God," he whispered and stared at her, all lush golden skin and killer curves in a wine-colored lace bra. "You're even prettier than I imagined. And trust me," he said with a slight smile as he tore his gaze away from her body to meet her eyes, "I've spent a lot of time imagining."

Lily might have stuttered out an unimaginative, "Ditto," if every drop of moisture hadn't suddenly deserted her mouth. Instead, she simply stared. But *ho*ly petunia.

His shoulders were wide, his arms were powerful, and his stomach was flat and ridged with muscle. But it was his broad chest that tempted her to check her chin to make sure the moisture missing from her mouth wasn't a result of having drooled it all out.

His chest was all sculpted brawn that looked harder than granite. But stone usually denoted a certain gray chill, and she already knew Zach's tanned skin would be hot to the touch. Flat copper nipples played peek-a-boo behind the fine fan of ebony hair that covered his pectorals, and Lily wanted to search them out and catch the tiny nail-head points of them between her teeth. More than that, however, she wanted to feel her breasts flatten against all that hard muscle, only this time without any clothing to separate them. Sitting up, she rolled onto her knees and reached behind her to unhook her bra. Peeling it down her arms, she knee-walked across the short space separating them.

"No, wait," he said. "Wait, Lily. I want to look at you."

But she didn't stop until she was pressed against him, and they both sucked in a sharp breath at the first bone-melting contact of hot, naked skin against hot, naked skin. Lily reached up and looped her arms around his neck.

She felt the quick wash of goosebumps that shivered over Zach's skin, but he didn't say a word. Instead, he tucked in his chin to gaze down at where her soft curves pressed against his solid muscle.

Lily discovered she liked watching him look at them. He clearly got off on the sight, for his bottom lip developed a sensual droop, his steel-colored eyes a molten heat. She didn't have to look down herself to envision the contrast between her curves and his planes, his tanned skin and her paler olive coloring. She felt the strength of him pushing her breasts back against the wall of her chest, and she undulated a bit to rub them against the smooth, bare skin of his torso.

Zach whispered a swear word and reached behind her to direct the movement. With the heels of his hands cupping her sides and his fingers splayed wide, it felt as if her entire back was enveloped within his hard-skinned grasp as he moved her against him in voluptuous circles. Then he widened the spread of his thighs to lessen the height disparity between them, and her breasts suddenly dragged over his hair-roughened pectorals, rasping heat into her nipples. Her head dropping back, she sighed.

"Ah, man, look at this," he said hoarsely, and Lily felt one of his hands slip forward. "*Pink*."

"Pink?" She couldn't seem to concentrate, and she blinked up at him. "What's pin—?" A high-pitched *uh!* exploded out of her when her left nipple was suddenly captured between Zach's finger and thumb and gently compressed.

"This," he said, watching as he tugged at the small, stiff crest in his grasp. "I wondered what color your nipples would be, and now I know." He flashed her a wolfish smile then went back to gazing at his captured bounty. "Pretty, pretty pink." He gave it another pinching tug, and Lily moaned.

Heat flared in Zach's eyes. "I want you naked," he growled and laid her back on the bed. "Now." Knees splayed wide as he knelt at her side, he bent to tease her nipple with his teeth and tongue as he reached for her waistband. But despite his words, he didn't immediately divest her of her jeans the instant he unfastened them. Instead he slid his hand inside the opening.

He stroked her stomach, and eased beneath the elastic band of her bikini panties. His fingers lightly brushed the downy stripe of hair on her mound before moving lower to cup her in his hand. He pressed with his fingers, then slid deeper to alternately cup and flatten his palm over her. She was so wet with arousal his actions caused a faint squelching sound, and her face flamed with mortification. But Zach groaned in wholehearted approval and insinuated his fingers between the dewy lips of her sex.

"Oh, God, *sweet*," he said reverently, and his eyes slid closed. They reopened almost immediately, but his eyelids remained at half-mast when he stared down to where his hand disappeared beneath her open fly. "This is exactly what I wanted—to feel you hot and wet." He licked his lips and raised his gaze to her eyes. "To feel you all slick." His fingers slid leisurely up and down slippery feminine folds, and every nerve in Lily's body screamed for more.

He gave it to her, too . . . but just as her breath grew choppy and the rocking of her hips began to strain upward in search of release, he eased his hand out of her pants. "I want you spread out naked beneath me," he said, and tugged at her pants.

"Do you?" Disgruntled at having been brought so close, only to be left hanging, she nevertheless lifted her hips to facilitate her jeans' removal. "How very macho of you. What happens if *I* want to be on top?"

"Then, honey, climb aboard and show me how you like it." He grinned at her. "You want on top, you get the top. You want the bottom, it's your choice whether you wrap your legs around my waist or prop your ankles on my shoulders. You prefer it doggie style, I'll grab those gorgeous hips and bark with the best of them. I'm not fussy about position, sweet thing, as long as you let me in." He finished peeling her pants down her legs, but ran into a snag when they puddled around her faux alligator Cuban-heeled shoes. There was no way the legs of her jeans would go over them.

"Damn," he muttered. "Guess I have to take these off you after all. There goes *my* big fantasy." He unbuckled the straps around her ankles and slid the shoes from her feet.

Lily laughed, kicked free of her jeans, and pushed herself to sit up, clad in only a minuscule pair of wine-colored panties. "Tell you what," she offered. "I'll put them back on while you make things a little more equitable by taking off your pants."

He climbed to his feet. "I like the way you think." He watched her put her shoes back on and fasten the straps as he shucked out of his pants. "You've probably heard this a lot, but you've sure got one killer body."

Pure pleasure suffused her, leaving no room for even a flicker of her usual compulsion to catalog her flaws. She simply flashed him a radiant smile. "Thanks." Watching him slide his hands beneath his jockeys and push them down his narrow hips, she blinked. Then she blinked again. And licked her lips.

"Wow," she whispered.

He gave her a crooked grin. "Thanks yourself. I'm hardly in Rocket's class, but I can promise you I've never had any complaints."

This time when she blinked it was in confusion. "You're not in a rocket class?"

"No, I'm not in *Rocket's*—" Smiling wryly, he shook his head. "Forget it. It's not important."

"Wait, are you talking about your friend John? *That* Rocket?"

"Yeah."

She stared at his erection so long it began to bob and weave, and he reached down to hold it still. Then she raised her eyes to his. "I don't know, soldier boy. If a guy came at me with something more than what you've got there, I'd probably run for the door. Seems to me that'd be a major case of overkill."

Damn. He dove onto the bed and snatched her up. Clearly surprised, Lily gave a shriek of laughter, and Zach found himself laughing, too, as he rolled them both over and over until they rocked to a halt perilously close to the edge of the mattress. The playfulness caught him by surprise. The kind of sex he was used to was all about being hot and driven and getting to the goal. He'd never thought of it as having fun. But this *was* fun. And when Lily, who'd ended up draped atop him with her fingers tangled in the hair on his chest, pushed up slightly to grin down at him as if she were queen of the mountain, Zach suddenly felt happier than he had in ages. For a brief moment the realization made him uneasy. Because it didn't pay to get attached to people.

Then he shrugged it off, telling himself not to be an idiot. Hell, he was about to get lucky, and it had been an age since that had happened. So big surprise he felt happy about it.

"You look good on me," he said and ran his hands along Lily's soft-skinned shoulders and down her back, appreciating the tinyness of her waist before smoothing his palms onto the voluptuous curve of her lace-clad butt. Her breasts rested warm and heavy against his diaphragm and they were full, pale, and pink-tipped. He slid his hands back up to cup her elegant little jaw, tunneling his fingers into the soft hair at her nape. "*Damn* good." Thumbs softly pressing her flushed cheeks, he exerted pressure to bring her face down to his. Raising his head off the mattress to meet her halfway, he kissed her feverishly and all the heat that had been banked between them exploded back into full flame.

Usually he was big on prolonged foreplay, but he wanted inside her—and he wanted inside her now. Luckily for him, Lily seemed to feel the same, for when the head of his dick brushed up against her wet, lace-covered heat, she slowly rocked against it. When she lifted her head and stared down at him, her mouth looked debauched, her blue eyes hot and slumberous.

"I don't think I can wait," she said breathlessly. "You have any protection handy?" She squirmed atop him. "I need . . . Oh, man, Zach, I need—"

"Satisfaction," he agreed. "I know. Me, too." Clamping her to him, he tipped them toward the edge of the bed. "Can you reach the nightstand drawer?" He sucked in a harsh breath when her stretch for it rasped her nipples across his chest. Then she pulled the drawer open. "Excellent. Inside there's a—"

"Got it."

Her hand emerged from the drawer clutching the tin foil packet, and he immediately rolled them back to their former position. Hands on her narrow waist, he scooted her up until one of her beaded, pink nipples was directly above his mouth. Raising his head, he gently bit it.

She cried out and dropped the condom. While he enjoyed himself nursing away the small hurt he'd inflicted, she swept up the protection and ripped it open with her teeth. Reaching behind her, she patted around blindly until her hand suddenly brushed the head of his cock.

She immediately glommed onto it, and then it was he

who rapped out a curse. His mouth went slack, Lily's nipple eased free, and she pushed up to sit astride his stomach. A second later, she climbed off as if dismounting a horse, and knelt by his side to roll the condom down his erect length. He hissed through his teeth not only at the feel of her small competent hands unfurling the rubber down his hard-on, but at the sight of them.

"Are you dead set on being on top?" he demanded, then gritted his teeth when she tightened her grip on him. He thrust up into her touch.

She seemed to have her work cut out dragging her gaze away from his erection as it pumped through her fist. "Hmm?" she asked vaguely. But then she blinked, gave her head a slight shake, and smiled up at him. "No."

"Good." And in a few efficient moves, he had her flat on her back beneath him. "Then let's satisfy *my* fantasy." He patted his shoulders. "Let's see those pretty shoes up here."

She laughed and started to comply, but before she could follow through he reached between them.

"Whoops—forgot to remove these," he said, and pulled her bikini panties off her hips and down her legs. Tossing them over his shoulder, he looked down at what he'd revealed and smiled. "And here I thought you were a natural blonde."

"I am," she replied dryly, then sucked in a breath when he eased his thumb into her silky-wet cleft and slid it up and down. "A natural L'Oreal number ten, Lightest Ultimate Blonde, blonde," she informed him breathlessly. Then her eyes lost focus. "Ohmigracious, Zachariah. Oh. My. *Gracious*."

He tapped his shoulder again with his free hand and

experienced a possessive sort of satisfaction when she immediately swung her feet up to prop her heels on them. Wrapping his hand around her slender ankle, he turned his head to press a kiss into her instep. Then reluctantly disengaging the hand that stroked between her thighs, he used it to grasp his hard-on and line up its broad head with her entrance. Leaning forward, he slowly pressed himself into her until he was buried to the hilt in her wet, furnace-hot, vise-grip depths. Pleasure shivered over his skin as he held himself still deep inside her. "Damn, you feel good."

"Oh, my gosh. Do I ever." She moved experimentally. "I. Feel. *Full*. So full. Which feels *won*derful. Except—"

He eased his hips back, then pressed them forward. "Except?" Eased them back again, and pressed them forward.

"Well, except, you're too far away. I want to hold you."

He dropped forward, catching himself on his palms on either side of her shoulders. It drove him deeper into Lily, and she moaned as her legs slid down his arms until they hooked on the inside bend of his elbows. She reached up and locked her fingers behind his neck. "Oh, please," she murmured. "Zach, please."

And he began to withdraw and thrust back into her, withdraw and thrust, with increasing speed and force. Lily started making desperate noises deep in her throat and her Cuban-heeled pumps bounced in the air with every slam of his hips. Zach stared down at her, and she returned his look with an unfocused, lust-blinded gaze. "Christ," he muttered, and lowered his head to catch her mouth with his own. She kissed him back hungrily and sank her fingernails into his shoulders. Then her soft moans began to escalate and grow higher in pitch, and she strained to meet his pistoning hips. Suddenly she stiffened all over, her pelvis thrust high, and hard contractions deep inside of her clamped and released around his dick, milking its length furiously.

Ripping his mouth free, he threw back his head. Then, grinding out her name, he slammed his hips forward one last time and in scalding, bone-rattling pulsations, he began to come.

And come.

And felt her climaxing around him all the while as he continued to come.

Until, finally, totally boneless and feeling like a homeless stray suddenly in possession of his very own hearth, he collapsed atop her.

15

LILY'S ARMS SLID AWAY FROM ZACH'S NECK AND flopped onto the mattress. Her legs, released by his collapse, followed suit and splayed bonelessly upon the duvet. Holy petunia. *So this is what really good sex feels like.* She was perfectly content to lie crushed beneath the weight of Zach's inert body—until it occurred to her that she couldn't hear him breathing and was far from sure if that was his heartbeat she felt, or merely the thundering of her own. Summoning all her energy, she raised her right hand and petted his damp, muscular back. "You still alive?"

"Dunno," he muttered into her neck. But one of his hands lifted to stroke her from armpit to hip, then eased into a slow return caress back up her side. "I think I may have died and gone to heaven."

That's nothing. I think I may have gone and fallen in lov—

No. Shocked, her hand dropped back to her side. *That's not true, so don't even think it.* It was simply a case of having a sexual experience beyond anything she'd ever known. *Don't confuse it for anything else, Lily.*

But it was hard not to panic when Zach, obviously reacting to her growing tension, raised his head to look down at her. "You okay?"

"Yes. Sure. It's just . . . you're kind of heavy, and I, um, have to use the bathroom." *Oh, jeez, you are such a liar. Not to mention a coward.* But she was still relieved when Zach immediately lifted himself off her. She eased to the side of the bed, then sat up with her back to him while she took a couple of silent, restorative breaths. When he suddenly ran his fingertips down her bare spine, she just barely refrained from leaping straight into the air like a spooked cat. Instead, she flashed him a smile made vague by the fact that she didn't quite make eye contact when she glanced back over her shoulder.

"I'll be right back," she murmured to his hard jaw, and rose to her feet, tugging the top sheet free of the bed and winding it around her as she padded to the bathroom.

A moment later found her with the door firmly closed between them, and her hands braced on the vanity as she stared at the worried expression looking back at her from the mirror. "I'm not falling in love," she vowed in a low voice. "I am *not* falling in love!"

"Did you say something?" Zach called.

"No. That is, I'm just talking to myself."

She heard him laugh and looked back at her reflection. *Dear God.* She met her own horrified gaze. *I'm falling in love.*

This was awful. If she had to go fall for some guy,

why him? He was the *worst* choice she could make—the complete and utter worst.

It was pure reflex that thrust her chin in the air. *So, big deal, then. The answer to that is don't. . . . Just don't fall in love.* A little distance, a little perspective, and she'd get over it. Heck, it was probably nothing more than a knee-jerk reaction to really good sex anyhow.

Oh, Lily, please. She blew out her breath. *Lie to Zach if you have to. But don't lie to yourself.*

She'd had good sex before. Maybe not as earth-shattering as what she'd just shared with Zach, but pretty darn great. The point was, she hadn't immediately gone from thinking *Dang, I feel good* to *I must be in love.*

Of course, she'd never tried to convince herself she lacked feelings for the current man in her life, either. Until Zach, she'd always gone into her admittedly limited relationships believing they were going somewhere. And if that didn't tell her something right there, she didn't know what would.

She was very much afraid this was the real deal. It might not make sense, but there you had it all the same.

The question was, what did she do about it?

For instance, even if he were to return her feelings—and face it, that was a mighty big if—was she willing to simply set aside her dream of opening her own restaurant to follow a soldier around the country?

No. Straightening, she dropped the sheet to reach for her periwinkle satin robe hanging from the back of the door. *Let's get real here for a minute.* Love was all very grand, but despite what the songs would have you believe, it wasn't always the be-all and end-all of every problem. Her dream was something she'd nourished for a *lifetime* . . . and that wasn't an aspiration one just blithely tossed aside. Not to mention she'd had her fill of moving every nine months with her parents and wasn't prepared to do it again.

Zach would probably be horrified in any case, if he had any idea she was in here attempting to decide their future. Chances were fair to decent that before he'd ever made his move, he'd figured the odds of her equating a roll in the hay with the chime of wedding bells. And considering she was a long way from anyone's idea of a starry-eyed kid, he'd undoubtedly come to the conclusion that she was old enough to know the score—that she could be trusted not to build fantastical scenarios out of thin air simply because the two of them had finally acted on the sexual tension that had been simmering between them since they'd first laid eyes on one another.

Tweaking her hair into some semblance of order, she pulled herself up to her tallest posture, then pulled her robe closed and tied the belt around her waist. She had to get back in there before he began wondering just what the heck she was doing. About all she could do at this point was take the situation as it came and live minute to minute if that's what it took.

Only, please, God, don't let me give myself away. All these new emotions left her feeling vulnerable and exposed, and she didn't want to look like a fool. It was the one thing she didn't think she could bear.

Zach was lying on his side with his head resting against the biceps of his updrawn arm when she walked back into the room, but he pushed up on his elbow the moment he saw her. "Are you all right?"

"Yes, sure. Absolutely." And his genuine concern made it easy for her to flash him a natural smile. He looked dark and powerful against the white sheet that had fallen to his waist. But for such a tough guy, he certainly was protective of her feelings.

In the next instant, as if fearing she might misread his solicitude, his eyebrows drew together. "Listen, Lily, I think we should talk about—"

Oh, gawd. Quickly crossing to the bed, she plopped down next to his hip and reached out to press her finger to his lips. The last thing she thought she could stand right now was the big, serious this-has-been-fun-but-let's-not-lose-perspective talk. "You don't have to worry that I'll expect too much from you," she promised softly. "We're both adults here, and I know the important thing right now is for you to get Glynnis and David back. So why don't we just keep things nice and easy between us?"

He wrapped his hand around her wrist and pulled her finger away from his lips. "I haven't nearly had my fill of you," he said harshly.

Lily thought it a pretty sad commentary that his obvious frustration lit her up like a mason jar full of fireflies. Good grief, was that a measure of how far gone she was, or what? But she managed to keep her voice light when she replied, "Good. Because I haven't had my fill of you, either."

"Then you can be damn sure we'll do this again," he said. "Only—"

"I know," she interrupted him gently, realizing she couldn't bear to have his reservations spelled out for her. Not right this minute, while she was still raw from all these new feelings. "You have Glynnis to rescue, and I . . . well, my priority is getting my dream restaurant up and running. So I understand, okay?"

"Yeah," he said roughly, and his deep voice licked goosebumps down her spine from nape to tailbone. Whipping his arm around her waist, he tumbled her flat on her back next to him and rose up over her. "Yeah," he repeated, looking down at her with those charcoal-rimmed, intense pale eyes. "Okay."

As the busy signal sounded in his ear yet one more time, it took everything Zach had to keep from slamming down the phone in frustration. Instead he replaced the receiver with exaggerated care, then turned to stare for about the dozenth time at the door connecting his room to the bathroom that connected to Lily's. It was a damn good thing she was downstairs preparing breakfast for everyone, he thought, because he had a wild hair up his butt urging him to go pick a fight with her.

The thought brought him up short. *Jesus, Taylor, what is your problem? Last night was fantastic—she pretty much handed you everything you could possibly ask for, all gift wrapped with a nice gold bow. So what's got you feeling so pissed off?* He plowed both hands through his hair. He wasn't so egotistical that he thought one hot session between the sheets, no matter how inspired, would motivate her to declare her love everlasting. On the other hand, they had shared something pretty damn special—and she'd been in an awful big rush to just blow it all off, hadn't she?

"Uh!" Loosening his fingers from his hair, he smacked himself in the forehead with the heels of his hands. What the *hell* was wrong with him? They'd fucked like minks all night long, and he ought to be relieved he hadn't needed to tell her not to expect a lot from him in the way of the emotional garbage that most women seemed to want. So why did the fact she'd beaten him to the punch have him all bent out of shape instead? Hell, she'd offered him the best of all worlds. She'd volunteered her kisses, and access to her gorgeous body, and all of her sweetness and smiles, without any of that messy, clingy, needy shit that usually went along with it. He ought to—

Screw ought to. Uttering another rough sound, he turned back to the phone and snatched up the receiver again. This time when he punched in Cooper's number, the phone on the other end of the line rang.

It was picked up on the third ring. "Yeah?"

"Coop, it's Zach."

"Hey, Midnight, how y'holding together? I imagine all this waiting around has gotta be a bitch, huh?"

Not as tough as it would've been without Lily's brand of distraction. The thought no sooner crossed his mind than he shook his head impatiently. "I'm hanging tough. I, uh, wonder, though, if I could ask you and John a favor."

"Sure. Shoot."

"We're supposed to hear back from the kidnapper on Saturday. Would you and Rocket lend a hand with the take-down? I could use some backup that I can trust—a reserve force that no one living in this heap of rocks knows anything about."

There was a momentary hesitation, and Zach, already sensitive at having to ask, asked stiffly, "Is there a problem?"

"Hell no. I'm just trying to think what I'll tell Ronnie."

What he'd—? For the first time that morning, Zach felt a smile crook up the corners of his mouth. "The Iceman has to ask the little woman if he can go out and play? Tell me it isn't true, Blackstock."

"It isn't true," Coop promptly replied. Then he laughed. "Shit. If I hear even a whisper of the word pussy-whipped, pal, I'll have to hurt you. But I know Ronnie, and she's gonna want to come along to lend a hand. I have to find a way to avoid that."

Zach was nonplussed. "What does she think she can do that three trained Marines can't?"

"Beats the hell outta me, but she'll want to help anyhow. In any case, count us in. We'll come up Friday and find a place to stay. Just pick a place for us to get together to work out the logistics."

"Thanks, Coop."

His friend made a rude noise. "Screw that. I'd want to be there when Glynnis gets home anyway, to check out her new boyfriend. Someone's gotta make sure the peckerwood's good enough for her." A voice rumbled in the background and Coop snorted.

"What?" Zach demanded.

"Rocket says the peckerwood's got money, and the way your baby sis runs through hers, that's at least a start."

A bark of laughter escaped Zach's throat.

"Here, John wants to talk to you," Coop said, and there was a faint shuffling sound as he handed off the phone.

A second later, Rocket's voice came down the line. "Hey."

"Hey, yourself." Then, too antsy for small talk, he demanded, "You have any luck with those background checks?"

"Depends on your definition of luck." At Zach's impatient sound, his voice turned serious. "Sorry, Midnight. But just once it would be nice to investigate a family who was less Borgia and more frigging Brady Bunch. I have information, but it doesn't narrow down the field much."

Great. Zach had known better than to expect an easy solution, but still his gut clenched. Squaring his shoulders resolutely, he blew out a breath. "So what are you telling me here—that the Beaumonts are all in bed together?"

John laughed. "No, it's not that bad. No machinations with incestuous overtones. As with most things, amigo, it pretty much boils down to money. The wealth in that family belongs strictly to Glynnis's David. He inherited the whole ball of wax when his father died."

"No shit?" Zach looked around the sumptuous room he'd been assigned. "*Every*thing went to him?"

"Looks like. Mama Bear receives a modest annual stipend, but all the rest—the family business, the family home—went to Baby Bear."

"Kinda makes you wonder how she feels about that, doesn't it?"

"Yes, indeed."

"How long since the father kicked?"

"Three years. David was barely twenty-three. Apparently our boy's got a head on his shoulders, though—not to mention a knack for making money. From all accounts, he took the family business and increased its net worth far beyond the original inheritance."

"This is a fairly small island whose only industry, as far as I can tell, is tourism. What sort of business are we talking about?"

"It has something to do with telecommunications and radio or microwave towers, or some such. I've taken a look at the annual report, but to tell you the truth I was more interested in the financial bottom line than whatever the product is they produced to arrive at it. So I'm not real clear if it has to do with cellular phones or satellite systems or exactly what the nature of the beast is. But I can tell you this much. It's not some hokey little nickle/dime operation. It has a net worth of over nine million dollars. The family property where you're staying is worth a couple of million more. If you want additional details, I can give it a closer look."

"No, the what isn't really the important issue. The point seems to be that David is the sole beneficiary of a sizable fortune. Do you have any idea who it goes to if anything happens to him?"

"Barring his getting married first, it all reverts back to Mama."

Zach whistled through his teeth. "Gives her a helluva motive, doesn't it? Especially now, with him on the verge of marrying Glynnie."

"I wouldn't count her out, that's for damn sure."

"But judging by your crack about the Borgias, I assume she's not the only one worth looking at?"

"Well, the whole friggin' family seems to have moved in with David and Mama following Papa's death. And I can tell you that Cousin Cassidy is in serious debt. She's racked up a small fortune on her credit cards and has had two Visas and an American Express cut off. Cousin Jessica's come up clean so far, and so has her husband and Cousin Richard. But if you don't ask how I got them, I'll tell you I managed to get my hands on the Beaumonts' phone records."

"And this is significant because . . . ?"

"Of the number of calls that've been made from there to a business competitor in California. They could mean nothing, or it could be that someone in the house is engaged in some industrial espionage. In other words, we don't know the significance. This is all strictly preliminary, so I can't give you any details yet. But you can bet your ass I'll get them, and meanwhile, I wouldn't remove damn near anyone from the short list. You never know what the hell's going to surface until I really start digging."

They hung up a short while later, and Zach rummaged through the small desk across the room until he came up with a piece of paper. Slapping it down on the desktop, he sat and divided it into sections, allotting one Beaumont per section. Next to the individual's name, he listed all the information John had given him for that person, plus his own impressions. The exercise didn't pop out anything that illuminated a big lightbulb over his head, but it did help cement the facts in his mind.

A short while later he looked up and saw by the clock

on the desk that he was on the verge of being late for breakfast. He promptly pushed back from the desk and rose to his feet, folding his sheet of notes into a small rectangle. He slipped it into his hip pocket as he headed for the door.

It wasn't until he was loping down the main staircase a moment later that the oddness of his own behavior suddenly hit him. Rushing off all eager for a meal, even one of Lily's tasty feasts, wasn't at all like him. He was a professional soldier, for crissake. If food was such a huge priority he never would have lasted eighteen years in the service.

With a sinking feeling he realized it was her. Lily. It was the prospect of seeing her again, being close to her, basking in the warmth of that generous smile. Just the thought of it had him panting like an overeager hound.

Well, shit.

The following evening Jessica raced into the kitchen and slapped a glossy page she'd torn out of a magazine down on the counter in front of Lily. "What do you think?" she demanded breathlessly, reaching for a white apron to tie around her hips. "Do you think that haircut would look good on me?"

"Goodness gracious," Lily said with a laugh. "I think I've created a monster." Then she leaned forward to peer at the picture, and her eyes rounded. "Oh. *Wow*. You're getting really good at this." She wiped her hands on her apron, picked the page up, and held it under the light to examine more closely. She looked up and studied Jessica for a moment, then went back to examining the picture again.

Jessica practically danced in place. "Well?"

"I'll say it again." Meeting her eyes, Lily grinned. "*Wow.* I think this would look *great* on you."

"Oh, God. Me, too." She laughed and gathered together salad fixings. Tearing romaine leaves apart, she tossed it in a bowl she'd rubbed with olive oil and a garlic clove, then reached for the knife and a green onion. "The model's face is the same shape as mine. And even better, the texture of her hair looks as if it might be similar."

"Yeah, and look what that style does for her neck. You've got that elegant swan-neck thing going for you, too."

"I'm going to call first thing in the morning and see if I can get an appointment." Jessica finished putting the salad together. "You want me to make a red-wine dressing for this?"

"Yes, that'd be great." Lily glanced over as she pulled a tray of browning game hens out of the oven to baste with cranberry vinegar sauce. "If you're able to get an appointment soon and the salon is in town, I'd love to ride along. I need to pick up some mushrooms for a recipe I'm thinking of trying."

"I'll let you know as soon as I find out when it'll be." As she went to set down the mixed dressing, she noticed a red stain spreading across her white shirt. "*Damn.*"

Lily followed her gaze. "What is it, wine? Oh, shoot, did that happen before or after you mixed it with the oil?"

Jess peered at the stain. "It doesn't seem oily, so I think it must have been before."

"Good, that's not quite so bad. Turn on the tea kettle." She made a shooing motion as soon as Jessica had done so. "I've got it covered here. Go change, then bring your shirt back down. As long as it's only wine, we can get it out with boiling water."

Jessica took the stairs two at a time as she headed up to her suite of rooms to change. Life had been so interesting the past few days. She felt prettier and infinitely more with it, and Christopher seemed to like the new her, too. He'd been chasing her around the bedroom steadily since her fashion epiphany.

She was grinning as she reached the room, but the smile dropped away when she opened the door and heard him hurriedly say, "Gotta go. I'll talk to you soon." He was hanging up the telephone as she walked into their bedroom.

He seemed to be doing a lot of that lately.

"Who were you talking to?" she asked as she peeled off her blouse and reached into the closet for a fresh one.

"No one," he said, and casually shrugged a wide shoulder when she turned to stare at him. "No one you know, in any case. Just someone about a project at work."

Her stomach squeezed. She loved him so desperately, and had never fully accepted her good luck in catching his attention. It seemed as if she'd spent the last two years waiting for the other shoe to drop, and she wondered if that's what was happening here now.

She didn't want to believe it, but something was definitely going on. The sad truth was, though, that whatever it was, she didn't want to know.

Christopher diverted her attention when his gaze tracked over her satin bra. His green eyes darkened.

"Look at you," he said, climbing to his feet and walking up to her. He trailed a long finger down her strap then traced the dip of the bra's cups between her breasts. "Did you come up here to give me a little pre-dinner appetizer?"

Muscles deep between her thighs immediately clenched at the idea, but she laughed and stepped away. "No. I just came up to change into a clean blouse. I spilled red wine all over this one. I need to take it back down to the kitchen to get the stain out."

He took the item of apparel she held out to him and dropped it to the floor without even looking at it. Then he bent to kiss her. His eyes were lambent when he raised his head again, and Jessica realized through a hot haze of arousal that he'd backed her up until the hollows of her knees brushed the side of the bed.

"I bet fifteen minutes one way or the other won't make a huge difference," he said. And with all ten fingers planted gently on her chest, he gave a little push. He was already reaching for his belt buckle as she tumbled backward onto the bed. "Whataya say we test that theory?"

She squeezed her eyes shut and hung on for dear life when he lowered himself over her. Whatever else happened, she thought dazedly, for now she at least had this.

☙16

Out on the veranda late Friday afternoon, Lily found a sunny corner sheltered from the wind and stretched out on a lounge chair to admire the view. It managed to stun her with pleasure every time she saw it. Spring flowers bloomed in profusion at the base of the veranda, and the emerald lawn swept in faultlessly groomed perfection to the rugged promontory. Water crashed upon the rocks at the foot of the cliffs and clouds chased across the sky, sending shadows racing along the channel. The ever-changing colors and the scattering of small tree-covered islands dotting the narrow passage held her enthralled as they had done ever since the mist lifted Tuesday afternoon and she'd caught her first glimpse of it.

Recalling that day took a little of the shine off her enjoyment. Tuesday was the night she'd acknowledged she was falling in love with Zach, and she wasn't proud of the fact that she still hadn't really dealt with the issue. Every night since then had found the two of them in either his bed or hers, wrapped around each other and making love that was sometimes wild and intense, sometimes slow and languid. He couldn't seem to stay away from her any more than she could from him, nor did he appear to be dealing with his emotions any better than she was hers. And if he harbored feelings anything like her own, he hadn't voiced them. For a couple of outspoken people, they were certainly being tight-lipped, and knowing she was in no burning hurry to rectify the situation left her feeling fickle, immature, and antsy. She appreciated the scenery all the more, therefore, because something about watching the capriciousness of nature, of seeing its elements blending in harmony one moment, then competing for supremacy the next, helped soothe some of her own plaguing indecisiveness.

"I thought I might find you here."

Lily looked up to see Jessica approach and smiled as her new friend swung a long leg over the chaise next to hers and collapsed onto its cushioned surface. "Yes, what can I say?" Her smile turned wry. "The sun feels so nice, and I adore this view."

"It is pretty, isn't it?"

"Um-hmm."

Falling into a companionable silence, they lounged side by side, exchanging only a minimum of desultory conversation over the next half hour. Eventually, though, Lily glanced at her watch and regretfully sat up. For several moments she simply perched on the edge of the chaise; then, with a sigh over the need to drag herself away from the drugging warmth of her protected little corner, she rose to her feet. "I'd better go get dinner started."

Jessica glanced at her watch. "This a little earlier than usual, isn't it?"

"Yes, but I'll need the extra time." She grinned down at the other woman, who shaded her eyes to gaze back at her. "You have any interest in learning to make risotto?"

"Oh, yes. Absolutely." Jessica joined her as Lily made her way down the terrace steps. The wind they'd been protected from in the lee of the mansion caught them as they rounded the corner, and Jessica's thick hair rose up and writhed like Medusa's snaky locks around her face.

With a frustrated sound, she attempted to anchor it down with her hands, but vagrant pieces caught in the wind and whipped across her cheeks. "That haircut appointment can't come soon enough for me."

Lily grinned at her as they dashed for the kitchen door. "It's not for another week yet?"

"Not unless they get a cancellation, in which case I'm on the list. *Please*," she implored humorously as they barreled through the door and banged it closed against the wind chasing them into the room. "Let somebody cancel soon."

The risotto garnered compliments when it was dished up a short while later, but dinner itself turned out to be a strained affair. Zach attempted once again to convince Mrs. Beaumont to call in the FBI to handle the ransom, but she remained stubbornly resistant. Although his manner remained courteous, Lily could tell he was frustrated and angry, and the moment she finished cleaning up the kitchen she headed for his room.

"Are you okay?" she asked as soon as he answered the door in response to her knock.

"She makes me crazy, Lily." He hauled her into the room, but once the door closed behind her he turned her loose and began to pace. "Not that we wouldn't have had to think twice about contacting the FBI anyway, since Rocket discovered the closest special agent in charge is a known glory seeker, but—"

"Then I don't get it," she interrupted, but found herself speaking to his back as he stalked toward the desk on the other side of the room. "If that's the case, why do you still keep trying to convince Mrs. B. to call them?"

He about-faced and strode back in her direction, his eyebrows lowered. "Because she doesn't *know* that, and I wanted to see her reaction. Usually leaving the authorities out of the loop is a huge mistake, and for all she knows, refusing to contact them could seriously endanger Glynnie and David." His stiff-set shoulders twitched restlessly. "I can't figure out if she truly believes the kidnapper will harm them if the feds are called in—or if that's exactly what she's counting on."

Lily recalled lying in his arms the other night while he'd told her what his friend Rocket had dug up. The idea of having to suspect anyone, let alone that sweet, dithery woman . . . "Oh, man, I hate this."

"Tell me about it. And just to make our day really special, I got a call from Coop earlier. He and Rocket are over on the dock at Anacortes."

"That's good news, right?"

"Well, it would be, except one of the ferries is out of commission, and it's Friday—which is a big travel day for the islands—so the schedule is backed up for hours. They'll be lucky to make the last boat." Agitated energy radiated off him in almost palpable waves as he paced back and forth, and the look he shot her was black. "Which means if the kidnapper follows the plan he laid out, that only leaves part of tomorrow to get together with Coop and John and plan the op. And that means I could lose whatever advantage having them in reserve will give me."

She walked over and grasped his hand, holding on with both of hers to halt his restless prowling. His skin felt hot beneath her fingers as she led him to the bed and pushed him down onto it. Climbing onto the mattress as well, she kneeled behind where he sat and began to rub his shoulders. "I'm sorry," she said. "But I'm sure everything will be all right. You'll feel better once your friends get here."

Zach felt some of the tension leave his shoulders, and he pushed back into her massaging hands. "Yeah, well. Not much I can do about it anyhow." He didn't know what it was about her, but she had a way of defusing the worst of his frustration. "Tell me about this dream restaurant of yours."

Her voice lulled him, and her enthusiasm made him smile. But the feel of her body heat shimmering between them soon distracted him, and he reached over his shoulder and snagged her hand. Pulling her around to his side, he flipped her onto his lap.

She batted her eyes at him. "Why, Master Sergeant Taylor."

He lowered his head to kiss her, got lost in her flavor, and had to rip his mouth free. Lust and the disquieting fear of letting her mean too much mixed uneasily in his gut as he looked down at her. "We shouldn't be doing this."

"I know."

But he kissed her again anyway—kissed her with

everything he had—before pulling back once more. His breath had begun to hitch. "Chances are, no one's gonna need me tonight. But if they do, I can't afford to be distracted."

"Wouldn't do to be found with your pants down around your ankles," she agreed, and stroked her lush butt up and down the rigid, aching length of his erection.

It responded by growing harder, a feat he would have sworn wasn't possible. "Right. Uh, Lily?" He sucked in a breath as she once again rubbed against him.

"Hmm?"

"Are my eyes crossed?"

She laughed that warm, wholehearted belly laugh that always made him want to grin back and then tuck her securely under his arm—well, either that or toss her flat on her back and kiss the laughter right out of her. "Beats the heck outta me," she said. "My own view at the moment appears to be limited to the tip of my nose."

"Ah, man." Helpless to resist, he kissed her again.

He had her cobalt chenille tunic unbuttoned and was working on the front clasp of her chocolate-colored lace bra when the bedside telephone shrilled. For just an instant, his hand tightened on the fastener as he contemplated ignoring it. Then swearing, he dumped Lily onto the mattress and reached for the phone. "Taylor," he snarled.

"Zach, come quick," Jessica said in a breathless voice that had him snapping to attention. "The kidnapper is on the other line. Or at least—"

Zach tossed the receiver back on the hook and ran from the room.

* * *

Thirty minutes later, he was headed out the door with a suitcase full of money and a jaw clenched tight against the desire to curse a blue streak.

He'd had plans for when the kidnapper called, and not one of them had panned out. First, he'd been set to demand that the kidnapper let him talk to his sister if he ever wanted to see one red cent of the ransom. But instead of an actual person on the other end of the line, he'd gotten a recording. A fucking *recording* that set out the terms of the exchange in a whispered, androgynous voice that left no room for bargaining or demands. It merely repeated the same spiel over and over again until the tape came to an end. Then, as if that wasn't headache-producing enough, for the life of him he couldn't figure out if David's mother was the most feather-headed woman on planet Earth . . . or wilier than a Wall Street shark.

He'd intended to hit *69 the moment he disconnected. Obtaining pertinent information from it was a long shot, since anyone with two brain cells to rub together would have used a public phone. But given the probability of this being an inside job, it was still worth pursuing. He'd barely depressed the disconnect button, though, when Mrs. B. had reached past him, punched the button for Richard's room, and then snatched the receiver from his hand, babbling hysterically into it the moment her nephew picked up. The next thing Zach knew, everyone except Cassidy, who'd gone out after dinner, was milling about the parlor all talking at once.

His jaw tightened even more at the thought of what

they wanted him to do. Climbing into the Jeep, he hunched grimly over the steering wheel as he reached for the ignition. This was not smart, and he'd argued against taking the ransom into a blind setup with no precautions in place—particularly without an assurance that Glynnis and David were still in good health and would be returned safely as soon as the money was dropped off. Money that just incidentally had been collected and put in the home-office safe that very afternoon.

And now, as if things weren't tense enough, he caught a whiff of Lily's scent where it had no business being, and his teeth clenched with such force he was surprised they didn't crack in two. "Christ," he muttered. That was just what he needed. If he'd had half a second without the Beaumonts all yapping at him, he might have thought to wash the smell of her off his hands before setting off. The woman was messing with his mind *way* too much, and it was past time he quit procrastinating and did something about it. It wasn't like him to let a female distract him the way he'd allowed this one to do.

And yet . . .

Where the hell had she disappeared to? He'd wanted to pull her aside and have her make note of who hung around the parlor while he was gone, and who disappeared for any significant length of time. When in the midst of all the hubbub he'd turned to look for her, however, she was nowhere to be seen.

Which should give you a clue. That's your entire life in a nutshell. Gunning the engine, he shot up the drive. *Barring your unit, which you know will always be here to back you up if they're able, you've got exactly one person you can depend on to be there when needed. That's you, bud.*

And no one else.

Miguel saw the master sergeant's SUV shoot out of the driveway and fishtail as it hit the road, and he jerked upright in his car. *Dios*. He'd begun to think he would fossilize here before anyone finally made a move. It had been the longest six days of his life, and as he watched the vehicle straighten out and then roar off down the road, he reached for the ignition key.

But his hand dropped back to his side before it connected, leaving the engine still turned off. He'd only seen one person behind the tinted glass of Taylor's jeep when it had passed beneath the light at the top of the driveway. *One*.

The master sergeant. All by himself. Which meant the man's woman had been left behind.

Ripe for the picking.

In the past week, Miguel had made careful forays around the estate grounds, trying to figure out what was going on. He'd hadn't been successful, but he had learned that there were seven people in residence.

And the only one he had any cause to worry about had just driven off as if *el diablo* himself was on his trail.

Miguel opened the car door and eased out, cursing under his breath when his legs, stiff from hours of sitting in one position, nearly buckled beneath his weight. But there was no need for profanity, he decided, as he bent down to scoop up the empty food wrappers that had wafted out in his wake and tossed them back on the seat with the others. This was the opportunity he'd been waiting for. And if he—how did the gringos say it?—played his cards correctly? Then his long wait was at an end.

Zach had emptied his mind of everything but the chore at hand by the time he entered Moran State Park, driving slowly beneath its white signature arch. As he approached the Midway camp area moments later, he turned off the Jeep's headlights, then coasted to a stop within the shadow of the shower house by the extra vehicle lot. He killed the engine and sat unmoving until his eyes adjusted to the night. Then he double-checked to make sure he was in the right place.

SITES 31–36, the sign read. His directions were to drop off the suitcase at Site 32, which appeared to be up the hill.

He reached up and flipped the overhead light switch to "Off." Then, picking up the money satchel from the passenger seat, he eased out of the Jeep and closed the door quietly behind him, glad to see the wind had died down. Cascade Lake lapped gently at the shore across the main road as he made his silent way in the opposite direction.

The spur road to the camp area climbed steeply for a short stretch before curving to the right around the hill, but he left it before reaching that point and cut up over the bank. The site he sought was likely to be second in line just around the bend, but marching up the road in search of it didn't strike him as the shrewdest move he could make. Doing what he was trained to do seemed to him a better bet. He picked his way through the woods with care, traversing damp undergrowth and downed trees as he climbed the hill.

Moments later he squatted in the deeper shadow of an immense evergreen on the knob of the hill and looked down on Site 32. Searching for signs of life, he gave the campground below a preliminary once-over.

It could be worse. At least the fire pit where he was supposed to make the drop wasn't accessible from all sides. The hill behind it was too overgrown to negotiate with any stealth, and he had possession of the rest of the knoll where it curved around to form the second side of the site. Woods separated the third border from the next camp, and he had a clear view of the approach in front. Crouching next to a tree, Zach widened his visual inspection to include the surrounding area.

It appeared deserted, but when it came to the woods at night, there were always places to hide. Hell, the eroded bank alone a few feet to his left provided countless pockets of darkness that even his exceptional night vision couldn't penetrate. There were simply too many shadows cast by the huge uprooted trees canting down the hill.

But if the kidnapper lurked in one of them, he'd have to come out sooner or later to collect the money. Zach eased back through the woods and down the hill, then made a production out of approaching Site 32 from the road. When he'd made the drop and left, he clomped down the road. But once around the bend, he raced with swift silence back to his place on the crest of the hill, where he hunkered down to keep the bag under surveillance. He had a wealth of experience in patiently blending into the background and waiting, and that's precisely what he intended to do now.

All night long, if necessary.

As it turned out, he didn't have very long to wait. He'd only been there minutes before he heard someone making his way up the road . . . and not with any particular stealth. The kidnapper didn't exactly march up the middle of the road like the redcoats coming to put down the rebellion, but he may as well have done. Soles scuffed occasionally against the blacktop, and toes came into obvious contact with pinecones, for three separate times Zach heard the distinct skitter of the latter as they rolled across the pavement. When whoever it was grew closer, Zach could even discern agitated breathing.

And he was torn. This was one of those situations in which a one-man watch sucked. You never, but *never* took your eyes off the object of your surveillance. But neither did you bypass the opportunity to find out all the information you could about your opponent, because the more you knew, the better you could maintain the element of surprise—and sometimes that was the only advantage you had. Unfortunately the two directives were diametrically opposed since he'd have to break the first rule to accomplish the second.

Shit. It really took two to affect an airtight stakeout in a case like this.

Then Zach mentally shrugged. So, big deal; who was it likely to be but the kidnapper? And if it was someone else, going over to check it out wouldn't put him so far from the ransom bag that he couldn't intercept an approach from another direction. Crab-walking foot by careful foot, he eased over to the verge.

The already undermined bank threatened to give beneath his foremost foot, and he edged back several inches. Pulling his nine millimeter from his waistband, he rested it against his knee and peered down to where the kidnapper would come into view any moment now, if the ruckus he made was any indication.

When the person suddenly did round the bend and come into view, however, every muscle in Zach's body went tight, and he had to bite his tongue against voicing the obscenities that rose up in his throat. But, shit fuck hell. He'd know that head of kiss-me-daddy hair anywhere. Not to mention that walk—simply changing from her usual four inch heels into a pair of strappy, flat-heeled sandals had done nothing to disguise it.

Lily.

When he'd smelled her in the Jeep earlier, apparently it hadn't been merely the residual scent transferred from their rolling around on his bed. Zach ground his teeth. What in *hell* did she think she was doing putting herself in danger, and screwing up his op? Shifting his weight onto his forward foot, he glared down at her.

A rock broke loose from the edge and rattled down the bank, and he moved back before he started an avalanche. Dammit, he had to get her out of here, but how was he supposed to do that and keep an eye on the ransom at the same time?

He was so focused on her that he didn't immediately heed the small hairs rising on the back of his neck. But they were an atavistic warning system that had stood him in good stead for eighteen years, and he didn't have to hear the faint crack of a branch on the ground behind him to realize that Lily wasn't the only one in the woods with him. Bringing his gun up, he was turning toward the sound when a light suddenly flashed on and caught him full in the face, blinding him. He aimed just to the left of the dazzling circle of light, but down on the road Lily screamed his name, and there was such fear in her voice that for one ill-advised moment he froze. Jesus. He couldn't see a thing.

He could hear the footsteps rushing him, however, and his finger once again exerted pressure on the trigger. But before he could squeeze off a shot, the light flared in an arc, and the side of his head exploded in agony.

Then everything went black.

🔓 **17**

AWASH IN A STEW OF FIGHT-OR-FLIGHT IM-
pulses, Lily froze. Seeing Zach spotlighted above her,
his profile fierce and a gun the size of a cannon to her
unaccustomed eyes in his hand, adrenaline shot through
her system with such force she thought her heart would
burst. As if she needed another reason to be scared out
of her wits! She was already completely freaked by how
out of her element she was—to have him suddenly pop
up on the hill like an illuminated commando frieze in
some avant-garde West Hollywood production darn
near made her wet her knickers.

That was nothing, though, to the moment when the
light shining on his face swirled sickeningly and he suddenly vanished. Her initial fear had been for herself.
Now her terror was for him. It was swiftly superceded
by a surge of red-hot fury at the thought of some face-
less coward hurting him, and her paralysis shattered.
Screaming at the top of her lungs, she charged up to the
campsite.

Keeping her eye on the knoll, she scrambled over the

woodsy debris that littered the area. When a darker shadow in a night already way too dark suddenly detached itself and hesitated on the ridge just above her, she slid to a stop, her heartbeat hammering in her chest, her throat, her ears. *Ohgawd, ohgawd.* Whatever had possessed her to think she could be of any earthly use to Zach? What seemed like such a good idea in the well-lit Beaumont mansion had revealed itself for the brainless folly it was the moment she'd crawled out the back of his Jeep. But the thought of him going into this all alone had been unendurable.

Now, more desperate to get to him than she was afraid of the kidnapper, she snatched up a rock to use as a weapon and forced herself to stalk toward the shadowy presence on the hill. It tossed its head like an enraged stallion, but then to her immense relief ran crashing through the woods in the opposite direction. The instant the kidnapper was gone, she stepped forward and hissed, "Zach!"

There was no answer and she called his name again, with a little more volume and a lot more insistence. Silence, broken only by creepy, shifty, nocturnal sounds, greeted her frantic demand, and shivering with pure reaction, she started up the hill, her feet sliding in their leather-soled sandals.

She paused when she reached the top, her breath sawing as she tried to reconcile where Zach's position, as seen from the road, was likely to be. Before she could figure it out, she heard a low groan to her right and, thrilled to hear evidence he was alive—and more shamefully, that she wasn't alone after all in the middle of the woods in the dead of the night—she headed that way.

She hadn't taken three steps when she tripped over something underfoot and fell hard onto her hands and knees. Her breath catching just shy of a sob, she pushed herself upright, feverishly brushed her hands against her jeans to free them of the muck clinging to her skin, then picked her way with more care over the uneven ground. "Zach?"

"Lily. Wha' the fu' cue doin' here?"

He sounded drunk, but she was so relieved to hear his voice she nearly wept. And when she finally located him and found him sitting up, gingerly palpating his left temple, she promptly dropped to her knees, threw herself against his chest, and clamped her arms around his strong neck in a fierce stranglehold.

"Jeez's cri," he protested in a harsh voice.

But his arms wrapped around her, and she shuddered in pure, unadulterated relief to feel their strength and the comforting body heat that accompanied his embrace. Clutching at him, she burrowed closer. "Oh, gawd, Zach, I was so scared you were dead."

"Prob'ly should be, letting myself get distracted like a freakin' raw recruit." He suddenly sounded much more alert . . . and furious. Clasping her chin in one hand, he tipped her face up and thrust his own down until they were nose to nose. "What the *hell* kind of irresponsible stunt was that, stowing away in my car? What did you think you were doing, Lily?"

"I don't know," she wailed truthfully. "Your friends were supposed to be here to back you up, and then when they couldn't be, it just didn't seem right that you should handle this all by yourself." Considering what a huge help she'd turned out to be, that sounded even dumber said aloud. She shrugged and admitted, "I didn't think, period."

He gave her an odd look. "You were watching my back?"

Her bark of laughter came dangerously close to hysterics. "Well, that was the plan, in theory. But it's so *dark* out here, and this much nature up close and personal scares me to death, so all I did was nearly get you *killed*."

The arm wrapped around her waist tightened. "You must have me confused with one of those Navy wusses—it takes more than a little pop upside the head to kill a marine." Then, releasing her chin, he felt around the ground near his hip. A moment later he gave a grunt of approval, and Lily caught a quick glimpse of a handgun before he tucked it out of sight behind his back.

He shrugged when he caught the direction of her gaze. "At least the kidnapper's not armed with my own pistol," he said and frowned. "I suppose it's too much to hope he didn't waltz away with the ransom money."

"I don't know. He wasn't much more than a shadowy form up here on the hill when I saw him."

Muscles tensing, Zach jerked erect, and reluctantly Lily loosened her grasp on his neck and moved back. Reaching out to grip her shoulders, he stared at her intently. "You saw him up here?"

"Yes, but not very well, I'm afraid. Just enough to think he's too tall to be a woman."

Zach shrugged that aside, obviously not finding it significant at the moment. "Where were you when you saw him? This is important, Lily."

"Down there in the campsite."

He gave her a brief, hard kiss. "That's my *girl*! Maybe all isn't lost, after all." He pushed to his feet.

When he started to stride away, Lily scrambled to her feet. "Wait! Don't leave me here!"

He reached back and grasped her hand. "Keep up." Despite the brisk command, however, a moment later he tightened his grip and said, "Watch that root."

"What root?" Aside from glimpses of his face when it was an inch away, she might as well have been in a cave. "How can you *see* anything?"

"Good night vision, remember? When people aren't flashing lights in my face, that is. Move a step to your left."

Zach led Lily down to the campsite, not releasing her hand until they reached the firepit. Squatting down, he felt behind it, and the tension knotting his gut since he'd regained consciousness unraveled slightly when his hand closed over the satchel. Maybe he hadn't fucked everything up, after all. His head felt like spikes were being driven behind his eyes, and his vision was the tiniest bit blurry, but those were things he could live with. Screwing up the drop and further endangering his sister weren't—but it looked as if he might have been given a second chance. And this time they were going to play by his rules.

"I can't believe I scared him off with a rock," Lily said, and he rose to his feet to see her glancing around nervously.

"I doubt you did. My guess is he didn't want you to see his face." Grasping the satchel handle in one hand and her hand in the other, he hustled them out of the campsite and back to his Jeep. But when he opened the passenger door for her a moment later, she dug in her heels, tilted her chin up at him, and thrust out a hand.

"Give me the keys."

"Don't be ridic—"

"Don't *you* be ridiculous," she interrupted and poked him in the gut with her extended hand. "I've had a rough night, and I'm darned if I'm going to get into a car with a driver who may have a concussion."

"I don't have a concussion." Hands on his hips, he bent his fiercest *I-hold-your-life-in-my-hands-and-you'd-be-wise-to-remember-it* master-sergeant look on her.

Without her usual skyscraper heels, the top of her head barely reached his chest. She obviously thought she was a giant, though, for not only did she not blink under a look that had sent men twice her size scrambling to do his bidding, she gave him another poke. "Give 'em here!"

He handed them over. As much as he hated to admit it, she was in much better shape to drive than he was, and pretending otherwise was dumb. He climbed into the passenger side, eased his throbbing head back against the headrest, and closed his eyes. He didn't open them again until Lily killed the engine what seemed only minutes later.

Surprised to find that he'd dozed off, he saw they were back at the Beaumonts', and the house was ablaze with light. Biting back a sigh, he reached for the door handle, only to pause when Lily touched his thigh.

"How do you feel?"

Like last week's K-rations. "Fine."

She made a skeptical sound. "You're not a very good liar, Zach."

"Yeah, well, would it make any difference if I said my head's pounding like a kettle drum? I've still gotta do what I've gotta do." He took a bracing breath, then opened the door, slid his thigh out from under her warm hand, and climbed out. But looking at her across the top of the Jeep, he admitted, "I could use your help on one thing, though, before we go in to face the lions."

Miguel had his ear pressed against the heavy wooden panel of a second floor door when the commotion broke out downstairs. Foregoing trying to calculate if it was safe to enter the room, he lifted his head and strained to make sense of the sudden babble of voices. But although the volume rose and fell, exact words escaped him.

He didn't know what was going on down there, but he knew he didn't like it. Even a floor away, he felt exposed, and since he hadn't heard any noise on the other side of the heavy door, he cautiously turned the knob. When no one promptly demanded to know who was there, he slipped inside.

The little bit of light that followed him into the suite showed it was another casually elegant, empty set of rooms. He couldn't believe this place. There were first-class hotels in Bogotá not half as beautiful, and he ran appreciative fingertips over the silky, striped chair in front of him. Then footsteps suddenly raced in his direction down the hallway, and he stilled, staring at the door that hadn't quite closed behind him and not daring to breathe again until the footsteps pounded past and on down the staircase.

Hotels didn't seem half as busy, either.

He should probably get out of here. After an hour of cautiously checking rooms, he still hadn't caught so much as a glimpse of Taylor's yellow-haired *puta*, and now a humming sort of agitation hung over the place, making it feel like a hive getting ready to swarm. That much activity couldn't be good for his chances of moving around undetected. And when a few moments later it occurred to him that he could barely even remember what Emilita looked like, he considered for an instant going back to Bisinlejo and just leaving this whole vendetta behind.

Then his chest puffed up. This wasn't about her. It was about *pride*, and his good name, and being a man. Besides, Taylor used to preach something about discretion being the better part of valor back when he'd been showing the men of Bisinlejo how to hold their own against the cartel. So he'd stay and see this through. But right now the situation called for a quick retreat.

Miguel headed for the door. Pulling out before the master sergeant returned was not a cowardly act. It was merely subscribing to the live-to-fight-another-day credo.

Just the way the U.S. Marines had taught him.

Lily felt her temper start to rise as she stood next to Zach in the Beaumont parlor. Richard was yelling, Mrs. B. was in hysterics, and Cassidy sat on the couch grinning as if this were an amusing melodrama put on strictly for her entertainment. Christopher kept inspecting Zach with narrow-eyed suspicion, and Jessica, in between bouts of attempting to calm her aunt, stared incredulously at everyone else in the room as if unable to believe their behavior.

Lily was having a tough time with that, herself. Pandemonium had been the rule ever since she and Zach had explained what transpired tonight in the woods. And after everything Zach had gone through for them, she neither understood nor appreciated the Beaumonts' attitude by half. His temple sported a vicious knot the size of a golf ball and his color was awful. He looked dead on his feet, but considering the new bombshell he'd just lobbed into the mix after Christopher asked where the money was, it seemed unlikely he'd get the rest he needed anytime soon. The only thing he had going for him, apparently, was the second of blessed quiet that had fallen in the wake of his reply.

Then Christopher moved forward to stand chest-to-chest with him. "What the hell does that *mean*, you've put it someplace safe?"

His aggression caused Lily to take a cautious step back, her lashes batting nervously. Zach didn't so much as blink.

"Exactly what it sounds like. I'm through letting you folks comply with every damn demand the kidnapper makes without taking a single precaution to ensure Glynnis and David's safety."

Surprisingly, Christopher's militance faded, and he stepped back. But before Lily could draw a relieved breath Richard pushed forward, demanding belligerently, "What kind of precautions *could* we take?"

"Insisting on speaking to your cousin before forking over his ransom, for starters," Zach snapped. "Jesus. You just sent me out with a boatload of cash and not so much as one lousy assurance as to the kids' safe return—not to mention a shred of proof they're even still alive."

Mrs. Beaumont's hysterical howling immediately grew louder, but Zach kept his attention focused on the two men. "From now on," he said flatly, "we do this my way."

"The hell you say," Richard countered, and Mrs. Beaumont screeched, "You'll kill him! You'll kill my darling David!"

Zach glanced at the older woman. "No, ma'am," he disagreed. "Blind obedience to an extortionist will kill him."

"Well, you can't simply commandeer our money and tell us we have no say on how it's used," Richard said furiously. "That's *thievery*."

"So call a cop." Zach pinned him in place with an ice-cold gaze. "I'd welcome it. In fact, you can all tell him where *you* were while I was out following your instructions."

"Listen, you—"

But when Richard took a menacing step forward, Lily's patience snapped. She inserted herself between the two men. "All right, that is enough! What's the matter with you people? Zach was knocked *unconscious* tonight trying to protect not only David and Glynnis, but your precious money as well, and all I've heard since we got back is complaints about how he handled the drop."

"Hey, he's supposed to be the big, hotshot expert," Richard sneered.

"Yes, and isn't it amazing how that only seems to apply when it comes to putting himself in danger? When he tried to give you the benefit of his expertise, however, no one wanted to pay attention. Well, shame on all of you! You can just sit around throwing hissy fits or wallowing in your self-righteous indignation until you turn blue for all I care. But Zach was injured doing what none of the rest of you were willing to do, and we're finished listening to your grievances. I'm taking him up to his room."

And with a final glare that dared anyone to stop her, she grasped Zach's arm and marched them from the room.

Okay, that was embarrassing. Lying in bed where Lily had stripped him down and bundled him a moment ago before heading off to her own room, Zach relived the way she'd jumped in to defend him from the Beaumonts' ire. He wasn't some grade-school kid needing his mommy to fight his battles for him. Yet he had to admit it was impressive as all get-out seeing a little five-foot-nothing blonde take on an entire household and leave everyone standing around with their mouths agape.

Of course the Beaumonts weren't the only ones whose mouths had been hanging open, and he was the one who'd allowed her to hustle him out of the room. So what did that say about him? That he was a grade-A pussy, probably—a guy who hid behind a woman's skirts. Still. He'd never had anyone stand up for him like that, and it was kind of—

Shit. The truth was, his head throbbed like a bitch in heat, and he didn't know what the hell he felt, aside from the fact that a persistent little kernel of warmth glowed in the region of his tough marine heart. And that wouldn't do. No one knew better than he how dangerous it was to let anyone come to matter too much. In the end no one ever seemed to stay.

Not that he'd let it become a problem in this instance. The trick was not to depend on having anyone's company for the duration, and he'd learned how to do that long ago. He didn't plan to get used to Lily's, either. As soon as he got his sister back and made sure Beaumont was good enough for her, he'd go back to figuring out how to spend his last two years in the service. And since little Miss Lily had big plans for her restaurant, no doubt she'd go her merry way as well without so much as a backward glance.

So when the subject of his thoughts suddenly slid back into his room wearing a little piece of satin and lace that could probably raise the dead, he had a noncommittal expression firmly in place. "I'm pretty hammered, sugar. I don't think I'm gonna be of much use to you tonight."

For just an instant her mouth dropped open. The minute she snapped it closed, however, it promptly morphed into a crooked smile full of genuine amusement. "Well, darn. And here I was, too, just dreaming about sex with a guy I could whip with one arm tied behind my back." She heaved a sigh. "I guess I'll just have to be satisfied with tending to your owie."

Only then, to his embarrassment, did he notice the small tray she carried in her hands, and he said flatly, "I don't require attending."

She nodded in complete understanding. "Because you're such a big, bad Marine." Climbing up onto the bed, she reached across him and carefully set the tray down by his hip.

"Damn straight." What the hell was she up to? He stared at her uncertainly as she carefully swung a leg to kneel astride him, then lowered her lush butt, settling on his thighs with a subtle little wiggle.

"Sometimes even marines need a little TLC," she said. "It doesn't mean they're like those Navy wusses or anything." She twisted to wring a washcloth over the bowl of warm water she'd taken it from, then turned back and cautiously dabbed at the knot on his temple.

For the next several minutes Zach watched her breasts sway and shift against her nightie as she administered to him, and stewed in his own confusion. He couldn't remember anybody ever taking care of him like this. When he was a kid and got hurt, his injuries had mostly been attended to with rough efficiency by a tribesman, since his folks, more often than not, had been out ministering to the natives. And in the service he'd always been doctored by medics. God knew in neither instance had anyone ever sat on his lap to tend him. Nor had they felt like this, nor smelled like this, and they sure as hell had never kissed the injury better once they'd finished bandaging it.

Man. What was it about her? He had a feeling if he didn't watch it she could make him come all undone. Between that body, that way she had of constantly surprising him, and her innate *niceness*, the woman was more dangerous than a vial of nitroglycerin.

But he was too damn tired to do anything more than feel grateful for the comfort he received a few minutes later when she put everything away, climbed into bed, and snuggled up against him. He pulled her a little closer, and sighed.

What the hell. He'd get himself straight in the morning. Right now he just wanted to let everything go. So he closed his eyes and concentrated on Lily's breath wafting across his chest, on the warmth of her arm draped across his stomach.

Then everything faded to black.

✂18

WHEN THE PHONE RANG THE FOLLOWING MORN-
ing, Lily snatched it up before it could awaken Zach.
She whispered a greeting into the receiver.

There was a second of silence, then a male voice
said, "Well, hey there. You must be Lily. Let me talk to
Zach."

She could hear a woman's voice in the background
chiding her caller about his manners, but she merely
said, "He's sleeping."

"So wake him up. Tell him Coop wants to talk to him."

"No."

"Excuse me?" He might have been Zach's twin, so unaccustomed did he sound to having his demands denied.

"No. I won't do that. The kidnapper moved things up
last night, and Zach ended up getting hit on the head.
I'm not going to distur—"

"Did he lose consciousness?"

"Yes."

"For more than a few minutes?"

"No."

"Did he have to go to the hospital?"

"Nooo." She drew the word out cautiously, pretty sure she didn't like the direction this was taking. "Zach said it wasn't necessary."

"Well, he's had enough experience to know."

"He has a knot on his head the size of a golf ball!"

"That's not necessarily a bad thing," Coop informed her, and his voice turned as comforting as a warm hug, momentarily soothing her fears. "If he hadn't had a lump you actually would have had more to worry about, because that often means the hematoma's pressing inward against the brain." Without warning, his voice developed snap. "Which means you can get him up and put him on the phone. It's not like he's some Navy wu—"

"What *is* this fixation you guys have with the Navy?" she interrupted hotly, feeling doubly betrayed because for a moment there she'd fallen for his show of concern. "He got smashed on the *head*, and I am not going to—"

"Lily." Zach's voice, scratchy with sleep, cut through her diatribe before she could really get rolling, and she twisted around to see the blankets slide down to pool around his waist as he pushed up onto one elbow. "I'm awake." He held out his hand for the phone.

She wanted to refuse to give it to him, to make him lie flat so she could check all his pulse points to assure herself of a good steady heartbeat, to go over his wound thoroughly until she was certain it hadn't gotten any worse. But his hand remained out and he met her gaze with level-eyed demand. With a sigh, she handed it to him.

It was a brief conversation. From Lily's standpoint, it

was also a frustrating one, since it was impossible to glean anything from Zach's grunts and *uh-huhs*. She snapped to attention, however, when she heard him say, "I'll be there in fifteen minutes."

"*No*," she protested as soon he hung up the phone, but could only watch in frustration when he ignored her and started pulling on his clothes. "Zach, be reasonable. You can't go running around with that wound on your head."

"My head is fine." A moment later he'd finished dressing and, against her continued protests, headed for the door.

She followed in his wake. "This is crazy."

"No, it's necessary. The kidnapper didn't get what he wanted last night, so he's bound to try again. This time we're gonna nail his ass."

"Not if you're flat on your back in the hospital because you were racing around with a concussion."

"It's not a concussion, Lily. It was a minor bump on the head, but I'm all right now."

A whistle of frustration escaped her. "You are so darn stubborn!"

He grinned and hauled her up against him, bending his knees until they fit in all the crucial places. Then he kissed her thoroughly. But even as he set her bare toes to curling against the floor and her body helplessly pressing as close to his as she could get, she felt him opening the door at his back in preparation to leaving.

"Oh!" Jessica's flustered voice exclaimed from the hallway. "I'm sorry, I didn't mean to intrude. I'm . . . oh."

Zach slowly raised his head. Licking his lower lip,

he stared down at Lily. "I prefer 'determined' to 'stubborn,'" he murmured, pressing a final quick kiss on her still parted lips. As she struggled to regain a modicum of intelligence amid a sea of jangling nerve endings, he turned to smile at Jessica, who stood on the other side of the door with her hand still raised to knock. "You're not intruding," he assured her solemnly. "I was just leaving."

And a second later, he did just that.

"Wow," Jessica said softly as she turned back from watching him stride down the hall. She stepped into the room. "He's feeling better, I take it." She inspected Lily, and a faint smile curved her lips. "I do believe your skin is smoking."

"Oh, my." A startled laugh escaped Lily. "It wouldn't surprise me." She looked at her friend. "How did you know to come here instead of my door?"

"I did go to your room first. You were just too preoccupied to hear my knock." Jessica flashed a crooked smile and shrugged. "When you didn't answer, I thought I'd try here."

Feeling her face heat, Lily decided a change of subject was in order. "Hmm. So. You're out and about early."

Jessica gave her a knowing grin. But she said politely, "Yes, I know. And I'm sorry to descend on you before you've even had a chance to get dressed, but the salon had a cancellation, and I've got an appointment in forty-five minutes to get my hair cut. You wanna blow off breakfast and come to town with me?"

Lily's sense of responsibility warred with her not-yet-lessened irritation with the rest of the Beaumonts for their treatment of Zach last night, and weighing the two opposing impulses, she gave a brisk nod.

"Sure, what the heck. Your family can fend for themselves for one meal. Just give me fifteen minutes to throw myself together, and I'll meet you downstairs."

Zach walked into the Kangaroo House Bed and Breakfast. No one manned the minuscule front desk tucked beneath the open staircase, so he strode straight into the living area and turned left by the craftsman style furniture grouped in front of the big stone fireplace. A few steps away was a door marked KATHLEEN'S SUITE, and he gave it a sharp rap.

Coop's wife, Veronica, opened the door, and her unexpected appearance made Zach blink. Then he smiled. Her usually sleek cap of shiny black hair was slightly tousled, but her white skin glowed with its usual pearlescent sheen. "Hey, Ronnie," he said. "Pretty as ever, I see."

She laughed. "And you're still just as diplomatic and sweet." She opened the door wider and stepped back. "Come in."

Beyond her, he saw Rocket folding a Murphy bed into the wall. As he stepped inside the sitting room, he noted a bathroom across the room to his right and an open bedroom door to his left. Coop strode out of the latter.

His friend was big, blond, and tougher than shoe leather, but his dark eyes went soft and his even darker eyebrows furrowed in puzzlement as he watched his wife step outside the room. "What are you doing out in the hall, sweetpea?"

"I'm going to go have breakfast and give you guys

some privacy to talk." She turned to Zach. "I'm so sorry about your sister," she said. "Please let me know if there's anything I can do. I know you'll get her back, but I can only imagine how worried you must be in the meantime." Then, murmuring a farewell, she pulled the door closed.

"Diplomatic and sweet?" John said the instant she was gone, raising his eyebrows at Zach. "Was she talking about the same hard-ass we all know and fear?"

"Hey, the last time I saw Veronica, she and Coop were about to be married. I just made myself scarce whenever Lover Boy here started messing with her in front of me."

"You must have spent a helluva lot of time making yourself scarce, then," John said sardonically, "because he's still at it every chance he gets." Both men turned to look at the subject of their discussion.

Coop shrugged. "What can I say? She's very messable."

"She must be," Zach agreed dryly, "if you couldn't leave her at home long enough to take care of business."

"You don't know the half of it." Rocket gave their mutual friend a pitying look. "He said, 'But honey, cookie, sugar. This here is men's work and ya can't come along.' To which she replied"—John's voice went falsetto— "'I'm going, Cooper Blackstock, and that's final.'" Then his voice dropped back down into its normal register. "And he caved, Midnight, he just caved. Hung his head and said, 'Okay, princess. Whatever you say.' Hell, she even got to ride shotgun on the trip up here."

Zach shook his head in sad disbelief. "Whoever would have thought we'd see the day the Iceman turned into a boy who just can't say no to the little woman?"

Coop snorted. "It wasn't *my* little woman who refused to wake you up this morning simply because you had a"—he inspected Zach's temple—"very minorleague knot on the head."

"Yeah, but some of us actually take charge once we regain consciousness from our extremely serious head injuries." Zach gave Coop a smile that was all teeth. "And you'll notice *Lily* didn't accompany me here." Not that she probably wouldn't have tried to if Jessica hadn't shown up in time to prevent the idea from occurring to her.

"If you two are through swinging 'em around," Rocket interrupted, "maybe we can get down to business." He gave the fly of his fashionable slacks a fond pat. "Besides, a show of size is about as pointless as the nipples on your chests, dont'cha think? Everyone knows who's got the big one in this group."

Zach and Coop looked at him. Then they looked at each other.

"Can't argue with that," Zach said and took a seat.

"'Course you'll notice he doesn't have a woman of his own." Coop pulled up the chair next to him and gave Rocket a nod as he sat. "But you're in the majors, Miglionni, no question about that."

Then he turned his attention on Zach. "So, what the hell is this I hear about the kidnapper calling last night instead of today?"

Lily picked up a few groceries, then stopped by the hair salon to collect the car keys and see how much longer Jessica would be. When she discovered it would be awhile yet, she left to stow the groceries in the back of Jessica's car, then headed for the drugstore to replace some of her items that were beginning to run low.

She was cruising the aisles when she suddenly ran across the condom selection. She stopped short, her heart dropping with a thud that was nearly audible. "Dear God," she whispered, her mind flashing to the lone condom she'd seen in Zach's zipper bag that night in the campground near Mount Shasta. They'd used it the first time they made love.

And hadn't used one since.

The romantic in her stood there bemused, staring at the display and thinking she was in big-time trouble if she was so moon-faced in love she'd bypassed something as basic as protection. Her bedrock practicality, though, took a more irritated stance. That part couldn't *believe* it hadn't occurred to her before now that they hadn't been using anything. Or to him either, since Zach was hardly the careless type. She was on the pill, so she wasn't worried about pregnancy. But he didn't know that, and he'd sure as heck never checked to make sure she had it covered. And for *both* of them to just disregard the most basic safety precautions—good grief, they hadn't even once compared health histories. She never took chances when it came to that, and knowing that she had with Zach made her feel like banging her head on the nearest hard surface.

Instead she selected a box and tossed it in her basket. It was probably locking the barn door after the horse had bolted, but until she knew Zach was safe, he could darn well suit up. It was his sole hope of ever getting his big ol' pride and joy anywhere near her again.

Still fretting about it as she left the store, she nearly barreled into a young man just entering. "Excuse me," she said, and gave the arm she'd grabbed to keep from mowing him down an apologetic pat. "I'm afraid I wasn't paying attention to where I was going." Then her eyebrows drew together. She knew that face from somewhere.

Just as quickly, however, her brow cleared. Well, duh. With that jet-black hair and those dark eyes, he was quite handsome, which undoubtedly was what she'd noticed about him when she'd seen him at one of the stores the last time she was here. Happy to have that cleared up, she gave him a sunny smile and stepped to the right to circle around him.

He stepped into her path, so she countered with a move to the left. When he mirrored her action, once again blocking her, she laughed. "Wanna dance?"

His eyes lit up, and it belatedly occurred to her he might think she was flirting with him. Fortunately, before he could say a word, Jessica's voice called out her name.

"Excuse me, gotta go." Holding up her hand like a traffic cop to stay him, she stepped around him. Then, catching sight of Jessica as her friend strode up the block, Lily immediately forgot the young man. She raced down the street as fast as her skyscraper heels allowed.

"Oh, my gosh," she said when they met in front of the jewelry store. "You look great!" She reached out to touch the soft brown wave that ended at Jessica's jaw. "How do you like it?"

"It's such a huge change, I'm kind of in shock. But I think I'm going to love it once I get used to it." She shook her head and laughed. "It feels so light!"

"It really suits you. It plays up the bone structure of your face and accentuates your eyes and neck. I give it the official Morrisette two thumbs up."

Jessica laughed, feeling weightless and pretty. She shook her head again just to feel her hair slide against her cheeks. "Oh, I do think I'm going to like it! It's so nice for once not to have great gobs of hair hanging in my face." She wondered what Christopher would think when he saw her new style. She'd deliberately not told him she was having it done, wanting it to be a surprise.

A few minutes later, as they were buckling themselves into the car, she looked over at Lily. "Would it be too awful of me if I didn't feel like going home just yet?"

Lily blinked. "Why would that be awful of you?"

"Well, I probably shouldn't be out enjoying myself when the kidnapper might call again at any minute."

"We've only been gone—what?—an hour? I don't see how treating yourself to another hour would hurt anything. And take it from me, it's not as if there's a lot you or I can do." Lily said the latter with such conviction it reminded Jessica of her spirited defense of Zach last night. But before Jess could pursue exactly what had occurred, Lily gave her a gentle smile and asked, "What is it you feel like doing?"

"You want to drive over to Olga? I'll show you the Orcas Island Artworks. It's one of the oldest cooperative galleries in the Northwest, and Lily, it has the greatest stuff. It offers everything from hand knits to the most exquisitely crafted glass. Not to mention the wonderful little café in the back." She wagged a persuasive eyebrow. "I'll buy you a goodie."

"Oh, very sly." Lily gave her a crooked smile. "You know me pretty well, I'd say, if you understand my appetite's the clincher. By all means, let's go. It sounds terrific."

"I can almost guarantee you'll love it. Plus, it's not that far away; it's just a mile or so the other side of Moran State park."

Lily shuddered. "Been there."

Jessica glanced over at her blonde friend as she maneuvered the car out of town. "How *did* you end up going along with Zach last night, anyhow?"

Lily described her stowaway adventure in the back of Zach's Jeep as they drove to Olga. With self-deprecating humor, she detailed her stint in the woods, painting herself as a witless city girl.

But Jess was filled with admiration as she took her eyes off the road long enough to glance at her friend. "You are so brave."

Lily's mouth dropped open. "Are you crazy?" she demanded. "I was scared to death!"

"Of course you were. But you followed through anyway."

"And nearly got Zach's brains bashed in for my efforts."

Jess pulled into the parking lot of the Artworks, killed the engine, then turned to face her friend. "Who's to say he wouldn't have gotten hit on the head anyway?"

Lily just looked at her.

"Okay, so I can't actually see Zach letting that happen without a distraction, but Lily, still! It was very courageous of you to try to help."

Lily laughed and reached for the door handle. "I have a feeling Zach wouldn't agree with you, but since I love having you believe I'm so stouthearted, I'll just say thank you and leave it at that."

Jessica's lips curled with pleasure as she walked

down the long porch of the old renovated strawberry packing plant that housed the Artworks. Opening the door, she held it for Lily. "This is my very favorite place on the entire island."

"Oh, my," Lily breathed as she stepped inside the beamed-ceilinged room. "I can see why."

The floors of the co-op were slightly uneven with their old hardwood planks, and windows spilled light into an interior crowded with fascinating goods. Straight ahead stood a display stand of multisized cubes holding pottery of various sizes and shapes. One exhibit led to another, from glass, to jewelry, to paintings, to a rack of wearable art, and Jess enjoyed watching Lily's delight every bit as much as she loved exploring herself. It was a crowded treasure chest filled with contributions from more than sixty-five artists, and there were always new things to discover.

She was trying on felt hats, admiring them with her new hairdo in a small mirror, when she saw Lily's reflection stop in front a display of small quilts that hung on one wall.

After several solemn, silent moments spent inspecting it, Lily turned to her. "You ought to be displaying your quilts here."

Instant delight suffused her, but accustomed as she was to downplaying her work as nothing more than a hobby, her instinctive response was to demur. Before she could say a word, however, a woman manning the central desk looked up with interest. "You make quilts?"

"Beautiful ones," Lily answered for her and walked over with a friendly smile. "They're quite different from these, but she's every bit as talented."

Face warm with both pleasure and embarrassment, Jessica joined them and found herself talking to the artist on duty about her work. Agreeing to submit some samples for consideration, she finally eased away and made her way down to the far end of the co-op, where she stood for a moment with one hand over her rapidly beating heart as she pretended to look at the handcrafted stationery and cards racked in front of her.

Once her pulse had settled down a bit, she walked over to peek into the café to check on the availability of a table. The silly smile, though, continued to play across her mouth.

It froze when she glanced toward the back corner of the café and saw Christopher seated at a small table near the door, talking intently to an unfamiliar woman.

Pain splintered through her with such ferocity she could barely catch her breath. Seeing him here when he'd specifically told her he'd be elsewhere, with a woman who was everything she wasn't, shouldn't have caught her by surprise. She'd known he was up to something—for weeks she had known that. Hell, sometimes it felt as if she'd been waiting for this very occurrence since the first night they'd met, yet nothing, she realized now, ever could have prepared her for seeing her worst fears realized. She numbly watched the single-minded attention her husband lavished on the other woman until Christopher's head started to lift. Then she scrambled backward, desperate not to be seen.

She would die if he saw her.

Lily glanced up as Jessica strode rapidly up the center aisle, and after one good look at her friend's face, frowned and went to meet her. "What is it?"

"I want to go now."

"Well, sure, but what's wrong. Are you sick?"

"Yes. All of a sudden I feel like I could die."

"You don't look so hot," she agreed. "Good Lord, Jess, you don't have a drop of color in your face." She took Jessica's arm and helped her out of the store, concerned when her friend leaned heavily in her grasp. "Give me your keys. Could you have food poisoning? Do you want me to take you to the clinic?"

"It's not food poisoning, Lily. I haven't had anything to eat since last night."

"Well, maybe that's it." She gestured back toward the café. "I could go get you—"

"No! I just want to go home."

"Are you sure?" Something about Jessica's stillness worried Lily, but when she gave a curt nod, Lily simply said, "Okay, then."

As she was settling Jessica in the passenger seat, she heard a car door close. She glanced up as she circled the hood to climb in the driver's side and froze for a moment as she saw the same young man she'd run into at the pharmacy.

The same young man, she suddenly remembered, that she'd seen before not in town, as she'd earlier assumed, but in a gas station parking lot on the other side of the state.

That was stretching coincidence way too far, and her heart began to thud anxiously. She had a bad feeling that something was very, very wrong here.

And suddenly she wanted to get back to the Beaumont estate every bit as much as Jessica did.

❦ 19

No one was around when they arrived home, so Lily escorted Jessica up to her apartment. After assurances from her friend that some rest would perk her up, Lily helped her into bed and dampened a washcloth to drape across her eyes. Hating to leave her, but getting the distinct impression Jessica wanted to be alone, she finally let herself out of the apartment. She stood indecisively out in the hallway for a moment, then went looking for Zach.

She tracked him down in the parlor, where she found him pacing with long-legged strides between the French doors and the fireplace. As she paused in the doorway, he completed his circuit to the fireplace, swept a small objet d'art off the mantel, and restlessly tossed it from hand to hand without apparent thought for its value. Thinking he looked lonely and stressed, Lily walked into the room. "Where is everyone?"

His posture immediately stiffened and, snapping the knickknack out of the air, he replaced it on the mantel. Then one broad shoulder hitched as he turned to face her. "Beats the hell outta me. Blown to the four corners of the earth, maybe."

"No one's heard from the kidnapper, then?"

"Not a word."

"I'm sorry, Zach. I know that must be difficult." She closed the distance between them and peered up at him in concern. "Are you okay?"

"Yeah, sure." Looking at her with those intense gray eyes, he ran his hand down her arm to her wrist, which he slowly circled with his fingers. He blew out a sigh and the tautness left his shoulders. "No, that's a lie. I'm frustrated as hell."

"I'm not surprised. Did you meet with your friends?"

"Yes." The faint smile tugging up the corner of his mouth told Lily that getting together with them had been good for him. He fiddled with her fingers. "We're ready to roll," he said, "if only the damn kidnapper would call."

"He will, Zach." Raising on tiptoe, she pressed a gentle kiss upon his mouth before settling back on her heels. "Meanwhile, try not to brood about it."

A distinct light entered his eyes, and transferring his hands to her hips, he pulled her in, bending his knees until their pelvises were snugged together. "Well, I don't know," he said. "Brooding's damn tough to avoid when you're worried. Seems to me if you don't want me caving under the pressure, you'd give me an activity to help pass the time. Take my mind off it." He swiveled his hips suggestively. "Ya know?"

That reminded Lily of her earlier discovery. Since she'd never gotten to her room to drop off her stuff, the pharmacy bag was still in her hand, and she handed it to him. "I've got something for you first. It kind of falls into that better late than never category."

"What's this?" He reached between them for the bag. Shaking it open one-handed, he peered inside. Then the hand still holding her hip dropped to his side, and he stepped back. "Oh, shit."

The set of his mouth turned grim as he stared into the open sack. "Christ, Lily," he said hoarsely. "I can't believe we've been having unprotected sex, and it never even occurred to me." Paper crackled as his fist suddenly cinched the top of the bag closed, and his gaze snapped up to pin her in place. "Is it possible you're pregnant?" A breath of derisive laughter escaped him. "Stupid-ass question; of course it's possible. We haven't used a damn thing to prevent it, and we've been fucking like—"

She winced at his wording, but said levelly, "That at least shouldn't be a problem. I'm on the pill."

"*Good.*" He blew out a breath. "Oh, God. That's good." Then, before she could decide if she was hurt by his obvious relief or perhaps the tiniest bit hacked off, he ran the backs of his fingers down her cheek, stared into her eyes, and said with soft intensity, "I'm sorry, Lily. I know what you must be thinking, but I promise you I don't make a habit of this. Hell, I can't believe I did it *this* time. I've never forgotten to wear protection in my life."

And just like that, she felt much better. She leaned into his touch. "I know what you mean. I've never been careless before, either. I don't know what it is about you." Okay, she did, but since Zach seemed to be pretty gun-shy when it came to emotional intimacy, she decided not to scare him off. She gazed at him solemnly.

"We probably ought to talk about this, though. I'd like you to know that the number of my sexual partners is in the single digits. And since it's been quite a while since the last one, and I have regular yearly exams, not only am I safe when it comes to pregnancy, but in all the other considerations, as well."

"Yeah. Me, too. My partners probably number more in the mid-double digit range, but—"

"You've slept with *fifty* women?"

"Hell, I don't know; it's not like I've counted. But I'm thirty-six years old, Lily, and I've been sexually active for twenty years. Let's be conservative and say I've slept with two women a year—that would still be forty right there." He shrugged. "So, realistically it was probably closer to a hundred."

"My gawd." Feeling her jaw drop, she said, "If a *woman* admitted to that much experience, she'd be labeled a slut. What the heck do you call a guy who has sex with a hundred partners?"

"A marine." He gave her a cocky smile, then sobered. "The point is, I was given a clean bill of health by the medics before I left for South America, and I, uh, haven't been with another woman since. Maybe that's why—"

He broke off and shook his head, a leery expression in his eyes as he looked at her. Then his sexuality slammed back into place, and Lily had the craziest notion he was using it like a shield. But when he smiled lazily and his breath misted warm against her ear as he murmured, "What say we take this box upstairs and see if we can't put a dent in the contents?" she forgot her momentary suspicion.

"Um, yeah. Okay. That would be good."

The next thing she knew, she was up in her room, divested of clothing and flat on her back in the middle of the bed, with an equally naked Zach propped over her kissing her from forehead to toes.

He was slow and thorough, and she was a writhing mass of inflamed nerve endings by the time he rolled onto his back, unfurled one of the new condoms down the length of his jutting erection, then lifted her to straddle him. Looking down as she found her balance, her heart slammed fast and furiously at the hot-eyed intensity darkening his pale irises. Then every corpuscle in her body stood at attention and shouted *yes*! as his rough-skinned fingers gripped her hips and slowly lowered her onto the hot, solid length pushing its way inside her.

"All those women?" he said hoarsely as she quickly found a rhythm and rose and lowered herself upon him. "They've run together in my mind, Lily, and I can barely remember anything about them."

Absorbed in the slight adjustment she'd just made that drove him deeper to touch a sweet spot high inside, bringing her closer, *closer,* to satisfaction, she barely heeded his words. She was striving for a shining goal just out of reach, and oh, gawd, she was nearly . . . she was almost—

Suddenly he arched his pelvis off the bed, and Lily cried out as mind-expanding pleasure exploded within her. Zach held her hips with a hard grip as he thrust up into her, and her climax roared through her body like sheet lightning, all but arcing and snapping as it went on and on and *on.*

But somewhere in the midst of it, she heard him say,

"I have a feeling, though, it's gonna be a long, long time before I ever forget you."

Jerking her chin down to study his expression, she found that he, too, had begun to come. His eyes were blind and his mouth mute as he held her tightly to him, so she wasn't certain if he'd actually said the words or she'd merely imagined them. Then she didn't care, for the look on Zach's face and the feel of that rigid source of pleasure throbbing powerfully inside her swept every other consideration from her mind and sparked a further round of contractions that were even sweeter than the ones preceding them.

She couldn't have said if minutes or hours passed before she became aware that the muscular body beneath her was losing its slackness. As some of her own post-coital lethargy dissipated, something important began to niggle at her memory. "Oh, shoot." She peeled herself off Zach's damp chest where she'd been lying limply. "I meant to tell you earlier: I discovered this morning that I might have another problem." Looking down, she was surprised to find his eyes wide open and, just for a second, vulnerable.

Then he blinked, and that endearing hint of confusion disappeared, leaving her wondering if she'd actually seen it at all.

Zach, fearing he'd just given something away, raised a deliberately sardonic eyebrow. "You have had yourself a busy day, haven't you?"

"It's sure as sugar been a long one," she agreed. "And it's not even noon yet."

He congratulated himself on successfully diverting her attention from whatever she'd seen in his face. But when she related the encounter she'd had with a young man in town, and told him how the youth had also approached her at the gas station on the Washington-Oregon border, Zach became all business. "I'm not a big believer in coincidence," he said flatly, and rolled her off of him. He climbed to his feet and bent to sweep up his discarded jeans.

"No. Neither am I."

He didn't care to admit to himself that it was almost a relief to have something to concentrate on besides the way he seemed to lose all control around Lily. But how the *hell* could he have forgotten to use condoms with her? Worse, why had he just been so tempted to continue doing so?

It wasn't an issue he was anxious to delve into, so he hustled her into her clothes, seated her in the chair in front of the desk, and hunkered down in front of her, his hands resting on the arms of her chair. "Okay, let's have it. Give me all the details you can remember."

"He didn't speak today, but that day outside the gas station and minimart, he apologized for his poor English and asked for my assistance."

"To do what?"

"Translate for someone having a difficult time with his accent, I think. At least that was the impression I got. But I'm not really sure, because you roared out a command to shake my tush or be left behind before we got very far into the conversation."

He ignored that. "So he's not an American?"

"No. Or if he is, English isn't his first language, although I didn't think it was nearly as bad as he seemed to believe."

"What nationality would you say?"

"Well, since he said *gracias*, and has that dark-haired, dark-eyed, handsome Latino thing going for him, my guess would be Hispanic."

An unlikely thought occurred to Zach, but he shrugged it aside as farfetched. "Do you have any idea who he wanted you to talk to?"

"No. I remember him waving toward either the mini-mart or the pumps on the other side."

Zach whispered a curse. If the initial encounter had been the extent of things, he might have blown it off as nothing. But his gut insisted this was definitely something. Orcas was a fairly remote island and mostly a rural one. What were the odds of Lily running into someone here who'd wanted to escort her to the unpopulated side of a minimart clear across the state?

Slim to frigging none. Pulling on his shirt, he headed for the phone.

She followed in his wake, standing so close he caught vagrant suggestions of her warm scent as he flipped through his dog-eared address book. She peered at the organizer over his shoulder. "Who are you calling?"

"Camp Pendleton." He paused in turning the pages to look at her. "When I came home from my last deployment, I brought back three South American nationals for a course of specialized training. I'd had a problem with one of them, but I thought we'd put it behind us."

"And you think this might be him?"

"I don't know. But I plan to make sure he's still where I left him." The line on the other end connected, and he pulled the receiver up to his lips. "Yes. Who am I speaking to?" The voice on the other end identified himself, and he said, "Corporal Sanford, this is Master Sergeant Zachariah Taylor. Put me through to Magnusson."

Put on hold, he had no problem hearing the hysterical squealing that broke out downstairs a second later. Actual words were indistinct, but the tone was clear, and he exchanged a look with Lily. Something was going on. The question was what?

Then Mrs. Beaumont's voice distinctly screamed, *"David!"* and he tossed the receiver back onto the hook and raced for the door. Lily's phantom stalker could be dealt with later. Right now it sounded as if they had a more immediate emergency on their hands.

Oh, man, he thought as he pounded down the stairs, his stomach churning anew as his sister's face floated before his mind's eye. *Let that have been a scream of joy. God, please, if You're up there, don't let this be bad news. I don't think I can bear to lose Glynnis.*

Lily was hot on Zach's heels, so when he came to an abrupt halt at the foot of the stairs, she was moving too fast and was too close behind him to stop. Slamming into his back, she bounced off with enough force to knock the breath from her lungs. The next instant found her sitting precipitately on one of the stair treads.

Zach didn't seem to notice. *"Glynnie?"* he said with soft wonder, and Lily's swimming head jerked up.

Dear Lord. Glynnis was here? Craning to see around Zach, she found herself blocked by the solid wall of his back, and to her frustration, it seemed to shift in synchronicity with her own movements. She started scooting her rear toward the banister.

Before she'd shifted enough for a clear view, however, she heard Glynnis's voice saying, "*Zach?* What are you doing here?"

He moved then, and Lily finally saw Glynnis, who looked every bit as stunned as she felt, but also hale and hearty, thank goodness. As Zach strode toward his sister, Lily saw Glynnis catch sight of her struggling to get up off the stairs. The younger woman's eyes grew even rounder, and she squeaked, "*Lily?* Holy shit—um, cow, I mean! You're here, too? What on earth is going on?"

Zach swept her into a hug so tight it lifted her feet clear off the ground, and burying his face in her dark hair, he rocked them from side to side. "God, Glynnie, I can't tell you how relieved I am to see you safe. I was worried sick."

"You were?" She pulled her head back to peer at him. "Why?"

Zach's brows came together and he set her back on her feet. "What do you mean, *why*? You think ransom demands for you and your boyfriend here aren't gonna cause a slight ripple of concern?"

"Ransom demands!" exclaimed both Glynnis and a deep male voice, and Lily's fascinated gaze left Zach and Glynnis to zoom in on David. Even as she watched, he disengaged his mother's frantic hold from around his neck and held her at arm's length to stare down at her. "You thought we were *kidnapped*? That's what you've been screaming about?"

"Yes," she sobbed, and collapsed against his chest again. Once more David gently disentangled himself from her embrace, but he slung a comforting arm around her shoulders and escorted her across the foyer to where the Taylors stood. He thrust his free hand out at Zach. "You must be Zachariah. Glynnis's told me a lot about you. But I don't understand. Why would you think we'd been kidnapped?"

"Because a ransom note was left in our mailbox," Mrs. Beaumont said as Zach's dark eyebrows gathered above his nose. "And we've gotten phone calls!"

"But that doesn't make a lick of sense." David looked baffled, but before he could say anything further, the front door opened and Cassidy strolled in. She stopped when she saw the crowd in the entryway.

"Well, well," she said in her I-have-terminal-ennui-but-am-still-terribly-amused-by-the-little-people voice. "What have we here, a military coup in the foyer?" She reached up to pull a bejeweled hatpin out of her beret. "Are you on the rampage again, Master Sergeant? How very macho of you—" Her arms froze overhead as the individuals comprising the group in front of her suddenly registered, and her mouth went round with shock. "David? Omigod, David! You're all right!" And with a peal of the most genuine laughter Lily had ever heard out of her, she rushed to close the space separating them.

"Cass. I'm fine. I'm just trying to figure out what the hell's been going on."

"Aside from that pesky kidnapping thing, you mean?" She gave him a fierce hug.

"We weren't—"

The front door opened once again and Christopher strolled in. Giving the group a curious glance, he closed the door behind him. Then he, too, went very still. "David." A smile broke out, making his face, already striking, downright gorgeous, and he closed the space between them, his hand thrust out. "It's good to see you, guy. Thank God you're okay. Jess is gonna be so relieved."

"Oh, for heaven's sake!" Glynnis snapped, and her let's-all-just-dispense-with-the-BS tone of voice was so like her brother's that Lily had to smile. "We were *not* kidnapped."

Lily had been getting that impression, but it was still a shock to hear it said aloud. And clearly she wasn't the only one who felt that way. Looking at David's relatives, she saw they looked as dumbfounded as she felt.

Cassidy was the first to recover. She slid her arms out from around David's waist and turned to give Glynnis a thorough perusal. "This must be the little girlfriend," she said and raised her brows at her cousin. "A tad simpleminded, is she?"

"Knock it off, Cass." Breaking away from her and leaving his mother by the parlor door, David made his way to Glynnis's side, where he slipped an arm around her shoulders. "She's telling the truth. We were never kidnapped, and I don't know why you would think we were. We've been in touch."

"With whom?" Mrs. Beaumont demanded incredulously.

David looked from face to face as if hoping someone would grin and say, "Gotcha!" But when all he received was everybody's rapt attention he shook his head and said, "Richard."

For one brief moment, Zach thought he probably should have figured it out for himself. Then he got real. Nothing had pointed to Richard, and Zach wasn't a man to waste time berating himself when there were more important questions to be asked and details to be gathered. So he shrugged his failure aside and looked over at Glynnis's boyfriend.

What he saw was a sturdy young man who carried himself well and had level eyes whose gaze tended to soften whenever they touched upon Glynnie. Zach gave a single terse nod of approval, then caught David's eyes. "You called here?"

"Yes. A couple of times."

"And you talked to Richard?"

David nodded. "I told him the first time that Glynnis and I had gotten caught up seeing the sights along the way and were going to be about a week later than I'd originally told Mother to expect us. He said he'd pass the message along and told me I'd better call him on his cell phone from then on because they'd been experiencing some difficulty with the land lines." David shrugged. "That often happens after storms here, so I didn't think anything of it."

"When did you last talk to him?"

"Yesterday. I told him we'd be home on Sunday."

Since this was Saturday, Zach simply raised his brows.

Glynnis bristled. "David's not one of your recruits," she said hotly. "So you can just quit using your Master Sergeant look on him. And in answer to the question you might have simply *asked*, we'd planned to spend the weekend in Seattle, but when we woke up this morning, I found myself more interested in meeting David's family and seeing his home than I was in playing tourist in the Emerald City."

"We figured we could always explore it another

time," David said, tightening his hold on Glynnis as he smiled down at her.

She gave him a fatuous smile in return, and Zach barely resisted the urge to roll his eyes.

"Right," she agreed. "So we checked out early and jumped in the car." She snuggled against David's side. "And here we are."

"The question is, where is Richard?" Zach glanced at Mrs. Beaumont and braced himself for her usual argument when he said, "We'd better call the sheriff's department."

To his surprise, she merely nodded, her mouth grim. "I'll do that right away." She began to turn away, but then swiveled back to face him. "I owe you an apology," she said. "If I'd listened to you, you probably never would have gotten hurt last night."

Glynnis's head came up. "You were hurt?" Pulling out from under David's arm, she raced over to Zach. "Where? Ohmigod, you've got a knot on your head!" She reached up to touch gentle fingertips to his temple. "Are you all right? Did you have a doctor check it out?"

"I'm fine, Glynnie." Clasping her hands in his own, he pressed them together, palm to palm. "It was pretty much a nothing little bump to begin with, and Lily fixed me up right as rain."

"But there's a knot!"

"According to Cooper Blackstock," Lily said, "that's actually a good sign." She cited the explanation she'd been given.

Glynnis craned her head around to stare at her. "*Coop* is here?"

"Not here, as in the house," Zach told her. "But on the island, yes. He and Miglionni."

"John, too?" She looked dazed. "My God. You called them in?"

"Yes."

"Because you thought I'd been kidnapped?"

He shrugged to cover the fierceness of his feelings. "I planned to get you back one way or the other."

"Aw, Zach." She kissed him on the chin. "I love you."

His heart clenched tighter than a fist. "Love you, too, baby sis." He grinned down at her. "So, I hear you're getting married."

To his regret, her eyes grew a little cautious, but he noticed it didn't prevent her from meeting his gaze squarely. "Yes. I am."

He looked past her at her fiancé for a moment, then returned his gaze to her face, feeling more grateful than he could express to have her back safe and sound. "David seems all right."

She flashed him a megawatt smile. "Oh, God, he is so much more than 'all right.' He's *wonderful*."

"Then if you're happy, I'm happy."

"I am." She hugged him. "I am *so* happy, Zachariah. And I gotta say, I'm delighted you're pleased for me. For a minute there I was afraid you might have come all the way up here to stop me."

"Who, me?" Zach shot a glance at Lily. She treated him to an ironic smile but kept her mouth shut, so he graced his sister with a cocky grin and kept up the feigned innocence. "And wreck the course of true love? Not a chance."

Out of the corner of his eye he watched as Lily and

Christopher put their heads together and spoke in undertones. A moment later the other man left, his forehead furrowed as he took the stairs two at a time. Mrs. Beaumont gave her son a final hug, and announced she was going into the parlor to call the police. Apparently at a loss for a snide remark, Cassidy said she'd go keep her aunt company. All of a sudden, the only ones left in an foyer that only moments earlier had teemed with people were Lily, David, his sister, and him.

Then Glynnis dragged Lily over by the front door to hold a low-voiced conversation, and the two men were left alone. The silence between them stretched out, and Zach began to feel as if he should say something. But, hell, it wasn't as if he really knew the guy or anything, so he could probably be excused for not having a lot to talk about.

On the other hand, David *was* going to marry his sister, and Zach noticed the younger man's expression when he wasn't doing the moony thing over Glynnis was pretty glum. Remembering the comfort he'd gained from Lily's condolences earlier, he blew out a breath and offered the younger man a light thump on the back. "I'm sorry about your cousin. Hearing what he's done has gotta be rough on you."

"I don't understand it. If he needed money so damn bad, why didn't he just ask? I would have given it to him."

"Well, it's never too late," another voice interjected. "I'll take it now."

Spinning around, Zach came face to face with Richard, who had entered unheard through the front door and now stood across the entryway behind Glynnis.

The shotgun in his hands pointed straight at her head.

❧ 20

•

ICE TRICKLED THROUGH ZACH'S VEINS, BUT HE kept his hands loose at his sides and his voice gentle and nonthreatening as he took a step forward. "I don't think you want to do this, Richard."

The younger man looked at him as if he were crazy. "Of course I don't want to do it! I never intended for anyone to get hurt. The plan was just to get the money and be gone before David got home." He glared at Zach. "But then you had to come along and fuck everything up."

Zach held his hands wide of his body in a shrug of entreaty as he edged a millimeter closer. "I thought my baby sister had been snatched. You would've moved heaven and earth, too, I'm sure, if it had been one of your sisters."

Richard made a rude noise and pressed the double barrels against the angle of Glynnis's jaw. Her eyes were huge with fear, but Zach was proud of her; she stood still and quiet in the midst of a situation where anyone could be excused for going all hysterical. Only her eyes moved, flitting between himself and David.

"Not frigging likely," Richard jeered. "My sisters are

up for grabs, as far as I'm concerned. Jess is nothing but a doormat, and Cass is a bitch."

"Who are you calling a bitch, you wormy little maggot?" Cassidy demanded as she strolled out of the parlor. "*I'm* not the lowlife thief stealing from my own fam—" She stopped just inside the foyer as if she'd run smack up against an invisible force field, staring in shock at the tableau that greeted her. "Oh, my God, Richard," she whispered, staring at her brother, Glynnis, and the shotgun. "What on earth are you doing?"

"Go back into the parlor," Zach said calmly, sparing her the briefest of glances, "and try to keep your aunt occupied. The last thing we want is her out here going into hysterics."

Cassidy nodded, but as she took a cautious step backward, Richard barked, "Stay right where you are." He glared at Zach. "How dumb do you think I am? As if I'm going to let her go where she can call the cops."

"Your aunt's already called the sheriff's department, so if you've got half a brain, you'll beat it the hell out of here while you still can."

"Yeah, right," the younger man scoffed. "Pull the other one, why don't you."

"It's true, Richard," Cassidy said. "Aunt Maureen is furious with you. She told me you're the one who kept reinforcing her fears that the kidnapper would kill David if Zach called the cops like he wanted to. So she didn't hesitate to call them on you."

"Fine." He gave his hair a nervous toss, adjusted his grip on the stock of the shotgun, and glared at Zach. "Give me the goddamn money then, and I'll be on my way."

"Just as soon as you let Glynnis go," David interjected. "I'll give you anything you want. But first, let her go."

Richard turned to look at him, but glanced back every few seconds to keep Zach in sight. He bent a scornful look on his cousin. "You always were a chump."

"Why?" David demanded. "Because I love someone and don't want to see her get hurt?"

"No, because you're such a frigging Little Lord Bountiful. You're just Mister Goddamn Generosity, aren't you?"

From the corner of his eye, Zach saw Cassidy open her mouth to protest. He gave an infinitesimal shake of his head, and to his relief she subsided. Richard had his attention focused pretty firmly on his cousin at the moment, and Zach wanted to keep it that way, since he was using Richard's preoccupation to edge nearer an inch at a time.

"Let me get this straight," David said incredulously. "You're pissed at me because I invited you to live with us and gave you a good-paying *job*?"

"Please. Like you did it from the goodness of your heart." Richard's laugh was bitter. "You're such a hypocrite. You invited us here and gave me a job because you get your kicks out of lording it over all of us and never letting anyone forget you're prince of the goddamn castle."

"That's bullshit!"

"The hell it is." As if sensing danger was approaching, he began to turn back toward Zach.

Lily, who stood on the far side of David, took a step forward. "You know what, Richard? You're a spoiled brat."

He turned to look at her. "Oh, that's good. So says the slut. Did I give you permission to speak, blondie? What are you doing out of the kitchen, meddling in the affairs of your betters, anyway?"

She met his eyes coolly. "I hate to burst your bubble, sonny, but I barely have an equal, let alone a better."

"Yeah?" His gaze did a slow slide over her from head to foot, lingering on her breasts. "Maybe I should take you hostage instead of the little princess here. Those lips look like they could suck the chrome off a trailer hitch."

If Zach's anger had been cold before, now it was red hot. He took the final step separating them and wrenched the shotgun from Richard with one hand while shoving his sister toward David with the other. "You're beginning to seriously piss me off, junior," he snarled and, flipping the weapon around in his grip, pointed it at the younger man. "Move over next to the bannister."

Richard didn't follow orders fast enough to suit him, and Zach gestured sharply with the shotgun. "March! You don't wanna test me right now, Ace, because trust me on this, I don't need much incentive to pump both barrels into your kneecaps."

Richard marched.

Zach didn't blink until he had Richard where he wanted him. "Lily, give me your belt, will you?"

She unfastened the narrow silk-cord-and-leather accessory and slid it off, dangling it a second later within his line of vision.

Zach traded her the shotgun for it. "This is the safety," he said, stroking this thumb over it as he passed her the weapon. "It's on, but all you have to do is push this little latch up, and it'll be ready to shoot. Blow his balls straight to hell if he so much as breathes wrong."

"Oh, believe me." She looked Richard directly in the eye. "That won't be a problem."

Zach's mouth crooked up, and he raised his eyebrows at the erstwhile extortionist, who was staring in horror at the shotgun trained on his crotch. "You're looking a little green around the gills there, Richie. I bet you're kind of regretting those crude sexual innuendos right about now, huh?" Staying out of Lily's way, he shackled Richard's hands to the ornately turned dowels connecting the bannister to the risers. Then he straightened and looked over at his sister, who was being held in a fierce embrace in Beaumont's arms. "You okay?"

"I am now." She clung to David, but brandished one of her sweet smiles at him. "Thank you, Zachariah."

"Hey." He shrugged. "You were the trouper here. And it was a group effort anyway. Everybody helped."

"Then thank you all." Her smile widening to encompass the two women, she snuggled her cheek into David's shoulder.

Zach heard car tires crunching down the drive just as Mrs. Beaumont walked out of the parlor.

"The sheriff is here," she said. She looked at her nephew, manacled to the banister with Lily's dainty little belt. "Well." She walked right up to him, and for a moment Zach thought she might slap Richard's face. But she merely looked him up and down and said in the coolest, most levelheaded tone Zach had yet to hear out of her, "You ungrateful pup. I hope you rot in jail."

Richard's lip curled. "Thanks, auntie. I guess asking you to post bail is out of the question then, huh?"

She looked as if she would hit him then. Her hand came up, and she took an incensed step forward.

But David said, "Mom," and she swung around to look at him.

"He's not worth it; don't waste your energy. Come meet Glynnis. I've been wanting to introduce my two favorite girls to each other for quite some time now."

Mrs. Beaumont turned back and looked at Richard for a long, silent instant. Then she gently patted his cheek. "He's right, dear. You aren't worth it." Ignoring the impotent fury that filled her nephew's eyes, she about-faced and walked over to the young couple.

A moment later, Zach watched Mrs. B. stroke a hand down Glynnie's dark hair and heard her coo, "Aren't you just the prettiest little thing?"

Shaking his head over her effusiveness for a young woman whose existence she'd had a hard time even re-membering a few short days ago, he went to let in the deputies.

Jessica jerked in surprise when the door to her sitting room suddenly banged open. Lifting the washcloth off her eyes, she pushed up on one elbow and peered at the bedroom door.

"Jess!"

Her heart began to bang against her ribs at the sound of Christopher's voice, and she had to steel herself against her usual melting sense of surrender when he strode into the room and crossed to the bed.

He sat on the edge of the mattress and reached out to touch her bangs. "You cut your hair." Then he shook his head, as if unable to believe he'd mentioned something so immaterial. "Lily told me you were sick."

God, he was handsome, and she wanted so much to pretend she hadn't seen what she had seen at the Olga Café. But she was through pretending; she simply could not do so any longer and still face herself in the mirror. She shifted away from his touch. "I am sick. Sick of this marriage."

"What?" He visibly paled.

"I saw you, Christopher."

"You saw me what?" He looked at her with baffled green eyes. "Where? What are you talking about?"

"Don't toy with me, okay? And don't play the innocent; it makes me want to scratch your eyes out." She shoved herself more fully upright and scooted back until her shoulders pressed against the headboard. Picking up a throw pillow, she clutched it to her roiling stomach. Then she met his gaze head on. "I saw you with that woman at the Olga Café today, after you specifically told me you'd be—"

He laughed.

Of all the reactions she might have expected, that wasn't one of them, and she felt as if something inside her had ripped away from its foundation. Tossing aside the pillow, she scrambled toward the far side of the bed. She felt as if she were bleeding to death inside, but damned if she needed to stick around and give him a front row view of the process.

Before she could slide off the other side of the mattress, however, he dove after her, catching her by the shoulder. "Jess—"

Years of being a good girl, of staying in the background and never making any waves, went up in smoke. She came completely undone and started kicking, scratching, and flailing. "Get away!"

"No." He wrestled her flat onto her back and rolled atop her to hold her down. Catching her wrists in his hands, he pinned her arms to the mattress above their heads. Then he pushed up slightly to stare down at her. "Jesus," he whispered, settling more firmly on top of her. "Jesus, Jessie."

Her breasts heaved as she tried to drag in enough breath to inflate her lungs. All the fight went out of her, and she returned his stare dully, her emotions a tangled web of loving him, hating him, and wishing herself a million miles away. "Let me go."

"I can't," he said hoarsely. "That's the one thing I just can't do."

Tears filled her eyes and silently overflowed.

"Oh, man, don't do that." Turning loose her wrists, he swiped at her cheeks with his fingers. "Please, baby, don't cry. I wasn't laughing *at* you, I swear I wasn't. I was laughing at the situation." His mouth slanted bitterly. "And you gotta admit it's kinda funny, in a twisted, dicked-up sort of way."

She just stared at him, and he insisted, "No, really, it is. This all came about in the first place because I knew you'd been unhappy for a long time, and I wanted to do something about it."

"So you thought you'd make me feel better by having

an affair with another woman?" she demanded incredulously.

"I'm not having an affair, Jessie. I'm getting a new job."

"You're—" She could feel her mouth working like a landed fish's, and snapped it shut. She shook her head in an attempt to clear it. But still all she seemed capable of doing was gaping witlessly. "What?"

"The woman you saw me with is the personnel director for a company called StarTek. Her name is Lynn Duncan." He blew out a breath. "You think I don't understand what's been going on here? Ever since I took the job with David things have gone to hell between us. I know you believe that's the reason I married you, but I'm actually damn *good* at what I do. I'm in demand, for crissake—corporations send their top headhunters after me on a regular basis." With each word he spoke, his golden eyebrows inched closer together, until they met fiercely over his nose as he glared down at her.

Then he seemed to collect himself, and his brow smoothed. "But I thought you wanted to live here with your family, so I took the job with David. I thought it would please you." He stiff-armed himself away to loom over her on braced hands. And he shook his head and sighed. "But I don't think you've been truly happy since the day we moved into this place." Rolling off her, he climbed to his feet.

For a minute all Jessica could think was, *It isn't another woman. It isn't another woman!* Then her own brow furrowed, and she turned onto her side, stuffing the throw pillow beneath her armpit as she propped her head in her hand. "Have you been any happier?"

He shrugged. "Not really, but I thought I was doing what you wanted."

Jessica's heart began to pound, with confusion, with hope. "Why didn't you ever tell me any of this before?"

"I don't know. Maybe I just hoped you'd trust me without having to explain myself to death."

"What do you mean, explain yourself to death? You've never explained yourself at all!"

"Yeah, all right, maybe I haven't." He thrust his fingers through his hair. "And that was wrong of me. But all my life women have looked at me and seen . . . my looks. I'll admit that wasn't a problem until I met you. When you seemed to see the real me, though, I discovered it's a lot more exciting being wanted for more than just my face or my studly butt."

"You can't simply take your looks out of the equation, though, Christopher. I knew within five minutes of meeting you that you were so much more than just a gorgeous guy. But the fact remains, you *are* a gorgeous guy. And I'm about as far from gorgeous as it gets. I'm just a mousy, average-looking woman."

"Are you kidding me? You're so beautiful, Jessie, both inside and out. And no one else can make me laugh the way you do. No one else makes me want to be a better man." His eyes darkened. "Besides, you've got those pretty eyes, and those legs up to here that make me so horny I can barely see straight. I fell for you like Adam from grace, and I thought we were going to live happily ever after."

But they hadn't. Somehow the ink had barely dried on the marriage certificate before everything had started falling apart. "What happened?" she asked.

He came back and joined her on the bed, stretched out facing her in a position that mirrored her own. "Remember how we used to talk to each other in our little apartment in Bellingham?"

"Of course. We never seemed to run out of things to say."

"Well, when we moved here, you quit talking to me. You quit laughing with me."

"So why did you never *say* anything? You don't seem to have any trouble telling me now. Why not before?"

"Why didn't you ever tell me *your* fears?"

Okay, looking at it from his perspective, she realized that the situation could be construed differently from the way she'd always viewed it, and she drew a deep breath. "I was afraid to," she admitted slowly. "I love you so much, but I guess I couldn't quite believe you could love me in return. I've just been waiting for you to take up with one of the gorgeous women who are always throwing themselves at you." She peered at him, a sense of wonder slowly filling her. "But you're never going to do that, are you?"

"Hell, no!" He reached out and dragged her across the small sea of bedspread separating them. Wrapping her in his arms, he held her tightly and pressed his mouth to the crown of her head. "You're the most important person in my life, and I've been trying to find a way back to you. I've been trying so fucking hard, Jess. For such a long time."

She spread her palms against his chest to absorb as much of his warmth and strength as she could. But she was desperate to hold him in return, and soon slid her hands up to wrap around his strong neck. "Why didn't you at least tell me you were looking for another job?"

"I wanted to surprise you." He gave a rueful laugh. "Don't ask me why, but it seemed like a good idea at the time."

"God, Christopher, I love you so much. And I'm such a coward for not trying harder. It's just . . . I've always felt so second-rate, and that's a hard self-image to break. First there was an entire lifetime spent trying to keep up with the Joneses, which is pretty futile when you flat out don't have the means to compete. Then, too, I've never been the life of the party, or even someone with an interesting career. And I'm certainly not pretty like Cassidy." He made a sound of disagreement and she tightened her arms around his neck. "I'm not. But you chose me anyway, and for a while I felt like a goddess. Then, when you seemed to jump at David's offer within months of the wedding, I didn't know what to think. I'm not proud that my insecurities made me suspect the worst possible explanation. And I'm even less proud that instead of confronting you with my doubts, I did what I've always done, and withdrew inside myself."

"I don't know, baby, I'd say your withdrawing days are numbered. You looked pretty kick-ass fierce a few minutes ago when you threatened to scratch my eyes out."

The corners of her lips curled up in a tiny smile. "I've felt a little more confident lately. A little less willing to please everyone—and a lot less passive."

He tucked his chin in and simply looked down at her

for a moment. "Because of Lily," he finally said, and a trace of sadness showed in the depth of his green eyes as he rearranged a tendril of her newly shorn hair against her cheek. "This is petty, but I wish I could have been responsible for some of it."

"Lily has helped me a lot. She's made me feel prettier by teaching me how to achieve a good look for me. It gives me self-assurance, Chris, because for the first time in my life I actually feel fashionable, instead of like some dowdy poor relation. And she gave me the gift of trusting in my quilting talents, too. But that's peanuts compared to knowing you love me." She tipped her head back to look him in the eye. "It's *nothing* next to learning you've been working to affect a change in our lives. That's gotta be the biggest confidence booster of all. It makes me feel invincible. In charge of my life. And I want that, Chris—I want to grab my life with both hands and shake it up a little. To be confident and unafraid to try new things."

He grinned at her. "Then that's what you'll do. And to start, what do you say to trying out this newfound confidence in San Diego?"

"Is that where the job is?"

"Where this offer came from, anyway. I've had a few interviews, but I like this company best. They seem the most ethical, and they're the only ones who didn't push when I told them bringing corporate secrets from David's company is not part of the package."

Joy bubbled up in Jessica's veins and, laughing, she pushed until Christopher rolled over on his back and she lay sprawled atop him. Stacking her hands upon his chest, she propped her chin on them and looked down at her husband. Then she gave him a dreamy smile. "San Diego sounds perfect."

⚬ɔ 21

THE SHERIFF WAS NOT HAPPY WITH MRS. BEAU-
mont when he learned she'd purposely not called him in
until matters had come to a head. But the same woman
who'd spent a great deal of time in the throes of hysteria,
Lily noted with interest, now met the lawman's condemnation with utter equanimity. Mrs. B. was apparently too
elated over David's and Glynnis's safe return to care if
the sheriff approved or not. And when he turned his ire
on Zach, she stepped right in to take full responsibility,
making it clear that she had acted contrary to Zach's
advice.

Lily watched the little drama unfold with fascination, but eventually pulled herself away to go down to
the kitchen to assemble a belated lunch. It was funny,
though, she mused, how people could rise to some occasions but completely fall apart on others.

A short while later she carried lunch to the dining
room. As she passed the parlor, she glanced in and discovered that although the sheriff had left with Richard,
others had arrived to take their place, and overall, the to-

tal number of people in the house had grown. Jessica, looking much improved, had come down with Christopher, and Zach's friends were there. Taking a quick head count, Lily unloaded her tray onto the dining room sideboard, then went back to the kitchen. It didn't take long, however, before she was headed back with additional servings. If there was one thing she was especially good at, it was making sure there was enough food to go around.

Zach must have spotted her on her second trip to the dining room, for his voice suddenly called out, "Hey, look! Soup's on! You want some help with that, lollipop?"

The entire boisterous group poured out of the parlor, and suddenly the dining room was alive with voices and laughter. Flashing her a sheepish smile, John Miglionni took the tray out of her hands. Jessica helped her set the table. Lily had barely straightened from arranging the last place setting of silverware when a big blond man with dark eyes and even darker eyebrows came over, hand-in-hand with a slender woman with glossy black hair and white skin. He introduced the two of them as Cooper and Veronica Blackstock, then gave her a thorough appraisal. His brown eyes were fiercely intelligent; the first words out of his mouth were not.

"*Hoo*-ahh," he breathed. "And you can *cook*, too?"

"Hey, that's exactly what I said the first time I saw her." John came up to join them. "The first part, anyway. I didn't know about the cooking." He grinned down at Lily. "It's a Marine thing," he explained. "A *complimentary* Marine thing."

Overwhelmed by the sudden wash of testosterone,

Lily blinked at the two men, and Veronica nudged her husband. "Once you've rolled your tongue back into your mouth, isn't there something else you'd like to say to Lily?"

"Huh?"

"Like how *sorry* you were to make her drag Zach out of bed this morning?"

He stared at her as if she were nuts. "Why would I say that? There was *planning* to be done, Ronnie, and Zach would've been one unhappy little buckaroo if I'd let him sleep through it just because of a minor bump on the head." He turned to his friend, who was approaching with a filched bread stick clenched like a Havana cigar between his grinning teeth. "Wouldn't you, buddy?"

"Hell, yeah."

"And let me guess," Lily said dryly. "That's a Marine thing, too."

"*Hoo*-ahh," Ronnie murmured, and the two women laughed.

Coop looked from them to his friends. "Women," he said, shaking his head.

Rocket gave a sage nod. "They're a mystery."

"Ain't it the truth?" Wrapping his arm around Lily's shoulders, Zach tucked her next to his side while he pulled her chair out from the table. He nodded at his friends over her head as he seated her. "There's just no understanding them."

All during lunch Zach teased Glynnis. He exchanged humorous insults with his Marine buddies, and was charming to all the women. And he laughed. He laughed so much it made everyone else at the table laugh, too, just from the sheer joyful sound of it.

Lily could barely keep her eyes off of him. She had never seen him like this. She had honestly believed she understood the depths of his distress over Glynnis's kidnapping, but what she'd seen must have been the proverbial tip of the iceberg, because this man at the table, this exuberant, head thrown back, happy-with-the-world man, was a whole new Zachariah.

A Zachariah who enthralled her.

And not only her, she discovered. After lunch, as she was clearing the table, Cassidy moved in and started flirting like crazy.

To Lily's disgust, Zach didn't seem to mind at all. Far from discouraging her, in fact, he laughed and flirted right back. Gritting her teeth and harboring hot thoughts about snatching a certain brunette baldheaded, she hefted her tray and headed for the door, suddenly feeling every bit the scullery maid Richard had labeled her. She pitied herself more with every step she took. Heck, even Jessica appeared to have deserted her this afternoon. Lily had caught a glimpse of her and Christopher heading up the stairs as if there were a four-alarm fire and they knew where the only extinguisher was kept. Feeling abandoned, she used her hip to ease open the dining room door.

"Here. Let me give you a hand with that."

Lily craned her head around to peer at Veronica as the slender brunette reached over her shoulder to hold open the door. "Thanks."

"You want me to grab the other tray over there?"

"Oh, please. That would be great."

Veronica followed her down the hall to the kitchen. "That was a fabulous meal."

Her mood lifting, Lily shot the other woman a smile. "I'm glad you enjoyed it. I just sort of threw it together, though, so I'm afraid it wasn't anything special."

"If that's the case, then I'd sure love to taste 'special,' because I thought it was fantastic." She set her tray on the counter and unloaded it with efficient competence. Pausing with the vinaigrette cruet in one hand, she looked over at Lily, who was loading the dishwasher. "Zach says you're a chef for a corporate yacht. That must be exciting."

"It's usually pretty fun," Lily agreed. "And on occasion it's a pain in the rear—depending on the guests, and to a lesser degree, the weather."

Veronica nodded. "Working with the public can be hard."

"Yeah. They can definitely make or break your day. And since the groups we take out tend to be mostly men, being the only woman aboard can occasionally be awkward."

"You get hit on?"

"Not by the crew. There's just three of us: the captain, first mate, and me—and Jack and Ben have never been anything but professional. But every now and again I have an incident with a guest. For the most part everyone is pretty cool—they usually take no for an answer with good grace. Only once did it turn into a real problem. Now, *that* was one of the not-so-fun trips."

"So, aside from the obvious of being on a boat, how does a yacht chef differ from being a chef for a restaurant?"

"It's much more intimate." Fitting the last glass in the top rack, she added detergent, closed the dishwasher door, and turned it on. As the machine began its gentle churning, she turned to lean a hip against the counter and gave her complete attention to Veronica. "In a restaurant patrons are there for maybe three hours, and only rarely does the chef come out to meet them. On the boat, we're thrown together for anywhere from three days to a week. And I'm a jack-of-all-trades there. In a restaurant, I'd have a kitchen crew and a wait staff, but the *Argosy*'s galley is minuscule and sleeping space is limited, so except for rare occasions I take care of everything myself. I plan menus and lay in supplies. Then I prep, cook, serve, and clean up." She waved a dismissive hand. "But enough about me. What do you do?"

Veronica had barely begun telling her when Coop poked his head in the door. "There you are," he said, gazing at his wife with a soft expression. Pulling his gaze away, he looked over at Lily. "Do you mind if I borrow her for a while? Glynnis is asking to spend a little time with her. She wants to get to know her better before we have to shove off." He shot her a cocky smile. "I think she wants to make sure Ronnie's good enough for me."

"Oh, by all means, then." Lily smiled at Veronica. "Thank you for your help."

"Thank *you* for the lunch."

"Yeah, it was great," Coop added. "Ronnie tells me my earlier compliment was—how did you put it, sweetpea?—'heavy-handed, chauvinistic pap'? So I take back the 'looking like you do' part. But you're still a killer cook."

She glanced at Veronica, and they both laughed.

Coop shrugged good-naturedly. "Still didn't get it right, huh?"

"Close enough," Lily said. "And thank you. I appreciate the sentiment. I just wish you guys were going to be around long enough for me to make you a meal truly worthy of these nice compliments."

Coop's dark eyebrows rose toward his blond hairline. "Tell you what. You get Midnight to bring you by our place on your way back to California, and we'll take you up on that. We'll supply the ingredients if you'll do the cooking."

"Deal." But when Lily thought about it after Coop and Veronica left, it plunged her back into a case of the poor-pitiful-me's. Zach was out flirting with Cassidy in the other room while she did the Cinderella-sans-the-prince thing here in the kitchen. What did that say about him wanting the kind of relationship with her that included spur of the moment side trips to visit his friends?

Not much.

She was taking her frustration out on a messy pan with a scrubby and a lot of elbow grease when two strong arms suddenly slid around her waist and a warm mouth pressed a kiss into the contour of her neck. With a startled squeak, she jumped.

"Hey, there," Zach murmured, bending his knees and snuggling up behind her. "You almost finished with KP duty?"

"What do you care?" She hunched her shoulder, dislodging his lips from the susceptible spot in her neck. "The last time I looked, you seemed pretty darn pleased to be otherwise occupied."

He stilled, and for a moment she thought he was going to withdraw. But before she could decide whether she would welcome or regret a retreat, a soft sigh escaped him and he rested his chin on her shoulder. "You're talking about Cassidy, right? Look, I'm, uh, sorry about that. I got the impression today that maybe she's not as bad as she'd like us to believe, and I was feeling my Wheaties, so when she started to flirt I just kinda went with the flow. *C'mon.*" Tightening his arms around her, he wiggled his pelvis against her bottom. "Don't be mad at me, okay? I'm feeling too good."

And because she'd seen that glimmer of humanity in Cassidy herself, and considering how enamored she was with this playful side of Zach, she relaxed her tense shoulders. "Hmm." She leaned back against him. "You *do* feel good."

He made a contented sound and went back to nuzzling her neck. "You always smell so fine," he murmured, kissing his way up the side of her throat. "Like lemon cookies, or something. It makes me wanna just eat you up."

She dropped the scrubby into the pan and reached for a towel to dry her hands. While she was occupied, he removed the belt that had been returned to her when Richard was released into the sheriff's custody, sliding it off and dropping it to the floor. Then his hands stole up over her ribs beneath her sweater. A second later warm fingers cupped her breasts.

"Oh!" She dropped the towel, and reaching up and back, curled her hands around the back of his neck, an action that pressed her breasts more firmly into his hard-skinned hands.

He sucked in air. "What color bra are you wearing today?" His voice was a husky rasp. "You always have the greatest underwear."

"Pink. Or maybe bronze. Lord, I don't remember." Reluctantly breaking contact, she turned in his arms. "We could check it out." And her hands went to the hem of her top.

Zach's own hands itched as he watched the soft material inch its way up, exposing first Lily's smooth-skinned, tiny waist, then the rounded undersides of her breasts, covered in some cobweb fine, sheer material. "Blue," he said huskily. "With green thready stuff."

"Embroidery." Which disappeared from view when she promptly dropped the top.

"Hey," he protested. "That's what's known as negative progress."

"It's all the progress you're going to see, though, buddy. Because if you think I'm taking my clothes off in the middle of the kitchen, you're deluded."

He looked around him. "Oh. Yeah. Good point." He bent to kiss her again, and was pleased to see the heavy-lidded arousal back in her eyes when he lifted his head to gaze down at her. Using his index finger, he rubbed the small slick of moisture left behind into her soft lower lip. "Wanna come upstairs with me?"

Still heavy-eyed, she gave him a sleepy smile and nodded.

Weaving their fingers together, he stepped back. For a second, he got caught up in the sight of her hand in his. It was all but swallowed within his grasp, and he found it amazing that so much competency could come out of something so delicate. Then he tightened his grip and headed for the door with her firmly in tow.

Before they could make their escape, though, the door banged open and Glynnis danced in. She stumbled to a halt a few feet away and eyed them speculatively for a couple of heartbeats. Her gaze dropped to their joined hands.

Zach fought a guilty urge to pull his free. Dammit, he was allowed a lov—that is, a sex life without accounting to his sister. He gave her a level look, quirking his eyebrows questioningly.

Her curled lips reminded him of a cat with a canary, but she didn't say a word about Lily's hand in his, nor did she ask any questions. Instead she met his gaze. "Coop and Ronnie and Rocket are getting ready to leave. You'd better come say good-bye."

He'd rather go upstairs with Lily, but all in all he felt too great to bitch about the interruption of something he should've known better than to start in the first place. Trying to sneak off in a house full of people—a good portion of whom were his friends—hadn't been his brightest move. Besides. He grinned down at Lily. It wasn't as if he were going to miss out altogether. He was simply putting off celebrating in his favorite manner until later.

Dropping Lily's hand but bidding her to come with them, he followed his sister back into the foyer, where he found his friends standing by the front door talking to David. The group turned at their approach, and Coop flashed Glynnie a smile.

"You found him, I see."

"I did, but he's not acting like himself, Coop. After lunch I saw him flirting with David's cousin. Then just now, I found him in the kitchen holding hands with Lily." Looking up at Zach, she shook her head. "I don't think I've ever seen you flirt with *one* woman, let alone two. And for a guy who's a Mr. Grumpy Pants half the time, you're frighteningly cheerful today."

"Yeah, Zach," John agreed. "You've gotta do something about this good mood you're in. You're scaring us."

Amid the laughter, Ronnie protested, "Hey, that's not fair. Zach has never been anything but easygoing with me."

"You tell 'em, sweetheart," Zach said, and adopted a look of injured innocence. "Why, I'm known far and wide for my cheerful disposition. Just ask Lily."

"You get to call him *Mister* Grumpy Pants?" Lily demanded of his sister. "Wow. That must be because you're related. He made me call him Master Sergeant Grumpy Pants."

"Hey!"

"But, come on, Glynnis," she continued as she nimbly dodged the fingertips he flicked at her butt. "Let's give credit where it's due here. If you find his behavior unusual today, you're the one who's gotta suck it up and be accountable. Because having you home safe and sound is what's got him—how did you put it a while ago, Zach? Feeling your oats?"

"My Wheaties."

"Yes, that was it, feeling your Wheaties." She flashed him a smile so brilliant it nearly stopped his heart in his chest. Then she turned back to his sister. "He's beside himself with happiness to have you back."

"I know." And grinning, Glynnis launched herself into his arms and danced them around the foyer. Stopping, she tilted her head back to meet his gaze and crowed, "I've got the power!"

She did, but he rolled his eyes in mock disgust.

"Power, schmower," he said. Waltzing her several steps up the foyer, he stopped abruptly and dipped her with theatrical drama. Then he snapped her back up against his chest, whirled her out in a fast spin that landed her in front of David, and turned her loose. "She's all yours, pal."

"Thanks." David tucked her under his arm. "I'll take her." The couple exchanged moon-faced-in-love smiles.

Shoving his hands in his pockets, Zach strolled over to his friends. "You just got here. Are you sure you have to leave so soon?"

Veronica nodded. "I promised my niece Lizzy I'd make her costume for her part in the spring program at school, and I only had it half done when we left."

"We could only get a single night at the B&B, anyway," Coop added. "And vacancies here on the weekends aren't exactly thick on the ground."

"There's a decent state park."

Coop snorted. "Ronnie's idea of roughing it is a hotel with no room service. There's no way in hell I could get her to camp out."

Lily beamed approvingly. "I knew there was a reason I liked you, Veronica. Why anyone would want to sleep in the dirt and do all the chores you do at home with none of the amenities is beyond me." She offered her hand. "It was so nice meeting you. I'm only sorry we didn't have more time to get to know each other."

"I told you," Coop said. "You come spend some time with us on your way home."

She shook hands all around, then touched Zach's forearm. "I'll let you say good-bye to your friends." But she gave them a final, friendly smile. "Have a safe trip."

Zach turned back from watching the swing of her hips as she walked away and found Coop regarding him.

"Hang on to that one," his friend advised.

He stared at Ice in surprise. "Whoa, buddy, you've got things all wrong. We're not—"

"I'm telling you, Zach. This one's got 'keeper material' stamped all over her."

"But, hey," John interjected cheerfully, "if you don't want her, just say the word. I'd be happy to take her off your hands."

His head snapped up. "Over my dead body, pal."

His friends laughed as if that settled it, and Zach just shrugged, unwilling to wreck his mellow mood with an argument.

But late that night, when he was hot and randy and seconds from making love to Lily, he gave his friend's assumptions a moment's consideration.

And wondered if there wasn't something to it.

He was shaking a condom out of the box she'd bought him when he noticed the rubber's dimensions written on the side. "What's this?" he demanded in mock indignation as he ripped open the foil packet. Rolling onto his side, he propped his head in his hand to stare down at her. "No Magnum extra large?"

She rolled her eyes. "Please. Do you realize the average condom has a stretching capacity of something like three liters? I read that somewhere." Taking the condom out of his hand, she pushed him over on his back, then bent to unroll it down his length until her capable fingers had him snugly protected. She held him in a firm, two-handed grip and pressed a kiss on the reservoir tip, then glanced up at him with small smile. "So unless you're Elephant Eddie and His Amazing Appendage, sizing is mostly a marketing ploy."

He'd never known a woman who could make him laugh even as she made the blood in his veins run hot enough to scorch from pure, unadulterated lust. And as he watched her swing a leg over his hips and felt her slowly lower herself down, down, *ah, sweet Jesus*, down on him, until his raging hard-on was seated deep inside of her hot, tight depths, he had to admit that Cooper had a point.

She did have "keeper" written all over her.

🔗 22

ZACH GAZED BLURRILY AT THE FLASHES OF *lightning outside the airplane window. His eyes felt gritty with fatigue, while his body ached from sitting. Glynnie slumped astride his lap, her arms limp at her sides and her head heavy on his chest. Every now and then a tiny snore rumbled out of her throat. She stank to high heaven, but since he wasn't about to risk waking her up to change her diaper he ignored it. They'd been traveling for thirty-four hours straight, with five stops and four plane changes, and she'd been awake and increasingly cranky for most of them. She'd howled nonstop during the layover in Atlanta, and by the time she'd finally dozed off on this last leg of the journey he'd been pretty tempted to put his head down and do some serious bawling himself.*

But he'd been charged with being a man and taking care of his sister, so he'd fought back the urge. Now, momentarily free of the need to be constantly vigilant, the desire to give in to his emotions suddenly roared back with a vengeance. Gritting his teeth, he blinked rapidly and stared out into the storm buffeting the plane.

Yet he couldn't seem to turn off his mind. Or stop wondering what was so wrong with him that his own parents didn't want him. In every village they'd lived in over the years, he'd seen evidence of the affection the various tribes held for their children. It was in the elders' voices and in their eyes. It was in even the most casual of their touches. Why didn't his parents ever tousle his hair as they walked by? Why had Father never swung him up onto his back? Or Mother rarely hugged him to her side?

Resting his cheek against the porthole glass, he decided that there must be something wrong with him. And now here he was, being shipped to the total strangers that were his grandparents, to another continent where he wouldn't even have the survival skills he'd had on the veldt.

But he'd learn. He straightened in his seat. He wouldn't rest until he knew this strange new place as well as he knew the high plains of Africa. Staring out into the storm, he clenched his jaw tight and vowed that while he couldn't control the actions of others or the way they viewed him, he did have power over two things. He could and would watch over Glynnie until he was certain she'd be all right. And he could take care of himself. As for his grandparents—well, the hell with them. He was done worrying whether they'd like him or not. From this moment on, he was through caring how anyone felt about him, through craving the things he couldn't have—like love.

Screw it. He didn't need anybody.

* * *

Zach came awake with a start, frowning as he stared at the shadowy outlines of the furniture across the room. *Shit.* What *was* it with all this dreaming lately? He flipped over in irritation, only to bump up against Lily's lushly rounded butt. She murmured a protest, but promptly wiggled close to spoon her back against his front, and he wrapped an arm around her waist. Burying his face in her hair, he breathed in her scent.

It was strangely soothing—if you were into that sort of thing, which he wasn't. It never paid to get too involved, and clearly this sudden spate of dreams was a wake-up call, a reminder of the hollowness he'd felt for too many years as a youth. They were a warning that he could easily feel that way again if he let things get out of hand with the curvy little blonde nestled against him.

The dread of losing his sister had forged a quick intimacy with Lily similar to what he'd experienced as a soldier in combat situations. Now that Glynnis's kidnapping had turned out to be a false alarm, he felt almost giddy with relief. But that didn't mean he should jump into a more serious involvement with Lily. She was every bit the keeper Coop had called her. Zach just wouldn't be the one keeping her. She deserved better than to be short-changed that way. Love, at least of the romantic variety, had never been part of his makeup.

The only bonds he'd ever had that lasted beyond a week or two were with Glynnie and the Corp. And face it, except for Coop and John, even his brothers in arms had come and gone in his life. He simply didn't possess the stuff tight relationships were made of.

But when Lily uttered a little hum of contentment in her sleep, Zach's arm automatically tightened around her waist and he snugged her a little closer. He blew out an impatient breath. Aw, hell. Why was he inventing problems where none existed?

So he didn't have a knack for relationships. Big deal—not all things were intended for all people. But that didn't mean he wasn't entitled to a little fling. He and Lily were adults; they knew the score. The two of them shared an eyes-wide-open, you-scratch-my-itch-and-I'll-scratch-yours type of arrangement. The fact it wasn't permanent was tacitly understood.

That wasn't to say he didn't care about her, though. Because he did—to his amazement, he realized he cared quite a bit. Somehow, of all the crazy, unlikely things, they'd ended up friends. But that's all they were, a couple of good friends looking to have a little fun while they could.

Having settled that to his satisfaction, he wrapped himself more tightly around Lily and sighed with the contentment of having her in his arms. Then, letting go of everything else, he allowed sleep to suck him back into its depths.

Things would work out fine, he thought hazily just before he drifted off. The only way matters could possibly get screwed up between them was if one of them were to go and do something stupid like fall in love.

And *that* wasn't likely to happen. He wouldn't let it. Should their relationship ever show signs of getting too serious, he'd do what was best for both of them and cut it off. And hell, chances were, if he wasn't quick enough to do it himself, Lily would do it for him.

Because if there was one thing he could count on, it was that practical, levelheaded Lily would never go all foolish and romantic on him.

23

LEVELHEADED WAS THE LAST THING LILY FELT the next evening as she followed the Compass Room host across Rosario Resort's most elegant dining room. She couldn't seem to stop smiling, and when she glanced over her shoulder and caught Zach eyeing the swing of her hips, she grinned even wider. She flashed him an *I saw that* wag of her eyebrows when his gaze lifted to meet hers, then quickly composed her features as the host stopped at a window table overlooking the bay and pulled out a chair. She thanked him as he seated her, then dismissed him from her mind in almost the same breath and leaned toward her date as he took his own seat across the linen-draped table.

Her *date*. She rolled the word around in her mind, jazzed right down to her pointy-toed, stiletto-heeled shoes that Zach had gone to the trouble of arranging this evening for them. She pushed aside the charger and plate in front of her and leaned toward him. Ordinarily, she'd be all agog to check out every aspect of the restaurant from its artfully folded linen napkins to the way the

traffic flowed throughout the room. But tonight her professional goals weren't foremost on her mind, and she
gazed at Zach's smooth-shaven countenance. "This,"
she sighed happily, "is so nice."

"Yeah, Jessica was sure you'd like it."

"Oh, well, yes. The restaurant, too." She planted her
chin in her palm and her elbow on the table, and gazed
dreamily past the small vase of fresh yellow rosebuds at
the man sitting so straight and tall across the table. "But
I meant this." She indicated the two of them. "You and
me—having an honest-to-gosh date. We've sort of gone
about this relationship backwards."

A look of what in any other guy she might have
termed alarm flashed across his face. But his expression
just as quickly cleared, and since he was hardly the type
to panic regardless of the cause—let alone show it—she
decided it must have been a trick of light from the tiny
lamp next to the roses. A deduction that seemed validated by the easy shrug he gave her.

"You've been cooking up a storm and handling all
the KP since we got here." He flashed her a smile that
was all gleaming white teeth. "And with the missing-
link Ernestine back in the kitchen now that Darling
David's been restored to the throne, I thought it was
time to give you a break. You've waited on everyone
else. Let someone wait on you for a change."

So it wasn't poetry. She didn't care. It was the kind of
autocratic-protective thing he usually reserved for
Glynnis, his *I-take-care-of-what's-mine* attitude, and
she gave him a crooked smile. "Works for me."

He sprawled back in his chair and gazed at her, his
eyes roaming to the hint of cleavage that showed above

her scooped neckline before raising to meet her own. He gave her a lazy, carnal smile, and when she felt his big feet encroaching on her territory under the table, she deftly unbuckled the ankle strap on her right shoe, slipped the pump off, and ran her toe up beneath the cuff of his slacks. Stroking him from ankle to shin, she enjoyed seeing his eyes darken, and continued to tease him even after the waitress arrived with the menus. The minute the young woman had taken their drink order and left, Zach leaned forward.

"You're playing with fire there, honey chile."

"Um-hmm." She stropped her toe up and down, up and down. "Don'tcha just love fires? They make a person feel so nice and"—she dropped her voice to a breathy murmur—"hot."

"Keep it up and I'll show you hot." His voice was a deep rasp that licked its way down her spine. "Right here on the table, in front of all these fine folk."

She made a moue but slid her foot out from under his pant leg and worked it back into her shoe. "Party pooper."

"Hey, I'm just trying to spare the other diners' sensibilities."

"Yeah, right." A laugh purled out of her throat. "I could tell that by your proposed demonstration on the tabletop."

"Honey, I've got a pole tenting the front of my trousers large enough to support a Big Top. The fire alarm goes off because of all this heat you're generating, and I'm going to give that blue-haired lady over there a heart attack."

Lily grinned. "Maybe. But it'd be from sheer envy."

The waitress returned with Zach's beer and her Chardonnay and offered to take their orders. Flushed by the sheer amount of raw sexuality she'd sparked, Lily hurriedly picked up her menu and made her selection. When the young woman departed, she made a conscious effort to dial back the tension by turning the conversation to less inflammatory matters.

Zach gave her a knowing smile, but fell in with the subject change. Over salads he challenged her to describe her ideal restaurant. Absorbed in trying to relate all her ideas, it wasn't until a seaplane's arrival in the harbor made hearing momentarily difficult that she realized she'd dominated the conversation throughout most of the meal. As the plane cut back its engines and taxied to the dock, she waved her fork and gave Zach a crooked smile.

"My, how I do go on. So now it's my turn to eat and your turn to talk. You said you're on leave." She sliced off a bite of salmon and studied him across the table. "What happens when you go back? Are you immediately off on an exotic new adventure?"

For just a second he stilled. Then his shoulders shifted in the faintest of shrugs. "Funny you should ask. I've been trying to decide that very thing."

"Whether or not you'll be sent on another mission?"

"No, what happens to my career when I go back." He pushed his plate away and leaned toward her. "You see, I've got two years left in the service, and I always thought I'd spend them the same way I spent the first eighteen. But lately a couple of my COs have been agitating for me to give up field work."

She studied him for a moment. "I'm guessing that

doesn't sit too well with you. Do you love it that much?"

"Yes!" Then he frowned. "Well, no—not really. I mean, it's a lot more exhausting and not as much fun as it used to be. But it's what I know—and what I'm good at it. And it's not frigging *teaching.*"

He sounded so affronted by the idea, she had to grab her chair to keep from climbing straight over the table to give him a great big hug. "Is that what they're suggesting you do instead?" At his terse nod, she loosened her grip on the seat in order to reach across the space separating them, touching gentle fingertips to the big hand fisted around his napkin. "This is not something you care to do, I gather."

"Are you kidding, Lily? Can you honestly see me as anyone's instructor?"

"Well . . . yes. Actually, I can." When he stared at her as if she were certifiable, she stroked the white knuckles beneath her fingers. "Zach, isn't that already part of what you do now? I mean, I know it's much more seat-of-the-pants and dangerous than any classroom situation could ever be. But you said your men are mostly in their late teens and early twenties—I would think dealing with that age group day in and day out must be an ongoing teaching process. I can't honestly envision you lecturing from behind a podium. But if you're talking about teaching practical application of the things they've learned in a class in more reality-based settings, then I can definitely see you doing that."

He looked startled. But he also looked thoughtful, and to her satisfaction his knuckles stopped displaying so much bone as his fingers relaxed beneath her hand.

He sat back in his chair and simply stared at her for a moment. Then he turned his hand beneath hers and enfolded her fingers in his warm grasp. Looking down, he seemed fascinated by the sight of his thumb smoothing over the back of her hand. "I think you're the one who'd make a good teacher," he said to the skin beneath his rough-tipped fingers. "I don't think it's escaped anyone's attention the way you transformed Jessica."

It was Lily's turn to be startled. "Oh, no. Really. I mean, we talked, of course, but Jess did all the work herself."

"Thanks to some major guidance and motivation from you." His pale, charcoal-rimmed eyes rose to pin her in place. "I don't think I've ever met anyone as patient or nice as you are."

"Oh. Oh, Zach." Her insides melted. She'd known since first realizing the depth of her feelings for him that sooner or later she'd slip and give them away. But she had always suspected it would be the mind-frying sex they shared that would undermine her defenses. Never once had she dreamed that hearing him call her *nice* while they were both fully clothed might be the agent to bring all her walls tumbling down. Yet her entire body yearned toward him as she felt every safeguard she'd ever placed on her heart crumble to dust. She squeezed the fingers wrapped around hers. "Oh, gawd, Zach. I am *so* in love with you."

His entire body stilled. "Yeah?" The tilt of his mouth looked pleasantly amused, but his eyes were suddenly guarded. "Well, if a little compliment like *that* floats your boat, I can hardly wait to see what kind of reaction dessert gets." His hand slid out from under hers, and he leaned back in his chair. Way back.

For about two seconds she was tempted to just let it go. She knew that's what he wanted—to pretend the elephant hadn't entered the room with them. But when she looked from her now-empty hand curled limply in the middle of the linen tablecloth to the man leaning as far away from her as he could get and still remain at the same table, she felt something cool trickle through the warm fuzzies she'd been immersed in all evening. And she knew she couldn't let it go—not after having just bared her soul. "Okay," she said slowly. "Not exactly the reaction I'd hoped for."

For a moment he looked downright panicked, but then he straightened, his face wiped free of all emotion. "What do you want me to say, Lily—that I love you, too; let's start looking for a rose-covered cottage?"

She kept her expression every bit as neutral as his while the cool trickle turned to an icy torrent. "Yes. I can't think of anything I'd rather hear."

"I'm sorry, but I can't. I don't do love."

Oh *boy,* did she disagree, but she merely said, "You do a first-class imitation of it, then."

"It's a pipedream, Lily—a concept invented by greeting card companies. There's lust, and like, and excitement, and that's no doubt what you feel too." Crossing his arms over his chest, he gave her an authoritative look. "Trust me. You're not in love with me."

Unfortunately, she was. But she didn't particularly like him right this minute. "And what makes you such an authority on how I feel?"

"Common sense." His arms dropped away from his chest and he leaned forward earnestly. "Look, you and I are really . . . compatible . . . in some ways. But in the long run we're interested in different things."

"That's funny, because despite the obvious differences between us, I could have sworn we had more in common than not. So what is it that interests me that scares you so much?"

"Opening the restaurant you've been saving a lifetime to buy, for starters. And it doesn't *scare* me. I'm just pointing out that you're ready to settle down in one place—and I'm in an occupation that has me constantly on the move."

"Yes, for two more years. That's nothing compared to how long I've already waited." But nausea roiled in her stomach at the look on his face. "I can see, though, that the last thing you want to hear is that I'm willing to postpone opening my place until you're out of the service." A chill raised the flesh on her arms and she rubbed her hands up and down them. "Gawd, this is almost funny. Not that long ago, I would have thought following a soldier around the country was the last thing I'd be willing to do too. But then I went and fell in love with you. I think we could have a phenomenal future together. You obviously don't feel the same." He didn't deny it, and she died just a little. "You said we're really compatible in some ways. You want to define what those are?"

He merely looked at her and the sickness increased. "*Sexually*? That's all I mean to you? Someone to fuck?"

He jerked. "Jesus, Lily. Don't talk like that."

A crack of bitter laughter escaped her. "Oh. That's

beautiful. You virtually tell me it's all you want from me, but I shouldn't *say* the word?"

"That's not what I meant. I've just never heard you swear." He shook his head impatiently. "But that's not important. You're *not* just someone to fuck—we're friends, you and I."

"But only as long as we're in the sack, apparently. Or—what? Were you thinking that when you've had your fill of me sexually, we oughtta get together every now and then for a beer?" Her voice wobbled embarrassingly on the last word and, feeling tears rising perilously near the surface, she shoved back from the table and snatched up her purse. "Excuse me. I've got to use the restroom."

He was hot on her heels when she pushed open the door of the ladies' room a moment later, but she turned with her hand on the knob to stare up at him. "Do you mind?" she asked. "If you're truly my *friend*, you'll give me a moment of privacy."

Dark brows gathering like thunderclouds over his nose, he stared down at her as if he had X-ray vision that would get to the truth of her emotions. But she refused him access to her thoughts, and with a sound of frustration he turned on his heel and stalked back to the hotel dining room.

She rushed to the restroom sink. Her dinner stayed down, but barely, and every time she thought of the way he'd said they were friends when he obviously believed their only real compatibility was in bed, the gorge rose anew. Standing with her hands braced on the countertop, and her head hanging low, she drew deep, steadying breaths and fought it down.

Finally, she raised her head and looked at her reflection in the mirror. When they'd arrived here this evening, she'd felt treasured and pretty. Now she thought she looked like a woman men only wanted for one thing, and she turned away from the sight. How on earth had she gone from Princess of the Night to Queen Slut in the space of so few heartbeats?

When she felt her composure was about as good as it was going to get, she walked out of the restroom and looked toward the dining room. Then she turned in the opposite direction and headed for the resort's front door.

The air was soft when she stepped outside and, had she not been wearing shoes so impractical as to make the notion laughable, she might have been tempted simply to start walking back to the Beaumonts'. Alternately, she wished for a moment, as she stared out over the parking lot, that her skills ran to hot-wiring cars. It would serve Zach right if she took the Jeep and left him high and dry.

But, no. Vindictiveness was all very warming to contemplate, but more often than not it only ended up biting the butt of the person who harbored it. Besides, running away was immature and ultimately wouldn't solve a darn thing. So she'd take a loop or two around the hotel to get her emotions in check. Then she might as well resign herself to heading back inside to face Zach like an adult.

Sometimes, though, being a grown-up bit.

She picked her way down the steps and once on the walkway, headed for the point side of the venerable old resort grounds. Tears kept rising to blur her vision, and between those, her skyscraper heels, and the occasional pine cone out to trip her, she had to be extra vigilant about where she placed her feet. The sun had gone below the trees, and as she rounded a curve, the twilit path became a stretch of deep shadow. She paused for a second to let her eyes adjust.

When she heard footsteps behind her, her first thought was that it must be Zach. Before she could decide whether she hoped for or feared the possibility, however, someone grabbed her by the arm, and she didn't need to see the person's face to know it wasn't him. Instinctively, she tried to pull away, but she stilled when something hard was jammed into the small of her back.

"I have a gun," a masculine voice said in her ear. "Make one peep, and I'll shoot you where you stand."

Well, that went just fucking swell. Zach sat rigidly upright in his chair, draining his beer, then reached for his coffee and knocked that back too while he waited for Lily to return. *Hard to believe you're actually supposed to be pretty good at negotiating your way out of tough situations.* The dinner he'd just consumed sat like gravel in his stomach.

His only excuse was that Lily had caught him off guard. But who the hell could have predicted she'd fancy herself in love with him? Or that she'd look so betrayed when he'd insisted she wasn't?

Who could have predicted that hearing him say they were friends would make her look as if she were about to throw up? Jesus. He found himself feeling pretty hollow-stomached himself.

His back grew even stiffer. Dammit, he would not feel guilty. He could have handled the situation much better, plainly, but he'd rectify the damage as soon as she came back. He'd make it clear it wasn't her—that he was the one destined to fail at the relationship game. No matter whose fault it was, though, the fact remained that ultimately it would never work, and it was better to clear up these misunderstandings from the start. It might not make either of them happy, but it sure as hell beat the complete mess matters would be in if he allowed them—*her*—to get in too deep.

What the Sam Hill was taking her so long, anyway? He wanted to go get her so he could begin making her understand it wasn't really love she was feeling. But he remained obstinately in his chair, refusing to chase after her. He'd done that already—damned if he planned to do so again.

When she still hadn't returned fifteen minutes later, however, he conceded that her stubbornness far out-shone his own tonight. He paid the bill and went in search of her.

It took another fifteen minutes to figure out she'd left. He sent a waitress into the ladies' room and searched the resort's public rooms himself. The bell captain remembered seeing Lily go outside, and Zach went over the grounds with methodical precision. Finally, furious, he headed for his Jeep. Clearly she had called Jessica to come pick her up. Of all the childish, vindictive, *bitchy* little stunts . . .

The first person he saw when he slammed through the front door of the Beaumont mansion a short while later was Jessica, who was descending the staircase.

"Well, hey there," she said with a smile. "How was din—"

"Where the hell is she?"

"Where is who?" Jessica's befuddlement was obvious, but even as it registered, Zach watched it segue into irritation. She loped down the last steps and strode straight up to him. Hands on her hips, she drew herself to her loftiest posture and thrust her narrow nose up at him. "What do you mean, where is she?" she demanded. "She was supposed to be with you."

"She was, but we had a . . . disagreement . . . and she took off. I figured she called you to come pick her up."

She stepped back. "Well, you figured wrong. And how dare you wreck her big night out, anyhow?"

A guilty sense of having done exactly that made him testy. "What the hell makes you assume it was something *I* did? Maybe she wrecked *my* big night out."

She just looked at him, and he rolled his shoulders uneasily. "Okay, I didn't handle something she told me very well." Then he snapped erect. "But that's no excuse to run away like some irresponsible little teenybopper, and if you didn't pick her up, then someone else must have. I want to talk to everyone."

Jessica shrugged. "Knock yourself out." She started to turn away, but then hesitated, a vestige of unease coloring her expression when she turned back to him. "Lily isn't exactly the irresponsible type."

"I know. But she was pretty upset." He heard Jessica mutter something beneath her breath, but since he was pretty sure he didn't want to know what it was, he ignored it and headed for the house phone in the parlor.

When he hung up several minutes later, he, too, was beginning to feel uneasy. Everyone was accounted for and no one would even admit to having spoken to Lily, let alone to having collected her from the resort. Jessica had followed him into the parlor, and he vaguely registered the weight of her stare as he pulled out a telephone book and flipped through its pages. Finding the number he sought, he punched it out on the telephone keypad. A moment later he was connected to Rosario's bell captain.

"My name is Zachariah Taylor," he said crisply as soon as the other man identified himself. "I talked to you earlier about—"

"The pretty blonde," the bell captain said. "I remember."

"Yeah, well, the pretty blonde didn't come home with me. I thought at the time she must have called someone else for a ride, but nobody here has heard from her, either. You told me you saw her go outside. Did she by any chance ask you to call a cab for her first?"

"No, sir. She came out of the ladies' room and went straight outside. It's possible she called one herself from a cell phone, though. We got busy about then, so I couldn't say whether or not a taxi actually arrived during that time."

Zach thanked him for his cooperation and slowly replaced the receiver. He looked at Jessica. "I don't like this," he admitted. "The resort didn't call her a cab and it's not like she could have called one for herself, since she doesn't have a cell phone."

Jessica made a skeptical sound. "*Everyone* has a cell phone."

"Except Lily and me, apparently. It's one of the things we talked about at dinner—how we seem to be the last two techno-dinosaurs on earth." Then out of the blue, he got a flash of the call he'd been in the midst of making to Camp Pendleton regarding a certain South American when his sister and David had shown up. Swearing, he took off for the stairs at a dead run.

"What?" Jessica was right behind him. "What have you thought of?"

He didn't slow down as his longer stride outstripped hers, but he said over his shoulder, "Call the cab company, Jess, just to be sure. I'll be back in a minute to explain." Meanwhile, he'd hope to hell he was wrong and this had nothing to do with Miguel Escavez.

He checked Lily's room quickly, just in case she'd somehow slipped into the house without being seen. But nothing had been disturbed and she'd clearly not been back. He went next door, grabbed his address book, and headed back downstairs.

Glynnie, David, and Christopher were in the parlor with Jessica when he walked in, and they all turned worried eyes his way. "Jessica says Lily's missing?" his sister asked.

Shrugging aside her question with a dismissive wave of his hand, he snatched up the phone and punched in the number from his book. But as the phone rang and rang, he realized it was long past office hours. He disconnected and dialed information for Jake Magnusson's number. As the man in charge of the Colombians' training, he'd be the fastest source of information.

Jake's home phone also rang several times, and Zach, on the verge of disconnecting, was trying to think who to contact next when the phone at the other end of the line was abruptly picked up. A deep voice growled, "What?"

"Maggie? It's Zach. Look, I'm sorry to bother you at home, but—"

"Where the hell have you been, Midnight? You picked one helluva time to go on leave—I've been trying to get hold of you practically since you left. We've got a problem with one of the nationals you brought back with you from Colombia."

Ice crawled through Zach's gut. "Shit. Miguel Escavez?"

"That's the one, all right. The boy's gone AWOL on us."

24

MIGUEL SHOT HIS CURVACEOUS PRISONER A triumphant glance as he drove slowly up Rosario Road toward the main highway. The sight of her bound wrists and the gratifying cautiousness with which she regarded him filled him with powerful satisfaction. He felt like dancing and singing, and it was all he could do to remain still in his seat.

"This is the third time I've seen you," she said when he glanced her way again and their gazes met. "Who are you, anyway?"

Intimidation was a potent weapon—the master sergeant had taught him that—and Miguel bestowed his iciest glare upon his enemy's woman and growled, "Your worst nightmare." Ha! He'd wanted to use that line ever since he'd heard it said on the television the night he'd played cards with the GIs.

Such a menacing statement deserved a respectful reaction—or at the very least something more deferential than the abrupt crack of bitter laughter that escaped his captive.

"Not tonight you aren't, pal," she said. "Ordinarily, maybe, since it's not every day I get abducted at gunpoint. But it's been a really lousy evening."

His wonderful threat was meant to instill terror, not disrespect. But not even the *puta's* refusal to give him his due could wreck his mood—he simply felt too good, was infused with too much power. He, Miguel Hector Javier Escavez, had accomplished his goal. And to think he'd almost given up!

He could only blame the low morale from which he'd suffered this afternoon on the sheer boredom of sitting around day after day after *day*, waiting for events that never happened. But that was of no consequence now. It had ceased to be important the minute the master sergeant and his woman had suddenly materialized, motoring out of the mansion driveway in the commander's black Jeep like a sign from *Dios* Himself.

Or not long after that, anyway. He had to admit that even then he had doubted the Divine One's intentions. But who could blame him? He'd found himself sorely disappointed on more than one occasion just when he'd thought his objective was in sight.

But he would never question his Savior again, for although he'd been afraid to depend on much in the way of results this time either, in the end his patience had been rewarded beyond his wildest expectations. He'd sat in his car and he'd paced the grounds, keeping an eye on Taylor's Jeep and the main door of the resort. But finally, just when he'd been sure his limbo would never end, who should exit the fancy white hotel all by herself but the master sergeant's woman?

A sign indeed. He hummed a snatch of a song that was popular back home.

His ebullient mood faltered, however, when he reached Horseshoe Highway and had to decide which way to turn. That's when it occurred to him that he didn't actually know what to do with the woman now that he had her. With an uneasy pang, he realized he'd never planned beyond the part where he took her away from the oh-so-high-and-mighty marine.

He turned on his left blinker, deciding to head straight for the ferry dock to catch the first boat off this island. Since the woman most likely hadn't even been missed yet, that would be the smart thing to do. But re-membering how long the wait had been on the mainland dock the day they'd caught the ferry coming to the is-land, he hesitated. It would be the smart thing only if he could drive right on a boat and sail away from here. If he got hemmed in on a crowded dock, that would not be so smart, for the ferry terminal was the first place Taylor was likely to check.

He turned right toward Moran State Park instead. He needed to get off the main road and find a quiet place where he could think.

Lily couldn't repress the shudder that raised goose-bumps all over her body when her abductor pulled the car into a secluded campsite several minutes later. But her reaction had more to do with the memory of her last time in this park than the fear of the man who held her captive. Swiveling to face him, she wondered why she wasn't more frightened. To be calm seemed just plain foolish, for here she was, back in the middle of these darn woods, with the last of the light fading fast, in the power of a young man inclined to do only God knew what.

Yet for some odd reason, although she was certainly apprehensive, she wasn't terrified. Maybe because her captor struck her as little more than a boy, and she didn't get the impression he was bent on murder or rape. Or maybe it had to do with the nagging feeling she'd been snookered. Believing his claim that he had a gun, she'd let herself be bundled into this messy car with its backseat full of empty food wrappers and beverage containers, and its smell of sweaty young man. To compound her error, she'd allowed him to bind her wrists with a grubby length of cord. And all without ever having seen so much as a glimpse of an actual weapon.

His apparent lack of a gun could only be considered a good thing. So why did it feel perilously close to the last straw instead?

Well, gee, she thought with simmering resentment, *you think it might have something to do with the fact you've had it up to your back teeth with being deceived by lying men?*

"I hate this place," she muttered aloud.

"What you like," he informed her, "matters not."

Her temper spiked right up to the red zone, and taking a deep breath, she concentrated on regaining control. This was no time to let her emotions get the better of her, but honest to God, it took every iota of willpower at her disposal to keep from venting her spleen. Between Zachariah and this arrogant young man, she was beginning to feel seriously abused and misused.

She quietly exhaled, however, and flexed her fingers.

Then, forcing a pleasant expression, she said in the most appeasing tone she could muster, "Please. Won't you tell me who you are?"

His chest swelled up. "My name is Miguel Hector Javier Escavez."

"That's a lovely name."

"*Sí.* I am—"

"My name is Lily Morrisette."

He stared at her as if uncertain what to do with the information, but she merely met his confusion with a gentle smile. She remembered reading somewhere that the more real a victim became in a criminal's eyes, the more difficult it became for him to harm that person. She was all for that. "Where are you from, Mr. Escavez?"

"Bisinlejo." His chest puffed up another notch. "Where my father is major."

Ah. It explained a lot. The good-looking son of a powerful man—the sense of entitlement was the same the world over, evidently. Keeping her thoughts to herself, she strove to project an air of fragile helplessness by giving him a vacuous smile and a slight flutter of her lashes. "I'm sorry, I'm afraid I've never heard of it."

He shrugged. "I would not h'expect you to. Americans' geography skills are very poor, and my village in Colombia is but a small dot on the map." Then he shook his head impatiently. "But that is—how you say—neither there nor here. Master Sergeant Taylor cost me my *prometida*—"

"*Promet*—?" Lily's high school Spanish was all but a distant memory. Then it clicked. "As in promised? You're talking about your fiancée?"

"*Sí.*"

She frowned. She'd pretty much worked out for herself that this was Zachariah's South American. Funny, though, that Zach had never mentioned anything about a woman when he'd told her that—how had he put it?—he'd had a problem with one of the nationals he'd brought back, but that he thought they'd put it behind them? Then impatient with her internal questions, she shook her head. No sense getting ahead of herself before she had all the facts. "Cost you in what way?"

"He is responsible for the stolen virtue of my Emilita."

Shock feathered icy fingers down her spine. "You're saying Zach had *sex* with your girlfriend?" *No.* The denial was pure knee-jerk instinct, but she didn't care. That couldn't be right. Any fiancée of this youth would have to be pretty darn young, and she simply could not see Zach messing with any woman younger than his own sister.

"The master sergeant didn't, no. But he was in charge, and he did *nothing* to punish the one who did." He spat out the window, then turned back to glare at her. "Instead, he stood in front of the entire village and told me she *welcomed* his soldier's filthy attentions."

And there was the rub, Lily guessed. Thanks to good old Tactful Taylor, Miguel had lost face. *God deliver me from young men's egos.* "So you have a beef with Zach. What does it have to do with me?"

"He is responsible for the loss of my woman. I am taking his from him in return."

What was she, a bone for a couple of scruffy mongrels to snap and snarl over? She felt the anger she'd banked flare back to life. But she managed to meet his gaze with reasonable calm. "I hate to burst your bubble, Miguel, but having me in your possession is unlikely to gain you what you want. Zach and I broke up tonight."

Outrage flared in his eyes. "I do not believe you!"

She shrugged. "Can't say as I blame you, since I can barely believe it myself. Yet, sadly, it's true. Why do you think I was outside without him?"

He sat and scowled at her for a moment. Suddenly, his gaze dropped to track over her figure, and she could practically see the lightbulb flash on over his head. "Then I will defile you."

"Ex*cuse* me?"

"Perhaps you are no longer his woman. But he would dislike it, I think, if another man were to make you his."

"Not half as much as I would, pal." A quick glance at his lap reassured her that the idea didn't have him all whipped into a lather either. But he was just arrogant enough to decide that since he'd decreed it so, the plan had merit, and darned if she intended to wait around for him to talk himself into the mood. Casually, she bent down and began fumbling with the ankle strap of her high heel.

He leaned over as well, peering down suspiciously as she clumsily unfastened the tiny buckle. "What do you think you are doing?"

She kept her head down to prevent him from seeing the rage she feared was much too close to the surface to disguise. "Taking my shoes off. My feet are killing me." The buckle came free, and she slid her right pump from her foot.

"That's because they are *estúpido*. No self-respecting Colombian girl would wear chews so dangerous and ugly."

"Excuse me?" She slowly straightened, turning the shoe between her bound hands as she sat back up. "Did you say *ugly*?"

"*Sí.*" His lip curled up in a sneer. "*Muy* ugly."

"You know," she said sweetly, "this has been a really crappy night. I put up with being dumped by my boyfriend, and I've been quite the sport, if I do say so myself, about being trussed like a turkey and thrown into this pigsty of a car by a self-important little chauvinist barely old enough to shave."

He blinked, clearly confused by the disparity between her words and the tone in which she spoke them.

"You think these shoes are dangerous?" she asked softly, favoring him with a great big friendly smile. "Let me show you just how dangerous they can be." And gripping the shoe between her hands like a high-fashion sap, she swung it with all her might at the young man's head.

He threw an arm up, blocking a fraction of the impact. She figured that was probably a good thing—otherwise she might have driven the spiked heel clear through his temple, and that was simply too gross to contemplate. As it was, it still connected with considerable impact, making a nasty, meaty sound that made her stomach roil, and she watched him collapse like a sack of wet cement over the steering wheel. Dropping the shoe into her lap, she grabbed a fistful of his hair and hauled his head back, gratified to see he was out cold but still breathing. She let his head drop, and reached to pull the keys out of the ignition. Then she bent at the waist to work the shoe back onto her foot, but didn't take the time to try to fasten it. Straightening, she twisted to reach for the door handle.

"Ugly, my Aunt Petunia," she snapped at his unconscious form. "I might've had to take all the other crap you idiots dumped on me tonight. But nobody, but *no-body*, junior, mocks my shoes and gets away with it."

Zach checked the magazine in his pistol as he headed along the second floor hallway. Seeing the group in the foyer as he started down the stairs, he shoved in the clip, slid the safety on, and tucked the nine millimeter into his waistband at the small of his back. His departure from the parlor in the wake of his conversation with Magnusson had been more than abrupt, and he halted at the bottom of the stairs in front of his sister.

"Okay, here's the deal. I have good reason to believe a South American with a grudge followed me up here and has abducted Lily. I want you to call the sheriff for me. Tell him the man's name is Miguel Escavez, and he's already approached Lily twice. Inform him he's probably driving a dark blue '83 Ford LTD with California plates." He recited the number.

Glynnis looked sick. "Oh, God, Zach. Will he hurt her?"

"I honestly don't think he will, Glynnie. But I'm operating under the assumption that he's dangerous all the same, and I promise you, I won't rest until we have her back."

"I know you won't." She squared her shoulders. "How did your friend manage to find out what kind of car he's driving?"

"Maggie said as soon as the word went around Pendleton that Escavez had skipped, a private came forward to volunteer that Miguel had won his car from him in a poker game."

"Okay, let me make sure I've got this straight." She repeated the information back to him, including the license-plate number, with no-fuss efficiency.

"Excellent." Hauling her into his arms, Zach gave her a brief hug, then held her at arm's length to look down at her. "The first time I met Lily, she told me you were a lot more grown up than I gave you credit for—and I can see that she was right. I'm real sorry I didn't do better by you, Glynnie."

"What are you talking about? You can be a giant pain in the butt sometimes, but you have *never* let me down." Grasping his arms, she gave him a shake. "Now," she said briskly, "where will you look first?"

"The ferry terminal. Does anyone have a schedule?"

"If you leave in the next five minutes, you should be in time to check the dock before the eight-oh-five loads," Christopher said. "The boat after that, which is the last to leave the island tonight, is at ten-fifty."

"Let Christopher and me check it out for you, though," David said. "Between us, we know most of the ticket takers, and we probably have a better chance than you of talking them into keeping Escavez's car off the boat if he's there."

"Thanks." Zach gave them a brief description of Miguel, then pulled his keys out of his pocket. "I'll head back to Rosario and see if I can pick up a trail to follow from there. Glynnie, can I take your cell phone?"

"You bet." She went into the parlor to collect it.

When she returned an instant later she handed it to him with a scrap of paper containing two telephone numbers. "The top one is David's cell and the bottom number is for the phone here. Keep in touch. I'll contact the sheriff, then let both of you know what he says."

Within moments the three men were climbing into their vehicles, and Zach followed David's car as it raced along the winding country roads. Reaching a crossroad, the other two men continued straight for the ferry dock, while Zach turned left onto Crow Valley Road to head to the east side of the island. Once alone, the hollow space in his gut began to spread, melting outward like a piece of old film caught in a projector. If anything happened to Lily—

Every word they'd exchanged tonight as a result of her evening-altering declaration played back in his head. He'd told himself that while he clearly could have handled it better, his succinct, dispassionate summation had been necessary to let her know in no uncertain terms that he could never love her. But who the hell was he fooling? That excuse was so full of shit it was a wonder there wasn't a cloud of flies surrounding it.

Lily had accused him of being afraid, and he'd blown the suggestion off. He wasn't a man who thought of himself as being afraid of anything that didn't result in death or dismemberment. But the truth was, he was terrified. He was scared right down to the ground that if he admitted to the feelings that had been growing ever since he'd realized how special she was—and then lost her when she discovered that he didn't have what it took to hold on to love—it would destroy him.

How the hell had he managed to keep the truth from

himself, though? He should have known the instant he'd awakened from his dream the other morning and found himself oddly comforted by her presence, realized when holding her had kept at bay the old familiar sense of abandonment the dreams usually left in their wake. He should have known when, beneath his towering relief upon discovering she couldn't possibly be pregnant, there had been the tiniest spark of disappointment that an excellent excuse for hanging on to her had been removed.

Shit. On some level he had known. He just hadn't want to confront it. Exposing emotions was too much like ripping off your armor in the heat of battle. It left you wide open for the knife's plunge or a bullet's destructive, ripping force.

But the raw fact remained, he acknowledged as he pulled into Rosario's parking lot for the second time that evening, that if anything happened to Lily tonight it would kill him every bit as much as it would have if he'd taken the chance and they'd lived together for months or years before she left him. The difference was, he would have had time to bask in her integrity, her honest sexuality, her sweetness.

Right now he had nothing but too few memories.

He didn't know what he expected to find by coming back here. He'd gone over the area pretty damn carefully earlier. But he'd been looking for her then; he hadn't been searching for a clue that might allow him to follow her trail. He headed along the path that led to the point.

A few minutes later, he paused beneath the dense stand of trees to let his night vision establish itself away from the lights. This was pointless. He was following a concrete path, for crissake—it wasn't as if he'd find holes from her spike heels to lead him to her. Bending his head, he dug his fingers into the tight muscles knotting his neck.

A second later he realized the darker shadow he stared at on the ground wasn't part of the tree trunk as he'd first assumed. He squatted and felt a hot zing in his gut when his fingers slid over the smooth leather of Lily's little purse.

Slowly he straightened, the small handbag clutched in his hand. And an icy calm settled over his nerves.

He couldn't afford to race around blind; he needed a plan. But before he could form one of those, he needed to know if Lily was still on the island. He pulled Glynnis's cell phone from his pocket and punched in David's number.

"What have you found out?" he demanded the instant his future brother-in-law answered.

"Chris is up checking every car that loads on the boat, but so far neither of us have seen one that fits the description of Escavez's. And no one remembers seeing either him or Lily."

The rush of relief had Zach's spine bowing for a second. Then he pulled himself back upright. "That's good. The longer we can confine Escavez to the island, the better chance we have of finding Lily. And where I was ninety-nine percent certain he had her before, now I'm a hundred percent positive. I just found her purse under the trees near that little park on the point."

The other man swore, and Zach said grimly, "As long as I'm over here, I'm going to drive through the park. It seems a logical place for Escavez to go."

"Try Mount Constitution," David suggested eagerly.

"There's a lookout tower up at the top—he might have headed up there for the night."

"Thanks. I will. Have you heard from Glynnie?"

"Not yet, but I'll call her to pass on your information, and one of us will get back to you."

They disconnected, and Zach headed for his Jeep. He was torn. Most of him wanted Escavez to be somewhere in the park, since it was a specific place to search and his best bet for getting Lily back as soon as possible. But there was a fraction of him that remembered how much the place had frightened her the last time they'd been there. Then he stuffed everything except the need to concentrate into the back of his mind and drove up to the highway, where he turned toward the park.

His sister called to let him know the sheriff's office would be on the look out for Escavez's car. With renewed purpose, he continued on, driving slowly and stopping to peer into anything large enough to shelter a car.

When he rounded a slight bend and his headlights suddenly picked out Lily, carrying her shoes and limping along the shoulder of the road, he stood on the brakes and stared, unable for an instant to believe his eyes.

Then sweet relief flooded his system. "Thank you, Jesus; *thank* you," he breathed.

She stumbled to a halt and threw up her hands to block the light from her eyes, and rage exploded in his gut when he saw the cord binding her wrists together. But before he could react or even open the door to go to her, a look of pure panic flashed across her face. And, pivoting on her nylon-stocking-clad foot, she plunged off the road into the woods.

25

LILY HAD SEEN TOO MANY SLASHER MOVIES. When the car lights found her by the side of the road she was so unnerved that the first thing to pop into her mind was the standard plotline of those films—woman gets hacked / slashed / chainsawed by resilient, utterly invincible killer. Fresh adrenaline roared through her and, since she'd already done the fight thing tonight, flight seemed the better choice.

And the worst of it was, it was her own darn fault. It hadn't taken five minutes alone in the dark, after her escape from Miguel, for her to realize just how badly she'd screwed up. Rather than taking the car keys to prevent the young thug from gunning for her the moment he regained consciousness, she should have just shoved him out of the car and taken the vehicle for herself. This pockmarked, rock-strewn, pitch-black wilderness was *no* place for a city-bred woman—particularly not one whose hands were bound and whose feet had been shod in her highest pair of heels until she'd fallen flat on her face trying to run in them down the goat-path that passed for a road.

Of course by the time she'd figured out her mistake, it had been too late to go back and rectify the matter. For all she knew Miguel might have already come to, and she hadn't wanted to be anywhere in the vicinity if that were the case. But after her second tumble to the rough ground, she'd started to rethink even *that*—until the vehicle with the blinding lights had slammed to a halt in front of her.

That's when her fantasy of taking over Miguel's car with its sturdy, lockable doors vanished, and the young man—who in her mind had been growing increasingly more easily conquered—suddenly morphed into a monster with foot-long steel blade fingernails. Dear God, he'd found her! Gripped by terror, she didn't stop to wonder how he'd managed to get the car started or why he was approaching from the wrong direction. She simply turned tail and ran.

Hearing her name called as she crashed through the underbrush unnerved her even more, but it was the sound of pursuit that really shot her panic up into the stratosphere. Ignoring the branches snagging her clothing and catching at her hair, she battled her way through the foliage, and when some small gleaming-eyed creature suddenly scurried in front of her before just as abruptly skittering out of her way, a sob pushed its way past the lump of terror clogging her throat.

A rebounding branch she'd turned loose too quickly whipped back and thwacked her left elbow, and a battalion of pins-and-needles charged down a pathway of nerves to her fingertips. One of her shoes tumbled to the ground, but she didn't dare stop for it. Instead, she desperately tightened her grip on the remaining one. She didn't have a clue how effective it would prove as a weapon now that the element of surprise had been removed. But it was all she had to defend herself, and she wasn't about to lose it, too.

The trees and undergrowth suddenly thinned, and her heart lifted at the prospect of picking up her speed—only to drop crashing to her stomach when she pushed into a small clearing and found the way in front of her blocked by an almost vertical rocky cliff. Whirling to the right, she discovered that avenue obstructed also by an impenetrable thicket of brambles and young trees.

Breath sawing in and out of her lungs, she swung around to examine her options, and found there weren't any. So she turned back to face her pursuer, whom she could hear rapidly closing the distance between them. When a nocturnal bird suddenly screeched on the bluff above her, she screamed.

Trembling as she teetered on the slippery slope of hysteria, she tried to regulate the speed of her breathing. To keep herself from tumbling into an abyss from which she feared she'd begin to scream and scream and never stop, she sucked air deep into her lungs and held each inhalation as long as she could before exhaling it. Then, her breath still coming too fast but feeling marginally more in control, she raised her shoe with its spiked heel out, ready to swing the makeshift weapon the moment anyone got too near.

That's how Zach found her, hair wild, eyes ablaze with equal amounts of terror and determination, her nylons in shreds, her clothing snagged and streaked with dirt. Blood was a black trickle down her right leg from an abrasion on her knee, and her hands and face sported a number of welts and scratches. She looked one scant nudge away from a total meltdown, but still she stood like a rookie up to bat, her stiletto-heeled shoe gripped between her bound hands, ready and willing to inflict damage on anything that came within reach.

Aw, man. And he'd actually thought he had a prayer of *not* loving this woman?

"Stay back!"

"Lily." He inched nearer, wishing he'd thought to grab the flashlight so she could see his face. "It's me, sweetheart. It's Zach."

"Stay away from me, I said!" Her voice wobbled and she adjusted her stance, lifting the shoe a fraction higher. "I cold-cocked you once, buster—don't think I won't do it again."

"It's not Miguel, honey; it's me. Shh, shh, shh, now," he crooned. "It's all right. You're safe and nobody's gonna hurt you. I just want to get you out of these woods."

It was the latter, he suspected, that finally got through to her. He watched as she blinked and then leaned forward, eyes narrowed, to peer suspiciously at him through the meager illumination provided by the fingernail moon drifting in and out of the clouds.

"Zach?" She took a tentative step forward, but didn't lower the shoe.

"That's right, baby, it's me." He eased toward her. "You're safe now, Lily. Let me take you back to the car."

The stiletto heel tumbled from her grasp. Her arms dropped, and she seemed to sag where she stood.

It only took him three strides to cover the ground between them, but even as he reached for her, she rallied. Her posture snapped erect, and she swung her clasped hands at his chest, connecting with a solid thump. "You wretch! You scared me to death—I thought you were *him*." Then she threw herself into his arms.

He held her tightly, aware of the rapid drumming of her heartbeat against his abdomen.

She rocked her forehead back and forth against his chest. "Of course, I also thought *he* was Freddy Kruger. I guess both assumptions were pretty stupid." A wild laugh exploded out of her throat. "Stupid seems to be the order of the night. I can't believe I lost it over my *shoes*, of all things."

He didn't have a clue what she was babbling about and didn't particularly care—he was just grateful to have her back safe and sound. He tucked in his chin to peer down at her. "Are you all right? Escavez didn't hurt you, did he?"

"No. I'm shook up, is all." She pressed closer. "Just hold me."

"Oh, yeah; I intend to." He'd forgotten how tiny she was without her four-inch shoes, and being reminded caused him to hunch over her protectively, tightening his hold. But her bound hands between their bodies kept him from enfolding her as closely as he'd like, and with an exasperated murmur, he swept her up off her poor abused feet and turned to stride back to the road.

Teeth chattering, she burrowed against him on the

short journey to the car, and stayed close when he set her on her feet.

He grabbed a knife out of the toolbox and cut the cord that tethered her wrists together, then watched helplessly as she rubbed the skin where the ligature had chafed. Guilt and love welled up in him and, reaching out, he gently smoothed back her hair, plucking bits of flora from it. "God, Lily, I am so damn sorry I got you involved in this mess. The instant I knew Glynnie was safe I should have checked up on Escavez's where-abouts. If I'd called the base sooner, you could have been spared all this."

She shook her head. "It's not your fault. And I was surprised that he's just a kid. To tell you the truth, I wasn't half as scared of him as I am of these horrid woods."

"Still, I screwed up. It was unprofessional of me, even if I don't understand why he fixated on you. But it's gotta be due to his grudge against me."

"He said you were responsible for the loss of his woman, so in return he was taking your woman from you." Her eyes cooled then, and she took a step back. "You needn't worry, though. I set him straight on that score."

Zach winced. He had really hoped to put off his grov-eling until he could put some thought into what he wanted to say, but it looked as if he was out of luck on that score. "Listen, about that. I owe you an apology for my behavior after dinner tonight. I was wrong, and I acted like a jerk. You, on the other hand, were one hun-dred percent right."

She blinked. "I was?"

"Yeah."

"Well, as much as hearing that is music to my ears, I'm not quite sure I understand just what it is you think I was right about."

He shifted uncomfortably, because this was uncharted territory and he was a man who liked to prepare. Still, he had to give it a shot. He owed her that, at the very least. "You know . . . love." He opened the passenger door of the Jeep and lifted her onto the seat, but sat her sideways, facing him. "The relationship thing."

"What about it?"

"I've decided I'm for it. I think we should have one." He eyed her expectantly.

To his dismay, Lily looked more confused than ecstatic. "Isn't that quite a turnaround?"

"Yeah, well, what can I say. I'm"—he cleared his throat, drew a deep breath—"crazy about you." He exhaled in relief. Whataya know? That hadn't been so damn difficult after all.

"Or perhaps just plain crazy," she said flatly. "And you sure as sugar picked the wrong night for it, because I am so, *so* not in the mood for your charity." Her chin came up even as her voiced cracked.

His head snapped back as if she'd slapped him. "Say what?"

"You sat across a table from me not more than two hours ago, and informed me in no uncertain terms that you don't—how did you put it?—'*do*' love, but now I'm supposed to believe you're suddenly wild about me? Don't insult my intelligence, Taylor. You think I don't recognize your overactive Mr. Accountability streak at work when I see it?" She crossed her arms over her breasts. "You've decided it's your fault I had a big, bad uncomfortable hour at Miguel Escavez's hands, so you're offering yourself up as consolation prize."

"That's a crock of sh—"

"The heck it is! But I've got news for you, Zachariah. Like I said, I'm not some charity case, and I deserve more than a pity proposal, or proposition, or whatever this is supposed to be. So I tell you what. You can just *keep* your big sacrifice. I don't want it."

I don't want you, roared in his head, and all his shields slammed into place. For one of the few times in his life he'd opened himself up and taken an emotional risk. Hell, he'd just offered her more than he'd ever offered another woman in his entire adult existence, and she'd tossed it back in his face. "Fine." Losing all expression, he essayed an indifferent shrug. "Whatever. I thought it might be fun. But if you're not interested, you're not interested. Damned if I'm going to beg."

"No," she agreed thinly. "Zach Taylor would certainly never do that, would he?"

Surprisingly, temptation was riding him with spurs of steel to do exactly that, but she obviously wasn't ready to listen and he wasn't about to toss his heart at her feet again—not when she seemed more inclined to stomp all over it with those needle-heeled shoes of hers than clutch it to her breast. He turned away and pulled Glynnie's cell phone from his pocket. "I'd better let everyone know you're okay."

His sister answered the phone and screeched so loudly when he broke the news that he had to hold the phone away from his ear. Once she'd settled down enough to carry on a coherent conversation, he said, "Is David back yet?"

"No, but he's on his way," Glynnis said.

"Okay, I'll see if I can intercept him. I need him to come pick up Lily."

"What, you got a hot date or something, that you can't bring her home yourself?"

"That's cute, Glynnie—a real knee slapper. And no. I don't. But I do have to go get Escavez and take him to the sheriff's office before he can slither off and find himself a hidey-hole to hatch a *new* plan to screw up my life."

"Oh. Yeah. Good idea."

"Can't tell you how relieved I am that you agree."

There was an instant of silence. Then she said, "Whoa," at the same time he muttered, "Sorry."

"Forget sorry," she snapped. "What's got your shorts in a wedgie?"

"Not a damn thing. I gotta go." He disconnected, and glanced at Lily. But she'd swung around to face front and didn't look at him. Pacing away, he punched in David's number. A moment later he disconnected again after giving the younger man a succinct update and directions on how to find them. Then he turned back to the Jeep.

He was all business as he grilled Lily regarding what direction she'd traveled since escaping from Escavez's car, but he didn't appreciate by half her own businesslike responses. As soon as David and Christopher arrived, he put her in the backseat of their car, but then stood holding the door open for a moment as he stared down at her.

This was freaking nuts. He loved her, she loved him, and he was ready and willing to make a go of it—why was she being so damned stubborn? Okay, now clearly wasn't the time to hash it out, but he couldn't just let her go like this. So he dropped to his haunches, reached into the car, and snagged a hand around the back of her neck. Pulling her toward him, he leaned in to meet her halfway, and planted a hard, hot one on her startled mouth.

Just as abruptly, he turned her loose. "I *will* do right by you," he warned her baldly as he rose to his feet. "You can take that to the bank." Then, closing the door, he slapped the car's roof to signal David to take off.

It didn't take him long to find Escavez's car. And miracle of miracles, something actually seemed to be going his way when he saw that the young man was still inside, head tipped back against the seat as he stared dully up at the roof liner. Zach opened the passenger door and slipped inside. "Hey, there, Miguel. I hear you and I have a little unfinished business."

"She took my keys," the younger man whined. "She hit me hard enough to break my head, and she took my keys. Just because I said her chews were ugly."

Zach nearly laughed out loud. So that's what she'd been talking about when she'd said she couldn't believe she'd lost it over her shoes. He didn't so much as crack a smile, however, and looking at the nasty lump on Escavez's temple, he shrugged.

"Well, see, that's your problem in a nutshell, Miguel. You don't know dick about women. But instead of owning up to it like a man, you blame everyone else. It was my fault that Emilita preferred another man to you. It's

Lily's fault that she didn't care to be tied up and taken to the woods and decided to change her circumstances."

Miguel roused to glare at him. "You shamed me! In front of the h'entire village you claimed that Emilita welcomed Pederson's touch."

"Oh, grow up. You shamed yourself. Yes, I probably should have told you in private, but if you recall, you're the one who made it public when you chose the town square to challenge my decision not to punish my soldier. And Emilita did welcome his attention. I'm sorry about that, but women dump men every day. It happens; get over it." He looked at the sullen young Latino, and shook his head. "You had potential, Miguel. You've got a good brain, leadership ability, and connections in your village. But instead of letting us teach you how to focus all that for the betterment of Bisinlejo, you tossed it away on some half-assed revenge trip because your fucking *pride* was bruised. Now INS will no doubt be called in and you'll be deported back to Colombia. I doubt anyone but you even cared about Emilita's defection. But when your compadres return to your village and are hailed as heros, you'll be the guy who went AWOL. That's the true disgrace here, and you've got no one to blame for it but yourself."

When Escavez merely regarded him as if he were full of it, Zach shrugged. "You just don't get it, do you? Lily was right—you're nothing but a dumb-ass kid."

Miguel slapped a hand on his puffed up chest. "I am a *man*!"

"Listen, amigo, if you were a man, you'd know it isn't about saving face. It's about sucking it up and getting the job done. But that's a lesson you're either going to learn for yourself or you're not. I've got better things to do than to sit here debating the matter with you." He tied Miguel's wrists together with a length of sisal he'd brought from his toolbox, and escorted his prisoner to his vehicle.

It took longer than he thought it would to get Escavez settled in at the sheriff's office and figure out who had jurisdiction over the young man's fate. But finally, Zach cut himself loose and headed back to the Beaumont compound, happy to devote the drive time to the topic that mattered most—figuring out the best way to handle the situation with Lily.

If he lived to be a hundred, he was pretty certain he'd still never understand the female mind. What the hell did they—did *she*—want from him? He'd said he was crazy about her, told her he wanted a real, honest-to-God relationship with her. What more was he supposed to do—drop down on bended knee and profess his eternal love?

Zach stood on the brakes, and the Jeep slammed to a halt on the dark country road, its headlights slicing through the night to illuminate towering evergreens, budding alders, and rural mailboxes. The silence outside his windows was broken by a lone cricket that was soon joined by others and then by the more distant sound of a bullfrog. Zach barely noticed.

Well, duh. Give the man a cigar. That's probably exactly what she'd wanted. But what the hell *had* he said to her anyhow? Shoving aside all the emotion his exchange with Lily had brought into play, he thought back to the actual conversation.

And could have happily sliced his own throat. Then

he laughed without humor. For he'd pretty much already accomplished that verbally, hadn't he? *Nice going, dumbshit.*

He'd never said he loved her at all. He'd managed to limp out the word exactly once, but hadn't linked it with "I" or "you" and had instead mumbled something about being ready for a relationship "thing." Christ on a cracker. No wonder she'd gone off on that tangent about not wanting his big sacrifice.

He had some freaking balls lecturing Miguel about letting pride get in the way. Although—he straightened—at least he knew he'd fucked up, and he planned to do something about the problem he'd created. He'd drop to his knees, if that was what it took. And Lily might not believe it, but he not only could but *would* beg if that was the only way she'd give him a second chance.

Feeling a powerful rush of euphoria, he put the Jeep in gear and gunned it down the road, anxious to get back. A stupid grin stretched his mouth—one that probably made him look like an imbecile on some kick-ass meds, but he didn't care. Because he had a sneaking feeling that once he got past the fear of saying "I love you" out loud, making amends might be a whole lot of fun.

He was surprised to see his sister come out of the parlor to greet him when he burst through the door a short while later, but he merely grabbed her up, whirled her in a circle, then set her back on her feet and headed for the stairs. He took them two at a time.

"Zach, hold up," she called after him. "I need to tell you something."

"It'll have to wait." He didn't break stride. "I've got to talk to Lily."

A second later he was rapping his knuckles against Lily's door, but he didn't bother waiting for permission before he reached for the knob and pushed the door open.

The room was empty, and when he strode into the bathroom, she wasn't there, either.

Well, okay. She was down in the parlor with everyone else. He was turning to go join them when a detail niggling in the rear of his brain stopped him. He looked back at the countertop.

It was as pristine as an unoccupied hotel room, with none of the girly clutter he'd come to associate with Lily. Euphoria fading, the muscles in his neck starting to knot up, he turned on his heel and marched into the bedroom, where he went directly to the closet. He yanked open the doors.

It was empty of all but a handful of hangers.

As he stood there staring at them, Glynnie arrived in the doorway. "I'm sorry, Zach," she said breathlessly. "That's what I was trying to tell you. Lily's gone."

26

LILY REFUSED TO CRY ANY MORE. SHE'D SHED
enough tears in the past however-many hours to keep a
small armada afloat, so she set her teeth and kept her
eyes resolutely torrent-free as she threw her belongings
into the boxes she'd dragged from the garage into her
bedroom at Glynnis's Laguna Beach house. Two of the
cartons were already heaped to overflowing with shoes—
when on earth had she accumulated all this footwear?
She'd swear she hadn't owned this much when she
moved in.

Like it's important, Lily. She gave herself an impatient shake. The only thing that mattered right now was
to be long gone by the time Zach returned from Orcas
Island. To that end, she was making steady inroads on
the packing, and she'd made arrangements with Mimi
to crash on her friend's couch for a few days until she
could find a place of her own.

She had a couple of restaurants on her string that
were usually more than willing to take her on as a fill-in
chef, and the minute she got settled at her friend's apart-

ment she intended to start making calls to them to see if she could pick up some work. Certainly sitting around for the rest of the time the *Argosy* was at dock was no longer an option. She'd go crazy if she had nothing to do but think.

Because, sure as sugar, her thoughts would head straight back to Zach. To how he saw her as someone he had to "do right" by. Or worse, to how he probably lumped her into the same category as Miguel—just one more person looking to screw up his life. She had never felt for another man even a fraction of the emotions she felt for Zachariah Taylor . . . and to him she was nothing but a burden.

Her teeth clenched tighter. She would *not* cry again, darn it!

She was straightening with an empty box in her hand when something sailed past her and landed on the bed. While she stared blankly at the lavender ruffle-edged tulip lying on the comforter, a variegated purple and white one landed next to it. She whirled around.

And her heart did the impossible, taking flight even as it sank to her toes. *Oh, gawd.* Zach stood in the doorway, one large shoulder propped against the doorjamb. In his left hand were more tulips.

"Let's get a few things straight right up front," he said, plucking another flower from the bunch and tossing it at her feet. "No man with a drop of red blood in his veins would ever consider you a charity case. That's number one." He appeared to consider, then shook his head as a deep purple tulip drifted to settle on the floor next to her toes. "No. That's number two. *One* is that I love you."

"You—"

"Love you," he repeated in that deep voice that always vibrated right down to the heart of her. He lobbed another flower. "I choked trying to get out the word last night, and then I acted like an ass when you didn't read my mind and immediately fall into my arms." More flowers rained softly around her. "But I love you, Lily. I love you like I have never loved anything or anybody in my life."

She knew she must be gaping like an idiot, but she couldn't seem to wrap her mind around the words coming from his mouth. Something deep inside of her obviously recognized them, however, for a warm glow, a brilliant light, began to unfurl in her breast.

He pushed away from the doorframe. "You were right when you accused me of being afraid." Stopping in front of her, he traced a blossom down her cheekbone and along her jawline. "I don't care to think of myself as a man who's afraid of much, but I was scared to death that if I trusted in your feelings for me, eventually you'd change your mind and . . . take them back."

Never. Before the denial could travel from her brain to her vocal cords, however, he dropped to his knees in front of her, shocking her into silence.

"You think I can't beg? Think again, sweetheart, because I would do anything, *say* anything, if that meant you'd give me another chance. So, God, Lily, *plea*—"

"Don't!" The dawning warmth and light exploded in pyrotechnics of joy so absolute she was amazed she didn't go up in flames. But even as they shot throughout her system to the farthermost tips of her fingers and toes, she realized that the last thing she wanted was to see this proud man humbled. "Zach, don't."

Clearly misunderstanding, his face twisted. "Dammit, Lily, you have to give me a second chance. I *love* you."

"Then that's all I need." When she couldn't tug him to his feet, she gave a strangled laugh and dropped to her own knees and plastered herself against him, wrapping her arms around his waist to hold him tight. It felt like coming home to be next to all that heat and scent and strength once again, and she stared up into his face. "I never wanted you to beg. All I wanted was for you to love me the way I love you. The way I'll *always* love you for as long as I've got breath in my lungs. That's not something I will ever take back."

"Ah, God." The thin scar bisecting his upper lip lost its whiteness, and bending, he pressed the most reverent kiss she'd ever received upon her lips. When he lifted his head, his pale gray irises had darkened. "I don't deserve you."

"And don't think I won't remind you of that every chance I get," she said dryly, resting her chin on his chest and gazing up at him. Suddenly her hand flew to her hair. "Ohmigawd! I look *awful*!"

He grinned crookedly. "Honey, you couldn't look awful if you tried."

But she'd seen herself in the mirror earlier. At the time she simply hadn't cared that her eyes were all bloodshot and her skin was ashy. She wasn't wearing her usual makeup to help disguise it, either, since what she'd applied yesterday had worn off ages ago, and she been too heartsick to bother replacing it. "I haven't been to sleep since I left," she admitted, then narrowed her lashes. "Which reminds me. How the heck did *you* manage to get here so fast? I just barely made the last boat off the island."

"I chartered a plane this morning."

"Well, aren't you Mr. Posh. I spent all night traveling, going from island to island to mainland, where I rented a car for the drive to Seattle. I got to the airport about two-thirty in the morning, and all I can say is thank goodness the air-traffic controllers' strike was settled, because frankly I'd forgotten all about it until I was almost there. But that turned out to be the last bit of luck I had going for me. I waited hours to get a flight home, then had to rent another car when I got to LAX—and the freeways, of course, were in their usual state of gridlock. But, gee." She smacked his chest with the flat of her hand. "How nice that *you* got to have a good night's sleep before tootling down here in a private plane."

When he bent his head to kiss her this time, there was nothing reverent about it. It was all fierce heat, and she dug her nails into the hard muscles of his chest to anchor herself. She was straining toward him in an attempt to meld their bodies by the time he lifted his head again.

"You think I just took the news of your leaving in stride, jumped in the sack, and slept like a baby?" A rude laugh exploded out of his throat. "Not only did I not sleep worth a damn, sweetheart, my head never even so much as touched a pillow! That frigging little airport in Eastsound was shut down by the time I called last night, and I spent every minute until it opened up again pacing my room, worrying that you'd be gone by the time I got here." His remembered frustration seemed to segue into something much more immediate as his fingers gently traced her puffy eyelids. "Dammit, your eyes aren't swollen just because you've been up all night. You've been *crying*." Regret filled his eyes. "I could cut my heart out."

"Oh, yeah. That'd do me a lot of good."

"But what if this isn't the last time I make you cry?" Worry etched his eyes. "Jesus, Lily, I know *zip* about this relationship stuff. I'm sure to fuck it up."

"No doubt you will." She cupped his face in her hands, appreciating the scratchy texture of his beard beneath her palms. "But so will I, Zach. I think that's probably the nature of the beast when you've got two people as different as you and I trying to make a go of it together."

"Great. So you're telling me we're pretty much doomed?"

"Heck, no. I'd bet all my restaurant money, in fact, that we'll get it right more often than we'll mess it up. And that's not even factoring in how stubborn both of us are."

He raised his eyebrows. "And this you see as a plus?"

"Well, if you define stubbornness as pretty much refusing to be swayed from a purpose, don't you think that ought to work in our favor when it comes to our relationship?"

"Yes." His smile dawned white, and his muscles visibly relaxed. "Yes, I do. And I suppose there's even something to be said for the occasional fight." His hands smoothed their way down to her hips. "I bet making up can be a whole lot of fun." He tipped his head. "So what do we do now? Do we get married?"

"Oh. Well. Marriage." Her heart gave a huge lurch and silently screamed *Want it! Want it!* "I don't know. There's still so much we haven't talked about. Like what happened last night with Miguel. And what you wanna do with your last two years in the service. Or the fact that if we marry, there goes my sweaty stableboy fantasy."

"Hey, I can be a sweaty stableboy." He spread his thighs to align the fly of his jeans with hers and rocked an impressive erection against the soft notch he'd opened up for himself between her legs. "Would madam care to ride the stallion this morning?"

Oh. Yes. Absolutely. Before she could slide her hands around to his muscular rear to clamp him in place, however, he eased back and scooped her up in his arms. She clutched at his shoulders as he rose to his feet and carried her over to the bed, where he flopped down with her on his lap.

"Before we play horsey, let's get the rest of this out of the way." He gently rearranged a few strands of her hair. "Miguel was collected by the MPs this morning to be transported back to Pendleton. It's out of my hands—men with more stars on their epaulets than I'll ever possess are in charge of deciding his fate now." He related the highlights of his conversation with the young man the previous evening. "As far as I'm concerned he was damn fortunate not to be turned over to the INS."

"I wonder if he's mature enough to appreciate his luck?"

"I doubt it, but that's not our problem. We've got considerations of our own to hash out." Zach tugged on her leg until she swung it around to sit astride him. He gazed at her, perched on his lap looking a bit pale and less pulled-together than he'd ever seen her, yet so pretty in his eyes that it made him ache. Love for her swelled in his chest. "Listen, I thought about this quite a bit on the way down here this morning. And I decided if you'd have me, I'd do what you suggested last night and see about teaching field work."

"Is that what *you* want to do?"

He hesitated, then nodded. "Um, yeah. Sure."

"*Zach*." It was her schoolmarm tone, and he knew better than to ignore it.

But he shrugged. "I don't know what I want, okay? That's been the problem—I'm a thirty-six-year-old who suddenly has to figure what he wants to be when he grows up."

"So take your time and figure it out. If you think the instructor thing would work for you, fine. But don't do it for me. Our relationship isn't contingent on you quitting reconnaissance."

"It can keep me away from home for long periods of time, Lily."

"And I'd miss you like crazy if that were the case. But I don't plan to give up my job, and it takes me away from home for a week or two at a time too." She kneaded his shoulders. "I guess what I'm trying to say is: if doing your thing in far off places is what makes you happy, then that's what you oughtta be doing."

"God, I love you."

She grinned at him, then wiggled her butt experimentally. His always-willing-to-be-aroused dick rose to the occasion, but he tried to ignore the messages it sent for a moment. "The truth is, honey chile, doing my thing in far-off places has been losing its allure for a while now. I just haven't figured out yet what I want to replace it with. But whatever that turns out to be could very well mean having to pick up stakes and move across the country. Your restaurant—"

"Can wait. I meant what I said last night, Zach. Two years just isn't that long in the general scheme of things. It simply means I'll have that much more time to save my money, which means I'll have a better cushion for when I start up my place."

"Sweetheart, if you want a cushion, I've got a *boat-load* of mon—" He broke off when he saw her expression. "Uh-oh," he said, giving the thigh that had gone rigid beneath his hand a squeeze. "I know that look. That's the look that makes me feel as if I've pissed in the middle of your tea party. I guess it'll be a pretty chilly day in hell before you accept my financial help, huh?"

The starch left her spine. "It's not that I'm adverse to helping you spend your money," she assured him earnestly. "Heck, if it'll make you happy, you can pay all the household bills—keep me in style. You can even support my shoe habit if you want. But, Zach, the restaurant has been my dream for as long as I can re-member—and I have to succeed or fail at it on my own." Her delicate eyebrows drew together. "Does that make me the worst kind of hypocrite?"

"No, ma'am. That makes you a woman of character."

"Oh, my." She rested her head on his shoulder. "I think I may just have to marry you after all."

Every corpuscle in his body screamed *yes!* but he managed to keep his voice light when he said, "So, what convinced you? I bet it was my willingness to play sta-bleboy, wasn't it?"

"Well, I have seen the stallion you're bringing to the bargaining table," she agreed, and wiggled upon the object under discussion. But when she framed his face in her hands and looked into his eyes, her own were no longer teasing. "Mostly, though, it's because I have never met another person with as much love to give as you have. I've seen what it's like to be the object of your affections, Zachariah, the lengths you'll go to for those you love. And I can't think of a greater privilege than to be your wife."

"Jesus, Lily," he said hoarsely. No one had ever made him feel the way she did. He never dreamed his heart could swell to such proportions that it downright amazed him the two of them didn't float right up to the ceiling. "I love you so freaking much. And I promise you this: I'll make you happy. I'm gonna make you so damn happy—and while I'm at it, I promise to give you one hell of a ride, too."

"I don't doubt that for a minute. And I've gotta confess: your offer to play stableboy *was* a consideration. Speaking of which—" She subtly rocked upon his lap. "Isn't it about time to bring out the stallion?"

"Oh, absolutely," he said with a tug of his forelock, and laughing, he rolled her onto the bed. "As madam wishes."

Who needs Buffy?

We've got adventurous women right here at Avon Books!

Yes, here at Avon we have heroines who would make Buffy think twice before going out at night . . . women who make Scarlett O'Hara look like someone who'd faint dead away at the sight of Rhett Butler. But, unlike Scarlett, Avon heroines know a good man when they see one . . . and they know how to treat him right. And, unlike Buffy, the guys they meet are *extremely* hot-blooded!

Meet the heroines of the Avon Romance Superleaders . . . and the men who are their matches!

Following are sneak peeks from four upcoming Avon Romance Superleaders. Some of these women are modern-day heroines . . . others face a world outwardly different, but actually much the same, as our own. For it doesn't matter if you're a Regency miss on the run from a bad match . . . or a contemporary woman looking for a happy life . . . these are gals who face life head-on—and who find love when they least expect it!

In January you'll get to gaze at. . . .

The Ring on Her Finger
by Elizabeth Bevarly

Lucinda Hollander was attending a big society blast with a dull-but-good-enough man one minute—the next, she's jumping out a ballroom window. Suddenly, this heiress is on the lam from the cops for a crime she didn't commit. So she "hides out" on a country estate, masquerading as a housekeeper . . . and finding herself attracted to a mysterious man named Max who everyone calls "the car guy . . ."

༄

"I don't think anything got broken," Lucy said as she hastened back over to where Max still sat on the floor, his arms hooked loosely over his denim-clad knees.

"Just my heart," he said under his breath.

"What?" she asked as she stooped to clean up—keeping her legs clamped together and turned to the side, he couldn't help noticing.

"Nothing," Max said, more loudly this time. "It was nothing." He knelt and began to scoop up what he could of the mess, trying to nudge Lucy aside. "I'll do that," he told her. "It's my mess."

"That's all right," she assured him, nudging him back. "I'm the housekeeper, remember? This is my job."

"But you've got something else to—"

"It's okay," she interrupted him. "I'll take care of this.

Go ahead and heat up what's left of dinner. I'm sure you're hungry."

Understatement of the century, Max thought. But he conceded to her wishes. Mostly, though, he'd only conceded to her wishes because he hadn't wanted to get into a nudging match with her. Two nudges and a collision with a woman were about all his deprived libido could stand these days. As it was, he probably wouldn't sleep a wink tonight, because he'd be too busy replaying those nudges and that collision over and over again. He was getting hot already just thinking about the replaying.

Oh, yeah. He had a full night ahead.

In February . . .

See Jane Score
by Rachel Gibson

Jane Alcott has no hesitations when she's assigned to cover the Seattle Chinooks hockey team—and tail their ace player Luc Martineau in particular. After all, she knows she's good for more than just writing a Single in the City column—and entering a men's locker room shouldn't be any problem for a fearless gal like her. But while she might not be intimidated by locker-room antics, she's a little taken aback by Luc's definite . . . attributes.

"Are you escorting me to my room?"

"Yep."

She thought of the first morning when he'd carried her briefcase, then told her that he wasn't trying to be nice. "Are you trying to be nice this time?"

"No, I'm meeting the guys in a few and I don't want to have to wonder if you made it to your room without passing out on the way."

"And that would ruin your fun?"

"No, but for a few seconds it might take my attention off Candy Peeks and her naughty cheerleader routine. Candy's worked real hard on her pom-poms, and it would be a shame if I couldn't give her my undivided attention."

"A stripper?"

"They prefer to be called dancers."

"Ahh."

He squeezed her arm. "Are you going to print that in the paper?"

"No, I don't care about your personal life." She pulled her plastic room key from her pocket. Luc took it from her and opened the door before she could object.

"Good, because I'm yanking your chain. I'm really meeting the guys at a sports bar that's not too far away."

She looked up into the shadows of his face created by her darkened room. She didn't know which story to believe. "Why the BS?"

"To see that little wrinkle between your brows."

She shook her head as he handed her the key.

"See ya, Ace," he said and turned away.

Jane watched the back of his head and his wide shoulders as he walked down the hall. "See ya tomorrow night, Martineau."

He stopped and looked back over his shoulder. "Are you planning on going into the locker room?"

"Of course. I'm a sports reporter and it's part of my job. Just as if I were a man."

"But you're not a man."

"I expect to be treated like a man."

"Then take my advice and keep your gaze up," he said as he turned once more and walked away. "That way you won't blush and your jaw won't hit the floor like a woman."

In March you'll be . . .

Getting Lucky
by Susan Andersen

Lily Morrisette felt anything but lucky when Zach came striding into her life—she wants respect . . . and Zach's not giving any to her. But amid a dangerous nest of secrets, Zach and Lily are pulled closer together than either thought possible, making them wonder if their meeting was better luck than either had ever dreamed.

❧

"Who are you?" he demanded, swinging an olive-drab duffle bag off his shoulder and down to the tiled floor. "And what are you doing in my kitchen? Where's my sister?"

His eyes were a clear, pale gray, the irises ringed in charcoal. Intense and unflinching, they narrowed between thick, dark lashes to rake over her, taking in her thin cotton, peppermint ice cream–colored drawstring pajama bottoms and tank top. The scrutiny served to remind Lily of every one of the extra ten pounds she could never seem to shed, no matter what. She set her glass down on the countertop with a sharp click, but refrained from responding in kind to his rudeness.

"You must be Zach." She stepped forward, extending her hand to Glynnis's brother. "She's away right now, but I'm Lily—Lily Morrisette. I've heard a lot about you since I started renting a room here."

"The hell you say," he growled, ignoring her proffered

hand. His voice was so deep she could practically feel its vibration through the soles of her feet, the way she always registered the bass thumping from the car of the teenage boy who lived down the block whenever he drove past. It was also nearly as frigid as those iceberg eyes of his when he continued, "Glynnis has always been a sucker for every con artist with a sad story to tell, but I didn't think she'd go so far as to actually install one in our house while I was gone."

"*Excuse* me?"

"I hope you got whatever you were angling for while the opportunity was ripe, lady." His gaze was so scornful it took all Lily's starch not to recoil. "But don't let that shapely little ass get too comfortable, because the free ride is officially over. Go pack your bags."

He thought her bottom was shapely? And *little*? Then she gave herself a sharp mental shake. Good God, what was the *matter* with her? His opinion of her butt was hardly the point. Straightening her shoulders, she tipped up her chin. "No," she said firmly, and crossed her arms over her breasts.

"What?" He went very still, as if no one ever contradicted him.

Perhaps no one ever did, Lily surmised, recalling that he was some hotshot Marine who specialized in reconnaissance missions. Then his mouth went hard, and part of her attention got distracted by the thin white scar that bisected his upper lip.

Funny the difference a few minutes and an insulting attitude could make. What she undoubtedly would have considered sexy as all get-out a moment ago struck her now as vaguely sinister. *Pretty is as pretty does,* Grandma Nell would've said, and for the first time Lily understood on a bone-deep, fundamental level exactly what her grandmother had meant. This guy's behavior wasn't pretty at all, and she refused to be the first to flinch in the strange game of chicken they played.

"What part of the word don't you understand?" she inquired sweetly.

In April experience . . .

Love With the Proper Husband
by Victoria Alexander

When Gwendolyn Townsend is left penniless and without prospects, she takes matters into her own hands and sets off to be a governess. So imagine her shock when this independent lady is told she has an inheritance after all . . . if she agrees to marry Marcus Holcroft, Earl of Pennington. Gwendolyn's not so certain she wants to marry at all—until Marcus manages to persuade her otherwise . . .

༄

"Good Lord, it's you!" Gwen stared in disbelief. This was Lord Pennington? The arrogant, sarcastic and admittedly somewhat handsome man on the stairs was Lord Pennington? Her Lord Pennington?

Not that she had given him a second thought, of course.

Besides, at the moment, he appeared more insane than attractive.

"Why are you looking at me like that?" she said cautiously, wondering if it was too late to retreat to the corridor. "And why are you grinning like a lunatic?"

"It is only that I feel quite mad with relief." He strode to her, took her hand and raised it to his lips. His gaze never left hers. It was most disconcerting. "It is a true pleasure to meet you at last, Miss Townsend."

"Is it?" She pulled her hand away. "Why?"

"Why?" He raised a brow. "I should think that would be obvious."

She shook her head. "Apparently not."

"Forgive me." The earl's forehead furrowed. "I assumed Mr. Whiting had informed you as to our connection."

"He told me of an arrangement between our fathers," she said slowly.

"Excellent." He nodded and the grin returned to his face. It was somewhat crooked and if his dark hair were a bit ruffled instead of perfectly in place, he would look more like a mischievous schoolboy than a gentleman of nearly thirty. She suspected it could be quite engaging under other circumstances. This, however, was not one of them.

"Then we can proceed with the arrangements at once. I will secure a special license and we can be wed by the end of the week."

Shock stole her voice and for a moment she could do nothing but stare. The man was indeed every bit as arrogant as she'd thought at their first meeting and far more high-handed than she'd ever expected. She had no intention of marrying any man, let alone this one. And even if she were interested in marriage, she would much prefer to be asked rather than issued a command.

"Miss Townsend?"

"I fear you have me at a disadvantage, my lord." She fixed him with a steady stare, the kind she'd perfected to intimidate children even if it had never especially worked. "I cannot be certain from your words, but is this a proposal of marriage?"

"A proposal?" Confusion colored his face, then his expression cleared. "Of course. How could I have been so thoughtless? You would expect that. Any woman would, regardless of the circumstances. I simply assumed . . . Well, it scarcely matters now, I suppose, but I do apologize. Allow me to start over."

He took her hands in his and looked slightly ill at ease. "I suppose I didn't think of it because, well, I am not especially polished at this sort of thing. I have never been in this position before. This is my first offer of marriage."

"How delightful to know you do not suggest marriage to every stranger you bump into."

"Indeed I do not." His eyes twinkled with amusement. "My dear, Miss Townsend," he cleared his throat and met her gaze. "Would you do me the great honor of becoming my wife?"

His eyes were the darkest shade of green, cool and inviting like the depths of an endless garden pool and for the briefest fraction of a moment, Gwen wanted nothing more than to fall into the promise they offered. Nothing more than to stare into those eyes forever. An odd fluttering settled in her stomach, as unsettling as the feel of his warm fingers wrapped around hers.

"Thank you." She drew a deep breath and pulled her hands from his. "But I must regretfully decline."